George Augustus Henry Sala

Notes and Sketches of the Paris Exhibition

George Augustus Henry Sala

Notes and Sketches of the Paris Exhibition

ISBN/EAN: 9783337094140

Printed in Europe, USA, Canada, Australia, Japan

Cover: Foto ©Andreas Hilbeck / pixelio.de

More available books at **www.hansebooks.com**

NOTES AND SKETCHES

OF THE

PARIS EXHIBITION.

BY

GEORGE AUGUSTUS SALA,

AUTHOR OF "MY DIARY IN AMERICA IN THE MIDST OF WAR," ETC.

LONDON:

TINSLEY BROTHERS, 18, CATHERINE STREET, STRAND.

1868.

LONDON: PRINTED BY WILLIAM CLOWES AND SONS, STAMFORD STREET
AND CHARING CROSS.

LONDON: PRINTED BY WILLIAM CLOWES AND SONS, STAMFORD STREET
AND CHARING CROSS.

TO

JAMES LORIMER GRAHAM, JUN.

OF NEW YORK,

IN MEMORY OF A THOUSAND KINDNESSES,

This Book

IS AFFECTIONATELY INSCRIBED.

CONTENTS.

CONTENTS.

THE PARIS EXHIBITION.

I.

PREFACE.

THE writer of this book will be spared, it is to be hoped, the accusation of having attempted, or proposed, or pretended to give, in the following pages, anything of the nature of a History of the Universal Exhibition of 1867, or anything even which lays claim to be a comprehensive panorama of the contents of that vast bazaar. I shall have a sufficiency of sins of omission and commission to answer for, even in the little I have striven to do, without incurring the risk of additional censure for undertaking a task far beyond the powers of any single writer. Were mere compilation and book-making the object in view, a solitary worker, in the course of, say seven years, might be enabled to produce an adequately voluminous and exhaustive record of the World's Fair of 1867; but the materials for such a purpose are not yet abundant enough. I am not desirous to "steal the thunder" or suck the brains of my brethren in journalism who may be intent, themselves, on republishing in book-form that which they have written in newspapers and periodicals concerning the Exhibition; and in her Majesty's government is vested, I presume, the copyright of the Reports of the Jurors, which have been published, with the addition of admirably-executed engravings, in the *Illustrated London*

News. Nor has anything in this volume been " taken from the French." It has been written, as country people put it, " out of my own head" entirely; and the head in question being of dimensions considerably smaller than the brazen one constructed by Friar Bacon, the amount of matter evolved from its cellular chambers has been necessarily limited. I could no more write a History of the Exhibition than I could compose an Encyclopædia, or build St. Paul's Cathedral. "Notes and Sketches of the Paris Exhibition:" such is the title I have affixed to my humble work, and its contents will, I believe, be found to bear out its name. I may have done too little, but I can certainly claim absolution from any charge of having sought to do too much. During a stay of five months in Paris, I noted and sketched as many things in the Champ de Mars as time and occasion would permit me to do, and those notes and sketches I transmitted in due course to the *Daily Telegraph* newspaper. By permission of the proprietors of that journal, I now reproduce the fugitive impressions of a very remarkable spectacle. Considerable additions have been made to them, and I have been enabled to recast and remodel very many considerations and conclusions at which, in the outset, I had at first too hastily arrived. As it is, the book will probably be found full of faults—in matter, in manner, and in meaning. The majority of these errors may be due to the troublesome fact that I do not possess Universal Knowledge. Indeed, I am persuaded that there is not one department of human science in which I have acquired even moderate proficiency. Such a persuasion—the confession of which is made, I entreat the reader to believe, in perfect candour and good faith— might, in the judgment of many critics, be held sufficient to have deterred me from writing about the Paris Exhibition at all. Unfortunately I am constrained to Live—although, of my living, those same critics, perhaps, following Cardinal Richelieu *in re* the lampoon writer, may not see the necessity—and, finally, I am not entirely my own master. I am one of the servants of a Centurion, and when he says "Go," I am fain to go, wheresoever the billet may be for. Since I last had the honour of addressing the public through a book-medium (in " From Waterloo to the Peninsula ") I have been compelled to go to a great many places. I was sent from the south of Spain to the north of Italy, and thence went from Trieste to Vienna. I came down again to Italy in June, when the Prusso-Austro-Italian war broke out; left my household gods in Venice, " in a state of siege ;" joined Garibaldi at Como, campaigned with him until the fatal armistice which gave Venetia to Italy at the expense of her honour ; and then, after wandering for two months longer up and down Lombardy and the Romagna, I returned to the Adriatic city to witness the triumphal entry of Victor Emmanuel and the Italian troops. I was sent from Venice to Florence, and from Florence to Rome, in time for the evacuation of that city by the French army of occupation. I wintered in Rome, and was enjoying the early days of spring at Naples, when a peremptory telegram bade me come to Paris at once, and " do " the Exhibition. I found two colleagues in Paris, one of whom had been at Sadowa, and the other, who had been with me in the Tyrol, is now in Abyssinia, whither I was only, myself, prevented from going, ultimately, by "urgent private affairs" which required my presence in England.

I do not allude to these personal matters and experiences with the slightest intention to show that such a Wandering Gentile as I have been was the person best suited to the work of a special correspondent bound to report the most noteworthy features in a Universal Exhibition of Art and Industry. My most appropriate functions, perhaps, would have been to assist Sir Samuel Baker in his report on travelling equipages and equipments, or to have drawn up a Memoir on the Phases of International Cookery endeavoured to be illustrated in the Champ de Mars—subjects concerning which I may be reasonably supposed to know something; but I have merely mentioned the foregoing facts to show what are the real exigencies of the management of a newspaper in view of a public whose appetite for graphic narratives of things passing in every part of the world grows more insatiable every day. To have selected persons possessing special knowledge of every one of the sections treated in the Paris Exhibition would have been, with the proprietors of the chief London newspapers, *theoretically*, an easy task. There are plenty of members of the Society of Arts, and other learned and scientific bodies at large—plenty of literate junior partners of commercial firms—plenty of studious clerks and mechanics who might have been welded into a staff to whom "no science" would have been a "mystery." For instance, the *Times*, the *Standard*, the *Daily News*, the *Post*, the *Advertiser*, and the *Telegraph*, might have sent to Paris so many painters, glaziers, jewellers, geologists, naturalists, cotton-spinners, carpet-weavers, engravers, paperstainers, photographers, pianoforte-makers, turners, dyers, mechanical engineers, soldiers, sailors, soap-boilers, wine-tasters, gold and silversmiths, modellers, chasers, die-sinkers, potters, surgical instrument makers, bell-hangers, carpenters, joiners, sculptors, and dolls'-eye makers, with instructions conscientiously and technically to describe the objects pertaining to their several trades and callings. This, I repeat, in theory— with a Senior Wrangler, or the President of the Social Science

Association, or the editor of the *Popular Cyclopædia*, to super-intend the labours of the accomplished body of contributors—would have been a matter of no very great difficulty. Unfortunately in practice the case is very different. There is a mob of gentlemen, and of ladies, too, who write with ease—the time may be approaching, as Lord Houghton once pointed out at a Literary Fund dinner, when literary acquirements may be so widely disseminated that it shall be hard to tell who is and who is not a man of letters—there are vast numbers of persons of both sexes and all stations who have gained special knowledge, and can write on their speciality clearly, sensibly, and fluently ; but all these things admitted, there remains the fact that newspapers, as they are at present conducted, demand a certain species of article, and that the persons who are able to supply such an article as will be accepted and appreciated by the public are exceedingly limited in number. These are the persons who are sent from a Funeral to a Wedding, from a Banquet to a Prize-fight, from a Campaign to a Coronation, from a Horticultural Show to a Hanging, from Pole to Pole, and from Dan to Beersheba; and who are expected, not to find all things barren, but to discover fertile themes for description in every rood of ground over which they travel. I do not maintain that such a state of things is either useful, or wholesome, or right; and were I a *Saturday Reviewer*, or a *Spectator*, or an *Examiner*, or a *Pall Mall Gazetteer*, or what not, I might sneer as sardonically as a natural tendency to mental dyspepsia might prompt me, at the desultory toil of the " Luca fa Prestos " of the press, hurrying from country to country, and from topic to topic, and gathering perhaps as little beeswax as honey from the innumerable flowers whose cups they search. The time may come perhaps when every paragraph in a daily newspaper shall be as gravely and deliberately excogitated from previous evidences and discussions as an article in the *Quarterly Review*; but that time has not yet arrived: and, meanwhile, I have only drawn attention to that which exists, and cannot, for the moment, be helped.

In conclusion, I may state that this book might have been swelled to thrice its size had I not, in the beginning, determined only to touch on subjects concerning which I had learned *something*—something tangible and technical. To science I make no pretensions; but I have been a workman, and I have dwelt occasionally on the details of workmanship. Whatever value these pages may possess will be due to the amount of earnestness with which I have been able to abide by this determination. I have not been "crammed" or "coached" in any one matter of which I have ventured to treat. I have borrowed from no authorities, pilfered from no "handy-books," and am indebted to "the kindly aid and suggestions" of no "obliging friends." Indeed, putting aside detraction and abuse—which have always done me good, and have incited me to work and to study harder than ever—I do not think I have ever been indebted to anybody for anything. The first book I ever wrote, a "Journey Due North," published ten years ago, was mercilessly tomahawked in the *Saturday Review*. I have written twenty books since then; and this, the twenty-second, will probably (if the *Saturday* condescend to notice it at all) be tomahawked as mercilessly as was my maiden effort. I have been enabled to live, and to make my way, and to pursue an arduous but delightful vocation, and to vary the labours of a coalheaver with the studies of a schoolboy, by a healthy, sanguine constitution, a good appetite, and the infinite mercy of Providence; and these I hope will not fail me until the end.

II.

DEFINITIONS.

ON the banks of the Seine, between the Avenue de la Bourdonnaye and the Avenue Suffren, there has been shown for seven months past Something which it would be paradoxical to term a microcosm—a solecism to entitle a panorama—a platitude to name a World's Fair. It has been called all these things, and a great many more besides. In attempting to describe its contents I have often, myself, been puzzled to know how to speak of it without falling into that "iteration" which has been so very empathically execrated by the poet. Persons of a serious turn have more than once likened it to John Bunyan's Vanity Fair: for did it not boast a Britain Row, and a Flanders Row, and a Portugal Row among its many concentric ellipses? and has it not been full, from morning to night, of piping and singing and dancing—of drinking and smoking and flirting, and of all manner of vanities? and have not the Lords of the Fair, in the shape of the members of the Imperial Commission, with Monsieur Le Play at their head, been ready to sit in judgment at their *Châlet*, close to the Avenue Rapp, on any rash Christians or Hopefuls who should dare to hint that this was not the grandest fair ever seen, and one eminently calculated to do honour to the world in general, and the Empire of France in particular? Again, there have been critics so cynical or so censorious as to declare the entire thing a Great Sham, an Iniquitous Job, and a Crying Scandal. Others, fond of picturesque verbiage and romantic associations, have spoken about it, enthusiastically or sentimentally, as the Universal Congress of Art and Industry? as the Giant Tournament of the Thinker and the Worker; as the infallible guarantee for the peace of the world and the brotherhood of nations. The wise and politic sovereign to whose initiative the great enterprise was due, and who is rarely disposed to be either enthusiastic or sentimental, would appear, himself, slightly to have over-estimated what the effect of this thing would be on the temper of humanity and the politics of the world. In one or more of his remarkable public discourses he distinctly stated that, in his opinion, the maintenance of peace was assured, and would be secured by the vast undertaking of which the beginning was to be on the first of April, 1867. *Humanum est errare.* The ruler who has achieved so many marvels—who has developed the resources of the land he governs to an extent undreamt of by the sagest politicians and the most thoughtful economists of the preceding generation—who, more successful than Augustus, has converted one of the uncleanest and most disorderly cities in the world into a metropolis whose wealth, whose splendour, whose convenience, whose ædility, and whose police are scarcely susceptible of enhancement or improvement — who has reduced the most turbulent and seditious populace in Christendom to the discipline of Sunday-school children and the docility of dancing dogs—who has metamorphosed a community once remarkable for their indifference to

monetary gain, and their supineness in commercial speculation (the nation whose cry was " *Vive la bagatelle,*" and who
reproached us with being a " Nation of shopkeepers "), into a
people of jobbers, and higglers, and hagglers, incredibly avid
of riches, unblushingly extortionate in trade, ceaselessly
hungering after francs and centimes;—this magician, who has
been able to do everything with France and the French
(the abrogation of profligacy and gambling, and the preven-
tion of decrease in the population excepted), appears likewise to have thought, or to have hoped, that by devoting the
Champ de Mars to a certain purpose, and giving that
purpose half a year's unlimited scope and verge, he could
manufacture a Millennium. The Imperial purpose has had
the very amplest scope and verge; but society is constrained
to own that the Millennium seems as far off as ever.

Meanwhile one labours under the same difficulty in
satisfactorily defining what has been this Something on the
banks of the shining river over against the Trocadero. The
Universal Exposition of 1867: that, you know well enough,
is the official designation. The " Great French Exhibition,"
that is the appellation given to it by some of the London newspapers. The " Transcendant Pageant of the Champ –
de Mars " might serve as a title if one wished to be
euphuistic. Or, to suit the sensationally comic mind,
such a name might be devised as " The Field of one
Million Footsteps;" or " The Globe flattened, and the Poles
brought face to face." I think myself, that, inscribing
" Notes and Sketches of the Paris Exhibition " on my title-
page, I shall be meeting the requirements of the case in a
sober and sensible manner, so far as my publisher's interests
are concerned. Mr. Mudie might not care about subscribing

to " Jottings from the Pont de Jena ; or "A Scamper through the Champ de Mars ;" or a "Trip to the Trocadero." Preserving then " The Paris Exhibition" as the practical basis of my book, I intend, while endeavouring to glean some scant inklings of its philosophical bearings and its real purport and signification, as an illustration of the civilisation of the age, to speak of it as a *Great Show*. I hope neither to overrate or to underrate the mark it has made in our social life, or the place it will occupy in the history which is to come. I trust that I shall neither exaggerate its faults nor amplify its merits. It has set neither the Thames nor the Seine on fire ; and the deceitful and desperately wicked heart of man will not be much softened, I am afraid, by the fact of the Legion of Honour being given to a Yankee pianoforte, or a gold medal conferred on the manufacturer of a beautifully-carved cupboard. Nor has the lion lain down with the lamb during the Exhibition, save with the intent of getting as much wool off his back as he was able ; nor have the nations, or rather the nations' rulers, after hearing Signor Rossini's hymn, abated one jot in their feverish desire, on the flimsiest pretexts, to send forth their fleets and armies in battle array for the purpose of cutting one another's throats and blowing each other to pieces. The great lessons of the Exhibition, whatever they may be, have yet, perhaps, to be gotten by heart ; and their value very probably will not be appreciated for many years to come : while whole centuries may elapse ere they bear good fruit in the regeneration of mankind. On the other hand, I do not feel at all inclined, because I have sat by this show, from its cradle to its grave—because I have watched its dawn, its noon, and its sunset—because I have been behind its scenes, and put my finger on its sore places—because I have noted the hollowness of many of its professions, and the meanness and rapacity of some of its promoters—I do *not*, I say, for such reasons, feel inclined to decry it as a job, or denounce it as a sham. It has been full of buffoons, and mummies, and conjurers, and mountebanks of every description—of dwarfs and giants, and quacks and toothdrawers, and Chinese jugglers; it has been full of beershops, and dramshops, and cookshops, and booths where all kinds of disreputable antics were played; it has been, throughout, the scene of the paltriest chicanery, and the *champ clos* of the dirtiest speculators; but all these scandals notwithstanding, it must never be forgotten that, tawdry and muddy as may have been the fringe, the mantle has been of the finest and richest texture the world has ever seen. Pushing through the Bartlemy Fair, in the exterior zone you entered a Palace replete with the most astonishing productions of the genius, the industry, and the skill of man; and it is not too much to say, that the bare fact of this show having contained such works as the paintings of Gérome, of Meissonnier, and of Rosa Bonheur; as the statuary of Vela, and the terra cottas of Leopold Harzé; as the bronzes of Barbédienne; as the porcelain of Sèvres; as the tapestry and carpets of the Gobelins and of Aubusson; as the jewellery and goldsmith's ware of Christofle of Paris and Castellani of Rome; as the mosaics of Salviati, and the enamels of Lepecq; as the furniture of Fourdinois and Gros— you see that I have abstained, for once, from that which is known as "British business," and have carefully abstained from alluding to one of my own countrymen—is sufficient to atone for all the mimicry and mummery, the vending of sweetstuff and photography, the droning upon bagpipes and drubbing upon tabors, which used to take place outside. In truth, although in the interior of the Palace a [vast quantity of rubbish was constantly on view,] and many sections of the show were inferior in quality of merchandise to what we can see every day for nothing in the Passage des Panoramas or in the Lowther Arcade, [there were scattered through the courts occupied by the different nationalities exhibiting, a prodigious collection of rarities and marvels which had never before been brought into juxtaposition. And in the instruction derivable from this juxtaposing of the products of various countries lies, yet latent, I think the chief benefit derivable from the entire Show.]

III.

LANDMARKS.

THERE could not have been chosen a better spot for the Peace Tournament of 1867 than the Champ de Mars, grand in actual area, grander still in the historical· remembrances. National assemblages, patriotic *fêtes*, the Federation of the Provinces, the Champ de Mai of the Hundred Days, reviews in the presence of great kings and mighty warriors—these are among the proud memories of Mar's Field in Paris. Again, it was here in the year 1798 that the first French Industrial Exhibition was held. The building was diminutive; the number of exhibitors was one hundred and ten; yet it is fitting for the giant to recognise his cradle, and wonder however it contrived to hold him.

Much fine writing has been lavished on the fact of a place dedicated from time immemorial to warlike exercises being selected as the site for a temple of Peace. I believe the Champ de Mars was fixed upon because no other area so vast or so convenient of access could be found; and, as for Peace and War, the smell of distant gunpowder hung about the Exhibition building from its opening to its closing day. Within its walls were an abundant display of engines of death and destruction; and by this time next year regiments will probably be trotting up and down Mars' Field with the Chassepot rifle, "which has done wonders," on their shoulders, as though the Evangelical Conference and the Society for the Protection of Animals had never had their "Exhibits" within its *enceinte.*

To M. François de Neufchâteau belongs the honour of arranging that '98 Exhibition of which I spoke just now, and which brought together only one hundred and ten exhibitors. At our Hyde Park Exhibition of the Industry of all Nations in 1851 there were 13,935 exhibitors.* At the Palais de l'Industrie in Paris, in 1855, the exhibitors rose to 28,954. In London, at South Kensington, in 1862, there were 28,653 exhibitors, and in Paris, in the Champ de Mars, in 1867, there were 42,237. The number of rewards distributed in 1867 was about 11,000. I take the number of exhibitors to be exorbitant, and the recompenses excessive.

There is no need to dwell upon the architectural appearance of the Exhibition building. It has been called a "Titanic creation of modern metallurgy." It was, certainly for the most part, constructed of iron and glass, was very huge and very unornamented, but exceedingly commodious. I am not

---

* Here is the ascending table of exhibitors at the various Parisian Exhibitions :—

		Exhibitors.	
Year V.	(1798)	110	23
Year IX.	(1801)	220	30
Year X.	(1802)	540	254
Empire	(1806)	1,422	610
Restoration	(1819)	1,662	869
„	(1823)	1,642	10,91
„	(1825)	1,695	12,54
Louis Philippe	(1834)	2,447	1,785
„	(1839)	3,281	2,305
„	(1844)	3,960	3,253
Republic	(1849)	5,494	4,000

much disposed to sentimentalize, but I can scarcely refrain from "wiping away a tear"—was it not the soldier who "wiped away a tear?"—when I think that the great Babel in which I passed the best part of so many months is being ruthlessly demolished as though it were of no more account than the filthy London hovels which are being pulled down to make way for the Holborn Viaduct.

When the Persian king reviewed his myriad army, he also burst into tears to think that a hundred years thence not one man among those legions would be alive. The sentimentality of Xerxes may seem affected, but there is, nevertheless, abundant food for sadness in the thought that anything is doomed to dissolution—that what we are proud or fond of is destined to go, to depart, to disappear utterly from the world. Shakespeare's "Tempest" might be performed by strolling players in a barn to an audience of bumpkins; but, however mean the show, however wretched the actors, however gross the hearers, there is always one speech which commands attention, and sinks deep into the heart—one speech that shines out bright, like the eyes of a lion in a dark cave—one speech that moves and impresses the actor who makes it almost as much as the clodhoppers who listen to it, It is the most eloquent sermon in the whole world, and the most re-nowned divines might strive in vain to preach a better. Nor Bossuet, nor Bourdaloue, nor Taylor, nor Wesley ever said anything so solemn or so true as that which the poet-player has told us—that the cloud-capped towers, that the palaces and pinnacles and temples, that the pride and ambition and luxury of Man shall dissolve, and "like the baseless fabric of a vision, leave not a wrack behind."

The Universal Exhibition of 1867 has already become a

thing of the past. It is over. The three last days of grace have expired. The doors of the edifice are now closed ; the auctioneer's hammer has been heard in the halls of the International Club, and the galleries of the Palace in the Champ de Mars have become a wilderness of packing-cases and a chaos of uprooted fixtures. Everything must go. Everything must dissolve. Picture and statue and carving, rich jewel and rare vase, pottery and goldsmith's ware, glass and iron—the porcelain of Sèvres and the tapestry of the Gobelins, books and photographs, microscopes and colossal steam-engines— the strangest assemblage of examples of ingenuity and industry ever seen must be scattered to the four winds of Heaven. Egyptian temples, Turkish mosques, and Tunisian bazaars, lighthouses and laboratories, conservatories and aquaria, the picture-gallery and the lapidary's workshop, the tavern and the theatre, the church and the coffee-shop, the Bible-stall and the showman's booth, the toy-shop and the library, the stable and the labourer's cottage—all the beautiful and curious and interesting objects brought together in the park must submit to one common lot, and come to one common end. They must be uprooted and demolished. Some of the edifices, indeed, their several pieces carefully numbered, may be put together again and rebuilt in other places, and countries remote and semi-civilized may rejoice in the possession of the *spolia opima* of 1867 ; but the spell is broken, and the wand of the magician is broken too. They will never possess the same interest, they will never impart the same pleasure and instruction. The whole is dissolved ; and what may be the fate of the parts becomes only a secondary consideration. As to the destiny of the Palace itself, one can only indulge in conjecture. The scheme of removing it bodily to Russia,

there to be used as a market, is said to have been abandoned.
Keenly sensitive as our neighbours are to the ridiculous, it is
not to be supposed that the Parisians would tolerate a re-
erected exhibition building in the environs of their capital.
Le ridicule tue in France; and when the Emperor compli-
mented M. Le Play on having built him a "magnificent
gasometer," the architectural pretensions of the edifice were
at once and definitively condemned. The most obvious
course to adopt with this vast structure of glass and iron is
to pull it down and sell the materials. Unkindly criticised
as its form and appearance have been, it is undeniable that
M. Le Play's palace has, on the whole, served the purpose for
which it was designed. Captain Fowke's Exhibition at
Brompton in 1862 was outwardly hideous and inwardly
incommodious; but the vast series of ellipses in the Champ de
Mars, mean and stunted as they looked, and deficient as they
were in the slightest approach to a handsome or an imposing
aspect, offered all conceivable facilities to exhibitors for the
proper display of their wares. Everything could be seen and
everything could be found. It was perfectly easy both to get
into and get out of the place. Nobody could lose his way in
the Exhibition. The radiating streets which centred in the
interior garden, the classification of the objects into groups, the
great raised platform which ran right round the Machinery
Gallery, were all original ideas, ingenious in conception and
most skilfully worked out. Those who studied the Exhibition
with any special purpose in view could at once fix upon the
department in which they desired to pursue their investiga-
tions. The man of system would take the Exhibition group
by group and ellipse by ellipse; the mere sight-seer would
saunter easily from France to the Antipodes, and find himself

led, by facile and and almost insensible degrees, to examine and compare the artistic and industrial treasures with which this house of marvels overflowed. It was very hard work to get through the Exhibitions of '51, of '55, and of '62; but '67 made sight-seeing easy, and opened a Royal road of instruction in technics and the applied sciences.

The records of this Exhibition will be famous to all time. The roll of its visiters literally blazes with splendour. Two Emperors and a Sultan and half-a-score of Kings came specially to see it. Princes were for months as plentiful in Paris as blackberries. With the exception of Victor Emmanuel, the Queen of Spain, and our own Sovereign, every crowned head in Europe was proud to pay homage at the shrine of Art and Industry. The Emperor Napoleon himself took from the outset the liveliest interest in the enterprise, and watched with the deepest solicitude over its development. Almost any afternoon during the heyday of the Exhibition, the Ruler of the French, leaning on the arm of an aide-de-camp, might have been seen strolling from stall to stall, examining, criticising, praising, purchasing objects of curiosity or rarity. The Empress also took the greatest interest in the display, and was its constant and most graceful patroness. And multifarious as the accusations brought against the Imperial Commissioners may have been—discourteous as some of their acts and patent some of their blunders undoubtedly were—grasping, rapacious, and greedy after lucre as they sometimes showed themselves, the very highest praise cannot be withheld from M. Le Play and his colleagues for their energy and skill in grappling with difficulties which, in many instances, seemed well-nigh insurmountable. It was said that in the scheme of the Exhibition too much had been attempted, and too much had been promised; but recalling the appearance of the palace and its surroundings in April, and contrasting it with the aspect presented in June, there was room for astonishment—there was room for the heartiest congratulation to the bold and skilful men who had at last succeeded in welding together all the parts of the gigantic machine, and putting it into working gear. The task before M. Le Play was immeasurably greater than that with which any of his predecessors in the organization of Exhibitions had had to deal. The retirement of Prince Napoleon from the presidency of the Commission was, in the outset, a heavy blow and discouragement; for the Prince was no merely "ornamental" President—his co-operation, his counsels, and his suggestions were eminently serviceable in 1855, and might have been of even greater value in 1867. The presence, too, of his Imperial Highness, at the head of the Commission might have softened down asperities, might have obviated the necessity for certain unpleasant acts, might have saved the commissioners from dabbling in many equivocal transactions. In the face of all these obstacles and all these difficulties, M. Le Play certainly achieved a success which, impartially considered, may be accounted a triumph.

The French people have throughout—and much to their credit—been the largest and most liberal patrons of the display of which France has so many reasons to be proud. Paris—unthinking, trivial, volatile Paris—was, it is true, very soon satiated with the spectacle of the Champ de Mars; and those who were neither exhibitors nor *concessionnaires* of *cafés* or *restaurants* speedily voted the Exposition a bore. The Parisian season ticket-holders were never very numerous; the only rush of the great world to the Palais de l'Industrie was to witness the distribution of prizes and to stare at the Sultan and the Prince of Wales; and no sooner did the heats of summer set in, than *gandins*, countesses, and *cocottes* trooped off to the watering-places; taking care, however, before their departure, to let their apartments at exorbitant rents to foreign visitors in Paris. The foreign visitors, even, did not come in that amazing numerical strength which had been anticipated. Most Englishmen of eminence, most Englishwomen of rank, many people of affluence or of easy means, probably took a run over to Paris between April and October; but vast numbers of the middle, and even a goodly proportion of the upper, classes of Britain stayed away altogether, deterred by the terrible tales narrated of inadequate accommodation, unsatisfactory dinners, and excessive prices. The Orientals, notably the Egyptians, made a fair show on the Champ de Mars; and picked and special men came in considerable numbers from almost every country under the sun; but the Italians, as a nation, were absent. They pleaded that they couldn't afford it. The Spaniards didn't " come in their thousands;" they alleged domestic troubles. The Germans didn't come up to the mark; they urged the gloominess of the political horizon. And a pistol-shot, fired by a crazy machinist in the Bois de Boulogne, withdrew from the Exhibition a large amount of Russian patronage. Even the threatened irruption of seventy thousand Yankees dwindled down to a modified invasion of not more than seven thousand.

In the face of these slight disappointments, the support given by provincial and rural France to the Exhibition was steady, continuous, and remunerative. There has been throughout the summer and autumn a constantly increasing influx of French country people into Paris. The shopkeepers of that rapacious city turned up their noses at the provincials, because they brought very little money, lived frugally, and preferred staring at the exterior of the Maison Dorée and the Café Riche to entering those abodes of luxury, and eating up a month's income at a single meal. The Louvre and the Grand, the Bristol and Meurice's, did not gain much from the advent of these tourists, who generally subsided into economical *maison meublées* in the calmest of bye-streets, and had a remarkable knack for finding out the very cheapest eatables and drinkables in the Commissariat of the Exhibition. But they *did* "come in their thousands," and they were precisely the thousands who should have come to such a Congress. The most wonderful old women, with the most wonderful mob-caps ever seen, perhaps, out of the caricatures of Daumier or Charlet; the most venerable patriarchs in blouses, and striped nightcaps, and *sabots;* farmers with fluffy white hats and "flower-pot" waistcoats; priests with crimson umbrellas; pretty Normandes, in their coquettish *cauchoises;* white-veiled and rosaried nuns; Dominican and Cistercian monks; shaggy mountaineers from the Vosges; savage-looking shepherds from the Landes; swarthy fishermen from the coast of Provence; loud-talking Gascons; smuggler-looking Basques; melancholy Bretons, with their long hair and baggy knickerbockers; hard-headed Northerners, never tired of assuring their acquaintances that Lille was in Flanders; all these represented, in the symposium on the quay of Jena, the Great French People. An analogous gathering of English provincials took place in Hyde Park in 1851, and at Kensington in 1862; and there is a story of a dapper engineer officer who was showing the lions of poor

Captain Fowke's palace to an ancient agriculturist in a smock frock, when Rusticus suddenly burst into tears, crying, "Lord ha' mercy! Such foine things beant for the like of I."

- The balance of profit and loss has yet to be struck, and the guarantors of the Exhibition may yet have to discover that those who come for wool sometimes go away shorn. The yield for the sale of season tickets may not have been wholly satisfactory; the takings at the turnstiles may not have come up to general expectation; the expenses may have far exceeded the calculations of the eminent financiers who framed the Exhibition budget. More than this, it cannot be gainsaid that there may have been, from first to last, a little blundering, a little pedantry, and, perhaps, a slight amount or jobbery in the guidance of the gigantic machine. It is certain, at all events, that no more vehement complaints could have been made against the Imperial Commission than were made in '62 against our own Royal Commissioners. Nor was the great French chair case, in which cookshop and coffeehouse-keepers went to law with M. Le Play on a question of joint-stools, much more scandalous than our own walking-stick and umbrella grievance, five years since, when her Majesty's representatives were dragged into the Brompton County Court by an indignant citizen, who conceived that he had been illegally mulcted of a few halfpence. It is probable, also, that a good many of the ardent and sanguine spirits who imagined that they were about to amass splendid fortunes from some speculation directly or indirectly connected with the Exhibition have burnt their fingers, and that the Tribunal of Commerce will in time be busied with the cases of these unlucky Alnaschars. But such consider-

ations sink into the pettiest insignificance when it is
remembered what the Exhibition really has been, and what
it really has done for France, for civilization, and for the
world. Its promoters perhaps undertook too gigantic a task,
and were unable efficiently to achieve all their dreams; but
that which was really accomplished was, it may be said
without exageration, stupendous. The park, with the edifices
scattered over its area, was an original idea, and may prove
to be unparalleled. No such assemblage of rare and beautiful works will ever be seen together as were shown in the
Gallery of the History of Labour. No such masterpieces of
painting and sculpture from every country in Christendom
will ever again be collected under one roof. No such
curious gathering of all nations will ever be brought together
in one European capital. No such Synod of Sovereigns
will ever be convened for the criticism of a mere show of
artistic and industrial products. This may not be, perhaps,
the last of Universal Exhibitions, but it has been assuredly
the largest and strangest our age has witnessed.

To complete the record of illustrious visitors to the French
Exhibition, it was necessary, perhaps, that the Prince of
Monaco should pay a visit to the Champ de Mars. The
Emperor of China was prevented by urgent private affairs
from coming to Paris, and circumstances over which he had
no control hindered the journey of the Shah of Persia to
France. The head of the House of Grimaldi—he is Charles
the something, the Seventy-third, we think—was wanting.
This was much to be regretted, for Monaco is a great prince
in Israel. He keeps a gambling-house. His fleet consists of
one felucca and a dingy. He has a standing army of eleven
gendarmes, with the largest cocked hats and the longest sabres

to be seen anywhere between Nice and Genoa, and they alternately officiate as sentinels at the palace gate and footmen at the palace dinner-table. Some people insinuate likewise that the general commanding and his brilliant staff of one sergeant occasionally take a turn as croupiers at the Monacal roulette tables. The coat of arms of Charles, Prince of Monaco bear, curiously enough, on a field argent, a number of lozenges *gules*, and the entire escutcheon has a striking resemblance to the ten of diamonds; a most appropriate cognisance for a potentate who makes such a comfortable addition to his income through foolish people's backing the red. Monaco is, however, just at this moment, under a cloud. The Exposition closed without numbering his Egregiousness— I mean his Serene Highness—among her guests. A carpenter who had sent in his bill to Monaco for the repair of a carriage, being unable to obtain his money—it was only thirty-five francs—sued the Prince before a *juge de paix* at Nice, and got judgment. He did not get the cash, however. Monaco snapped his fingers at the Nizzard *juge de paix*, and, moreover, expelled the presumptuous carpenter from his dominions. One kick would, perhaps, have been sufficient to attain that end. I can hardly, however, imagine that Monaco can be so very short of money as to be unable to pay a carpenter's bill for thirty-five francs. The gambling-house is said to be doing pretty well; but perhaps Monaco has been forestalling the allowance he receives from the manager, or has taken to playing at his own tables, and, backing the red, has been brought to confusion. At all events, if Monaco be wise, he will pay up. *Noblesse oblige.* The Grimaldis should be above the seductions of " tick."

IV.

TRANSFORMATION.

THE Second Empire has been fruitful in surprises, political and social; but of all the strange things which have been seen in Paris during the last fifteen years, few can equal the extraordinary transformation which was taking place in February in the Champ de Mars, and in view of the approaching Universal Exhibition. I came straight from Naples to Marseilles to behold the extraordinary transformation here. The Parisians have no New Zealander who can be summoned from Oswego, and perched upon a shattered pier of London Bridge, with a sketch-book on his knee, whenever a moral is to be pointed or a tale adorned; but M. de Voltaire had an "intelligent Huron," whom he occasionally trotted out when strong social contrasts were to be drawn. The Voltairian Huron was in Paris about a hundred years ago, and may have visited the Champ de Mars when the Ecole Militaire was really a military school, destined to receive, a few years later, a young military graduate from Brienne, by the name of Napoleon Bonaparte. What would the intelligent savage have said to the Field of Mars in its aspect last February? But for the imposing façade of the academy which has long since been changed into a barrack, he would have barely recognized the great sandy plain which for so many centuries has been devoted to the art of war, and in which, perhaps, fifteen hundred years ago, the legions of Julian the Apostate were wont to manœuvre. We may send our intelligent Huron, however, back to his native wilds, and take a more familiar type of observant humanity—the "Oldest Inhabit-ant." In few cities do people seem to live so long as they do in Paris. The reason may be that the French are fond of retiring from business so soon as they have realized a decent competence. They live on their *rentes*, and annuitants are proverbially long-lived. The "Oldest Inhabitant," then, duly inscribed on the Grand Livre, decorated, white-haired, slightly bent, but quite healthy and cheerful, and giving promise to draw his dividends for an indefinite number of years to come, might well have held up his hands in amazement when he surveyed the rapidly progressing works of the Universal Exhibition, and reflected upon the changes which he had seen, not only in the march of events and the manners of the time, but in the actual configuration of the Champ de Mars; for so old may we assume this annuitant-inhabitant to be, that he may remember being taken by his papa to the spot, when Louis XVI. was still King, but was to be converted into a Constitutional Monarch, and, in the presence of half a million, more or less, of his subjects, was to swear a bran new oath to a bran new constitution, at a bran new altar in the Champ de Mars, converted for the nonce into one colossal amphitheatre. Then, as in February, thousands of workmen had been toiling night and day for months at the metamorphosis of the great sand plain. Some dim outlines of the artificial ridges of earth built up for seats may yet be traced on the outskirts of the field. The builders were not only hired day labourers, but soldiers, schoolboys, priests, noble lords and fair ladies, and waiting women, who cast by their embroidered coats and powdered wigs, and laid down their fans and scent bottles, to ply pick and shovel, and delve sods, and trundle barrows. Mr. Carlyle has, in match-less language, described the vast army of volunteer navvies who embanked, and swept, and garnished the Champ de Mars for the great ceremony of the oath of federation—a federation which was to regenerate France and the world. And from the remembrance of that solemnity our Inhabitant may turn to the period when the Red Flag made the circuit of the Champ de Mars, streaming, as Lamartine said, with a nation's blood; and to the bleak wintry day when, on the other side of the river, but in view of the field, the virtuous Bailly, after being subjected to the last degrees of indignity and outrage, was done to death by savage men. Or, again, the Inhabitant may call to mind the Champ de Mars when it was a *Champ de Mai*, and the First Napoleon, in a plumed hat, a velvet doublet, and silken hose, mounted the steps of a new altar to promulgate yet another new constitution— the end of which, six brief weeks afterwards, was Waterloo. Or, finally, our ancient observer may remember when, under the restored Bourbons, the mound of the Trocadero opposite— the sham monument of a sham victory—was heaped up, and all that blazing fireworks could achieve was done to make the people, in whose memory Austerlitz and Wagram were yet fresh, believe that the Duke of Angoulême was a great general, and the Spanish military promenade of 1822 a glorious campaign. It is not idle to assume that there are people alive and hale in Paris who have witnessed all these mutations of the Champ de Mars; but its last transfor-

mation may excite almost equal astonishment in the present
generation. Apart from the absorption of the plain itself
by the Exhibition buildings, gardens, and park, the entire
environment of this huge space has been changed since
Napoleon III. has held sway, and Baron Haussmann has
officiated as Prefect of the Seine, and architectural magician
in ordinary to the Empire. Great gaps of waste have been
filled up, and now loom grandiose with many-storied mansions.
The Trocadero itself, on the opposite bank of the Seine, has
been transformed. It was wont to resemble a kind of
Primrose-hill in difficulties; it is now a species of Renaissance
Acropolis. The houses formerly surrounding the field at
irregular intervals were either mean hovels, shady cabarets,
and rickety soap factories, or those peculiarly ugly, gaunt,
and ghastly blocks of houses which, with their tall, bare
fronts spotted with black windows, gave to the outskirts
of Paris an odd affinity to a city built of dominoes set on end.
The double-sixes and double-fours, with here and there a
double-blank in the shape of a dead-wall, have all disappeared,
and in their place rise the stately structures of new Paris,
slightly redundant in decoration—slightly garish, if you will
—but still a vast improvement on the bleak and tasteless
structures of the Restoration and the Monarchy of July. All
this, however, is but a drop in the ocean of transformation
I saw last winter. The Campus Martius had itself been
swallowed up. It had vanished. Mars had no longer anything to do with it. Minerva ruled the roast. No Julian's
legionaries, no veterans of the First nor hosts of the Third
Napoleon, could manœuvre any more in a field, every rood
of which was now dedicated to the arts of peace. The plain
was still sandy, and worked up as it was with a compost

of brickbats, limewhiting, and sawdust, proved not very conducive to comfort in walking, or to the preservation of neatness about the lower extremities; but there was nothing
else to remind the spectator that he was on the famous
ground so intimately associated with some of the most moving
events in French history. Where the Chinese were rearing
their porcelain tower, Imperial Cæsar may have sworn his
oath; and the refreshment bar from which Messrs. Spiers and
Pond dispensed such teeming stores of dainty viands, and
inexhaustible floods of generous beverages, might have been
on the very site of the high altar where Talleyrand, Bishop of
Autun, said mass, grinning and with his tongue in his cheek.

The visitor who approached the Exhibition building with
any preconceived notion of a Crystal Palace, or, indeed, any
kind of palace, would scarcely fail to be disappointed at the
appearance of the structure; but if, before crossing the bridge
of Jena, he had just glanced over the plan of the building
and its approaches, published by the *Illustration* newspaper, and mastered the general topographical bearings
therein marked out, he must have been hypercritical indeed
to dispute the merit of the architects and engineers employed
by the Imperial Commission in having contrived a series
of buildings eminently convenient and practicable, and in
every way suited to the purpose for which they were designed.
That can scarcely be termed ugly which lays no claim whatever to æsthetic merit. A locomotive engine, as it is, cannot
be called ugly; but a locomotive with a composite capital
to its funnel, and lion's-head bosses on its axle-boxes, might
be a very hideous construction indeed. Our Crystal Palace
of '51 was an inspiration at once happy and unique; but in
the infinite variations and elaborations of the idea conceived

by Sir Joseph Paxton, and so wondrously worked out by Sir Charles Fox and Mr. Henderson—variations and elaborations attempted from one end of the world to the other— the progress made, from an æsthetic point of view, was certainly retrograde.   Captain Fowke, with a really commendable capacity for plain-sailing work and the best intentions in the world, attained the bathos of bad taste at Brompton in '62; and the French architects, after trying their very best with the Palais de l'Industrie in the Champ Elysées seem to have arrived at the sage conclusion that modifications of the Crystal Palace were, at best, but a mistake, and that it was preferable for the future to keep the shell of the Exhibition nut entirely subordinate to the development of its kernel.   They provided shelter for the treasures of the World's Fair of 1867, and they did not profess to do more; but few can deny that the shelter afforded was ample, was well arranged, and was so simply symmetrical as to have become, in its *ensemble*, decidedly handsome, if not strictly beautiful.   Thus, there was no towering dome, serving no earthly purpose, and failing to please the eye which it endeavours to strike.   There were no towers, designed mainly to flank a *façade;* and no *façade*, erected expressly to afford an excuse for two towers.   The programme set down before the architects by the Imperial Commission was rigorously imperative, but admirably simple: " An area with two main entrances.   Manufactures and products of cognate natures to be arranged in concentric bands, with a garden in the middle.   The different nationalities to intersect these bands by lines or avenues radiating from the centre."   This was the theorem propounded, and on this the Exhibition buildings were strictly constructed.

The form of the entire area was that of a quasi-ellipse. To speak more plainly, it was of the shape of a Pie-Dish, Around it ran a series of concentric galleries, cut into so many blocks by the radiating avenues. Take your dish, as Mrs. Glasse would say, and place an oval of spinach in the middle—there is your garden. Range round your spinach, at equal distances, as many rows of tit-bits as you like, at equal distances and with equal spaces between them, and there are your galleries. Set down the dish in the midst of the drawing-room carpet, and call the chiffonnier, the chairs, the fender, the footstool, and the work-table, annexes, belonging to China, Turkey, Russia, or Egypt, as the case may be, and there you have the plan of your Universal Exhibition.

It need scarcely be said that in a building constructed on such principles the attainment of any general and magnificent *coup d'œil* was a simple impossibility. We had no colossal and commanding sweep of vista in which the eye could embrace at one glance an Australian gold pyramid, a majolica or a crystal fountain, a Keith's silk trophy, a great organ, a forest tree, a daïs, and a throne.

Many thousands of workmen were of course employed, and were busier than any bees in finishing the interior. When I first came to the place little remained to be done in the way of galleries and pilasters, trusses and girders, so that the workers in brass had mainly disappeared from the scene, and given place to painters and glaziers, and especially to carpenters and joiners, whose avocations diffused a universal odour of warm glue and new deal planks through the building. The smell of the latter, albeit eminently terebinthine, was not unpleasant; and so soft and mild was it that the Parisian faculty began to recommend promenades in the enormous workshops to consumptive patients. Whether to assist a curative treatment, or to satisfy a legitimate curiosity, or to kill time, great numbers of ladies and gentlemen daily availed themselves of the leave granted to visit the works by the Imperial Commission. The admittance was not given as a matter of favour, but was procurable by every person who chose to pay the sum of one franc at the turnstiles. Such an innovation must be held as wholly unprecedented, and it certainly worked admirably. There is no nation so thoroughly wedded to the doctrine of social equality as are our gallant allies. A Frenchman detests the bare idea of favouritism, and scouts the notion of a privileged class. Did caste prevail in France, caste would obtain its special passes of admission, and the non-Brahminical sections of the community would be excluded from the Exhibition; but, under the happily imagined one-franc *régime*, the senator or the marshal of France, the workman in his blouse and the *grisette* in her plaited cap were alike free to inspect the progress of an undertaking destined for the recreation and instruction of the whole Empire. At home our first care, when we set about making anything national, is to post up placards, with " no admission except on business;" or to plant policemen wherever there is anything to be seen, with instructions to order off the inferior classes.

The grand or Imperial entrance to the Exhibition was on the Quai d'Orsay, facing the Bridge of Jena. There was a species of triumphal arch at the foot of the bridge, formed by four columns sixty feet high, from which floated banners. The distance from the bridge to the Exhibition building was about five hundred yards, and the whole of this was roofed in by a vast awning, sixty feet broad, and at a height of thirty feet from the ground. The underside of the velarium was of green cashmere, powdered with golden bees. This superb canopy was supported throughout its length by thirty pilasters, ornamented with scutcheons bearing the arms of France and the flags of all nations. Thus the most beautiful portion of the park was traversed under cover, with France on the left and England on the right-hand side—a right generous compliment to us, and one worthy of a people who are as courteous as they are brave. In the distance, on the French side, loomed the East with her minarets and her cupolas, her mosques and her bazaars. On the English side, the West, with all her arts and all her industry, filled the perspective. Entering the palace by the large bay at the extremity of the velarium-covered avenue, the visitor entered the immense nave occupied by machinery. At the end of this was the central garden, from whose green glades radiated all the intersecting avenues of the fabric. France branched to the left, England to the right. From the middle of the great machinery nave branched on either side an iron staircase, leading to a wonderfully-constructed gallery, or rather platform, of iron, supported on highly-ornamented pillars, fifteen feet high. This platform served as a promenade, and was occupied, besides, by the workpeople engaged in duties complementary to those of the machines below. At intervals along this platform, which formed one of the concentric wings of the grand ellipse, there were staircases for ascent and descent.

Among the multifarious systems of artificial memory by means of which, in all ages and countries, ardent but impatient scholars have striven to bridge the Straits of Hard

Work, and build a royal road to the Temple of Knowledge, there is one known as the " topical," of Greek origin, and, presumably, some three thousand years old. No book, or implement of any kind, is required, and the system is best acquired in bed, and in the dark. The student has merely to imagine that, in his mind's eye, he sees a rectangular apartment. Then—always in imagination—he must divide the ceiling, the 'floor, and the four sides of this apartment into any number he chooses of squares. In every one of these squares he must place permanently some object, letter, or sign, which by a subtle mental process can be made to associate itself with the thing he wishes to remember. Thus, after a little practice, the square occupied *en permanence* by, let us say, a goose, will serve to recall the birthplace of Haydn, the date of the last Punic war, and thirty-three, Wood-street, Cheapside ; while a pair of scissors may come to mean the destruction of Troy, and a lamp-post the population of the State of Ohio. It may be hinted that the mental process involved is so very subtle that few are able to master it, or to retain it when it. has been mastered ; and that this system of artificial memory, like many other notable devices for shortening labour, is good only so far as it goes, which is not far. It is as when drunken men, in their over-cunning, hide their money, but are unable when sober to remember where they hid it. A tremendous accumulation of facts may be stowed away under the " topical " system ; but when you want a fact the chances are ten to one that you cannot find the key of your store cupboard. Should any modern lady or gentleman, however, feel ambitious to effect that which the old Greek philosopher puzzled his brains over, perhaps to their destruction—for it is said that quite as many persons have gone mad from the study of artificial memory as from that of the Apocalypse—I might advise them to take the Universal Paris Exhibition as a good solid foundation whereon to build a modification of the "topical" system. Let them try to attain some conception of its arrangements and of its probable contents by means of artificial memory; for it is quite certain that they will gain but a very vague notion of the building, the park, or its approaches, either through reading or through learning by heart any description of them, however detailed. They may be advised to purchase, for a franc, an engraved bird's-eye view of the Champ de Mars in its transformed condition. Having pinned this cartoon against the wall, let them sit down and stare at it, regularly, for, say three hours and a half every day. By degrees they will find that the bird's-eye view, colour, distant perspective, marginal references, and all, will have become durably burnt, etched, stamped, or carved on their memory. If they stare long enough, they will always have the Exhibition in their eye, as the hypochondriacal gentleman of the last century had the skeleton. They will go to bed with a bird's-eye view, and get up with a bird's-eye view, and take it with them to church, to the theatre, or on railway journeys. Being once provided with this indelible proof of nature-printing, they have only to furnish each one of the curvilinear blocks or slices into which the interior of the building was partitioned with some familiar object or sign, with which—by means of the "subtle mental process" mentioned above—they may associate the different countries exhibited and the different products to be exhibited. After that they may go to the catalogue with what appetite they may. The perusal of Humboldt's "Cosmos" is said to comprise a thorough educa-

tion; and if the mere schedule of classification published by
the Imperial Commission is to be taken as a sample of what
is to come afterwards, an entire lifetime may be devoted to
the perusal of the Exhibition Catalogue. If at any stage of
this somewhat trying intellectual curriculum the student
should happen to break down, it need only be hinted that
the Maison de Santé of Dr. Blanche, in the vicinity of Paris,
leaves, in comfort and the attention shown to the mentally
afflicted, nothing to be desired.

"Egypt's Place in Universal History" is, as all students of
M. Ernest Bunsen must be aware, as vast as it is mysterious;
but there was no mystery about Egypt's place in the Paris
Universal Exhibition of 1867. The energetic and apparently
enlightened Viceroy spared no effort to glorify his dusky
dominion in the eyes of all the world in Paris. The countries
which are generally assumed to be the most backward in
civilisation attempted to prove, so far as outward show and
glitter went, in the Champ de Mars, that they were leading
the van rather than bringing up the rear of the march
of Progress; and among the old and seemingly worn-out
countries determined to show that they have grown young
again, Egypt occupied a very prominent place. She distanced
Turkey; she gave Tunis twenty, and beat her; she threw
Algeria into the shade; she even eclipsed America and
Australia. The reproach has ere now been flung in the teeth
of Spain that she is in Africa, which continent is said to begin
at the Pyrenees. The Egyptian Viceroy ventured on a bolder
geographical paradox. He strove to convince the Giaours
that Egypt is in Europe. The Commissioner-General for
Egypt was M. Charles Edmond. To M. Mariette-Bey his
Cairene Highness confided the direction of the archæological

department; for ancient as well as modern Egypt was represented, and the Viceroy contributed to the Exhibition the .
choicest treasures in his museum of antiquities. He could
not, it is true, send Cleopatra's needle to Paris, since that
interesting monument belongs to the British Government,
who have unaccountably neglected, during more than half a
century, to take formal possession of the venerable relic,
which is undoubtedly their property, and which would be
eagerly accepted by any other European State. What a
superb central ornament to the courtyard of the British
Museum would Cleopatra's needle make! It remains, however, baking in the Egyptian sand, the cynosure only of
donkey boys and of tourists, who—as inquisitive as the down-
east gentleman who, when he was shown the knife with which
Charlotte Corday slew Marat, asked to see the fork, if it was
" on hand "—inquire, when they see Cleopatra's needle,
whereabouts she kept her pins. In default, however, of an
obelisk, the Viceroy sent a good stock of mummies and a
liberal batch of rolls of papyrus, covered with hieroglyphics,
of which photographs, and an explanatory key in French,
were published and sold in the Exhibition building. M. Mariette-Bey, an Egypto-Frenchman, very long resident in
the land of the Pharaohs, had for his right-hand man
M. Drevet, a well-known French architect; and the sculpture
and mouldings of the Egyptian buildings were undertaken by
the firm of Bernard and Co., under the artistic supervision of
M. Mallet, a rising sculptor, who, in his working blouse and a
chisel in his hand, gave every day a practical denial to the
libellous report that modern sculptors are able only to handle
clay or wax, and are compelled to leave the absolute hewing
out of the block to marble-masons. A great deal was done

to the Egyptian department in the way of decorative painting; and the chief artist employed was M. Bin, "second
grand Roman prizeman." Fancy a Royal Academy gold
medallist doing decorator's work at an Exhibition, or an
Academy travelling student touching up the private box
panels of the New Adelphi, or an A.R.A. painting the ceiling
of a music hall in fresco. Honest lovers of art may hope to
see the day when such fancies as these may become realities,
and when the foremost artists of England shall not be ashamed
to paint the walls of a coffee-house, as the foremost artists of
France have not been ashamed to do in the *Grand Café*—
nay, by doing which they have gained great honour and
many score thousand francs. The Royal Alhambra Palace,
redecorated by Sir William Powell Frith, R.A.; the Charing-
cross Railway terminus, with water-glass paintings eight
hundred feet long by Mr. Daniel Maclise; the *loggie* of some
new baths and washhouses by Mr. Holman Hunt; the dry
arches of Waterloo Bridge, with encaustic paintings by Mr.
John Everett Millais: why not?

The Egyptian outdoor section was situated at the eastern
extremity of the grand park, skirting the avenue, and
opposite the Porte Desaix, between the covered gallery
which divided the palace and the grand alley forming the
limits of the United States park. Close by were the Russian
and Persian *villegiature*. Monumental Egypt was represented
by four distinct edifices, the Viceroy's Palace, the Temple,
the "Okel," and the stable for dromedaries. The viceregal
palace was in the most gorgeous arabesque, or rather
alhambresque style, and contained some enamelled mosaics
vying in beauty with those in the mosque at Cordova,
and in the tombs of the Caliphs at Cairo; mosaics at

which Dr. Salviati, of Venice, might hold up his hands in admiration, though not in envy ; for the works of the master mosaicist, Salviati—witness what he has done in St. Paul's, and in the Prince Consort's mausoleum—are of the very highest order of merit.   One suite of the apartments in the Viceroy's palace were reserved for the exclusive use of his Highness.   In the remaining saloons were exhibited divers curiosities and articles of *virtù*, and a remarkable series of plans in relief of Egyptian topography, *à la* Baumgartner, the work of Colonel Mincher.   The Temple was a genuine sepulchral chamber, the exact reproduction of one recently excavated at Saghara, by Mariette-Bey, which, for all its four or five thousand years of existence, is stated to look as fresh as though it had been built yesterday.   It is indeed the peculiar characteristic of Egyptian monuments and of her Britannic Majesty's lineaments on the coinage and postage stamps to be eternally young. The Egyptian monoliths, which are so plentiful in Rome, and the youngest of which must be some twenty hundred years older than the Cloaca Maxima, have a fresh, crisp, and shining look, as though they had just been hewn from the quarry, and covered but half-an-hour since with inscrutable processions of dickey birds and short-petti-coated Egyptians, with their beards in boxes. They are older than anything in old Rome, yet they are the only objects which appear modern in that oldest of cities.   The Egyptian asp forms a conspicuous object in the decoration of this sepulchre, and the capitals of the enormous columns are sculptured in the likeness of Athor, Goddess of Night.   Light has been admitted to this sepulchre by means of a huge lantern in the roof, which, much to the consternation of sticklers for purity in archæology, the architects have been compelled to glaze.

In this respect the courts of our matchless palace at Sydenham
have, or had rather, a decided advantage over all that
imitators or adapters could do elsewhere. Our Owen Joneses
and Digby Wyatts were not driven to outrage propriety by
glazing in the area of the Pompeian house or the Court of the
Lions in the Alhambra. Paxton had provided an artificial
empyrean, in the shape of the glass roof of the palace itself,
and to that simulated sky Pompeii and the Alhambra could
be open. The sepulchral chamber at Paris was dedicated to
two personages named TI and PHTHΛOTHEP—great
"Mokos" no doubt in their day, and now very completely
forgotten. So may it be with the descendants of those who
came over with the Conqueror. What is fame? Names
remain ; but those who possessed them fade clean out of
human memory. Who was Magg—not Meg—and what was
the " diversion " for which he was so noted ? And what can
history tell us about Dickens—not the renowned novelist,
but the tradesman who was so unlucky in disposing of his
dishes ; or Ludlam, who had a dog so lazy that he was fain
to lean his head against a wall to bark ? TI and
PHTHΛOTHEP had no doubt the entry to Pharaoh's back
stairs, or were very thick with all the Ptolemies ; but where
are they now ?

The "Okel," or caravanserai, was built from designs by
M. Drevet, made from suggestions furnished by Mariette-Bey.
It comprised numerous divisions, a courtyard planted with
palm-trees, and sleeping chambers for the guardians of the
place. Covered galleries ran round it, in which ostensibly
genuine merchants from Cairo were installed, who offered
rich stuffs, precious gems, brilliant carpets, and all kinds of
Oriental curiosities for sale. Without the slightest desire to

be censorious, it may strike the observer that in a few trifling particulars this Exhibition professed too much; and, to be candid, the scheme of the Cairo merchants to be installed in the stalls of the caravanserai smelt rather too strongly of the Algerine nicknack shops of the Boulevards and the Rue de Rivoli, with their cheap and nasty chibouks, their sleezy burnouses, their gimcrack bracelets, their unsound carpets, and their unwaterworthy coffeepots. It is to be presumed that certificates of baptism or of nationality were not exacted from the live Cairo merchants, although it was as likely as not that they were genuine Egyptians. There was a strong desire to make this an exhibition not only of universal raw produce, manufactures, artistic objects, and live stock, but also of universal humanity. Some of the proposals made in this regard were so eccentric as to trench on the ridiculous. For instance, the city of Valence is said to have petitioned the Imperial Commission to be allowed to exhibit twenty of its prettiest girls. As the possession of the prettiest women in all France has, from time immemorial, been claimed by Arles —although the claim is stoutly disputed by Nismes and constantly cavilled at by Montelimart—other southern towns would probably have sent consignments of female beauty, marked " fragile, with care," had the demand of Valence been acceded to. However, setting aside the Cairene merchants, who did *not* include a barber with seven brothers, a little hunchback, and three one-eyed calendars, sons of kings—the Damascene confectioner who makes cream tarts without pepper was in the Turkish section of the park, and very nasty his tarts were—it was extremely edifying to the Parisians to see what a real Eastern caravanserai was like. The travellers who have described it as one of the dirtiest and most comfortless holes in existence — a wretched place where you obtain shelter from the fury of the elements, and not always that; and where you have a fierce squabble with an itinerant cookshop-keeper to obtain a skinny fowl and a little boiled rice for your *pilaf*—these travellers are, of course, utterly unworthy of credence; or is it that in the Champ de Mars we saw an animated panorama, not of the world as it is, but of the world as it ought to be?

A curious exhibition was on view on the first floor of this caravanserai, and one which would have infinitely interestd a Lavater, a Gall, or a Spurzheim. It was "anthropological," and consisted of above six hundred human skulls, many of them belonging to the very remotest antiquity. What a cargo to bring to France! We all know the prejudices entertained by seafaring men against the conveyance of anything of a charnel-house nature on board ship. They will not sail with the dead if they can help it. Even the defunct governors of colonies have had to be brought home as grand pianofortes, or casks of prime mess beef. Perhaps the six hundred Egyptian skulls were shipped from Alexandria as Dutch cheeses. The summit of the caravanserai was occupied by a "moucharabien," or terraced gallery; and attached to the establishment there was an Egyptian café, where coffee was prepared in the Oriental fashion, pounded, and not ground, and served up, grouts and all, in cups of the size of egg shells. At night the entire Egyptian quarter was brilliantly illuminated. There was a feast at Bairam, and a fast -at Ramadan; and all the feasts meant the extortion of francs and centimes from a confiding public.

Strolling through the Exhibition park, gardens, and annexes, and watching the multifarious devices in progress of completion there, the student of Perrault or the Countess d'Anois might have been reminded of the pretty scene in " Riquet with the Tuft," when the side of the mountain yawns, and legions of little cooks are discovered hard at work over their casseroles and frying-pans. In the Champ de Mars, indeed, the preparations were for the most extraordinary banquet at which ever Imperial Amphitryon invited humanity at large to sit down. There was to be every dish ever dreamt of by the concocters of cookery books. There were to be viands unrecorded by Francatelli, and left obscure even in the late M. Soyer's " Pantropheon," a most erudite and exhaustive work, which began at Adam's apple and left off at a sirloin of beef for the annual dinner of the Royal Agricultural Society. Roast and boiled, stewed and fried, grilled and carbonadoed, hashed, curried, bashawed, toasted, steamed, baked, iced, pickled, and preserved ; there was no stage of coction, or rather of manufacture, in which the products of civilisation were not to be exhibited at the great festival of 1867. Nor need metaphor be very violently strained when the huge place was likened to a kitchen. The Official Guide read remarkably like the bill of fare for the Lord Mayor's feast—the contents, of course, of the *menu* being multiplied to infinity. We were promised so many thousand fat capons, so many hundred bowls of calipash and calipee, so many hundred dozen of ruffs and reeves, so many score hogsheads of iced punch; and, in such a banquet of universal fraternity as this, it may be presumed that the loving cup surely would not be forgotten. The fraternisers, however, very nearly got to fisticuffs before the feed was half over. But would the dinner be ready in time ? It is when this reflection occurred to the spectator that the culinary metaphor stood him in best stead. Enter

E

the kitchen of any great City confectioner some three hours before the splendid banquet is to take place, and, to the uninitiated eye, there will seem but scant likelihood that the hospitable boards at Guildhall, or the Fishmongers', or the Clothworkers', will " groan " under all the " delicacies of the season " at the appointed time. Everything has an embryonic, an inchoate, a chaotic look. The glacial, the volcanic, the antediluvian period of creation may be traced; but there is no promise of anything being fit to eat by six o'clock. There are caldrons, furnaces, ovens, pots and pans innumerable, and many men in white calmly peeling raw vegetables, or smearing raw meat with yolks of raw eggs, or rolling raw paste, or even coolly plucking fowls and crimping cod, as though there were plenty of time, and the dinner was not to come off till the day after to-morrow. There *is* plenty of time given, plenty of provisions, plenty of hands, and plenty of skill and perseverance on the part of the chief cook; the dinner will be done to a turn, dished to a T, and served up to the minute as the clock strikes; and the *chef* will be able, by eight o'clock, to occupy his accustomed stall at the Opera.

But the things they were doing in that park! I told you that the suave warmth of the odour of freshly-sawn wood in the palace had been recommended to persons of delicate lungs. There was another department, however, of the Exhibition where the perfume of turpentine and sawdust might be enjoyed in even greater perfection. This was in the famous Russian village, or *sloboda*, which was built in the park, close to the Avenue Suffren, not only from Russian designs, but by real Russian workmen. Here you might see, daily growing in picturesque completeness, the timber houses in which Russian peasants live. The pine logs were laid horizontally,

and the extremities intersected at right angles as blades of
opened scissors might do. This "criss-cross" arrangement
gave to each log the appearance of having four ends, which
we know, in a log not being miraculous, is impossible. The
interstices were filled up with tow, and the cornices beneath
the shelving roofs were curiously carved. The staircases of
these cottages were, as usual in Russia, on the outside, and
led to the upper chamber, called the *isba*, in front of which
there was a wooden balcony, and beneath which enamoured
youths in sheepskin coats were supposed to serenade their
innamorate to the dulcet but mournful strains of the *balalaïka*.
This village was one of the most prominent lions in the Exhibition. The Russian section of the park occupied about one
thousand metres. It comprised, first, a large *hangar*, or shed,
on the ground floor of which agricultural machinery was
exhibited; while in an apartment above were haylofts, and
lodgings for six Russian peasants or *moujiks*. They were
prize peasants, of course. They failed however on fine summer evenings to "speak a piece," after the manner of Mr.
Artemus Ward, reciting, in choice Sclavonic, odes *àpropos* of
the abolition of villenage in the Russian dominions. Nor
did they dance, or sit round the *samovar*, quaffing brick tea,
and intoning hymns in praise of St. Isaac and St. Sergius.
They neglected, too, to get up private theatricals, and perform
the admired drama of "A Life for the Czar." Opposite the
hangar was the office of the Russian Commissioners to the
Exhibition—a pavilion in timber, highly ornate, "in the style
of the Eastern boyards." It is to be feared that the style of
the Eastern boyards would be deemed in England a sad con-
travention of the Metropolitan Building Acts; and indeed
there were very many structures in the park of the Champ

de Mars at which cautious district surveyors would have shaken their heads. Then came the *isba*, or peasant's cottage —a complete habitation for the laborious and useful, but poorly-paid, person, whom Mr. Carlyle calls "our conscript," who is sometimes termed a "proletarian," and who was anciently known as a husbandman. To judge from the Exhibition *isba*, the tiller of the soil must be excellently well lodged in Holy Russia. He has an immense stove in terra cotta in one corner of his parlour—a stove not unlike York Minster in miniature; and towards the close of the Exhibition, as the evenings grew chilly, the brave *moujik* obliged the visitors by going to bed *à la Russe* on the top of the stove, and wrapped himself in his sheepskin, the skinny side out and the woolly side in, an arrangement which, with reference to another article of apparel, was found "mighty convanient" by Mr. Bryan O'Lynn. The Exhibition stove likewise served as an oven for the baking of Russian bread, and for heating water for the Russian bath. The process of ablution took place, it is to be presumed, *in camerâ*. Attached to the cottage there were stables and coach-houses; and, finally, there was a tiny wooden pavilion, very coquettishly arranged to serve as a guard-house. The punishments of the knout, the stick, and the rod having been abolished by the humane Sovereign of all the Russias—always excepting the Polish exiles in Siberia, who, like "*le meere Irishes*" mentioned by the old Norman-French law writer, "*non avez le bénéfit de la ley*" —there was no necessity in the Martian *sloboda* for the erection of a police station, with a convenient arsenal of whipcord, leather, birchbroom and willow-pattern sticks, and a garrison of strong-armed officials in grey greatcoats ready to chastise the brave *moujik* for his soul's health when he had taken too much *quass* or *vodka*. The good old times seem to have entirely vanished in Muscovy; unless indeed this *sloboda* was a toy village—a highly imaginative type, twin-brother to the pasteboard simulacra run up by the wily Potemkin by the roadside, when the Czarina Catherine made a progress through her dominions. It is a pity that the Russian commissioners did not lay on a *starosta*, a head man of the village—a venerable personage in a long beard and flowing caftan—to discharge municipal functions during the Exhibition. The wooden watch-tower to give notice of conflagration was not visible—an indispensable edifice in all Russian villages; but there was a real Russian verst-post, the substitute for a milestone, painted in the national colours, and a *yourta*, or tent, thirty-six feet in diameter, made of rushes sewn together, and resembling an enormous beehive. There was a hole in the top to let the daylight in and the smoke out. The *yourta* is said to be the ordinary habitation of the Cossacks and the nomadic Tartars. It may be mentioned that in a series of stables, quite sumptuously arranged, were exhibited twenty-six horses of different races, most of them indigenous to Russia; and in the coach-houses adjoining were the *telegas*, *tarantasses*, and sledges for which Russia is famous. In all these edifices there were used neither screws nor nails. Everything had been beautifully dovetailed and morticed by the joiner's art, under the superintendence of M. Gromoff, one of the most eminent timber merchants of St. Petersburg. Quite as curious as the Russian log-houses was the spectacle of the Russian mechanics at work upon them. They were fine-looking fellows, hirsute and rubicund enough about the chin to make Frederic Barbarossa, were he alive, desperately jealous. The Parisians were never tired of staring at them and their picturesque national costume — baggy knickerbockers of velveteen, vests of violet flannel, high boots, and Astracan caps. They used scarcely any implement in their varied labours but the hatchet. Persons who have seen a real Russian village building in Russia, or who have watched the miserable creatures in dirty *touloupes* slaving on the quays at Cronstadt, may be apt to think that the representative Russian "proletarian" in the Champ de Mars was slightly idealised for the occasion.

Next to the Russian *sloboda*, with the carpenters and joiners in violet waistcoats and velvet breeches, the work-men from Tunis, who were decorating the charming little kiosque destined for Tunisian products, must be accounted among the chief attractions of the Exhibition out of doors. It was quite marvellous to watch them cutting out, with the aid of nothing but a delicate saw, the most beautiful and intricate arabesque patterns on the bare plaster of the walls. There must surely have been some preliminary tracing, some guide line; but it was not apparent. They used neither pencil, charcoal, stencil, pin, compass, plumb, nor square, but continued tranquilly honeycombing solid blocks of plaster into the most exquisite imitations of point lace. You began to understand what kind of workmen they must have been who decorated the Hall of Ambassadors in the Alhambra, and the Courtyard of the Maidens in the Alcazar; but still, although you stand close to the workman with his little saw, it is as difficult as ever to understand *how* he does it. Is it merely assured discipline of eye and hand, due to long experience and constant practice; or is it a secret, or a magical art, known only to true believers, and not to be mastered by the giaours? The Liliputian palace where they were working their wonders was an exact reproduction, or rather reduction, of the palace of the Bey of Tunis—a very good sovereign, as sovereigns, especially Mahometan ones, go; and of whom nothing more injurious has ever been heard than that he once purchased a team of white horses for his state carriage, and had them all painted a lively pink, to match the coach, which was of a rosy hue. The master arabesquist, if such a term may be coined to designate the dexterous person who carved plaster into lace, was said to be a member of a family renowned for centuries as adepts in this art, and was the son of the decorator who some twenty years since filled the saloons of Alexandre Dumas's evanescent Monte Christo château at St. Germains with mauresque devices. The model of the Bey's palace contained bath-rooms on a very elaborate scale, and on the ground floor was a tiny bazaar for the sale of Tunisian articles. M. Alfred Chapon, the young French architect to whom the erection of this pretty toy was confided by the Tunisian Government, so built it that it might be taken to pieces in real toy-puzzle fashion when the Exhibition was over, packed up, and trans-ported, *à grande vitesse*, and without the slightest risk, per Lyons Railway and Messageries Impériales steamer, to Tunis.

And the Isthmus of Suez had an exhibition to itself in the park. Incorrigible sceptics will, it is to be hoped, at last admit that the Suez Canal is a great fact—that Ptolemy may in future hide his diminished head, and vanquished Father Nile ride off into obscurity on the back of a hippopo-tamus. M. Chapon was likewise the architect of the Suezidal erection. It contained a plan in relief of the isthmus, a panorama of the canal, and models of all the dredgers, canal boats, steamers, hooks, baits, and other machines employed in the accomplishment of this gigantic work. The edifice did not contain photographic portraits of the shareholders in this remarkable enterprise; but, without hazarding any opinion on the chances of success of the Suez Canal, it may be justifiable to hint that M. Ferdinand de Lesseps at least deserved a statue on the very top of the edifice, as a slight testimony to the pluck, perseverance, and ingenuity he has shown for more than a quarter of a century, under almost every conceivable kind of difficulty and discouragement. So far as persistent endurance is concerned, M. de Lesseps's hobby is no mean rival to one of the bronze horses of St. Mark at Venice.

The International Club, for there was a club in this park—what was there not, from mosques and British and Foreign Bible stores to derricks and steam ploughs ?—covered a very extensive space. The club, or *cercle,* was presided over by the Duke de Valmy, and within its walls it was intended to bring together the exhibitors of all nations, as well as amateur visitors. The enormous hall on the ground floor was to serve as a kind of artistic and industrial exchange; but means were adopted to prevent its conversion into a locality for ignoble *tripotage* and Bourse gambling. The Electric Telegraph had branch offices here for the transmission of orders for porcelain towers to Nankin, and the striking of bargains, per Atlantic cable, with lucky mortals who have " struck ile " in Pennsylvania, and wish to admit partners, at a premium, to their oleaginous bliss. On the first floor was a dining-room for fifteeen hundred guests, and the basement contained kitchens on a commensurately gigantic scale. The two wings of the club-house were formed by galleries of iron and glass, which were fitted up as shops. These shops were not much bigger than birdcages, but the amount of rent fixed for their occupancy throughout the duration of the Exhibition was thirty thousand francs, or twelve hundred pounds sterling. I have elsewhere stated to what complexion the International Club came at last.

V.

OPENING OF THE EXHIBITION.

WITH effect although not with splendour, with success although not with solemnity, the great festival so long and so anxiously expected, was consummated on the first of April, and the Universal Exhibition of 1867 became a fact. Not a wholly accomplished one, however. There were many and grave shortcomings; but it was hoped that those omissions would very speedily be remedied, and that ere the commencement of the summer, when the fullest concourse of tourists and holiday-makers from all parts of the world might be looked for, that which was in April barren and incomplete might be rendered worthy of France and of the French. A nation so ingenious and so accomplished, it was pleaded, could not afford failure. They *must* succeed. *Noblesse oblige,* the vain admirers of heraldry say. But there are traditions far more obligatory than those of nobility and long descent. A people who, for a thousand years, have been as illustrious in arts as in arms—who have won the brightest of laurels in the field of intellect and taste—whose genius and whose dexterity have rendered them the admiration and the envy of surrounding communities—should be ashamed as well as amazed, should blush as well as murmur, to find that the most colossal work of Peace which this century has witnessed had, through indolence, through procrastination, or through mismanagement, been but a semi-success and a truncated triumph. These auguries did not fail to be fulfilled. The first two months of the Exhibition were a season of incompleteness, confusion, and general deficiency; but, by the beginning of June, the " installation," as it was termed, came to an end; the last barriers and the last scaffoldings were removed, and painters, glaziers, carpenters, and decorators, left the place.

However, although there was not much to see behind the doors of the Palace in the Champ de Mars, they were duly thrown open, in accordance with official announcement, on the first of April, and that was one step in advance. It was opened at two o'clock in the afternoon, by the Emperor Napoleon in person, and although really the next best thing to be done would have been to shut up the palace and grounds until the works were finished and the place fit for the inspection of the public, there was some room for congratulation in the mere fact that the opening had occurred at all.

The morning of Monday was lovely. After the detestable weather we had been enduring in Paris, the sudden change experienced was not only a delight but a surprise. It hailed during the last week in March, and rained, snowed, and fogged, and froze, and thawed, and froze again, and blew stiff gales, and did everything that was abominable and disagreeable. The soil of the Champ de Mars had become resolved into the usual compost of mud and slush; but we woke up on the morning of the first to find everything dry, bright, and sunny. In uniformity with the laws laid down by the Imperial Commission, the gentleman guests invited, some thousands in number, had duly arrayed themselves in sable garments and white cravats ; and as every possessor of a ticket was anxious to reach the Exhibition in good time, the necessary consequence was that from an early hour Paris presented the appearance of a city in which there had been a *bal masqué* overnight, and nobody had gone to bed. On closer examination, however, of the innumerable persons in black and white who pervaded Paris with pink tickets in their hands, the absence of claret-stained linen, rumpled kerchiefs, battered hats, and dusty boots, quite banished the masquerade notion. Every one was evidently dressed in his best. The ladies were *en grande toilette de ville*—bonnets, or the minutest apologies for bonnets, being permitted—and by ten o'clock the roadway on the quays, the foot-pavements of which were thronged by holiday folk, was filled with continuous streams of vehicles of every grade in the hierarchy of wheels—from the lordly ambassador's carriage, with its sumptuous lacqueys and plumed chasseurs, to the humblest *fiacre*.

The crowd of idlers in the palace and grounds on the previous Sunday had been greater than ever. At one period of the afternoon the ladies and children very nearly had the whole of the avenue of stained glass to themselves. The white tickets or *billets de favour* presented by the I.C. to their friends and acquaintances seem to have been delivered with indiscriminate generosity. An equally liberal use was made of the passes granted to workmen, and one gentleman brought in no fewer than four ladies in the tallest of *chignons* and the shortest of skirts of mauve plush, on the score of their being *ouvrières*. " *Vous voulez me dire que tout ça va travailler ?*" the *sergent* on duty murmured, as, somewhat reluctantly, he gave ingress to the party. The throng began to laugh ; but soon there came a fresh rush of free admissions to the gates, and the *sergent de ville* had his hands full, and was far too busy to pursue his inquiries as to the industrial qualifications of the ladies in mauve plush. It is my firm belief that, in addition to the people who had obtained white tickets, a vast number managed to get into the Champ de Mars without any tickets at all. You had simply to walk in through any gap in the hedge or hiatus in the hoarding you might discover—for the turnstiles * were not yet erected—and wait until you were stopped. This very seldom happened, and the consequence was that towards sunset the palace had become a very Fair, and the noise and dust attained tremendous proportions. In the English department alone did

* The manner in which money was taken at these turnstiles during the Exhibition season was sufficiently droll. "They manage these things better in France," we are accustomed, sometimes appositely, but more frequently idiotically, to say. The money-taking in the Champ de Mars was not a very bright specimen of management. At each *tourniquet* were two cash-takers ; one took your franc ; the other raked it towards him with a kind of *croupe*, let it fall into the slit of the box, and touched the mechanism which allowed you to pass through. This division of labour was beautiful in theory ; but the practical idea of the thing was, that two money-takers were placed there in order that one should make sure that the other did not "frisk the till," by pocketing an odd franc now and then. Could the authorities have laid on brothers (twins preferably) at all the gates, this system might have worked admirably, for brothers seldom agree ; but in a little while dark rumours got about that an *entente cordiale* existed between each pair of money-takers, and that they played into each other's hands. So a *sergent de ville* was set to watch each couple. Presently it was whispered that the *sergent* was "squared," so a *gendarme*— usually supposed to be an incorruptible functionary—was posted to watch the muncipal. Eventually, I believe, an *escouade* of detective policemen were detailed to watch the entire party. Who watched the detectives I never ascertained. On the whole, the system was repugnant, illustrative of the old saying, "who shall keep the keepers." It is certain that temptations were many, and that there was an enormous amount of roguery about.

something like order and Sabbath stillness reign. The British exhibitors had succeeded in getting the heaviest portion of their labour accomplished by Saturday night, and no more work than was absolutely necessary was done on the Sunday. The passages between the stalls had been swept clean, the veils had been removed from the fronts of the glass cases, the hangings which decorated the principal avenue of the English courts—hangings which were of white-figured muslin, and, albeit, looking very clean and smart just then, bore an inconvenient resemblance to bed curtains—had been put up. The furniture courts of Benham, and Gillow, and Holland, and Jackson and Graham; Defries' chandeliers and Dobson's engraved glass; Benson's giant cathedral clock, and Hancock's gems, and Harry Emanuel's silver swan—which promised to eclipse in fame the automaton duck of Vaucanson *—Watherston's goldsmith's work, Grant and Gask's display of drapery; and, in particular, the industrial and artistic treasures of the Indian department, were all in full working gear, and ready for the inspection

---

* The dear old duck! It is still extant; it still quacks, plumes itself, waddles, cranes its neck, drinks, and digests. I have known it these twenty years past, in Russia, in Denmark, in Holland, and the South of France. The last time I had seen it, at Avignon, about five years ago, it was in a lamentably shabby and dilapidated condition, and had scarcely a web foot to stand upon; but I was delighted to see it turn up, with a bran new coat of feathers, and fresh clockwork in its stomach, as lively as ever, as a show on the Boulevards this year; admission, fifty centimes. It was styled "*Le Canard de l'Exposition : chef d'œuvre de l'immortel Vaucanson.*" The automaton flute players were there too; but they had lost many of their fingers, and their tootling was very weak; and, likewise included in the small charge of fivepence, was the automaton letter writer; the gaily attired young lady who writes any name demanded, and pursues her task with such an utterably inane expression of countenance and such a vacuous simper, that you might almost fancy she employed her leisure hours in writing fashionable novels.

of the most exigent of jurors or the most clamorous of season ticket-holders. The praiseworthy exertions of Mr. Cole— the best-abused man of his time, rather an arbitrary, rough-grained, "cranky" official, I take it, but a clear-headed, indefatigable worker, for all that—who had not yet absolutely expired from bodily and mental fatigue, but who must have been near it—had been equally successful in pushing on the works in the English Picture Gallery, and in the Science and Art Court devoted to the exhibition of articles from South Kensington. The booksellers and publishers also were perfectly ready. Bradbury and Evans's case glowed with poor John Leech's coloured cartoons and the inimitable frontispieces to the pocketbooks of Mr. Punch, although I failed to discern, surmounting the Whitefriars stall, that monumental effigy of Mr. Punch himself, coloured according to the life, like Shakspeare's bust at Stratford-on-Avon, and "in his habit as he squeaked," which we had been promised. It may be that M. Le Play had remonstrated against the proposed apotheosis in the Champ de Mars of the great humourist of Fleet Street; for these are perilous times, and the memory of Prussian King William's laurel-crowned statue so close to the Bridge of Jena was yet fresh and rankling in the Gallic mind. At any rate, I looked for Mr. Punch's statue in vain. It was on its way, however, with the nine thousand and odd packing cases belonging to different nationalities which were still anxiously expected, but which still failed to come to hand. On the whole, England —could our respect for Sunday have permitted such a thing —could have thrown down its barriers on the thirty-first of March, and with becoming pride invited the universe to inspect her products and manufactures. England, however,

very properly did her best on this the last day of admission
of the great unpaying to keep the public out. Mr. Cole and
his exhibitors had a wholesome terror of the thousands of muddy
boots, of prying eyes and inquisitive fingers, of the great unpaying aforesaid ; so a pretty strong force of police agents had
been provided. Boards inscribed *" Entrée interdite "* were
plentifully planted at the entrances to the courts, and unless you
really had business in connection with the English Commission
you were not permitted to enter the forest of iron columns on
whose shafts the British crown and the initials " V. R." were
eloquent as to the business-like promptitude of the loyal
subjects of her Majesty Queen Victoria. Mr. Cole had
certainly as many difficulties to contend with as any other
foreign commissioner. In some instances the obstacles to be
surmounted were exceptional, and well-nigh unprecedented ;
but perils and impediments vanished before the pluck and
endurance of the sturdy organiser from South Kensington,
and the result was that Great Britain and her colonies made
certainly a completer display in the Champ de Mars than
any other competitor in this enormous *concours.** It was

* The British Commissioners, home and colonial, used to abuse the
British Commission in general, and Mr. Henry Cole, C.B., in particular,
roundly. The British Jurors, on the contrary, got up a kind of Round
Robin to Mr. Cole, stating that he was one of the nicest men with whom they
had ever come in contact ; but as the attributes of the jurors and delegates
were in the main confined to walking about as gentlemen at large, and
getting fifty pounds apiece for writing reports on the classes, which (with
a few exceptions, notably Mr. Beckwith's admirable report on fermented
liquors), were either dull or imbecile, the unanimity with which they
cheered the " honourable gentleman in the chair," need not excite astonishment. As I have said, the great body of British exhibitors were never
tired of girding at Mr. Cole. He did not do enough for them, they cried·
I believe that he did as much as ever he could, frankly, zealously, and conscientiously ; and I know that for weeks before and weeks after the opening
of the Exhibition he worked harder than any convict ; but I think he

only in the park that—owing to the weather, the workmen's strike, and the dilatoriness of contractors—Britannia in the beginning of April was somewhat behindhand. The curious structure which was termed by the English Commission the "Test-house," and where everything that could conduce to the internal decoration and external convenience of a dwelling-house was experimentally exhibited—but which the French nicknamed "*La Cottage Anglais*," or more irreverently "*Le Goddam*," and which they persisted in regarding as a typical specimen of English domestic architecture—was not completed by the opening day. It was certainly a very curious and incongruous pile of chimney-pots, cowls, gutters, drain-pipes, ornamental tiles, terra-cotta mouldings, tesselated pavements, revolving shutters, ventilators, wire fences, improved cooking stoves, spring latches, patent bolts, improved door handles, and other domestic contrivances. But it answered its purpose, and was true to its real title; for outside and inside its walls all that ingenious manufacturers could do to perfect the thoroughly British institution known as "comfort" could be applied and tested. Then there were our gun-shed, our boiler-house, our Trinity House pharos, and other English edifices too numerous to mention, in the park; but many days elapsed before these were finished. Inside, our machinery gallery stood in most advantageous contrast to the foreign machine departments, which, late on Sunday evening, looked very much like the London Docks

---

would have been able to do a great deal more had the British Commission kept on decently amicable terms with M. Le Play and his colleagues of the I. C. "Instead of which," as the judge remarked in the celebrated duck-stealing case, "the British and Imperial Commission squabbled most fiercely and most scandalously from the beginning to the end of the show."

F

mixed up with Rag Fair, with a Manchester cotton mill and
a sugar bakery added by way of supplement, and a railway
accident, a conflagration, and an earthquake thrown in to
complete the picture of disorder and unreadiness. America
was putting her best foot foremost all day Sunday; but
although the decoration of the United States Courts was
completed, and the counters were ready, and the glass
cabinets prepared, the United States packing-cases were not
yet emptied of a tithe of their contents. I saw, however, a
great many Transatlantic articles exhibited to which I gave,
at a more advanced period, extended notice. Amongst
others were some sumptuously-carved chimneypieces of
Vermont, Tennessee, and California marble; the last as rich
in colour as onyx, and beautifully veined with gold in its
natural state. There was also a really astonishing machine
—I need scarcely say that it was of New England manufacture—for the simultaneous composing of type and forma-
tion of a matrix for stereotyping, the type being stamped
into a thickness of soft blotting paper, from which the cast
can subsequently be taken. The compositor sits before a
species of keyboard strongly resembling that of a pianoforte.
His foot works the pedal; in fact, you might think that,
while he is really "setting up" the constitution of the United
States, he was some boarding-school miss practising her
exercises on an instrument whose keys had been carefully
muffled out of consideration for the nervous lodger next door.
In its remaining portions the United States department—
through the non-arrival of merchandise—was in a regrettable
state of backwardness. At all events, however, America had
something to show, which was not the case on Sunday afternoon with Italy, with Portugal, and with Brazil. Those

countries had unpacked nothing, and seemed hopelessly behindhand.

I have said that towards the close of the day the yet un-opened Exhibition had become crowded with interlopers, and resembled nothing so much as a fair. The most "fairy-like" aspect of the place was, however, in the "Food Department" —the external ellipse looking on to the park. Here the cafés and beerhouses were all in full swing, and the legion of smokers and drinkers were most thickly congregated. They had not yet opened Quevedo's café, from the Puerta del Sol, Madrid, where, in due time, you are to be served with "*helados*" or ices, "*bibidas de naranja*" or orangeade, and "*refrescantes de varios suertes*"—"fancy" drinks mainly, I apprehend; for so far as my personal experience extends, the staple article of consumption in a Spanish café is cold water; but it began to *fonctionner* on the morrow. On the other hand, the Russian restaurant and tea-house were in full operation. A preparatory banquet had been given by the proprietor to the most distinguished Russian residents in Paris. The guests were regaled on *stchi*, or cabbage soup, *sterlet* from the Volga, *caviare* from Astracan, *pirogues*, or meat pies, and other national Russian dishes, with copious libations of *vodka* and *quass* to wash the dainty dishes down. If they had not all that they had, at least, a profusion of roast chickens and plenty of champagne; but I can vouch for the fact that they were waited upon by servitors in caftans of pea-green, purple, and maize-coloured silk and satin; and after this, after the dirty rascals in dirtier shirts, who really wait upon you in Muscovite houses of entertainment, one could not help admitting that between the real and the ideal there exist a very vast difference. The *couleur locale* of

Russia was, however, kept up by the dispensation to the guests of perfumed caravan tea, served out in tumblers from the traditional *samovar*, and flavoured with slices of lemon.

But the ceremonial of Monday now demands attention. I was early afoot and made my way to the grand avenue leading to the Bridge of Jena entrance, whence branched off the staircases leading to the iron staging which follows the course of the machinery department. One of those staircases led to the French, the other to the English section. I chose the latter, and pushed through intervening municipals and staging, and eventually ascended the platform, where I found myself among British commissioners, jurors, naval and military officers, and so forth. It was clear that I had no business there ; but I presume that the chief authority, seeing that several of my colleagues of the press * were likewise present, did not like to turn us out. I stood, then, at the brink of the staging leading to the British platform. A

* To push one's way into the society of gentlemen from whom you have not received an invitation would, at the first blush, appear an act of impertinence. In explanation, however, I remark, that as I happened to be the representative of a London newspaper, and that many thousands of persons expected to read on Tuesday morning a full, true, and particular account of the opening of the French Exhibition, it was absolutely necessary that I should "push my way," in defiance of all rules of etiquette. I may add that in England, on similar occasions, special seats in special tribunes are always reserved for the correspondents of the newspapers, who are generally regarded as the ambassadors of the people; but in France a journalist, unless he is the parasite of a statesman or the *ruffiano* of a prince—in which case he may become senator, deputy, or millionaire—is treated with the utmost contumely and neglect. From the Imperial French Commission the representatives of the English press in Paris received nothing but rudeness and discourtesy. I certainly, by dint of sheer bullying and threatening to appeal to the highest powers, obtained a season-ticket for myself; but many of my colleagues were forced to pay every day for admission at the turnstiles.

handsome green carpet had been laid at the base of this stair-case—more than had been done on the French side—while the space was flanked by British sappers and miners, standing in amicable propinquity to the French municipal guards. There were also two regular British men-of-war's men, attached to her Majesty's gunboat Dasher. These gallant tars were under the command of Captain Hoare. I think there were five British commissioners and about fifteen jurors present.

At a quarter past two o'clock a grand clangour of martial music was heard. The drums beat to arms. The troops presented, and we could hear the cries of "*Vive l'Empereur!*" from the crowd outside. Looking through a wilderness of girders and through the outer circumference of glass into a confused perspective of waving hats and shakoes and banners and glittering bayonets, I could see three open *calèches* and the Imperial liveries of green and gold. The Emperor's cortége was advancing from the Bridge of Jena, under the canopy of cashmere powdered with golden bees, towards the grand entrance. Anon a *posse* of policemen entered the vestibule. These were followed by a numerous band of gentlemen, the monotony of whose funereal-looking evening vestments was relieved by the orders they wore. To these succeeded the members of the Imperial Commission wearing *bandeaux* of green and gold at their buttonholes. Three persons of more exalted rank made their appearance in the train. There was M. Rouher, looking remarkably rosy and cheerful, and not at all discomfited by his recent passage of arms with M. Thiers; there was M. Béhic, looking com-mercial, agricultural, and ministerial; there, in excellent "fettle," was the champion of French free-trade, M. Arles-

Dufour; and there, tall, white-headed, and hung thick with orders, with a little page boy carrying a camp stool behind him, was the Baron James de Rothschild, Patriarch of Finance and *Pontifex Maximus* of the Temple of Mammon.

And now the Emperor. His Majesty, on whose arm the charming Empress leaned, looked well, although not very strong; but it was a sad disappointment to those present— especially the French portion of the assemblage—to observe that his Majesty was clad in plain evening costume, wearing the Grand Cross of the Legion of Honour for sole decoration. The public had hoped that the Emperor would appear in the uniform of a general of division. Even a morning frock, light trowsers, and a coloured scarf would have been better than that desperately lugubrious suit of black. Surely a reformer, an agitator is wanted to put an end to black dress coats and white chokers in the daytime. They give to the most joyous ceremonials a "Funerals performed" aspect. Victor Emmanuel was ushered into Venice by persons clad in the costume of waiters at the London Tavern. And I remember an English gentlemen telling me that journeying once from Trieste into Dalmatia with a view to a little sport, and the contemplation of the picturesque costumes of that wild and primitive region, it was discovered from his passport at some out-of-the-way village that he was an M.P., and had once been an under Secretary of State. Forthwith the Hospodar, or the Waywode, or the Starosta, or whatever else the head man of the village was called, and who had been dawdling about in his national costume of sheep-skin caftan, baggy boots, fez cap, and embroidered leggings, with a cherry-stick pipe in his mouth, rushed into his house, and, speedily returning in a black swallow-tail and pants, and a white choker, insisted on reading an address in the Maraschino patois to the astonished M.P. The absence throughout of uniforms and gay costumes at the opening of the Exhibition was unpleasantly remarkable, nor can it be denied that the entire performance bore an unwelcome resemblance to the ceremonial of the *Pompes Funèbres*. A bevy of chamberlains, ushers, equerries, and pages, down to footmen and *chasseurs*, swarmed after the Imperial train, and the Emperor and Empress, who were closely followed by the Princess Mathilde, slowly ascended the French staircase, where with the curve of the ellipse they were eclipsed. We had then to wait, cooling our heels on the high-level iron bridge, for full three-quarters of an hour. We could hear the successive peals of applause as the Emperor passed from one section of the platform to the other, and was received by the members of the different commissions. In the United States and in Egypt his reception was most enthusiastic. At length he came towards England. British and Colonial commissioners, jurors, officers, and gentlemen ranged themselves in Indian file, and the illustrious although not brilliant group advanced. The Imperial face was lit up with a very kindly smile when he met Mr. Cole, with whom he very warmly shook hands, and to whom he addressed some very gracious and friendly words. The Empress also conversed with the British Commissioner with her wonted and most charming animation. The Emperor evidently recognized Lord Houghton as an old friend, and, after a few more gracious words, Cæsar and his fortunes went by.

The Imperial party then made successively the round of all the picture galleries, ending with that of England, and about three o'clock, amidst a storm of cheering, took their departure by the same gate, and in the same order in which they arrived, and then everybody rushed off to lunch, and Rouzé and Gousset, Bertram and Roberts, and Spiers and Pond drove an amazing trade.

I returned to the Champ de Mars later in the afternoon, and it was in the highest degree curious to remark the change which had taken place from the bustle and turmoil of the morning to comparative stillness and quiet. The "roaring looms of time" seemed to have suspended their labours. No hum of human voices was audible; the courts echoed no more to the tramping of footsteps; and even the sound of jingling glasses, and clinking knives and forks and plates, and popping corks, was hushed. Luncheon had been taken in plenty; but very few persons seemed to have chosen the Exhibition as a place to dine at. I was bidden myself to a grand banquet given by a well-known art connoisseur, at the Cercle International, or Exhibition Club; but, after experiencing the very greatest difficulty in passing through a *cordon* of *sergents-de-ville* drawn across the only entrance thereto, we found the club in a dreadful state of incompletion, the walls still unpainted and dripping with damp, the scaffolding still unremoved, many of the windows still unglazed, and the flooring of the outer rooms still littered with planks and sawdust.* However, we dined very merrily, and

---

* This club was an awful fiasco. In its huge *salle des pas perdus* the exhibitors of the whole world were to meet and discourse of trade and commerce. But the exhibitors displayed a remarkable reluctance in paying a hundred francs' subscription for membership to the club, and the *salle des pas perdus* became a Hall of Eblis. It was afterwards turned, but with indifferent success, into a promenade concert. Dinners and lunches were tried at the International, but they were dear and bad: and the last time I went there, in August, the originally numerous staff of *garçons* had so wofully declined that I was led to conjecture famine had done its work,

I came back into the Exhibition grounds with contentment in my heart and a cold in my head.   By this time the cafés

---

and that the waiters had eaten one another.   Whether the last two servitors took to a knife and fork combat, "*aux chats de Tipperary*," has yet to be disclosed.   Yet there the club was as big as a barrack, and it will have to be sold as rubbish.   The International Theatre was another collapse.   The manager paid nobody.   He had engaged a large number of English ballet-girls, who were reduced literally to destitution by the non-payment of their salaries; and one poor girl, who was not quite alive to the admired French doctrine that the wearing of pink tights and the leading of a vicious life naturally go together, absolutely starved in a garret till she was removed to an hospital.   The fate of the *vestiaires*, or cloak and umbrella leaving-rooms, was as luckless, but not quite so tragic.   It was found that nobody left their cloaks and umbrellas, their overcoats, or their sticks.   Why should they, since they were allowed to take those articles into the Palace?   The *vestiaire* keepers, who had paid large sums for their concessions, were at first dismayed, and contemplated hanging themselves on their own coatless pegs; but speedily taking heart of grace, and accepting as a wink the acquiescent nod vouchsafed to them by the commission, they turned their cloak-rooms into drinking shops.   The change was one quite of the "hey, presto!" order, and the mouldy females who had been engaged to take charge of the coats and umbrellas that never came were instantaneously metamorphosed into fascinating young ladies in blue satin skirts and pink satin boots, and with their hair dressed in the approved bird's nest and lobster-salad fashion, who speedily began to sell the "Beer of the Allied Emperors," and the "Nectar of All Nations," and the "International Cream Sodas."   One of these transformed cloak-rooms being right opposite Spiers and Pond's buffet, those eminent refreshment contractors evidently thought it very hard that *their* "concession," for which they had paid even more heavily, should thus be impinged upon, and that the "exploiter" of the young ladies in the blue satin skirts and the pink satin boots should thus steal their thunder; but *que voulez vous?*   The Imperial Commission was all powerful, and could do whatever it pleased.   It seized hundreds of chairs belonging to the cafés and restaurants in the exterior zone, and thus reduced the takings of one establishment, of which I am cognizant, by no less than forty pounds a day, while other and smaller enterprises have been wholly ruined by its act of spoliation.   And all this was done in pure spite, simply because the commission had been worsted in a lawsuit with a pertinacious person named Bernard, the "concessionaire" of the right of sitting down.   The Imperial Commission could, however, be tolerant, and liberal—to the extreme bounds of catholicity—when it chose.   It tolerated and restaurants in the outer zone had all concluded operations. Where were the crowds of eaters and drinkers of all nations who were to have lingered in these places of entertainment until the closing hour—ten o'clock? They were all gone, and in the empty cafés great piles of chairs turned on end looked like mournful sepulchral monuments raised to the buried hopes of French, Italian, and Spanish proprietors, who, with rueful countenances, stood at the doors which no strangers cared to besiege, jingling keys in their pockets instead of halfpence. The English luncheon bars are said to have done remarkably well until sunset, and so had the Russian tea-house—the *badauds* being delightfully astonished at the aspect of the serving youths in parti-coloured caftans, and in particular at the rich and rare appearance of a beauteous Russian dame, all pearls, silk, velvet, tinsel, and spangles, and wearing a towering *kakoschnik,* or diadem headgear, and a novel, elaborate *sarafan.* It is as likely as not that the Parisians assumed this to be the ordinary costume of Russian ladies, and were not aware that, in the cities of Holy Russia, it is worn only by wet-nurses. The costumes visible during the day were wofully few and far between. The dead level of black coats and white cravats all but swamped that which might have been striking and picturesque. Of French military uniforms, usually so plentiful when anything public is going on in France, there was a most remarkable scarcity; indeed, I think that for martial

---

a giant, a Japanese dwarf, and a Chinese lady with small feet within its barriers; and it even extended the ægis of its patronage to one Sallot, nick-named Casque de Fer, an itinerant tooth-drawer, recently tried for murder, and acquitted. The late inmate of the dock became quite a lion; and he was exhibited in the " *salons Français* " of the Universal Exhibition of all nations, at the small charge of half a franc for each visitor.

show the palm must be given to the British Commission, several of whose attachés appeared in the Royal and the Volunteer Engineer uniform, and looked very gallant and comely indeed in their bright scarlet. For the rest there was a party of Egyptians, whose attire was wild and desert-looking enough; but it was somewhat dangerous to come between the wind and their oriental nobility. I had not been aware until that moment that the Egyptian cuisine contained so large an element of garlic. These children of Egypt subsequently perambulated the grounds, singing doleful strains, which reminded me forcibly of the comic song, supposed to be a hymn, sung by the coloured gentlemen from Africa who, on a recent occasion, took part in the speech-day exercises at the Propaganda, Rome. They likewise produced most admired discordance from musical instruments, among which the homely but popular banjo, and the familiar but abhorrent tom-tom, were most prominent. Gathering round the Egyptian café, they howled, and twanged, and thumped for full half an hour, while a venerable person of chocolate complexion, with a tarbouch and a flowing beard, distributed cups of coffee gratuitously to the spectators nearest the musicians. I could not exactly make out whether this was to be taken as an act of graceful hospitality *à l'Egyptienne,* or whether it was an artful advertisement designed to puff the new coffee-shop. As I was some paces distant from the banjo and the tom-tom, and did not get any gratuitous coffee, I suspected the latter to be the case. I may be prejudiced, but am I quite alone in hinting that this enterprise has been from the first somewhat "over-shopped," slightly over-puffed, and a little too much devoted to the thoroughly national institution of *La Blague?*

We had one or two "Chineses," too—affable creatures, with black currants for eyes—harmless specimens of potichomanie and perambulating porcelain—animated teatrays in poplin and cardboard clogs. The civilisation, however, of the Flowery Land tends, as we all know, to the effete and the decadent; and our Chineses were completely eclipsed by the Japanese, who, quite as affable, but twenty times more sharp and shrewd-looking than their continental kinsmen, strutted about with their double swords and their tunics of the hue Lady Morgan used to call "dun-duckety mud colour," and their hair knotted into very feminine chignons behind, and apparently wooden platters on the tops of their heads, tied beneath their chins with white tape. There was a Persian, too—a grave and courteous gentleman, with a beard at least two feet long, and seemingly of black floss silk, and with a lamb's-wool kalpac on his head. There were several Turks, whose red fezzes shone among the black hats and coats like holly berries in a pine clump; and there was a Siamese, a most wonderful being, of the precise complexion of a West Indian shaddock, and whose costume was irreverently described by a bystander as being the "latest kick from Bangkok." He wore a waistcoat which was, like Joseph's coat, of many colours—a very bowpot of radiant tint. His nether limbs were swathed in bandana handkerchiefs of the brightest hues. He had a coat of blue velvet, trimmed with yellow window cord, and on his head was the exact duplicate of an English jockey's cap, surmounted however at the top by a formidable spike at least six inches long. I am very glad that I saw him, for it is clear that until I go to Bangkok I shall not look upon his like again.

By eight o'clock the palace was entirely deserted by

visitors, and was left to darkness, the *pompiers*, and the *sergents-de-ville*. I have only to add that, although there was no very unusual crowd on the Boulevards at night, some of the principal shops, such as Giroux's and Tahan's, were brilliantly illuminated. The *Moniteur du Soir* did not contain a word about the ceremonial of the morning, at which it is computed there were about thirty-five thousand persons present.

VI.

THE FINE ARTS.

IT is extremely questionable whether picture and sculpture galleries should be permitted—for their own benefit, as well as for that of their surroundings—to form integral parts of an Industrial Exhibition. When such an exhibition, as in the instance of 1867, lays claims to be Universal, and must, to some extent, have its claim allowed, it may indeed be pleaded that universality cannot be attained without a due representation of every department of human work, and without an impartial admixture of the ornamental with the useful. This plea is valid so far as it goes, and it will not go very far. To banish from an exhibition the fine arts in their secondary phase—I mean as applied, and as aids to manufacture—would be absurd and virtually impossible. Glass, porcelain, jewellery and goldsmiths' ware, furniture, tapestry, metal-work, woodwork, leather-work, must all lean, more or less, on the assistance of the draughtsman or the modeller; and even in the most desperately prosaic and practical machine, there is often present the idea of a Doric column as a support, of the germ of an arch, of a moulding, or a "bead" of colour, suggestive of the difficulty of entirely divorcing art from industry. The working-drawings for engines cannot be made without the employment of drawing paper and pigments and Indian ink, and parallel rules, and the cognate paraphernalia of the artist ; and if a bas-relief of the royal arms of England appears on some newly patented engine, it is clear that some one at the first must have drawn those arms tastefully and symmetrically, and that the matrix for the relief must have been artistically executed. My Lord Mayor's state coach may be, as a whole, only a piece of skilled mechanics' work ; but it is not complete until the aid of the modeller and the chaser has been called in to achieve the silver bosses on the hammercloth, and until the herald-painter has lavished all his wealth of blazonry on the panels. These illustrations are almost tritely obvious; but it is necessary to bear them in mind when we are discussing the relations of Art to Industry, and the propriety of drawing a distinction between the fine arts primarily and secondarily considered : between their application to manufacture and their state of isolation and independence as monuments, more or less abstract, of beauty and truth.

I repeat, however, that the expediency of the introduction of paintings and statuary to an Exhibition of industry is questionable, principally for the reason that both art and industry must suffer in a greater or smaller degree from each other's propinquity. In the Paris Exhibition, while crowds gather round Vela's "Napoleon," round Marshall Wood's "Needlewoman," round this "Pietà" and that "Bacchante," whole streets of stalls devoted to the display of textile fabrics, of silks and woollens, and alpacas and calicoes, are all but entirely deserted. While the picture galleries are rendered wellnigh impassable by curious sightseers, expatiating over the excellences of a Meissonnier, a Frère, or a Rosa Bonheur, the machine galleries never number, at any time, more than a few thin groups of spectators. The jurors have, of course, passed through in the exercise of their functions; special men, mechanics, and engineers, equally of course, devote hours to the patient study of particular machines. But the general public either avoid this department of the Exhibition altogether, or pass rapidly through it, declaring that the whirring wheels or the "roaring looms"—by the way, with all due respect to both Goethe and Carlyle, I never heard a loom "roar;" it rather clinks and clatters—make their heads ache, or are induced to take some temporary interest in mechanics by some contrivances for fabricating felt hats by steam, or cutting pretty devices out of blocks of oak with a circular saw, or engraving visiting cards by the instantaneous process. Now, one or another interest must suffer by such a state of things. I say that the machinery and the textile fabrics suffer. Their exposition has been meant not alone for mechanics and specially practical people, but for the whole world. There is no reason why we should not fall into ecstacies as enthusiastic over a Stephenson's locomotive, or a Fairlie's " bogie " engine, as over a cavalier by Meissonnier, or a bull by Bonheur. They do not enjoy their proper position of importance. " Dry goods " in the immediate vicinage of pictures and statues do not receive their proper meed of attention. Nor are they alone in the endurance of injury. The Fine Arts, abstractedly, suffer as bitterly and unjustly. I ask whether a visitor with his head full of centrifugal pumps and steam dredgers, of cocoa-nut matting and seamless carpets, of patent flat-irons and waterproof goloshes, of ever-pointed pencils and improved cooking ranges, of Chickering's pianos and Distin's saxhorns, of Fry's cocoa and Colman's mustard, and Dunville's "V. R" whiskey, is in a fit and proper state to proceed to the calm and temperate examination of a picture or a statue? I answer that he is not. And all students of art will, I think, agree with me.

To all this the projectors of Universal Exhibitions in the actual condition to which they have sunk (for I hold them to be in decline, and verging upon fall), have one reply which I suppose they think unanswerable. The pictures and statues are, in a superlative degree, "attractive." They bring the mob. They bring the shillings; and the mob and the shillings are the things most dearly desiderated by the projectors. Wonderful, interesting, edifying as are the products of useful industry, it would be difficult to persuade the public to "come in their thousands" and gaze on a special exhibition of the boots and shoes, the knives and forks, the plates and dishes, the ploughs and harrows, the coats and trousers, the candles and rushlights of All Nations. There is the rub. The public must be "attracted." "All very nice; *but it wants a piano*," said Douglas Jerrold, when Thackeray asked him what he thought of his first lecture on the "English Humorists." If the many-headed monster be not tickled with attraction he will not come, and the concern will not pay. There is too, I hasten to admit, among the rudest and meanest of mankind, an innate love, an often unconscious appreciation of beautiful and tasteful things. The admirable gentlemen who, in England, have care of the insane, can testify how instrumental in soothing the agonies of madness have been the beautiful engravings with which the munificence of Mr. Henry Graves has covered the walls of Bethelehem Hospital; and in asylums not so favoured it is well known that the possession of a number of the *Illustrated*

London News is a boon and a blessing to the afflicted. In my own fantastic and of course impracticable opinion, all human things, to the wickedest and the most degraded, may be softened and bettered by Art ; and I even dare to think that were an engraving, say after Rafaelle's " Madonna del Sisto," or Domenichino's " St. Jerome," or Murillo's " San Juan de Dios," stuck up, in lieu of the gaol rules, in the solitary cell of a convict at Pentonville, there might be in time instilled into the mind of the brutish inmate some ray of light, some dim idea of love and mercy, some tiny seed— God save the seed, and let it grow !—of sorrow and repentance. But these are idle fancies, not to be recognized by the Inspectors of Prisons or by her Majesty's Secretary of State for the Home Department. We will be practical, if you please.

From the Great Exhibition of 1851, painting, *per se,* was excluded ; and this exclusion was decreed with the full cognisance and complicity of the Prince whose love and reverence for Art was patent to all the world. Sculpture, however, as an element of attractiveness, had a place conceded to it. What was the result ? What were the most popular objects in the World's Fair of '51, next to Osler's fountain, and Gulliver and the Liliputians, and the Comical Creatures from Wurtemburg ? Why, Rafaelle Monti's veiled statue, and Hiram Power's Greek Slave. The attractiveness of Art, for Art's own sake, was more forcibly exemplified in 1857, when a triumphant success, commercial as well as moral, was achieved at the Manchester Exhibition of Art Treasures, in which, with the exception of a few pieces of ancient tapestry and a few suits of armour from the Tower, there was nothing to be seen save pictures and statuary. I own then, unreservedly, that if we are to regard an Exhibition as a show and a spectacle, and nothing else, it must have its "attraction," and that the best attraction is Art; but I do not recede one whit from my former opinion, that the unity and utility of any Exhibition must be injured by the contiguity of pickles blacking-brushes, cigars, cognac, and corduroy trousers, with the most exquisite examples of human thought and genius. Cunningly as you may arrange your groups, and elaborately as you may tabulate your classes, the grand result will be general confusion in the mind of the spectator. The father of Robert Houdin the conjuror used to exercise his son in the art of visual memory by making him stop before a shop window, bidding him take a rapid view of the contents, and then close his eyes and tell him "what he had seen" an instant before. But if you took a sightseer fresh from the "Ten groups" of the ellipses in the Champ de Mars, and asked him rapidly what he had seen, he would begin to stammer out, photographs, cork legs, marble statues, sewing machines, stuffed lion and tiger, jade cup, perambulators, organs, lay figures, majolica:—his mind would be in a hopelessly hetero- geneous state. For this reason, if for no other, I trust that the Congress of 1867 will be the last of Universal Exhibitions which this age will witness. Of the confusion of ideas brought about by a frenzied assemblage of incongruous things, we had a sufficing illustration when the Duke of Manchester wrote to the newspapers, pointing out as one of the articles which had principally struck his gracious mind, the automa- ton figure of a monkey playing on a fiddle. Of the half grotesque, half scandalous blunders into which projectors, in their ambition to achieve universality, have fallen, we have an adequate proof in the actual aspect of the Champ de Mars, which has assumed, in equal proportions, the likeness of a bazaar, a museum of art, a provincal " everything 'shop," a country fair, an eating-house and a tavern, and where cheek by jowl with painted canvas and Parian marble are giants and dwarfs, barbers and blowers of the bagpipes, rope-dancers and sword-swallowers, flower-girls and newsboys, patentees of cough lozenges and vendors of corn plasters.

Could we shut ourselves out, however, from the incongruous surroundings which here compass art about and mar our thorough appreciation of its beauties—could we pass blindfolded through the Bartlemy Fair of the Park, and stop our ears, as did the heathen man of old against the syrens of the sea, as we passed through the gallery of machinery in motion, enough might be found in the galleries devoted to painting and statuary to occupy half a lifetime for study and reflection. This is the first time that an attempt has been made simultaneously to measure the art progress of the whole civilized world. The measurement is not complete, certainly, for the materials, bountifully copious from some countries—such as France, for instance—are wofully meagre with respect to others. England, in particular, does not show one tithe of what she can do. But the attempt has been made nevertheless. The painters and sculptors have been brought face to face, and the untravelled spectator may, in these countries, wander from country to country, and enjoy such advantages of examination and comparison as have never before fallen to the lot of human student. I have not, by any means, forgotten the analogous attempt made at South Kensington in 1862. We originatd the idea of an International Picture Gallery, but, as usual, we got very little credit by it, nor, for a variety of reasons, were we enabled to carry it out on a scale even remotely approaching completeness. The French borrowed our idea, improved upon it, and, I daresay, are by this time fully persuaded that the notion is their own.

The conclusion at which most impartial critics will arrive, when they have accomplished the long journey which is commenced at the French Fine Art Gallery, and terminates in the English section, will be, I apprehend, that there are in the world, three schools of art—the French, the German, and the English. The French school would seem to be, at present, in a transition state. It is no longer rigidly conservative, or classic, as in the days of David and his immediate successors; but it has also ceased to be outrageously heterodox or romantic, as in the epoch immediately preceding and immediately following the Revolution of July, when Hugo in poetry, Delacroix in painting, and Gautier in criticism, boldly flung their gauntlet of revolt in the face of the lettered mandarins of the Academy and the Ecole des Beaux Arts. As it is, classicists and Romancists in France seem to have agreed upon an armistice until some great treaty of art peace can be concluded. The erst combatants do not, however, sulk in their entrenchments. They visit each other's camps and exchange courtesies, as did the allies with the Russians before Sebastopol, while Orloff and the other plenipotentiaries were negotiating peace at Paris. Nay, they sometimes condescend to make excursions to Simpheropol and Batschi-Serai, and see what the Crim-Tartars—I mean the English—are doing. Hitherto the French have been afflicted with, or have professed the profoundest ignorance, as to the existence of a British school of art. *"L'école Anglaise! qu'est ce ? que c'est que ça,"* the shabbiest *rapin* of the Rue des Saints Pères would exclaim, if you talked to him of the

English school. There were a few better-informed French-men—Guizot, Maxime Ducamp, Louis Viardot, for example—who had heard that we had a Landseer who painted dogs and horses tolerably well, a Stanfield who was clever with his pencil at seascapes, and that we once possessed two really eminent portrait painters, whose names were Reynolds and Lawrence. Beyond this, all was thick night. In 1862, at a literary dinner in London, I had the honour to propose the health of M. Théophile Gautier, one of the most brilliant of French prose writers, and certainly the ablest of French art critics. In returning thanks, he reciprocated the compliment, as is the custom with his countrymen, and "carried a toast" to the health of Turner:—*"grand peintre poetique, jadis inconnu en France:"* so he qualified him. He did not know that the painter of "Calais Pier" and the "Building of Carthage" was dead; and he confessed that, until his visit to South Kensington, he had never heard of Turner. Some of our living men, Millais, Mulready, Ward, Webster, especially made their mark at the Paris Exhibition of '55; but acquaintance with English masters is yet in the earliest stages of dawn in the French mind. This year they are beginning to abuse us; and abuse is one of the best tests of celebrity and success.

The amicably dissident condition into which the republic of art in France has fallen, claims, however, some further notice. There can be no doubt that the Imperial French Academy at Rome, with its large subsidies and its cornucopia of honours and rewards notwithstanding, the "Grand Style," the severely academical manner no longer enjoys supremacy in the polity of French art. The *Grands Prix de Rome* are still eagerly sought for and proudly cherished; the *pension-*

naires of the Villa Medici continue to forward to Paris their "Nativities" and "Entombments," their "Continence of Scipio," and their "Orestes pursued by the Eumenides;" the State continues to feed the returning prizemen with liberal commissions for the decoration of churches and public buildings; but it is easy to see that the empire of the grandiose-devotional and the colossal-historical has passed away. Even in battlepieces, of which in a country like France there must always be a profusion, the whilom gigantic canvasses of Vernet and Bellangé, and Gèricault and Gros, have dwindled down to the pretty *camera-lucida*-like battle scenes of Meissonnier. There is a rumour that this unrivalled micrographer intends for the future to devote himself to the production of historic works with figures the size of life; and that his illustrious compeer Gérome, who has hitherto excelled in the classic-sensuous, bordering sometimes on what M. Taine, following Rétif de la Butonne, disdainfully styles the "Pornographic," has threatened to paint nothing in days to come but religious subjects on the largest scale. Should either carry out his promise, however, it is to be feared that their amended style will find but little appreciation among French patrons of art. The *petits bonhommes* of Meissonnier, those delightful little puppets, who had they been subjected to the criticism of Louis XIV., might have been dismissed as disdainfully as when the great king, turning his back on a Teniers and Ostade, said, "*Ôtez moi ces magots là*"—the charming liliputian cavaliers and dragoons, and marquises and spadassins, so trimly attired, so cunningly lit up with varied *chiaro-oscuro*, so exquisitely finished, to the minutest frill in a laced *jabot*, to the last tag and button on an embroidered doublet, to the last feather of a plumed hat, to the last seam in a boot of Cordovan leather, these homuncular marvels will always be eagerly sought for in France, and may continue to command, as they do now, more than three times their weight in gold. For in the "Rixe," the "Man Choosing a Sword," the "Bravoes waiting at a Door," the "Orderly," the "Wayside Inn," the "Souvenir of 1813," the "Man Etching," the "Good Friends," the "Reading Party at Diderot's," is there not, to excess, that quality displayed—prized as almost inestimable in France—the quality of *chic?* It is to be feared that David, or Gros, or Proudhon, would have had, for a Meissonnier, contempt equal to that which the Grand Monarque displayed for the Dutch masters—and contempt, let me add, quite as foolish and unjust. Gérome, again, would have met with but scant favour from the austere and haughty professors, whose "Rape of the Sabines" was as stilted and decorous as a Minuet de la Cour, whose battle pieces were as glittering and about as genuine as the sham fights at the Cirque Napoleon, and whose heroes, and sages, and poets, and virgins of antiquity, were quite as well proportioned, quite as shapely and comely, quite as cold and lifeless, as the wax figures at Madame Tussaud's. And, to come nearer our own time, what would Ingres—what would the rigid and virtuous painter of "St. Symphorien," and "Angelica," and the "Cherubini" of the Luxembourg, and the "Odalisque"—the great defiance to the romantic school, the most decorous piece of indecorum perhaps ever produced—what would the melancholy and ascetic Ary Scheffer, the dreamy mystic whose "Mignon," whose "Dante and Beatrice," whose "Francesca," whose "Christus Consolator," seem to bear about them something of the vague, wild, wailing music of an Æolian harp—what would even the superb and chivalric Paul Delaroche, the Velasquez of his day, the hero who delighted more in the portrayal of noble personages and grand deeds—what would these Conscript Fathers of art have thought of a public running mad ·after Meissonnier's puppets and Gérome's Phrynes and Queen Candaules?

It is a plain and patent fact, however, that the "grand style"—dependent on severely academical drawing, conventional drapery, conventional attitudes, conventional composition, and conventional colour—that is to say, a prevailing pink, grey, and drab, and, throughout, chalky hue, has ceased to find favour in France. There are the usual governmental and municipal commissions given for altar-pieces, hemicycles, the spandrils of arches, the *cieli* of cupolas, the walls of council chambers and staircases; but the orders of the state are ordered spiritlessly and reluctantly. They *are* executed, for artists, at the outset of their career, must have bread; but so soon as they can emancipate themselves from the patronage and the censorship of the ministry of fine arts, we find the academically-bred painters striking out new paths, seeking fresh associations, *jettant leurs dépoques aux orties*, like dissolute monks, and plunging into all the delights, and sometimes into all the license of liberty. It is perhaps better for all painters, whatever may be the department in art to which in future they elect to ˙devote themselves, to have, as a basis of instruction, a thorough course of academical discipline—to go through the whole stony curriculum of free-handed and instrumental geometry, of linear and aërial perspective, of the theory of shadows and the laws of curves, of plastic and comparative anatomy, of the doctrine of foreshortening and the axioms of pyramidal composition: —that they should learn to model and to etch before they

presume to paint. Such a thorough and painstaking theoretical and practical education can do them no harm, and it
may do them a vast amount of good. At least it will make
them, artistically, scholars and gentlemen:—and an analogous plea may be advanced in favour of subjecting our
English youths, who are afterwards to become lawyers, statesmen, divines, surgeons, physicians, or even soldiers and
sailors, to an eight or ten years' course of Greek, Latin, and
mathematics. The number of artists, however, as of scholars,
who persist in the continually up-hill career of erudition, is
limited. Only blockheads can really forget that which they
ever learnt at school; and, as a rule, when you find a man
declaring that he has "forgotten his classics," it will generally
turn out, on inquiry, that he never knew any. Still we are
apt to merge our original book-learning into a common stock
of subsequently-acquired and *viva voce* knowledge. We
dread the imputation of pedantry; and, indeed, we often
find that book-learning, unless it be Applied—unless it be
absorbed in and made to subserve actual technical attain-
ments—will prove rather a hindrance than a help to our
advancement in life:—that it will cause us to be intolerably
conceited; and that it will fail to make us useful. A good
mathematician, who is also a good carpenter, is twice a man.
A good carpenter, without mathematics, is a man; but a
mere puzzler over problems and chalker of diagrams, who
cannot do anything to earn five shillings a day for himself, is only half a man. For example, I may have a conviction that, as a man of letters, I have pretty well said my
say—that I am growing stupid and prosy—that I am coming
to the end of my stock of ideas; that young men are growing
up around me who are brighter, cleverer, more industrious

than I am. But I learnt in early youth to engrave visiting cards and tradesmen's billheads on copper and steel; and if I find the bright and clever young men pushing me from my stool, why, I can emigrate to Canada, or Australia, or California, knowing that wherever trade and commerce thrive, there is a demand for card-plates and billheads; and that I may at least get my bread and cheese without either robbing, digging, or begging.

A survey of the works of art in painting and drawing, exhibited in the French sections of the Champ de Mars, and a comparison of those works, not alone with those which the English have to show in Paris, but with those which, from memory and experience, we know to exist at home, forces on us one dominant and melancholy conclusion:—that the French, however much they may vary in their status as painters, do, as a rule, draw admirably; and that we, although often excelling in colour, and in the taste, the pathos, and the humour we instil into our pictures, do as a rule draw infamously. The "free hand" is manifest in almost every French picture, although, as a painting, it may be next door to a daub. By the "free hand" I mean the unmistakable presence of a knowledge of draughtsmanship on the part of the designer. He knows the proper proportions of the human figure. He has had the canons of Vitruvius and Albert Durer drummed into him. He has mastered, long years ago, the grammar, the theory, the thorough-bass and counterpoint of art. He knows not only where are the muscles, but where that invaluable scaffolding *beneath the muscles*, the bones, should be. His muscular and bony markings, although broad, are in essentials correct. Knowing what is the latent appearance of the human form, he is enabled, with the very slightest assistance from models, to cause his drapery to fall in easy and natural folds. Having been taught the law of shadows, he knows how to give to each round or flat surface its proper quota of light, shadow, and reflection. Having learnt perspective at school —not as a mere "extra" or supplement to artistic instruction, but as an integral part of mathematical education, he knows how to manage the planes of his picture, and how to set, not only his trees and his houses, but his horses and his human figures, in their proper visual aspect. In English pictures, while the landscape and architecture are frequently in strict accordance with the laws of linear perspective, the figures, from the absence of early geometrical training, are monstrously out of proportion, or, if they are foreshortened, present their *raccourcis* at impossible angles when compared with surrounding objects. Finished with wonderful carefulness and nicety, sweetly and tenderly coloured as they are, the best of English pictures rarely fail to excite in the mind of an educated spectator a sentiment of indignation. They are so vilely drawn. They sin so crassly against the very first rules of mathematical truth; and, for all their meretricious stippling, and glazing, and scumbling, and tickling, and touching up, you can see from beginning to end the painter would have been able to do nothing without human or still-life models. Take away Mr. John Gilbert, and there is scarcely an English figure painter of note who is "free handed," and who is not an abject slave to his models.

VII.

THE TERRA COTTAS OF LEOPOLD HARZÉ.

SAMUEL FOOTE, the famous actor and wit, once took it into his head to invest some money in a brewery, as wits in all ages, and often to their destruction, have been curiously apt to do. The beer that Foote brewed was very bad. Those whose sides had often ached at his wonderful mimicry and his jests frequently found, after patronising his tap, that the aching sensation extended to their stomachs. It chanced that he was bidden to dine one evening at the house of a great lord, in whose servants' hall beer from the Foote brewery, much to the discomfort of the domestics, was drunk. The lacquey who opened the door recognized and scowled upon him as on a personal enemy. The butler who poured out the actor-brewer's Madeira probably wished that he could fill his glass with his own abhorred swipes, instead. But the banquet proceeded, and Foote began to be funny. He let off, that night, some of his choicest jokes. The table was in a roar. The guests, as M. Guizot afterwards related of Sydney Smith, laughed "while he spoke, after he spoke, and before he spoke." He surrounded himself with a blaze of verbal fireworks. My lord was pleased to be pleased. Even the moody butler chuckled; and as for the little black boy who waited behind the actor's chair, he so grinned with delight that his ears nearly met at the nape of his neck. That black boy went down subsequently to the kitchen, and laughed till he cried. When he had recovered his breath and his composure, and had related a few of the richest *facetiæ* he had heard upstairs, he made before the assembled servants this memorable remark—"*He is a great man. I will drink his beer.*"

Now, in the kingdom of Belgium, so gently and honestly ruled by Leopold II., there is one dreadful and abhorrent thing—one detestable and maleficent product to which I have sworn these many years past eternal enmity. I allude to the hateful stuff called Faro Beer. To say that Faro is at once sour, bitter, acrid, vapid, and mawkish—that it has neither body, nor bones, nor muscle, nor sinew—that in hue it resembles black dose which has turned pale at the memory of its own misdeeds, that in odour it might remind the curious in bad smells of a vinegar factory next door to a bone-boiler's, with a tanyard over the way and a tallow-melter's round the corner—that it is infinitely worse, even, than the revolting beverage called "clink," made from the gyle of malt and the sweepings of hop-bins, and brewed especially for the benefit of agricultural labourers in harvest time (four gallons of "clink" per diem are considered a pretty "tidy" allowance for a bold peasant, his country's pride, in districts where cider cannot be procured): to say all this is not to mention a tithe of the unpleasant things which can be said about Faro Beer. The *braves Belges* drink prodigious quantities of it—I think the retail price of Faro is about three halfpence a quart—usually in conjunction with hard-boiled eggs and loud-smelling cheese; and they are bold enough to assert that even foreigners, duly acclimatised, will come in time to be fond of Faro. Ay; but did not Mithridates feed on poisons? and have I not seen, in Barbary, negroes who could digest with equal facility the rind of a prickly pear, a live lizard, and a red-hot poker? Are there not people who delight in assafœtida biscuit? and others who drink themselves to death with the nauseous and brain-killing absinthe? Be it as it may, I never could stomach Faro, and I never was acquainted with a virtuous or reputable person who could. But, in view of certain Belgian products to be seen in the Paris Exibition—in view of certain beautiful works of art over which I pored for days, and of which I now purpose to pen a brief account—I am prepared to retract all the hard words I may have said against Faro. On the principle laid down by Foote's black boy, I will do my best to drink the Belgian beer, for the sake of a "great man" who lives in the Rue d'Ixelles, at Brussels. I will forget all my grievances for the sake of the terra cottas of Monsieur Leopold Harzé.

A terra cotta is, as you know, only so much baked clay. The process of baking is a most delicate and difficult one, for the clay model always shrinks in the "firing," and with even greater frequency "flies" or cracks. Probably not one in ten of the beautiful models produced by the facile hands of sculptors as *matrices* for the future bronze or marble can be baked with satisfaction or security. In large figures they are compelled by the laws of gravity to use "supports"— that is, to prop up and strengthen the clay internally by means of wires and sticks. The foundation for a figure of colossal size is often a perfect skeleton of wood or iron. But such models do not go to the furnace; they are cast at once in plaster, and in the process of casting the original clay is generally broken to pieces. In a model meant for the oven, props or supports must be used most sparingly, and it is far better, if the subject will possibly allow it, to do without them altogether. The clay in drying shrinks, the supporters are thus naturally isolated, and what sculptors call *un mauvais vieux* is thereby produced—*i.e.*, the figure is bereft of cohesive solidity, and the slightest concussion will shatter it. The most that prudent modellers will venture upon is to plant a slender wire—a hairpin will suffice for a small figure—in the clay while they are fashioning it, just to keep their work steady; but this metallic spine or wire should be withdrawn before baking. It is obvious, then, that in a case where adventitious aids can be so grudgingly employed, variation of attitude or hardihood of design in a terra cotta becomes exceedingly dangerous. The modeller can take very few liberties with the *pose* of his figure. He is altogether dependent on its centre of gravity, and he must take care that the limbs he models shall be in proper balance with the centre to harden without supports. There are, however, a number of attitudes of the superior extremities, and a few of those of the inferior, which are not dependent on the laws of gravity, but which, in the living subject, are produced by muscular volition. Many of these defy plastic skill to reproduce them; and even in so strong a material as marble, and in the most consummate of the ancient statues—the Meleager, the Youth with the "Strigil," and the Belvedere Apollo, for instance—we can see where the sculptor has been forced to prop up an arm or an extended foot with a short bar or ligament of marble, absolutely indispensable, but most unsightly.

Another difficulty in the art of modelling in clay for baking is that which environs the attainment of any elaborate detail. For busts, or reliefs of anything of a bold nature, with plenty of broad surfaces, the clay will serve admirably; but for "niggling" finish clay—carefully as it may have been kneaded—is too coarse. Such things as feathers, curls and ringlets, whiskers, eyelashes, lace, ribbons, foliage, and the gewgaws and trinkets of women, are, generally, but clumsily imitated in clay. For broad, sweeping, heavy folds of drapery it is excellent; but when the modeller comes to such niceties as a lace shawl, or the underskirts of a dancer, or a filigree necklace, he is puzzled, and wellnigh despairs. There are truly some wonderful examples of veiled figures extant both in ancient and modern sculpture, in which the most exquisite finish has been attained. Monti's "Veiled Slave" astonished the world seventeen years since; and an even more astonishing example of what has been unkindly termed "the art of imitating a wet towel" may be seen in the "Dead Saviour" of the San Severo Chapel at Naples, and in some Spanish wood carvings in the Church of the Caridad at Seville. Almost superhuman patience is required for the execution of these simulacra, and the result is, after all, but a negative one. The material in which the most exquisite elaboration of detail can be attained is wax—a substance which, seemingly intractable at first, becomes, as it gradually warms and is handled by a skilful modeller, exquisitely ductile, supple, and pliable. One need only point to the wax flowers in the London shop windows, and to the marvellous Mexican wax figures—the manufacture of which in England has been so successfully practised by Madame Montanari and by Mr. Rich, of Great Russell Street

—to show of what wax, properly treated, is capable. As an axiom, it may be laid down that it is susceptible of twice the amount of finish that can be achieved with clay; and for this reason the most delicate statuettes, the most cunning arabesques, the tiniest figures of animals or flowers, afterwards to be executed in gold or silver, are first modelled, not in clay, but in the seductive though sight-destroying material known as *cire rouge*, or wax mixed with some red pigment in powder. I saw last winter, in Rome, in the studio of an eminent English sculptor, Mr. Cardwell, a very ingenious and successful compromise devised by him for combining the substantiality of clay with the ductility of wax, and at the same time obviating the perils to eyesight which arise from poring over the reddened wax. He had mixed clay and wax together, with some boiled oil as a diluent, and the result was a compost emiently plastic, but exquisitely fine and capable of application to the minutest details; such, for example, as the fur of animals, the intricacies of foliage, and the reticulations of net-work. The material, with proper care, promised to be indefinitely durable; but it could not, of course, be baked.

The illustrious John Flaxman, too, was accustomed to model with a mixture of putty and sand ; and I think it is John Thomas Smith—" Nollekens " Smith—that most amusing antiquary, gossip, and legacy hunter, who speaks of some beautiful *alti-rilievi* in putty and sand with which the good man, whom crazy William Blake used to call " Sculptor of Eternity," decorated the walls of his studio. In this material great sharpness of outline was procurable, and intense hardness set in when the compost dried; but it was a most repulsive substance to knead, and—as in every case where lead is a component—was injurious to the health of

the workman. Those who have seen the "bread seals" made
by schoolboys know that a well-kneaded morsel of new
bread will take very sharp impressions, which when dried
becomes as hard as stone, but the bread should be mixed with
a little gum-water, which renders it disagreeably sticky to
the fingers, and both this and the cognate material of papier
mâché are more serviceable for pressure into metallic moulds
than for absolute manipulation as models.   With all our
devices, we are compelled to revert to first principles, and
the beginning of all plasticity is clay.   The illiterate urchin
kneads his "dirt pie," and Phidias with all his learning must
fain do as much for his Venus.

M. Leopold Harzé, of Brussels—a gentleman whose name I
candidly own I never heard before, and of whose antecedents
or individuality I have not the vaguest knowledge—appears
to have surmounted, in a most astonishing manner, the
manifold obstacles which lie in the path of the artist in terra
cotta ; and he has produced a series of works in this material
that, for skilful modelling and careful finish, may vie with
the rarest of the wax figures from Mexico ; that surpass the
well-known booty-dividing brigands and guitar-playing and
macaroni-eating beggars in which the terracotians of Naples
have attained such celebrity ; and that leave a long way
behind even the delightful little papier mâché statuettes of
toreadores, contrabandistas, chulos, and *aguadores,* which you
purchase at Malaga and Alicant.   Mr. Harzé exhibits ten
groups in terra cotta, numbering each from two to six
figures ; and it is not alone by their finish that they are
remarkable.   They are all replete with a sly humour, almost
Hogarthian in its finesse.   There is a scene from "Tartufe,"
and never was a more hypocritical villain immortalised in

clay than has been moulded by M. Harzé.   There is the duel
scene from the "Bourgeois Gentilhomme," with the sauciest
soubrette and the drollest *bourgeois* M. Jourdain ever conceived.
There is a paraphrase—an unconscious one, I dare say—of
Mulready's " Wolf and the Lamb " :—a big, ruffianly boy, who
has bullied and beaten a smaller one, but is suddenly overtaken by Nemesis in the shape of another boy, the biggest
and most ruffianly of all three.   There is a cottage scene,
which looks like one of Jan Steen's interiors put into high
relief, and in which Béranger's charming ballad of the blind
mother and the pair of sweethearts—" *Lise, vous ne filez
pas* "—is illustrated. There is a Trial Scene with a thief—*such*
a thief! with *such* a beard and *such* a blouse.   I am sure it
must have been a case of " *vol avec escalade et effraction.*"
This rascal is arraigned before three stern judges, while the
Procureur du Roi reads the act of accusation.   Then there
is Doll Tearsheet sitting on Falstaff's knee, while the naughty
old fat man is bidding her sing improper songs, and telling
her that he shall receive money on Thursday, and asking her
what stuff she will have a kirtle of. You can almost hear
Mrs. Quickly in the corridor, and "Sneak's noise outside," and
the pressure inwards of the knight's fat jowl by Doll's hand
is a triumph of plastic observation in what the Italian's call
morbidezza, or the " art of fleshiness."   There is a charming
rustic scene entitled—" The pitcher goes often to the well, but
gets broken at last "—a young girl at a fountain with Love
hiding among the bushes, till he snuggles close to her and
whispers perilous stuff in her ear.   And there is a wonderful
composition of a painter's studio : an old dowager in hoop
and brocade, sitting for her portrait, with a self-satisfied smirk
on her countenance, and her little dog asleep on her knee.

The dowager, however, is wholly unaware that there is some one else asleep in the studio ; the painter to wit, who, overcome by fatigue, has sunk into a sound slumber, with his head against the canvas on his easel. The rogue ! it is easy to see how it is that Somnus has overtaken him. On the floor beneath his chair are perceptible a pair of very coquettish satin boots, while his own *pierrot's* costume and the most unmentionable portions of a *débardeur's* costume, complete the evidence of this tale of guilt. The wretch ! *There is somebody else asleep in an alcove not far from that studio.* I said the boots were of white satin. You may ask how, the material of the whole being terra cotta, I could have arrived at such a conclusion ? I answer that the evidence, quite unmistakable, of this and other facts, is due to the marvellous texture which M. Harzé has given to clay. He seems to be able to do everything with and in his stubborn material. Lace, filigree, embroidery, the pile of velvet, the ribbing of silk, the sheen of satin, the embroidery on a ribbon, the nap of cloth, the dull softness of felt, the harder surface of leather, the roughness of stone, the smoothness of ivory, the fluff of feathers, the embossed mosaic of Berlin wool, the very grain of wood and veining of marble, the exquisite anatomy of leaves and ferns, the blading of grass, the petals of flowers, the down which is under the wings of birds—all these he has imitated in baked clay. His figures have backgrounds, too, with curtains, pictures, bird-cages, busts, bookcases, candlesticks, sheets of music, the very crotchets and quavers accurately noted. I hold these terra cottas of M. Leopold Harzé to be the most admirable specimens of purely imitative art that have been seen these thirty years.

Ere I dismiss the subject of terra cottas I must say a word

concerning three very admirable works in baked clay in the United States courts. These should properly have been in the Fine Arts gallery; but for some unaccountable reason they are jumbled up with Chickering's pianos, and dentists' chairs, and billiard tables, glass bottles, cast-iron clocks, Californian and Vermont marble chimney-pieces, surgical instruments, patent plumbago pencils, and stuffed birds and beasts. "The Oath and Rations" is the title of the first group. A Southern lady, young, comely, graceful, but desperately poverty-stricken in appearance, has come, with her little child clinging to her skirt, to the "Freedman's bureau," to "draw" a sufficiency of bread and meat to sustain life. But before she can draw her rations she must take the oath of loyalty and allegiance to the United States of America. You can see, in her every lineament, that from the bottom of her heart she hates the United States. A spruce young Northern officer stands with a volume of Scripture in hand to administer the oath. He is a polite young Northerner, and raises his forage cap as he points out the dire necessity of swearing. What is the poor Southern lady to do? It is clear that her little child must be fed. So her philosophy must be the converse of ancient Pistol's. She "swears," but eke, she eats. Another story, quite as pathetic, but not so painful, is told in "The Charity Patient"—a good old doctor prescribing for a sick baby drooping in its mother's arms: and in "Uncle Ned's School"—an old negro shoemaker teaching, as he cobbles, a mulatto girl to read—there is a wonderfully humorous figure of a little nigger boy, who sprawls at the dedagogue's feet and tickles his toe, even as he teaches.

VIII.

M. FRÉMIET'S STATUETTES.

SOME of the choicest things in the Exhibition have been hidden away in corners undiscoverable save by considerable detective astuteness and untiring perseverance. Has not this been the case in all Universal Exhibitions? What crowds of persons went away from Hyde Park in 1851 without setting eyes on that exquisite tableau of Captain Lemuel Gulliver and the Liliputians? It would be a sad pity, if, in the exercise of my duties as a cicerone, I omitted to guide the steps of the visitor (he may be in Hong Kong or in Hawaï, and never have set foot in the Champ de Mars; but I ask him to travel with me in the spirit) to these remote regions, these shady nooks and corners, where the gems of the Exhibition lay more or less *perdu.* One day I passed a stout English matron, who, with her feet slack-baked by the hot asphalte-laid pavement of the palace, wisely determined to give herself, on a broiling May day, as little trouble as possible, and was being gently drawn along in a Bath-chair. The lady's French was susceptible of improvement. " *Voo allez long, très long ;*" thus she exhorted the attendant. " *Voo prenez votre temps, et vous montrez moi tous les jolly shows.*" She had a meek English companion with her, in deep mourning—are ladies' companions always expected by their employers to have suffered a recent bereavement, necessitating the wearing of sable garments?—who, in an under tone, suggested first the picture galleries, and then the jewellery. But the British matron declared that she had had enough of jewels, and that the pictures made her head ache. You will scarcely credit me when I tell you that the chairman had the hardheartedness to drag her to the machinery department, and to come to a halt before a great whirring steam-engine, as though *that* were a *jolie chose*. I should have dearly liked to volunteer my services as an amateur guide to the pretty things; but you must be on your guard in offering the slightest courtesy to the fair sex—especially when they hail from the British Isles. I remember coming on a lady once in Regent Street whose strings and things were coming down and trailing behind her. I ventured to hint at her mishap, and she told me I ought to be ashamed of myself. I remember seeing a lady in a brougham in Piccadilly, who was splitting her glove and bruising her pretty little hand black and blue in ineffectual efforts to turn the obstinate handle of her carriage door. I turned the handle for her, and she looked as though she would have liked to box my ears. Altogether, in presence of an inflexible and implacable sex, I the rather incline to the canon laid down by a Yankee philosopher. "If you see a man drowning," says this sage, "and you haven't been introduced, *throw a rail at him*."

Misadventures well-nigh as terrible have occurred to me when, unauthorized, and from a mere stupid blundering wish to do service, I have ventured to show the lions to a person of my own sex. In the Tribune at Florence I got into trouble with a "stout party in a shovel"—I almost fancy he was a bishop—to whom I was bold enough to whisper, having heard his loud-voiced criticisms, that the Dancing Faun was not one of Canova's Boxers : those twin-pugilists, Creugas and Damoxenus, being at Rome, in the Vatican. So too, at Rome itself, being in one of those incomparable cabinets surrounding the Cortile of the Belvedere, I made last January—I declare I couldn't help myself—a terrible hole in my manners. I had been satiating myself with the contemplation of the "Lord of the unerring bow," of that matchless embodiment of the idea of manly beauty of whom we are never tired of quoting Byron's lines :—

> But in his delicate form—a dream of love,
> Shaped by some solitary nymph, whose breast
> Long'd for a deathless lover from above,
> And madden'd in that vision—are express'd
> All that ideal beauty ever blessed.
> The mind within the most unearthly mood,
> When each conception was a heavenly guest,
> A ray of immortality—and stood
> Starlike, around, until they gather'd to a god.

I was cogitating over Visconti and Winckelmann's theories, as whether the work was Roman or Greek, and wailing, as every art lover must wail, over Mortosoli's miserable restorations of the right ankle and leg—what a righteous fury John Bell the anatomist fell into with the clumsy botcher !—when there entered to me, from the cabinet of the Laocöon, a party of English tourists. Papa, dogged, surly, trudging onwards, and I am afraid praying inwardly ·for a " point steak," and a " pint of cooper," and the *Pall Mall Gazette*, at the Cheshire Cheese, in lieu of " kickshaws " artistic or otherwise. Mamma, fagged to death, half asleep and unutterably dejected. Eldest daughter supercilious, and principally concerned for the dragging skirt of her dress, for we had much wet weather, and the Cortile was slightly sloppy. Youngest daughter, aged thirteen, and with her frizzy hair floating over her shoulders, simply dazed, and, for the time, idiotic; thinking however, very probably, that after all these big saloons full of big stone men and women without any clothes on were preferable to Miss Pinkerton and the lesson-haunted school-room in Montagu Square. Finally, there was a long, drooping, vapid, inert, lethargic, conceited, washed-out English swell, tremendously whiskered and moustached, but of a hue so florid that he looked like Lord Dundreary dipped in red ochre. I can stand a good deal, but I couldn't stand the whole party sailing by without condescending to cast one glance on the "Lord of the unerring bow." I couldn't stand the long swell yawning, and then halting to examine the heel of his boot, into which a pebble had inserted itself, and "craunched while he walked." I went up to him, lifted my hat, and said, courteously: "Excuse me, sir, but *that* is the Apollo Belvedere." He looked as though he would have eaten me. The whole family stared. It was my usual luck. I blushed and withdrew.

Now, here, in a quiet little nook behind one of the French furniture courts, is a collection of pretty things—the prettiest you could hope to find in a summer day's march, and which, for want of a discreet guide, you might altogether escape. There is no harm, I hope, in drawing the abstract idea of a lady in a theoretical Bath-chair, and volunteering one's services to a kind public whom we may never know and never see. Please, then, to permit me, whom *you* may not know, and whom *you* will never see, to direct you to the modest glass case which has for its sole insignia a printed card, bearing no artist's or manufacturer's name, but simply inscribed, " Class 14 and 15, 144."—In this case are grouped a series of the most beautiful little statuettes—either in wax or in papier mâché, but so artfully are they coloured I cannot positively tell which—I have ever seen. They are illustrative of the costumes and equipments of the French army and their auxiliaries. There is a Chasseur de Vincennes, there is a Zouave, there is a trumpeter, there is a drum-major, there is an old drummer giving lessons to a *petit tambour*, there is a Spahi in full Oriental gear, there is an *invalide* with a wooden leg, there is a Sister of Charity, there is a gendarme reading a passport, there is a gendarme on horseback, there is a mule with a mountain-howitzer on his back, there is a *bât* pony, there is a lancer with his martial cloak around him, there is a French sailor; and, finally, there is a most marvellously-executed model of a field-piece, with its carriage, caissons, horses, gunners and drivers complete. The charm of these works is twofold. First, the modelling is most excellent, the attitudes are spirited and unconstrained, the faces lifelike and full of expression. Next, the execution is so astonishingly faithful to the military originals, that these models might be preserved in an ordnance bureau, or in the museum of an army clothing board, as exact patterns and exemplars of the uniform and campaigning gear of the Imperial French army in the year 1867. Not a button, a trace, a strap, a buckle, a girth, a mess-tin, a knob, or a clasp has been omitted. The minutest accessories of the soldier's dress have been preserved. The very drumsticks have evidently been scrupulously copied from the originals. Every plait in the Sister of Charity's gown, every square in her snowy veil, every bead in her rosary, are there. The *sapeur* looks as though " *rien n'était sacré*" for him. The gendarme reading the passport has the true inquisitorial, suspicious mien of the police-soldier. You might wager that he was about to discover that the document was out of date, or that it was deficient in a *visa*, or that the *signalement* did not correspond with the personal appearance of the bearer. As for the drum-major, he is a perfect study —gorgeous, solemn, and insufferably conceited, and with his plume reaching, figuratively, to the Seventh Heaven. He seems to be murmuring, " *Roi ne puis: Pékin ne. daigne·* *Major suis.*" " I cannot be a king; I scorn to be a civilian; therefore I am a drum-major." The greatest exuberance of finish is lavished however on the field-piece, with its horses and mounted artillerymen.

There is a story told of the admirable French painter, Monsieur Raffet, one of the best delineators of modern military costumes, that during his sojourn in St. Petersburg he executed and presented to Count Dolgorouki a very careful study of one of the grenadiers in the Preobajinski regiment of Guards. This drawing came into the hands of the late Emperor Nicholas, who was delighted with it, and inquired the name of the artist. Subsequently, M. Raffet was commissioned to make drawings of the uniforms of some score of the regiments of the guard. He was liberally recompensed, but urgent private affairs requiring his presence in Paris, he took the liberty of applying, in the usual form, for his passports, and permission to quit the empire. He was informed, in reply, that the Government of his Imperial Majesty appreciating, as it did in the highest degree, M. Raffet's talent, was very sorry, but that it could not possibly think of suffering him to pass the frontiers before he had made drawings of the uniform and equipments of the officers and soldiers of all grades of the entire Russian army—horse, foot, and dragoons artillery, engineers, and gendarmerie, Cossacks, Khirgese Tartars, Circassian bow-and-arrow-bearers, pioneers and all. When a Romanoff commands there is nothing left but to comply, and I know not how many years M. Raffet remained in Russia, or how many thousands of roubles he earned against his will. No such coercion, however, has, I should say, been exercised towards M. E. Frémiet, the artist of the remarkable collection in " Class 14 and 15, 144." The work has evidently been a labour of love with him; and the entire series of military models has been, I am informed, presented as a gift to the Emperor Napoleon.

IX.

BRITISH SCULPTURE.

SCULPTURE being, in its final phase, an art which is carried out by cutting a hard substance, the official gentlemen to whom the task of classification in the British Fine Art Department has been assigned have consistently " lumped " sculpture together with dye-sinking and stone and cameo-engraving.   However, there are very few British sculptors in the Paris Exhibition to grumble at the order of precedence which has been fixed for them.   Only fifteen sculptors, properly so called, exhibit.   Mr. G. G. Adams has two busts of Prince Teck and the late Lord Palmerston.   Mr. William Davis has a plaster statuette of Clyméné, a well-modelled embodiment of female form, but a great deal too delicate and ethereal, I think, for the robust daughter of Ocean and Tethys, and the mamma of those remarkably bouncing boys, Atlas, Prometheus, Manetius, and Epimethæus.   For any-thing there is in this statuette to tell us of the character of a lady, who for the rest is entirely mythical, and has never been charged, even by the poets, with any other attributes save those of prolific maternity, Mr. Davis might just as well have called his statuette Clytemnestra, or Cleopatra, or Clitie. But it would seem, in the baptism of works in sculpture, the system is akin to that adopted by the parish authorities of Mudfog, at the instigation of Mr. Bumble, the beadle, in the nomenclature of the parish foundlings. You christen your statues alphabetically, beginning with Aphrodite and ending with Zenobia.

Miss Susan Durant exhibits her pleasing series of medallion portraits of the Royal family, forming part of the decoration of the Wolsey Chapel at Windsor; and of the three works presented by Mr. P. de Epinay is a curious marble bust of one "Asunta, wife of Dambrosio la Pruella, brigand, condemned at Rome, November, 1865." Now, I have nothing to say against this work, artistically; but will Mr. P. de Epinay allow me to ask him one little question? I will assume him, for the sake of argument, to be a married man. I will assume, always for the sake of argument, that some of these days he gets "into trouble," say for high treason, and is condemned to be hanged, drawn, and quartered, which sentence, the Marquis of Abercorn being at the time Prime Minister, is duly carried out. Now, I will ask Mr Epinay, how would he like to have the marble bust of his widow exposed in a public picture gallery, with a note in the catalogue drawing particular attention to that unfortunate transaction at the Old Bailey? For aught that is known, his Holiness the Pope may have organised some excursion trains this autumn from the Eternal City to the Paris Exhibition. Imagine the horror of Asunta, wife of Dambrosia la Pruella, at finding herself "busted" in the middle of the Champ de Mars, with an explicit allusion to her late husband's "misfortunes." I am afraid that one of the things which artists who travel to Rome do *not* learn, is that the picturesquely attired contadini who wait in the Via Sistina, or on the Trinità di Monte steps, to be hired, are human beings, and that if you prick them they will bleed, and if you pinch them they will squeak.

The illustrious English sculptor, Foley—one of our strongest, brightest, most earnest artists—is poorly represented in Paris. There is but a statuette of Caractacus—the property of the Art-Union of London—from his hand. M. Louis Gardio should be, by his name, a Frenchman; but he should have a British welcome for the sake of his vigorous bronze bust of the late Captain Speke. A plaster statue of the "Fugitive," by Mr. Lawlor; a bust, in terra-cotta, of the late Captain Fowke, by Mr. Woolner—in Mr. Woolner's well-known manner; a statuette of "Mercy," by Mr. Edward Stephens, likewise the property of the Art-Union, do not call for any special remark. Mr. T. S. Westmacott has a model for a statue of Alexander the Great, to which, without disparaging its artistic merits, there may be applied a remark analogous to that made by Voltaire to Jean Baptiste Rousseau—not Jean Jacques—when that indifferent poet insisted on reading his "Ode to Posterity" to him. "It will fail to reach its address," observed the pitiless M. de Voltaire. So, very probably, is Mr. Westmacott's well-meant model destined never to become a statue. It is rather too late in the day to think of erecting statues to "Macedonia's madman." The artist might indeed get his model off his hands if he painted it coffee-colour, and offered it to M. Alexandre Dumas, in whom, as is well known, all the glories of all the Alexanders, from the king to the coppersmith, are summed up.

Mr. Reuben Townroe—a new name, but one that deserves to be better known—has modelled, for the panels of some bronze doors at the South Kensington Museum, a series of figures of Davy, Newton, Watt, Bramante, Michael Angelo, and Titian. This assemblage of great men is about as incongruous as that of "Shakspeare, Heliogabalus, and Jack the Painter;" but I will let that pass.. They are good figures, well draped, firmly handled, and posed. They are the more interesting, as having been modelled after sketches left by the late Godfrey Sykes, one of the most accomplished, and certainly the most promising, decorative draughtsman the Victorian age has seen. He died quite "too young for friendship, not for fame;" and, indeed, there would seem to be some mysterious pestilence going about among our young painters and draughtsmen, smiting them down as they emerge from the dark chambers of struggling poverty—laying them low on the very threshold of fortune and renown. Godfrey Sykes was a toiler in the Philistine's mills at South Kensington; but away from there he will be best known by the admirable title-page he designed, about seven years since, for the "Cornhill Magazine." That frontispiece of black and orange is by this time as familiar to English eyes as the green covers of Mr. Dickens's serials; and as a work of art, in the grace and symmetry of its design, poor Godfrey Sykes's vignettes may vie with Mr. Maclise's famous frontispiece to the "Chimes," or the more elaborate illustrations of Kaulbach to the "Sleeping Beauty," and the "Song of the Bell."

I cannot tell why there are no marbles here from the graceful and fertile chisel of Alexander Munro; and why, as examples of the genius of the sculptor to whom we owe so many noble and beautiful works, there should be only a plaster alto-relievo of a "Boy asleep," a plaster bust of "Joan of Arc," and a medallion of the Duchess of Vallombrosa. The promise of the English Fine Arts Gallery, when set against its performance, is enough to make one mad; and groups of grinning Frenchmen are going about, jeering and chattering, and shrugging their shoulders, and saying that "decidedly the English have no sculptors." No Gibson, no Baily, no M'Dowall, no Cardwell, no Noble, no Thornycroft. The question may be well asked, "Where are our sculptors?" From Munro only a medallion; from Foley only a puppet; and if we yearn for Durham or John Bell, we must go to Copeland's porcelain stall, or Hunt and Roskell's stand of goldsmith's ware. It is not the less suggestive that, among the twenty-two works exhibited by the fifteen sculptors who represent British plastic art at the World's Fair, no less than fourteen are marked in the catalogue as being the property of "the artist." Her Majesty the Queen, Madame B. Delessert, the Art-Union of London, and the South Kensington Museum seem alone to have condescended to lend the art treasures in their collection for exhibition in Paris. It is said, I know not with what truth, that art-collectors and patrons have grown tired of lending their *chefs-d'œuvres*; that scant gratitude has been shown them by those they have obliged; and even that, in many instances, the almost priceless works they have temporarily surrendered for the public benefit have been disgracefully maltreated. Be these facts or not, one thing is very certain, that if Great Britain was not in a position to make an adequate display of the works of her foremost sculptors in Paris in 1867, Great Britain should have carefully abstained from making in this department of art any display at all. It is better to stay away altogether from the evening party to which you have been invited, than to enter the drawing-room in a dirty shirt, and with scandalous rents in your elbows and the knees of your pantaloons.

Taking from among those actually present Mr. Foley, Mr. Woolner, and Mr. Munro, as three of our most eminent living sculptors—in three widely divergent branches of their art—it cannot be concealed that all and each of them make in Paris, through no fault of their own, only a pale and shadowy appearance. One more sculptor, however, remains to be noticed, and I have reserved until the last my comments on his performance. Mr. Marshall Wood has been enabled, in his noble marble statue illustrative of Thomas Hood's "Song of the Shirt," to do himself and the country to which he belongs all but entire justice. I say all but entire, for the unfortunate construction of the English Fine Arts Gallery, situated as it is at the very sharpest curve of the penultimate ellipse of the palace, has surrounded the hanging of pictures and the disposition of statuary with all but insuperable difficulties, and both Mr. Cole and his assistants deserve the very highest praise for having done so much with the limited and unpropitious means at their command. As it is, wherever Mr. Marshall Wood's "Needlewoman" might be placed, and with whatever adventitious adjuncts of screens or reflectors it might be environed, it could never enjoy its due and properly balanced share of light, and some of its most exquisite points, notably in the head and bust, must consequently be bereft of the salience which is essential to them.

Mr. Marshall Wood's "Sempstress," it must be admitted, is a pure idealism. It might not please the fanatics of realism. It might be objected to by those who swear by Mr. Woolner. You miss the fingers weary and worn, the eyelids heavy and red, the unwomanly rags, in which Hood's garret martyr is clad. Behind her is no blank wall—so blank that she thanks her shadow for falling there. There is no

rickety table, with the coarse candle in the battered sconce—
the candle purchased with the price of a meal, in order that
she may sit up all night and do her sewing. Strict realism,
applied to Hood's heroine, would bring with it a hideous
entourage of pawnbroker's duplicates—duplicates for the
miserable woman's boots and flannel petticoat—of mouldy
bread and the rind of a Dutch cheese—of the Whitechapel
slopseller chaffering over the careless hemming of a wristband
—and of the landlady banging at the garret door for her
rent. Such realism was essayed in the picture of the " Death
of Chatterton ;" and the picture, albeit a beautiful, must
always be a repulsive one. Such realism was attempted in
Mr. Egg's picture of the " Death of Buckingham," and
the result was failure. The apartment in which lay the
expiring Villiers did not look like the " worst inn's worst
room ;" the floor was not of plaster, nor the walls of dung ;
the George and Garter failed to dangle in sufficient contrast
in the squalor of " the bed where tawdry yellow vied with
dirty red." You merely saw a handsome pallid cavalier
reclining on a capitally-painted couch, surrounded by care-
fully-painted accessories. Mr. Marshall Wood's aim has
been, at once, more and less ambitious. He has not attempted
to render wretchedness palpable and starvation tangible ;
but he has succeeded in idealising in marble a most moving
and pathetic picture of human suffering and resignation. He
might have expended more labour in chiselling the " seam
and gusset and band, band and gusset and seam " of the
garment which lies on the woman's knee ; he might have
insisted, with greater particularity, on her gaunt cheeks,
her sunken eyes, and the bones protruding almost through
her skin ; and he might have made his statue awful and

terrifying as Dante's word-picture of Ugolino; but his idealism is, nevertheless, a genuine triumph of art. His needlewoman is every inch the woman who stitched, stitched, stitched, from weary chime to chime, and who with a voice of dolorous pitch uttered that memorable cry :—

> O men, with sisters dear!
>   O men, with mothers and wives!
> It isn't linen you're wearing out,
>   But human creatures' lives.

And the shirt, in this beautiful statue, becomes indeed a shroud, and the mists that veil the shrunken limbs and scanty raiment of this poor creature are indeed those of the valley of the shadow of death.

X.

ILLUMINATIONS.—THE WARDS,
OF BELFAST.

I HAPPENED to be, about two years ago, in the energetic and hospitable town of Belfast; and, although it rained incessantly from the Saturday when I arrived until the Tuesday when I went away, and although on the Monday night my nerves had been somewhat rudely shaken by well-directed volleys of "Kentish fire" discharged at my head by about fifteen hundred gentlemen congregated at the Ulster Hall, whose political opinions did not precisely square with mine, I don't remember a pleasanter sojourn in a strange land. I had emphatically what the Americans term a "good time" of it. "Kentish fire" doesn't hurt much if you stop your ears, and the political ire of my audience halted a good way on this side dead cats and ginger-beer bottles. Those who, in the exercise of their vocation, *have been pelted*, know well how to draw distinctions in these manifestations; and Mr. Macready is said to have silenced an American abolitionist, who was complaining of a tarring and feathering with which he had been favoured down South, by asking him if he knew what it was to have oyster-shells and red-hot halfpence thrown at him by a "Forrest faction" during the performance of

Hamlet. Well, everybody in Belfast was very kind to me; and among the sights I was taken to see was the establishment of Messrs. Marcus Ward and Co., of the "Minerva Works"—a very hive of art and industry. The Messrs. Ward are a purely Irish firm, employing Irish hands, and have made Belfast the seat of a number of beautiful and humanising crafts, of which we are too apt to assume that the monopoly must be looked for in London, in Paris, or in Vienna. They have also an establishment in Dublin, and are about to open a depôt in London; but in Belfast is their real home. They are fancy stationers, bookbinders, photographers, manufacturers of writing-desks and account-books; but their real speciality is a much more exalted one than any of the foregoing. From their *atêlier* have proceeded some of the most sumptuous and tasteful works of illumination on vellum which this century of revival of a noble and beautiful art has seen.

I must own that the busy Belfast studios, full of artists and artisans in the unromantic costumes of the present day, furnished with every modern appliance for illuminations— "fine Siberian hair-brushes in quills," "round sables in albata," "heraldic tinctures," "shield and banner models," "vellum block books," "Bristol board," "ink erasers," "Cumberland lead pencils," "China slant-tiles," "gold and aluminium shells," "agate burnishers," "platina-paper," and "extra thick gold-leaf,"—all the paraphernalia, in a word, which make Messrs. Winsor and Newton's price-list read, to the amateur, as deliciously as the "three hundred and sixty-five *menus*" of the Baron Brisse read to the *gourmet*—did not convey to my mind any definite notion of the mediæval *scriptorium* set up by the good old bishop at Winchester. It gave me no distinct idea of the quiet cells attached to countless monasteries in England and on the Continent, from Byzantium to Blackfriars, in which—while, outside, statesmen were plotting, and cardinals intriguing, robber-barons plundering, ravishing, and murdering, courtiers hating and poisoning, poets fawning and flattering, and high-born dames gallivanting in the great, wicked raree show—the tasteful, skilful, patient, self-contained hermits, whom it has pleased modern ignorance and intolerance to term "lazy monks," devoted their long, calm lives, half to the praise of God and half to the production of works of almost inconceivable elaboration and of imperishable beauty. How did they do it? How did they contrive to perfect those marvellous tomes? Their tools must have been few, their pigments rare, their chemical knowledge infinitesimal. They had no "cocoa-handled erasers number five," no "patent moist water-colours in porcelain pans," no "permanent Chinese white: a preparation of white oxide of zinc." "If you wante a Rubber," says an old treatise on illumination, "you must take a Dogge's toothe, and set him in a Sticke." It may be, perhaps, that some of the most exquisite "diapers" in mediæval illumination were traced with no more complex instrument than a fish-bone; and that some of the most delicate "scrolls" in body colour were pencilled with a brush gathered newly from the back of the conventual tom-cat. There were no artists' colourmen in those days. The gold and silver for gilding were beaten into leaves by hammers wielded by monks' hands on monkish anvils. Even as the nuns of St. Agnes weave from the wool of the lambs which have been blest on the altar the *pallium* for the new-made bishop, so, very likely, the vellum needed for the missal or the book of hours was manufactured within the convent walls. The monks kept sheep. They wove themselves frocks and cowls from the fleeces; they ate the mutton on feast days; they made the skin into parchment; and, if unkindly critics are to be believed, they sometimes used the small knuckle-bones for playing the profane game called by the moderns " dibs." Their vassals ground the colours, which they themselves had extracted from the earth, or from plants, or from worsted yarn. Their lay brethren pounded in the mortar the subtle stucco used for " raising gold," and the secret of whose recipe was for long ages lost. And, finally, they bound their illuminated books themselves; for in how many " side-backs " of old missals have we not seen pasted scraps of monkish chants and canticles, emblazoned in red and black, the music-lines as broad as magnum bonum pens, the breves as big as horse-beans? Rude and simple were their means and resources; yet they did their work somehow —did it in a patient and loving spirit, spending hours over the petals of a flower, days over the scales of a lizard, months over the rays of a celestial nimbus, or a cherub's wing; but doing it always honestly, conscientiously, and *thoroughly*. And who shall blame these anchorite-artists if, in the end, they became convinced, not only that their work was delightful to the King's Highness or my Lord Bishop, but that it also met with the approbation of the Saints and the countenance of Heaven ! " A Prayer for the Rambler " was found among the papers of Samuel Johnson; and we need not sneer at the fervently pious invocations with which some of the Spanish and German friars began their illumi- nating labours, praying that their raised gold might not flatten, that their diapers might not be effaced, that their high lights might not turn brown.

I have travelled many thousands of miles since my visit to the Belfast *scriptorium*, where clever and facile artists were endeavouring to emulate the achievements of the monks of old. I have seen, dragged from the dusty cupboards of the Escorial, and pawed by a seedy and cigar-smoking old *custode*, the marvels of Spanish illumination, and the even more wonderfully minute work brought from Flanders by Charles V. I have seen all that the Ambrosian at Milan or the Imperial Library at Vienna has to boast of. In the library given by the son of Christopher Columbus to the city of Seville I have seen some works of Arab poetry and devotion so gorgeous and so refined in their embellishment that you might have thought you were looking on the field of a camera obscura at the reflections of the arabesqued alcoves of the Alhambra and the Alcazar. And, finally, in the Vatican I have seen the four great treasures of Italian illuminating art, the "Vatican Virgil" of the fourth century, with its fifty miniatures, debased in design and rude in execution, but still glowing with colour, and priceless as exponents of ancient manners and customs; the "Bembo" Terence of the ninth century; the "Greek Book" of the Emperor Basil, a tenth-century work, mainly in silver on purple-stained velum; and the "Life of Francesco della Rovere," with miniatures by Giulio Clovis.

Nor, while expatiating on the art treasures of foreign countries, do I forget what magnificent specimens of mediæval illumination are to be found in our own country—in the British Museum, in Dublin, in the Advocates' Library at Edinburgh, and in the cabinets of such instructed and appreciative collectors as Mr. John Ruskin and Mr. Digby Wyatt. To the last-named eminent architect belongs, indeed, the

glory of having practically revived the art of illumination
in England. Chromo-lithography, and the tried skill and
experience of Messrs. Day and Son, enabled him to issue a
work on illumination, the number and the splendour of
whose examples did towards the vindication of mediæval art
that which Mr. Owen Jones's "Grammar of Ornament" has
done for the exemplification of the purest canons in colour
and harmonious design. Mr. Wyatt, indeed, has been not
only an exhibitor of patterns, but an actual guide and instructor
in illumination. To the plain and definite rules laid down
in his writings has been due the gratifying development in
English society of a long-neglected and all but forgotten art.
It has grown to be fashionable to practise illumination. A
"five-guinea box" from Winsor and Newton's has become
as essential an item in the objects of recreation of an accomplished lady as was formerly the tambour frame or the
crochet needle. Illumination is an art peculiarly suited to
the feminine mind and the feminine hand. Who can set the
most delicate stitches? who are more skilful than any others
in embroidery? who are better judges of colour and harmony?
who are fonder of pretty things? who like gold and silver
and gems better? who are the most patient, delicate, dutiful
creatures in the world? Why, women. The combination
of nearly all the qualities I have hinted at above are necessary to produce a good illuminator; and (to increase the
fitness of the art as a lady's employment) it is one that
demands the utmost neatness and cleanliness, and that is
best carried on in a back drawing-room. The good house-
wife hates dust, noise, and hurry; and hurry, noise, and dust
are sworn foes to excellence in illumination. Of course male
artists are frequently engaged in this work—are there not

gentlemen who earn handsome incomes by designing trellis-work for ladies' "Garibaldis" and borders for ladies' petti-coats?—and I believe that the majority of the illuminators in the employ of the Messrs. Ward are of the sterner sex. The reason given to me for this was a very obvious one. The ladies are capital hands at any work they like to put their pretty fingers to, only they cannot be depended upon in the way of completing it. Now, we will assume that an order is received for a testimonial to be emblazoned or a book illuminated within a given time. What are you to do if it occurs to—say four out of ten young lady workers to go away and get married? It is thus with domestic servants. The moment you have succeeded in manufacturing a dawdling "slavey" into a neat-handed Phillis—the moment you think that you have succeeded in producing a "thorough servant," she levants with a corporal in the Foot Guards, or marries the baker's man. The monkish illuminators of old were bachelors, perforce; but you cannot introduce the rule of celibacy among lady artists. In our houses I wish sincerely that we could have "serving sisters" under the rule of St. Bridget, enjoined to "poverty, chastity, and obedience." We would pay them no wages, but make handsome donations to their convents. If they were naughty we should have no occasion to scold them, for St. Bridget's inflexible rule would of course impel them, when they were peccant, to wear horse-hair Garibaldis next their skin and unboiled peas in their shoes, and to castigate themselves morning and evening with knotted cords or fresh-gathered nettles. So everything would be very nice and comfortable, and a "character" given to a "serving sister" by the lady abbess would be as unim-peachable as a banker's reference—perhaps a little more so.

But, dear me! dear me! how would it be if some fine morning Sister Veronica threw her veil and her rosary over the area railing, and murmuring the dulcet strains of " I'm off to Charleston," once more proved that " history is continually repeating itself," by running off with the young man who brings the quartern loaves?

I was very glad, wandering in the labyrinths of the English courts in the Champ de Mars, to find that the illuminators of Belfast had made a display of the choicest works in their *scriptorium*.   As examples, not only of careful and really artistic design and colour in illumination, but also of gorgeous bookbinding, the performances of the Messrs. Ward are entitled to the very highest praise.   Their ingenuity has also enabled them to answer a question which is very often and very spitefully put to those who admire and those who practise this luxurious art.   It is the terribly cogent question—" *Cui bono?*"—" Of what use is your illuminated vellum when you have finished it?" the objectors ask.   "What purpose does it serve?   What end does it further?"   The Messrs. Ward have hit upon a means by which illumination may be made to serve a thoroughly practical end.   Taking a hint, perhaps, from the gorgeous blazonry upon patents of nobility and genealogical pedigrees, they have applied illumination to the embellishment of the multitudinous addresses, testimonials, and so forth, which in modern life are continually passing between landlords and their tenants, pastors and their flocks, professors and their pupils, and—sometimes, but not often—companies and their directors.   In fact, some hopes may be entertained of the illuminated testimonial superseding the service of plate. It is cheaper, it is much more beautiful, and there is no danger of seeing the tribute of "fervid admiration" or "undying attachment" turn up, about a year after its presentation, in Mr. Attenborough's shop window.

Messrs. Marcus Ward are the originators of this novel mode of giving permanent and additional interest to such records, and have applied the revival of an ancient art in this direction so as actually to create a new artistic industry in Ireland.   Some of their works in illumination are superb. They exhibit specimens lent by the Prince of Wales, by the Lord-Lieutenant, the Marquis of Abercorn, by the Marquis of Donegal, and by Lord Kimberley.   There are eight most sumptuously-illuminated volumes presented to the Earl of Hillsborough by the tenantry of his father, the Marquis of Downshire, each volume containing beautiful vignettes illustrative of localities referred to in the text, with the armorial bearings belonging to the particular estate whose tenantry have presented it.   These volumes are all bound with lavish splendour, but with consummate taste.   Even more ambitious, but quite as successful, are the two magnificent testimonial volumes presented to Sir Benjamin Lee Guinness on the completion of the work of restoration in St. Patrick's Cathedral, Dublin—a restoration due to the munificence of that illustrious Irishman.   One of these volumes expresses the gratitude of the citizens of Dublin; the other emanates from the Dean and Chapter of St. Patrick's, and both are decorated throughout with borders, in gold and colours of unexampled richness, and with miniatures—really works of art—representing scenes in the Irish records of the Cathedral and in general Irish history.   The magnificence of the binding equals that of the contents.

In devoting so much space to the notice of purely Irish

work, on purely Irish subjects, conceived by Irish brains, executed by Irish hands, and put forth, in rare completeness, by an enterprising Irish firm, I have been prompted by a double motive.   First, that of rendering justice to some really surprising examples of artistic taste, patience, and skill; next, that of saying, at this time, above all others, a good word for Ireland.   She wants it; not in pity, not in contempt, but in frank friendship and cordiality.   These beautiful things of Marcus Ward are as thoroughly of Irish device and manufacture as Irish linens or Irish poplins; and it behoves us, in these bitter days, to say all we can that can do good to Ireland.   It behoves us to remember by what a gifted and genial race she is inhabited; and how mean, against the bulk of Irishmen, north or south, Catholic or Protestant, should be reckoned the knot of knaves and fools who, in their wickedness and folly, have done their best to drench a beautiful and peaceful country in blood and tears.

XI.

LAY FIGURES.

THE proverbial locution warns us that we never know what we can do until we try, and this warning should surely be an incentive to continued experiment and effort. It is *not* so, unhappily. For the reason that we have never done a certain thing, we too often assume that we should utterly fail in the attempt to accomplish it, and so we sit supine, and, folding our hands, and smiling complacently, permit other nations to carry off the prize for which we are, not too indolent, but too feeble in confidence in ourselves, and too shamefaced to compete. And we allow the foreigners to set us down as ignoramuses or as deficient in the "*feu sacré* of genius" in this or that department of art, quite unmindful of Buffon's definition of genius—that it is a "great power of attention," and of Johnson's—that it is "a general capacity directed in a particular channel." For my part I intend, before I die, to acquire the Basque language, to learn to make salmon flies, perambulators, and *potage à la reine*, to play the *cornet à piston*, and to dance a Rigadoon—if I can discover any professor of choregraphics who knows what a Rigadoon is, and can teach it me. If I fail—as I very probably shall—it will not be for want of trying. In the contest between the tortoise and the hare it was, as every one knows, the slow but steady old Hard Shell that won the race; but how about that *pococurante* Mole who just looked out of his burrow and blinked lazily at the starters, and was fast asleep when the number went up at the post, and Tartaruga claimed the stakes? *The Mole was one of those people who never try.* If "the little gentleman in black velvet" had put his best foot forward, he might—the hare being winded—have made a decent second. Although a mole, he might be able to do something if he tried. One of his ancestors did contrive to kill William III. I firmly believe in an infinity of things in which we might attain proficiency if not pre-eminence, but which, in our stolid *mauvaise honte*, we abandon to strangers, as though they had a greater number of legs and arms, or more thew and sinew, or more pluck, or better brains than we. I believe that we could produce artistic bronzes if we tried, and that it is only for the lack of trying that we allow the French to distance us in cheap clocks, and chimney ornaments, and wall paper. I believe we could make tapestry not much inferior to Gobelins work. I know that our Copelands and Mintons *do* make porcelain not inferior to Sèvres, and that our Kidderminster manufacturers have distanced Brussels and Aubusson and Beauvais. I believe we could make Parmesan cheese without being dependent on Signor Bartovalle, and Russian caviare without going to Fortnum and Mason's for it. I have tasted, in America, *pâté de foie gras* of more exquisite flavour than ever a patriotic goose contributed to a Strasbourg *terrine ;* and I know that the *pâté* never came from Alsace, but was an inspiration of the "genius" of Mr. Hiram Cranston's head cook at the New York Hotel. But then the Americans are always trying ; and, if they fail, they " recuperate " and try again, harder than ever.   I am sure, if we only tried, we could make Chartreuse more delicious than any to which Grand Prior Garnier has affixed his signature, Maraschino more luscious than any that has ever come out of Zara, and Curaçoa to the full as pleasant as that which you get in the Dutch island of Curaçoa itself, where full fifty per cent. of the liqueurs consumed are imported from Holland.

Now, why should we not try our hand at the manufacture of lay figures for the use of painters and sculptors? *Do* we make any? No. Could we make them if we tried? I say yes. An artist's studio is nothing without a lay figure ; and in these days, when realistic details are so much insisted upon, the possession of a well-made *mannequin*, on whose limbs drapery can be tastefully adjusted, is of the first necessity. I have heard it stated, ere now, that both Sir Joshua Reynolds and Sir Thomas Lawrence disdained the use of lay figures. It must be remembered that both these illustrious artists were essentially portrait painters, that their greatest care was lavished on their faces, and that, the countenance once terminated, the clothes, draperies, and accessories were thrown in very loosely and carelessly. The carelessness, indeed, of Lawrence in this respect bordered on slovenliness. The envious, of course, declared that he could only paint heads ; that hands, even, were beyond him ; and that he had no knowledge whatever of the anatomy of the human figure, or of the proper manner in which the folds of drapery should be arranged. It was, perhaps, to disprove these slanders that Sir Thomas ventured on his large full-length sitting portrait of George the Fourth. His Majesty is represented in those closely-fitting nether garments which the satire of Mr. Thackeray—satire slightly cruel, and not altogether just, when we come to dissect it—has made immortal, and the royal legs are encased in black silk stockings, which, in their too symmetrical form, their smoothness, and their sheen, bear a laughable resemblance to the legs of a grand pianoforte. Sir Thomas's whole length of John Kemble is better drawn, and stands admirably, and the artist must have had the "life" or a good lay figure to study from; but, as a rule, Sir Thomas was happiest when he was only called to paint a head and shoulders, or when, in the whole length of a peer, he could take refuge in the flowing robes of the Garter, which are like charity, and cover a multitude of sins. The obvious reply, when the dearness and scarcity of lay figures is represented,—amounts to this—that the artist can go to Nature. He certainly can; but he is in the position of the caller of spirits from the vasty deep. Nature will not always come at the bidding of the painter of moderate income. Miss Etty, it is true, used to delight in seeking out fleshy nymphs for her brother to paint from; but William Etty was a frugal man, and his only extravagance was in models. Artists' wives, too, sometimes object to have any female models admitted to their husband's studio. Decorous Mrs. Nollekens was accustomed to declare that she would have "no such bold-faced hussies trapesing about the house;" and it was only on her husband's representation that he should lose a five hundred guinea commission from my Lord——, if he were not allowed a living model for his statue of the "Bather," that one of the patient sisterhood was allowed to enter the studio. Even then Mrs. Nollekens put her head in at the door every five minutes, and exclaimed that the Bather ought to be ashamed of herself, for a saucy jade as

she was. But it was mid-January. The weather was very
cold. Nollekens was penurious, and his fire burnt low. Mrs.
Nollekens, although her notions of decorum were somewhat
rigid, was a woman, and had the heart that could feel for
another. About one o'clock she bounced into the studio
with a basin in her hands. "Here, you poor ——," cried the
British matron—I decline to transcribe the epithet, but it
might be applied without offence· to the sister of my little
dog Ponto—"Here, you poor ——, there's some hot mutton
broth for you." It must be remembered that this little
scene took place nearly eighty years ago, and that ladies
were then far more free-spoken than they are now.

There have been painters who had wives so complaisant as
to sit for them and serve as models. Rubens was so fortunate
as to possess two—both fat, both fair, and not forty—and
they disport themselves in plump exuberance on scores of his
gigantic canvasses. But an artist requires a model draped as
well as a model *au naturel,* and you cannot expect the wife of
your bosom to sit for you for seven consecutive hours every
day while you are imitating with pre-Raphaelitic minuteness
the gloss of a white satin robe or the "water" of a moire-
antique jacket. Professional models are to be had ; but they
are dear even at the traditional tariff of a shilling an hour—a
tariff against which, I dare say, they have long since struck.
Moreover, photography, which has been by turns the slave,
the tyrant, the friend, and foe of art—which now lends the
young painter five shillings and now robs the engraver of a
thousand guineas—photography, which may be termed the
gunpowder of peace, for its lightning expedition and its
terrific force, we cannot do without it, and yet we managed
to slay our men, on canvas, before it was invented—photo-

graphy is making, every day, deeper inroads in the ranks of professional models serviceable to painters. The venerable prophets, with long white beards, have found out that they can earn more money in five minutes by sitting as blind fiddlers and grand masters of Odd Fellows, in the *tableaux de société* of the Stereoscopic Company, than by attitudinising for five hours while McGuilp, R.A., is fagging at his grand scripture piece. Hercules, normally of the Life Guards Blue, prefers being represented in his undress uniform in a stereoscopic slide, to being modelled *in cuerpo* from his occiput to his tendon Achilles; and the dryads and hamadryads, the bacchantes, and the bathers, find it much more comfortable to be rapidly "focussed" in low-necked dresses and ample crinolines, in the act of taking tea in the front parlour, and stepping into omnibuses in *cartes de visite*, than for a moderate wage to have a chalk mark drawn round their feet, and, holding on by a rope from the ceiling, stand as bare as a robin on a red baize throne in a "Life" academy, to be sketched in chalk by fifty aspirants in art. Finally, the haste, the bustle, the excitement of this feverish age render those who have their portraits taken impatient of long sittings in a painter's studio. Mr. Claudet keeps us only five minutes; John or Charles Watkins takes off our head as rapidly as though we were Richard the Third's Duke of Buckingham. Why should our Grace or our Major-Generalship sit hour after hour, in "full fig," while Mr. Lawrence or Mr. Sant copies the embroidery on our Windsor uniform or the plumes in our cocked hat? So his Grace's body-servant brings down his Grace's uniform in a carpet bag, and the Major-General sends his compliments and his cocked hat in a neat japanned tin box, and, with the aid of a lay figure, Mr. Lawrence or

Mr. Sant must get out of the dilemma as best he can. There are some people who cannot sit long. Napoleon could not. David was obliged to "shoot him flying," as it were. Gros used to employ a young man to read Ossian to the Emperor while he sat for his portrait, and while he was listening to that clever forgery the hero would remain tolerably quiet. When he sat to Gérard, the only possible way to keep him still was for Madame Bonaparte—he was not Emperor then—to force the conqueror of Marengo on to her lap, and hold him tight round the waist with both arms. Haydon declared the Duke of Wellington to be a good sitter; but, Goya, the Spaniard, to whom he sat at Madrid after Vittoria, declared he was the worst that ever entered his studio, with the exception of the Duchess of Alba, who used to dance the Jota Aragonese when she should have been as still as a mouse. To be sure, the terrible painter-bullfighter was a difficult person to sit to; and if we are to believe his latest biographer, M. Charles Yriarte, Goya snatched up a carving knife and offered to murder the Duke, because, in his blunt way, the great captain declared that his portrait wasn't a bit like him.

I have said enough, I think, to show the usefulness, and indeed imperative necessity, of good lay figures for artists' use. Until within a very recent period, a *mannequin*, life-sized, properly padded and covered with silk, and quite new, was a luxury quite out of the reach of a struggling artist. I have heard of so much as a hundred guineas being given for one. They could be hired, at so much per month, from such establishments as that of Lechertier-Barbes in the Quadrant; but hiring lay figures is something like hiring piano-fortes—you are pretty sure to get into some trouble before you have done with them. Even second-hand lay figures could not be obtained for less than fifteen or twenty guineas. A cheaper and far less expensive article in wood has within the last few years been imported from Germany. These *mannequins* are to be found at every artists' colourman's. They vary in altitude from half life size to that of your thumb, and in price from a guinea to half-a-crown; but they are stiff, ungainly, and incapable of assuming a tithe of the positions into which the human limbs can be bent or extended. They may occasionally suggest an attitude, but the suggestion is of the vaguest and most rudimentary nature, and at the best these figures can only be regarded as a superior kind of Dutch dolls. The lay figure requisite to an artist should be of life size, or in no case less than half life, so that the drapery thrown over it may fall in natural masses and folds, and not in the stiff and angular manner which is inevitable when the *mannequin* is of diminutive size. Albert Durer, it is said, used to study from small dolls, which he attired in draperies made of paper soaked in gum-water. He could thus crumple up his paper togas into infinitesimal folds, but as the gum dried the paper naturally assumed that sharp but stiff and spiky appearance so characteristic of Durer's draperies. The advantages of a life-size figure are obvious for purposes of modern study, seeing that it can be dressed from our own wardrobe, and does not require to have clothes made for it like a doll. It should be preferably, too, in the female likeness, for a woman can wear man's clothes and look perfectly graceful in them; whereas a man can never be anything but abhorrently repulsive in the garments of the opposite sex. Lay figures are now made of both sexes, male and female, and epicene (by which last, following the doctrine laid down by M. Fourrier, I mean children); but the painter must be a "glutton" in art who could not rest content with one good lady lay figure. There are some lay figures, too, which will stand, when accurately balanced, without any artificial support; and the impalement, indeed, of lay figures on truculent-looking spikes and hooks of iron has ere now appalled many an inexperienced visitor to the studios; but unsupported figures are apt to get weak in the knees, and to tumble off their feet without notice when a door is violently slammed, or a van-demon from the Great Northern Railway comes rattling and rumbling under the window. Unsupported lay figures, too, sit badly. They can be made to assume the sedent position quite gracefully, with no other aid than the spike before mentioned. I am not aware how the gentleman—said by some to be a dancing dervish become sedentary—who used to sit upon nothing, and in mid air, many years ago, at the Colosseum in the Regent's Park, contrived to manage it. It is an art, perhaps, like walking on the ceiling; but I have heard, on not untrustworthy authority, that even actual impalement is not so very disagreeable. There are Turkish gentlemen alive who have been impaled, and have risen subsequently to be pashas of three tails. I have been told of one—who was not so fortunate, however, as to survive—who, being brought to that last state by the Governor of Anatolia—it was in the time of the Sultan Mahmoud—bore the infliction with great equanimity and, indeed, serenity of countenance, reciting *in medias res* many passages from the Koran and Hafiz; the pasha, meanwhile, who had caused him to be impaled, sitting not afar off, smoking his chibouk. The impaled gentleman, towards sunset, began to make uncomplimentary remarks about the father and mother of the pasha, and their respective graves, whereupon the pasha, a hot-tempered man cried out, " Give the dog some water, and let him die." He drank, and immediately died ; but had he not taken that draught he might have been alive to this day, to witness if I have told truth.

This, however, is but a digression. There is one most tangible advantage in supported lay figures, inasmuch as they can be placed in the position of flying, of running, and in falling attitudes which the unsupported *mannequin*, being inanimate and incapable of volition, cannot assume. The iron support plays on the impaled figure the part of the Will. An admirable opportunity is afforded of testing and comparing the various capacities of lay figures in that part of the French section in the Paris Exhibition which is devoted to the display of objects pertaining to the liberal arts. Three eminent manufacturers of lay figures compete. The house of Le Blond, of the Rue Du Val, Ste. Catherine, show a male and female figure, life size, and a pair of dimensions about one-sixth those of life. They are of wood and indiarubber, stuffed, wonderfully true to natural form ; but their covering, or " skin" seems to me needlessly loose, and, when the limbs are bent, forms most ungainly creases. To this it may be answered that lay figures are only intended to be studied when dressed. The *mannequins* of Le Blond have iron supports. Bonel, of the Rue Blanche, Ste. Catharine, has a male, a female, and a child figure, perfect marvels of symmetry of form, and covered with fine silk. These figures might almost be photographed as portraits of " Meess Menken "—about whom the French went so very crazy— without the slight apology for pantaloons, in which the charming Amazon delighted the amateurs of the Gaîté. So beautiful, indeed, is the finish of these figures—which are wholly unsupported, *et se tiennent sur leurs jambes* precisely as human beings do—that the exhibitor has been compelled to cover them with a semi-diaphonous veil of oiled silk, and very droll indeed do these lay figures look beneath that covering. It is quite needed, however, for the public—all prayers, entreaties, and commands to the contrary—*will* touch ; and the havoc committed by human fingers is supplemented by the dust which is continually whirling round the concentrics of the Champ de Mars in simooms, siroccos, and Sahara waltzes. The third exhibit of lay figures is that of the curious *mannequins perfectionnés* of Galibert: articles of very recent invention. They are constructed of a kind of *carton pierre*, and somewhat after the manner of the carapace of a lobster, and are not stuffed. The attitudes into which they can be put are innumerable and wonderfully human, and indeed the matrices for these *mannequins perfectionnés* are modelled, I am informed, on the human figure. They are supported on irons; and the supports strike me as being rather too complex and liable to get out of order. They have one great advantage, however, over their stuffed rivals, in being very cheap. A *mannequin perfectionné* may be purchased for 225f. (or £9), whereas a silk-covered Bonel or Le Blond would be worth, I conceive, double that sum.

Of course there are no English exhibitors of these curious but highly useful art adjuncts. There is an eminent practitioner in Cork Street, who makes artificial limbs; but he has not yet thought it worth his while to construct entire figures. I may be accused by the unthinking or the malevolent of having wasted too much time over "dumb dollies" and

joint stools; but those who love art, and understand its
requirements, will see my drift and do justice to my motives.
I want English artists to be in a position to obtain good,
cheap, and serviceable lay figures; but I do not see how this
consummation can be brought about when we are forced to
import them from France, and to pay, perhaps, a profit to
one, two, or three middlemen, commission agents, or colourmen. I mentioned lay figures in connection with pianofortes.
I believe you can buy a cottage piano, a good working
instrument, for something like twenty guineas. An artist
should be able to get a good working lay figure for ten. But
to render them obtainable at such a price they must be made
at home. We can make dolls; we are good anatomists, and
bird stuffers, and articulators of skelctons,—why should we
not make an essay in the manufacture of lay figures?

XII.

DOLLS AND TOYS.

A REVIEW of the remarkable development which within the last ten years has taken place in the French doll trade, not only as regards the manufacture of the puppets themselves, but in the artistic taste and ingenuity lavished on the decoration of objects essentially puerile and intrinsically worthless, might strengthen the position of those who argue that the most palpable fruits of the actual era of French civilisation have been dissipation and frivolity, senseless luxury and frenzied prodigality. It is reported that Baron Haussmann once met a meek remonstrance against the cruelty of pulling down the squalid, but inexpensive dwellings of the poor, in order to erect sumptuous boulevards suited only for the occupation of the wealthy, with the cool and heartless rejoinder that he did not want anybody in Paris with an income of less than 50,000f. a year, and that persons whose revenue failed to reach that minimum had better seek accommodation elsewhere. The story reminds me of an observation I once heard from a waiter at Bignon's, at the corner of the Chaussée d'Antin—one of the costliest restaurants in Paris, if not *the* very costliest—who, while he was pouring my after-dinner coffee from a silver *cafetière*, confidentially remarked,

"One cannot afford to live like this every day." The man deserved to be kicked for his insolence, but he was entirely right. It is clear that *I* could not afford to dine at Bignon's every day, even if I doubled the Haussmannic standard of income. It would really seem as though the dolls of the Second Empire had been manufactured in strict accordance with the financial ethics of the Prefect of the Seine. They are wholy out of the reach of people with less than two thousand a year. The *blanchisseuse* would decline to wash for these aristocratic dollies at lower rates than four francs for a frilled petticoat and fifty centimes for a pair of silk stockings —the lively tariff now being charged by the extortionate despots of the Paris washtub. These are the dolls to dine with the Marquis de Cocodés, or the Vicomte de Petit-Crêvé, at the Café Riche, or Durand's, or the Moulin Rouge. They must have their open *calèche* to drive in the Bois, their *coupé* for nocturnal conveyance to a *baignoire* at the theatre, their *berline*, with postilions in jackboots and powdered wigs, for "down-the-road" trips to the race-course at Longchamps or Chantilly. These are the dolls who, in the heat of summer, levant to "*les eaux*," who promenade the bathing *plage* at Dieppe in costumes between that of a *débardeur* and a harlequin, who pick their way among the rocks of Biarritz and San Juan de Luz, with the aid of tall bamboo canes, gold and amber-headed,— who dance at Baden, and gamble at Monaco, and follow the hounds at Pau in the Pyrenees. These, finally, must be the kind of dolls for whose *beaux yeux* duels are fought, on whose account suits *en séparation de corps* are frequently brought, and for whose smiles the flower of the French youth squander their patrimony, rush into the spider webs of usury, and either make an end of it by blowing out their brains in the very cabinet of the Maison Dorée, where they have paid for so many *petits soupers,* or expire of atrophy and *dépérissement de la moelle épinière,* "the disease of the epoch," in a *Maison de Santé.*

A dozen years since Paris, and, indeed, the whole Continent, found content in the simple old-fashioned dolls—with their waxen, meaningless, simpering faces, their round, staring blue eyes, their little pudgy hands and arms, and their tiny stumpy feet (tiny in proportion as the "golden lily" hoofs of a Chinese belle), with the blue kid shoes and the openwork socks. A doll undressed was a sight which would not have raised a blush to the cheek of the most prurient prude. Dolly was a mere bifurcated bag of bran. Sometimes she had pink kid legs, but they were entirely innocent of calves. She had a waist, but no purist would accuse her of wearing a bustle. She was a doll, in fact, made to be nursed, and tossed, and tumbled about by little children—to be dragged about in a go-cart, and occasionally to be run away with in the mouth of the big dog. If you sat upon her it did not much matter; if you poked her head between the bars and burnt off half her nose—as was the case with the dolly in the "Rejected Addresses"—the mischief could be mended. In those primitive days five francs were thought a good deal for a doll, and a louis *un prix fou.* There were very rich people for whom more costly dolls were made—prize dolls, plump and pink and inane as prize pigs, who, on being squeezed, emitted the words "pa-pa," "ma-ma," in a sepulchral squeal, and with whose draperies you were forced to take most unseemly liberties in order to find the string the tension of which impelled them to move their eyes. But these dolls were rich and rare, like the millionaires who purchased them. They were made only for princesses of the blood and the daughters of contractors for Russian loans; and even when purchased they passed the major part of their existence wrapped up in silver paper in the decorous retirement of a chest of drawers, and were only brought out to be nursed and admired by poorer children on high days and holidays. Finally, in those unsophisticated times there prevailed a sensible custom, now all but extinct, of presenting children with undressed dolls. The happy possessor of the bag of bran with the waxen extremities forthwith set up as a milliner and dressmaker on her own account. Her mamma "set" her the fashions, and she went to work with a will. All kinds of scraps and remnants of textile fabric were pressed into the service, and many bitter tears were shed, I have no doubt, over bonnets and bodies that would never fit. But little girls learned to be neat and tidy and handy, which was something. In these days I fancy the young ladies of France no more dream of making dresses for their dolls than they do of making dresses for themselves.

I have always thought that the chief offender in bringing about that which I cannot but consider as a decline of manners and a corruption of taste was a person who, soon after the Crimean War, started a "doll's wardrobe shop" in the Rue de Choiseul. The shop was a very little one, and the stock-in-trade of a correspondingly diminutive nature. The whole display was extravagantly absurd, but irresistibly fascinating. The doll's *marchande de modes* discovered that dolly required a parasol, a pocket-handkerchief, a reticule, a scent-bottle, and a huswife-case—things which had never been dreamt of under the old bran-bag *régime*. Then they found out that she wanted a trunk, with a movable tray, for her fine linen, a toilet-table and looking-glass, and brushes with ivory backs, a pack of cards to tell her fortune, a purse to hold her donations to the poor, a fan when she was warm, a railway-rug, symmetrically strapped up, when she travelled, a prayer-book when she was pious, and a birch-rod when she was naughty. The climax of absurdity was reached when she was provided with a lapdog, of about the size of a baby white mouse, and a doll—a doll for her who was a doll herself! This shop in the Rue de Choiseul was the parent of at least two hundred establishments of a similar nature which are now scattered all over Paris. I found one doll's wardrobe shop in the Rue Scribe recently, and watched a pale overworked needlewoman who had brought home a bundle of dolls' "garibaldis" full of most elaborate "insertion." There were at least two dozen of them. It was a sight, and not a very joyous one, to see the portly mistress of the shop turning over these tiny falbalas, severely examining the cut and workmanship, and now and again scornfully rejecting one as quite unfit for a doll moving in the first circles. In the name of Folly and Frenzy, what next, and what next? Fancy the "sweating system" applied to dolls' clothes! Fancy the woman clad in unwomanly rags, and, with fingers weary and worn, stitch, stitch, stitching in her garret over these whimwams, and, in a voice of dolorous pitch, singing the song of a doll's chemise!

What would you have? It is a merry age, a dancing age, a jovial, lighthearted, devil-may-care age. *Vive la joie! Vive la bagatelle!* Long live the Café Riche and the Jardin Mabille, and the Closerie des Lilas, and the Thirteenth Arrondissement! Let us paint our faces, and put black under our eyes, and pad our haunches, and wash our hair in a solution of soda till it turns red, or, if we have not enough hair of our own, let us unthatch the heads of the dead for our *chignons* and our false curls. When we grow tired of sham red hair let us smear our pates with dark unguents, and stain our skins with walnut juice, and become sham brunettes. 1 am tired of girding and carping and sneering. What did the Danish prince say of times that were out of joint? To set them right shall be no cursed spite of mine. I acquiesce, I obtemporate, I perpend, I retract, I "cave in." Everything is right. Things could not be better. Let us wear boots with heels as high as the column of the Place Vendôme, and gowns with tails that trail a mile and a half behind us, or, being come to forty years, let us have short skirts like those of school-girls, and strive to persuade the Marquis de Cocodés that we are fourteen. Hurrah!

If you think I have said anything too severe, or have shown the slightest tendency towards exaggeration, I entreat you to consider Group IV., Class XXXIX., and see what Rémond, and Huret, and Lonchambon, what Dessain, what Verdavainnc, what Fialon, what Bontemps, what Loiseau, what Simonne, what Andrina, what Schuctze, and what Schanne, all of Paris, have to show in the way of dolls and dolls' toilets, gutta-percha dolls, wax dolls, articulated wooden dolls, porcelain dolls, dolls' furniture, hosiery, millinery, underclothing, jewelry, and kitchen utensils. Let me first render to these eminent manufacturers of toys all that which they really deserve credit for. Their mere *bimbeloterie* is capital. Their toys, as toys, are wonderful. Never were there seen such ingenious specimens of mechanism as the new *poupées articulées*, which are so cunningly jointed that they will stand without any adventitious support, and can be put into almost every position proper to the human being. They wellnigh rival the mannequins, or lay figures, for the use of artists, which have always commanded large prices; and these articulated dolls, undressed, are sold at least a hundred per cent. below that asked by the artist's lay-figure maker. For grace and symmetry of form the old bifurcated bran-bags cannot, of course, compare with them, but it is their toilettes that cost the money. It is their mahogany and rosewood furniture, their mirrors and consoles, their chandeliers and their Aubusson carpets that ruin the young prodigals of 'Sixty-seven. If you buy a doll in Paris now-a-days you must not only put her *dans ses meubles*, but furnish for her a luxurious boudoir in the Pompadour or the Empire style. She must have a carriage. She must have a saddle-horse. She must have a "ghroom" and a "jockei." She must have a grand piano from Erard or Pleyel. Her gloves must come from Madame Causse, her bonnet from Jenny Navarre, her watch from Leroy, her diamonds from Mellerio. She must have seventy-two petticoats, like the Russian countess who lives at the Hôtel Bristol. She must bathe in milk of almonds, or *sang de menthe*. And I am very much afraid that, if you are suddenly called away, and return, in about a fortnight, unexpected, you will find your doll drinking champagne with your "ghroom." Don't think I am talking about real men and women. I am, discoursing simply about the dolls, who, in the French *Bimbeloterie* Court at the Exhibition, are flirting, lounging, waltzing, jingling on the pianoforte, surveying themselves in mirrors, and ogling each other through consoles. The old child-doll type seems entirely lost. The French toymen have taken to the manufacture of adult dolls. They look like dolls that have vices—dolls that don't care much about the Seventh Commandment—dolls who, to feed their own insatiable appetite, would eat you out of house and home, mortgage your lands, beggar your children, and then present you with a toy revolver to blow out your brains withal. They are so terribly symmetrical, so awfully lifelike; they carry their long trains, and nurse their poodles, and read their *billets doux*, and try on their gloves, and gamble at lansquenet with such dreadful perfection, that you would not be at all surprised at last to find a male doll cheating at cards, or a female doll running a long milliner's bill and forgetting to pay it. And this is the chief count in my indictment against the modern French dolls in the Exhibition. They have nothing to do with the happy, innocent, ignorant time of childhood. They look like dolls who know the time of day, and whom no young man from the country—or any other man—can get over. The old wizards used to make to themselves waxen dolls in the likeness of persons whom they hated, and into these effigies they stuck huge corking pins, every puncture of which inflicted corresponding torture on the living original. I never look upon the grown-up dolls in the French *Bimbeloterie* Court without thinking of Mr. Barham's story of "The Leech of Folkestone."

But there are dolls and dolls, and puppets themselves are, I suppose, just as old as the world, or reach back at least to the time of the first children of humanity. When Eve was tired of stitching her fig-leaf apron, it is probable that she set herself to work to make, out of a gourd or a pine-cone, something pretty for her little ones to play with; and Cain and Abel squabbled, I dare say, very fiercely over their playthings. The first dolls were presumably constructed for those mythical young ladies whom Mr. Solomon Gessner has introduced, in order to balance his *dramatis personæ*, into the " Death of Abel," the sweetest, silliest pastoral ever written, and one which reads, after the terrific " Paradise Lost," as currant wine might taste after hot brandy and water. Leaving the mythical ages, there are plenty of ancient dolls which have come down to us; and the simplicity and purity of taste characteristic of antique art may be verified in these its simplest productions. For this age, in which mental impressions are so forcible and so lasting, it would seem that our boasted civilisation has still much to do. Instead of engrafting bad taste in the minds of those little beings who will one day become men and women, by imposing on them by means of toys the pernicious companionship of vicious forms, should we not sedulously watch over the design and conception of their playthings? Might not we endeavour to give in our dolls some reflex of the calm contentment of domestic life, of the peaceful happiness of the household, of family joys and family cares? The Roman dolls are as innocent as sucking pigs. There is not a tinge of the *ceinture dorée* about them; and from Latin playthings at least the meretricious and the " pornographic " are banished. Prince Biscari has compiled a very sumptuous collection of engravings, the *Antichi ornamenti e trastulli de' bambini* ; and, apart from a few *pantins* of the " grimgribber " or hobgoblin type, these two thousand-year-old playthings might claim a place in any modern *Kindergarten*. In the tombs of children in the *Columbaria* of Rome pretty little *pupæ*—whence the French *poupées* and the Italian *pupazzi*—are continually turning up. Most of these are articulated, and rather weak about the knees and elbows, but they are often most delicately proportioned. In fact, the ancients do not seem to have been able to do anything clumsy or tasteless. Sometimes, also, dolls have been discovered of a material of which the Romans appear to have made a use as frequent and various as we make of gutta-percha—to wit, *terra-cotta ;* and these earthenware puppets have often been mistaken for Lares and Penates, or at least declared to be such by obstinate antiquaries. There is no human being so obstinate as an antiquarian, except, perhaps, an entomologist, who would risk bloodshed for the sake of a beetle. Many very beautiful dolls have likewise been found in the excavations of the Acropolis of Athens; and others, dug up in the south of Italy, have been supposed to represent the handmaids of Flora and the village belles of Campania. I am inclined to think that they were meant to be dolls, and nothing but dolls. The ugly puppets have generally tremendous noses, squinting eyes, pot-bellies, spindle shanks, hands in an exaggerated attitude of supination, like those of Guy Fawkes, and flop-ears, like unto those of an ancient sow. Were these hideous images caricatures of unpopular senators, or were they designed to frighten into propriety the naughty little boys and girls of consular families?

Jumping unceremoniously from B. C. to A. D., and returning to our toys of 1867, I find no reason to abate my strictures on the French *poupées,* skilfully as they are made and gorgeously as they are apparelled. They are not infantile dolls. There is nothing natural about them. They look like *cocottes,* and they leave an unpleasant taste in the mouth. Unmingled praise, however, may be awarded to the French, for their puppet automatons—monkeys playing on the fiddle, bears performing on the harpsichord, hares beating on tabors, and the like. Some of these are really surprising specimens of skill, and the expression of many of them is irresistibly comic. There are also some admirable toy locomotives, railway-trains, steamboats, and models of animals, in the French department.

Germany has always been pre-eminent in the manufacture of mechanical figures, such as Mr. Thiodon has been for so many years exhibiting in England—I mean those profile figures, which, by an ingenious mechanism concealed behind the painted background, are made to go through a variety of droll movements common to humanity. Thus we see an indignant papa kicking the sweetheart, of whose attention to his daughter he does not approve, downstairs; a schoolmaster caning a squalling urchin; a cobbler drawing his double thread, winking his eyes and lolling out his tongue meanwhile; an old black man busily sweeping; a bootblack polishing a gentleman's upper-leathers; a girl milking; an old woman coercing a refractory pig, and the like. The funniest effect is produced when a number of frames containing these mechanical tableaux are placed together. Then the cruel parent kicks, and the pedagogue scourges, and the urchin squalls, and the cobbler sews, and the old negro sweeps, and the bootblack polishes, and the girl milks, and the old woman drives the pig to market—all in unison. If you come back in half an hour's time they are still hard at it. If you revisit the German Court in a week, or a fortnight, or a month, you will still find the same thing going on. You begin to think at last that perpetual motion has been discovered, and that these automata will continue kicking, and thrashing, and polishing, and milking, and sewing, for ever and ever.

The number of military toys in the German courts is very remarkable. There are whole *corps d'armée* in tin, lead, and zinc; with encampments on the vastest scale of which miniature is susceptible, squadrons of cavalry, parks of artillery, and gabions, fascines, and pontoon bridges without number. It is significant to note that the smaller German States contribute the largest number of these bellicose playthings. The Prussian toys are comparatively peaceful. The Austrian are miscellaneous, and, if chiefly tending towards miniature furniture, are excellent throughout. But to the fierce martial display of Bavaria, Hesse, and Würtemberg there is no end. Those misguided small Germans! Much better would it have been had they thrown themselves into tiny locomotives and hansom cabs and windmills. They have brought their cavalry and infantry, their parks of artillery, their pontoon bridges—and their pigs, too—to a fine market.

Great Britain shows but one toy-maker, properly so called, Mr. W. H. Cremer, jun. Jeffries and Malings, of Woolwich, show some capital rackets and balls and shoes for racket playing; Lillywhite, Brett, and Co., of Newington Causeway, are strong in cricket bats and balls; so, likewise, in the same paraphernalia of the "noble game," is J. Lillywhite, of Seymour Street, Euston Square. Nicholson, of Rochdale, sends croquet apparatus; and croquet the French are just beginning dimly to understand. Up to a very recent period they seem to have imagined that it was either a kind of needlework or something to eat. But for "dolls, toys, and games," Cremer, junior, is alone in his glory. Proudly he challenges the French with a doll's house—complete, from attic to basement. Now the French are not up to dolls' houses. How should they be? they live in flats. As proudly he throws down a gage of defiance in the shape of a rocking-horse. These wooden steeds are quite out of the French attributes as playthings; for, unless a Frenchman be a dragoon, a Bois de Boulogne dandy, or the Postillon de Longjumeau, he is generally quite a stranger to the.art of equitation. Mr. Cremer's doll's house has evidently been furnished regardless of expense, and it is to be hoped, for the sake of the young couple who inhabit it, that Messrs. Jackson and Graham won't send in their bill for the furniture, Mr. Dobson for the glass, and Messrs. Rippon and Burton for the kitchen utensils, yet awhile. The young couple are visible in perhaps the most virtuous-looking bedroom ever exposed —by the simple process of taking the front off—to the gaze of the profane multitude. The happy bridegroom, leaning his manly arm on a mantelpiece covered with beautiful china, is reading his morning newspaper. His blooming bride, in a sweet morning wrapper, holds by the hand a charming little boy in knickerbockers, whose hair has apparently just been combed, and who, to judge from the expression of his face, has not been altogether satisfied with the operation. Perhaps soap has been the sorrow which has his young days shaded, and some of the brown Windsor, a cake of which may be seen on the adjacent toilette-table, has got into his eye. Altogether, Mr. Cremer's doll's house is a great success; so are his yachts and his fishing-rods, his doll's *trousseau* and his doll's *batteries de cuisine*, his parlour croquets and lawn billiards, and multifarious appliances for the inno-cent recreation of youth.

XIII.

POTTERY.

Pottery—I use the generic term in its widest sense, for the potter may make either a penny pipkin or a Palissy dish worth its weight in guineas, a bedroom ewer or a Sèvres vase, *bleu du roi*, a Dresden shepherdess or a Delft chimney tile, painted with the story of Joseph and Potiphar's wife— pottery may be regarded as one of the oldest and one of the newest of human industries: at once the most venerable and the most juvenile of crafts. Of its existence the memory of history, even of tradition, runneth not to the contrary. The potter's wheel might be almost that of Time ; and so soon as man was made from clay does he seem to have taken the kindred earth into his hands, and moulded, and fashioned, and baked it into a pot. I saw a poor creature once, in a great madhouse, who was allowed, for his recreation, to keep a diary. He showed me some of the entries. Against one of the days he had scrawled this comforting announcement— "The Devil died ;" but against the very next day he had entered, "Born again." The demented man was not alto- gether wrong in his generation. "Nothing is created since creation ; nothing has been lost since the first was found," says Lavoisier : and the new Reform is only the old good, and the new grievance only the old evil in another form. The art ceramic seems to die, too, sometimes. The Goth crushes the eggshell vase beneath his ruthless heel. The bull of barbarism bursts into the china-shop of civilisation, and smashes everything to bits. Rubbish is shot over the cities of Etruria, and mountains of ignorance 'and stupidity rise over buried treasures. Components are lost, glazes forgotten, colours mislaid. Whole centuries pass, and mankind are fain to endure the coarsest shards, or to eat from wooden platters. But the morrow always comes, and the ceramic is born again. Now it is a Bernard de Palissy, and now a Josiah Wedgwood, who may be permitted by Providence to act as the revivifying magicians. After all, pottery seems to contain in itself something defiant of destruction, which, by an innate force, surmounts oblivion and neglect. It is the Antæus of arts, and acquires fresh strength every time it comes in contact with the earth. It meets kaolin, and is born again, in Saxony. It meets phosphate of lime and barytes, and is born again, in England. Granite may disintegrate, and diamonds may be resolved into the ordinary condition of normal carbon, but you shall not kill the potter's ware. The twin brother to a potsherd is a brickbat, and out of bricks they built the Pyramids.

A very few words—as hints and indices, technical and historical—may not be out of place in a rapid notice of some of the principal works of porcelain and earthenware in the Paris Exhibition of 1867. "Porcelain," the first condition of whose being is that it should be translucent, is said to derive its name from the *porcellana,* a shell sacred to the Venus called "Impudica," or Naughty. The characteristics of porcelain, otherwise " china," are the fineness of the paste,

the brilliancy and durability of the enamel, varnish, or
" glaze," which last should be so hard as to resist the action
of a knife. There are two kinds of porcelain—the hard and
the tender. The basis of the hard is kaolin, discovered in
Saxony in 1710. The first "old Saxony" was made at
Meissen. In 1765 the discovery of kaolin at Saint Yrieix,
near Limoges, gave birth to the manufactory of hard porcelain in France—a manufacture which has since become so
famous in connection with the Imperial establishment at
Sèvres. That which is called "old Sèvres" was "tender"
porcelain with an argillaceous calcareous base, and a "frit"
of silicious sand, soda, and nitre. It may be recognized, not
only by its ornamentation, but by the unctuous appearance
of its glaze. It is heavier than the hard porcelain. The use
of porcelain in China and Japan may be traced back to the
first century B. C. ; but it was only towards the middle of the
sixteenth century that this beautiful oriental ware was imported to Europe by the Portuguese. Chinese porcelain
may be known by the prevalent bluish tinge of the glaze,
and the Japanese is often enamelled black. For the rest,
the leading points in the history of pottery may be summed
up very briefly. By the "Ceramic" art is meant the assemblage of the divers crafts and mysteries relating to the fabrication of all kinds of pottery ministering to the wants or to
the luxury of mankind. The object of those who first made
pots or vases of clay was to render them watertight and
fireproof. The most ancient pottery is porous, with a dull or
"mat" surface, fragile, and ill-baked. The Romans, however,
must have possessed well-constructed ovens for the production
of the enormous jars in which they stored their oil and their
wine, and the sight of which, with symptoms of their contents

still clinging to them, as you ramble through the houses of Pompeii, always puts you in mind of the story of Morgiana and the Forty Thieves. That which the Etruscans did in the way of ornamental pottery, thousands of years since, is patent to all the world. They, however, were surpassed in purity and beauty of design by the Athenians. All this pottery was of course opaque. The Romans seem to have excelled more in the production of statues and bas-reliefs in terra cotta; but in the latter days of the Empire a ceramic manufacture, probably resembling in some measure that which we term "majolica," must have made great strides. Domitian's turbot—the beastly glutton!—was served in an earthenware dish six feet in length; and his rival in gormandising, Vitellius, had a dish made of the same dimensions, after the fashion of the shield of Minerva, to hold his memorable mess of livers, tongues, and brains of rare animals and birds. Alexander the Great had brought from Asia the use of gold and silver plate, but in the remotest East the Chinese had already attained excellence in the manufacture of translucent and durable porcelain. When the Roman Empire went to pieces, and throughout the dark ages, the ceramic art died again the death, and it was not until the thirteenth century that the discovery of a varnish or glaze made from lead revived the seeming corpse. Faenza, in Italy, was the first place on the European continent where the new glazed earthenware was made: the kind known as majolica is said to owe its title to the island of Majorca, whose Arab conquerors were great potters. There are no more beautiful samples of enamelled earthenware in the world, perhaps, than are to be found in the walls and pavements of old Moorish houses in Seville and Cordova; and these were made by the unbelieving Moslems during these so-called "dark ages," when the rest of Europe was sunk in one huge slough of ignorance and barbarism.

In the consideration of the potter's art, it would be as well to observe the broad line of demarcation between the two chief branches. Porcelain and earthenware run in parallels, and may be continued to infinity without meeting. "Porcelain" *must* be translucent and semi-transparent; "earthenware" is wholly opaque.

It is not from any wish to be over-complimentary that I address myself, first, in these remarks to the Imperial Porcelain Manufactory of Sèvres in the department of Seine-et-Oise. To take this renowned *atélier* before mentioning the ceramic manufactures of other countries is but an act of simple justice; for, while rendering every due recognition to what Saxony, what Würtemburg, what Madrid, and St. Petersburg can do, and even what such master-potters as our own Wedgwoods, Mintons, and Copelands have achieved, it is still undeniable that in the production of "great pieces," in abundance and splendour of decoration, in brilliancy of colour, and in lavish gilding, Sèvres china is still the first in the world. As respects the quality of the paste and the durability of the enamel, I am not potter enough to award the palm. Indeed I have heard that, from a pure potter's point of view, competent persons are of opinion that Staffordshire may pit itself, without any fear of the result, against Sèvres; and more than one critic, while admitting all the abundance and splendour of the decoration, all the brilliancy of the colour and prodigality of the gilding, have stigmatised modern Sèvres as being only a kind of scene painting *in excelsis*—very gorgeous to look at, but still so overlaid, so redundant and so florid, that the painting kills the porcelain, and might as well be executed on panel, on canvas, or on copper, as on china clay. Be this as it may, Sèvres must still take the *haut pas* in the hierarchy of ceramics. It could not well be otherwise. It must be remembered that the organisation of the establishment is historical, and as mathematically adjusted as that of the Polytechnic or the Cavalry School at Saumur. Its financial resources are unlimited; for it is the State which is its capitalist and its best customer. It is not compelled to produce cheap articles. Its products are meant only for the alcoves of queens and the banqueting halls of princes and ambassadors. It is not obliged to consult the public taste. That taste it commands. It has vast and innumerable appliances for facilitating the labours of the workshop, the oven, and the studio. It manufactures its own colours, which it refuses to sell. *La palette de Sèvres* is richer in tints than that of any private factory; and although the artists' colourmen eagerly imitate its hues, there are some few preparations, of a most valuable nature, still belonging exclusively to Sèvres, and rigidly kept secret. The tender but melancholy hue known as "Céladon," and the curious process termed *pâte sur pâte*, a kind of very low relief on the porcelain, analogous to that which has been done in black and white glass on the Portland Vase, may be considered indigenous to Sèvres. Finally, Sèvres, from its celebrity, and the governmental patronage it enjoys, can always command a supply of the best porcelain painters in France—ladies and gentlemen who are artists in the truest sense of the term—professors such as Béranger, Jacobbert, Fragonard, as Constantin, Develly, Robert, as the Schilts, father and son, as André, and as Mesdames Jacottot, Ducluseau, and Laurent. I do not say that our English manu-facturers have not in their employ artists to the full as accomplished as these. The copies of the old masters on Minton's tablets, the Wedgwood Etruscan, the Copeland flower paintings, will match with anything that Sèvres can show; but the proficient "porcelainist" is in England an exotic, an importation, rich and rare. The English manu-facturers who have brought over foreign artists, and paid liberally and even munificently for the work of their pencil, deserve the highest credit; but I wish to look still further ahead. I wish to see the day when neither French nor German artists, at enormous salaries, shall be needed in the potteries, but when South Kensington, and the schools of art all over England, shall be in a position to send to Burslem or Stoke a sufficient supply of Browns, Joneses, and Robinsons, of Tomkinses, Smiths, and Greens, both male and female, to suffice for all our needs. As regards ceramic statuary we are getting on capitally; and I hold it much better that our embryo Phidiases and suckling Praxiteles should take a leaf out of Mr. Durham's book, and diligently produce forms of beauty and grace for the potteries, than that they should break their hearts because they cannot afford to buy a block of Carrara as big as a six-roomed house, wherein to carve a statue of "Satan Falling from Heaven," or "Eve discovering a Bunion on her Foot" (nude), or "The Mayor of Hole-cum-Corner refusing to support the local rate for putting the Police into Cocked Hats."

Sèvres had, in the Universal Exhibition, a whole saloon to itself—a most gorgeous apartment, the walls appropriately hung with tapestries from the kindred manufactory of the Gobelins, also an Imperial enterprise. These tapestries, mainly copies from the old masters, will demand notice elsewhere. Limitation of space will not permit me to dilate at length on the magnificent specimens of ceramic art exhibited here; nor, perhaps, is extended criticism very much needed. The productions of Sèvres are familiar, both for size and quality, to the whole world. There are the same towering vases, the same enormous cups and plateaux and centre-pieces every sightseer has gazed upon at Versailles, at St. Cloud, at Windsor—in the Library of the Vatican, in the Palacio Real at Madrid, in the Burg at Vienna, in the Palaces of Dresden and Munich, Florence and Naples. Sèvres furnishes the regalia of pottery, the crown jewels of china, to all the monarchs of Christendom. Its catalogue is an *Almanach de Gotha* in earthenware. Simulated jasper and jade, onyx and porphyry, chalcedony and sardonyx, beryl and malachite, alabaster and cornelian, turquoise and opal, glow from its polished spheres. All the flowers from all the hothouses of Schönbrunn and Tsarskœ-Selo seem to have been strewn over its vases. And when Sèvres condescends to do anything small, what is it but to produce a cup and saucer worth five thousand francs, or a tea and coffee service cheap at twenty-five thousand—dainty little porcelain gems entombed in white satin and morocco cases— charming tit-bits of luxury, to be exhibited only in the boudoirs of duchesses, and sometimes of demireps? Altogether, the productions of Sèvres may be pronounced, as are some masterpieces in picture galleries, as *hors concours.* Competition between the Imperial manufactory and the humbler enterprises of private commerce is all but impossible and is not quite fair. Sèvres, moreover, exhibits less proof of what she can do than replicas of what she has done. Her reputation is made. Her laurel crown was won long ago. She is a "modern antique." You have no right to show the Portland Vase against your grandmamma's teapot. Thus Sèvres, from an Exposition point of view, must be regarded simply as an adjunct and accessory, as part of the *décor* or pageantry of the display. She no more exemplifies any stage of progress or development than a *cent-garde* in full uniform represents the improvement of military tactics, or the Koh-i-noor the latest novelty in jewellery. She is not obstructive, not retrograde; but she is as perfect as she can well be: as perfect as St. Peter's is in architecture, or Windsor Forest in sylvan beauty.

Of private French porcelain and earthenware manufacturers, both for luxury and for common domestic use, the name was legion, and the display of their productions was highly satisfactory. Of the French proficiency in decorated and ornamental china—albeit their style is a trifle too "stagey" and meretricious—it would be superfluous to speak; but, passing from all their beautiful nymphs and fauns and nereids, their satyrs and their bathers, their dryads and their hamadryads, their Cupids and their Psyches, it is quite as pleasing to notice the advance they have made since the last Exhibition in fresh, truthful, quiet landscape-painting, as applied to porcelain. The spirit of Lee and Creswick, and of our admirable Birket Foster, seems to have been abroad among the French; and verdant nooks, and purple distances, and cool rills, and moss-grown cottages are beginning to peep on their porcelain through the swarms of heathen gods and goddesses and impossible shepherds and shepherdesses of Arcadia. Arcadia! Did you ever see a shepherd on the Sussex downs eating a hedgehog for his dinner? Did you ever assist at the filthy operation known as sheepwashing? I think *that* would sicken you of poor Arcadia for a considerable period: to say nothing of Jeremy Taylor's remark on "the noise of the Arcadian porters." I say that the landscapes and the flowers, which the French are painting more skilfully every year, are gradually driving the deities of Olympus and the pastorals of M.M. de Florian and Parny out of the field. It is time, indeed, that the admirers of art enjoyed a surcease from these eternal pink Cupids without clothes, and pinker nymphs with ne'er a rag on; and the rising school of French artists would do well to study, in this regard, what the philosopher Diderot has said of Boucher and Vanloo, and their disciples, the great-grandfathers of the pink Cupids and pinker nymphs.

Henri Ardant and Co., of Limoges and Paris, show some delightful services in pure white porcelain, chaste in design, and full of unaffected grace. They should be cheap, too; and that is the chief need in France. Few things are more beautiful than expensive French porcelain; few more hideous than the common, heavy, lumbering cups and saucers you get at the cafés. Michael Aaron has some very charming terra-cotta statuettes; and on Ardant's stand I noticed also some wonderfully lifelike figures in Parian of Zouaves and Chasseurs. To Gille *Jeune* should be given great praise for his red terra-cotta figures, many of very large size, and surprising both as specimens of modelling and of successful baking. The porcelain of Abel Monvoisin, of Bagnollet, is commendable for its extreme elegance and lightness. Schucht Brothers, of Besançon, make an admirable display of vases, cups, dinner services, and flower-stands, in painted porcelain, earthenware, and crystal. Véry and Baratte are prominent in vases, lamps, and liqueur-stands; and Machereau, of the Faubourg du Temple, has been very successful in works of *pâte tendre* porcelain mounted in bronze. In flower-painting Dartout and Pinot are pre-eminent. L. Coblentz shows some remarkable samples of porcelain decorated by the chromo-lithographic process. It is always pleasant to see anything done which can contribute to the keeping alive of lithography, the birth of which pretty art was about concurrent with the revival of wood-engraving, but a little prior to the invention of photography. Between them, wood-engraving and photography have almost murdered poor Aloys Senefelder and his charming pictures in stone.

There are but fourteen exhibitors in Class 14, that of the English pottery, and, although Wedgwood—*clarum et venerabile nomen*—might well claim precedence on the score of seniority, I will transcribe my notes in the order in which I took them, and begin with the work of W. T. Copeland and Sons, of Bond Street and Stoke-upon-Trent. They exhibit porcelain vases, ceramic statuettes, earthenware, and glass. Their *pièce de résistance* is the gorgeous dessert service manufactured for the Prince of Wales. The highest praise to be awarded to this sumptuous assemblage of chinaware should be that of its entire and perfect originality in design. No models, save those of beauty and good taste, have been consulted. The gifted artist, who has covered the delicate and glistening surfaces with glowing clusters of flowers, has gone neither to Paris, nor to Dresden, to Sèvres, nor to Berlin, for his inspiration. He has looked only to Nature, and his close study of natural grace and harmony has been amply rewarded. The artistic execution of the paintings is superb, and the mingled monograms of Albert Edward and

Alexandra most dexterously conceived and woven out. Looking at the service technically, at the turning, the adjustment, the sharp yet firm cutting of the perforated borders, the treatment of every line and curve and interlacement, it is impossible to deny that the good artist has been seconded by as good an artisan. A potter would say that the whole is capitally "potted;" that is to say, the cut of the garment and the excellence of the workmanship are equalled by the quality of the cloth. In the centre rises a beautiful piece of ceramic statuary, consisting of draped female figures, representing the four quarters of the globe. Of these the modeller is Mr. Joseph Durham ; and from the plastic hand of the same famous sculptor the Messrs. Copeland have obtained numerous other exquisite specimens of ceramic statuary ; amongst others, a charming figure of "Chastity." Of these ceramic statuettes the Copelands may be said to have almost a monopoly. The delicacy and elaboration of their finish derive additional attraction from the strength of the material, which is wellnigh equal to that of stone ; and it is well to bear in mind the serious difficulties which encompass the production of works such as these, shrinking as does the moulded clay in the kiln during the process of baking to the extent of one-third from its original size. A colossal vase, a very triumph of flower-painting, and from original designs, several beautiful *tazze*, and a marvellously-engraved glass claret-jug, looking more like the enlargement of an antique gem than a work of modern hands, also demand attention. Let me also say a word for a cut-glass goblet remarkable chiefly by its entire colourlessness. It is pure white "metal," and that is the highest eulogium which can be passed on glass. With one passing note of admiration for

Durham's statuette of Santa Filomela, suggested by Long-
fellow's poem in honour of Florence Nightingale—you remember those touching stanzas:

> A lady with a lamp shall stand,
> In the great history of the land,
> A noble proof of good,
> Enduring womanhood;
>
> Nor even shall be wanting there
> The sword, the lily, and the spear,
> The symbols which of yore
> St. Filomela wore.

—and with a glance at the reduction of Monti's " Morning,"
a wonderful turquoise vase, a mauresque tazza, which might
have come from the Alcazar, and some capital imitations of
Limoges, I will pass from the Messrs. Copeland to the stand
of Minton and Co., likewise of Stoke-upon-Trent.

That some degree of rivalry should exist between three
manufacturers of pottery so eminent as the Wedgwoods, the
Mintons, and the Copelands is natural, and all but inevitable.
Rafaelle admired Michael Angelo very sincerely, but he ran
him as hard as he could, for all that. It is certain that Sir
Edwin Landseer has the highest appreciation of the works of
Rosa Bonheur; but were the Duke of Northumberland to
commission from *"la Grande Mademoiselle"* of art a new
lion in lieu of the deformed poodle which now wags his tail
above the chimneys of the Percies' palace, it is probable that
Sir Edwin would not be displeased to hear the critics maintain that the Nelson lions were superior to Rosa's. There is
no necessity for us to hate our rival, or stretch a string across
his path to trip him up; but we must keep up with him, and,
if possible, distance him. The race is very close indeed
between Copeland, Minton, and Wedgwood. The betting is

even. Fortunately, no section of the betting world need be "hit hard" by the victory of any one of the competitors, for the taste and comfort of a whole empire are benefited by their energetic contest for supremacy. Again, the acrimony which is too often the companion of emulation is, in this case, tempered and all but obviated; first, by the honourable and straightforward feeling which prevails among English traders, and next, by the fact that each of the three earth-masters I have named has his "speciality," his department of art, to which he has devoted the greatest attention, the strongest energy, the largest capital, the most cultivated taste, and in which, if he be not unrivalled, he is surely unsurpassed. If the spiteful Goddess of Discord had only thrown down on the dinner table of the gods three golden apples instead of one, that false shepherd on Mount Ida might have made a better award, and been hailed the prince of arbitrators. Surely each of the three divinities entered for the Beauty Stakes must have been superior to her sisters in something. Hera had a deuce of a temper, but she had beautiful back hair; Aphrodite had a cast in her eye, but she had an exquisite complexion; Pallas was thin and wore spectacles, but she could write like George Eliot. Why couldn't the shepherd give them a pippin apiece? He could not, for the obvious reason that Discord was the giver of the stakes, and that Discord wished the goddesses to squabble among themselves and Troy town to be ruined. But, as Concord and not Discord should be our object here, the "choice of Paris" with respect to the potters involves a triple prize. Give one to the Copelands for their ceramic statuary; it is the best. Give another to Minton for his majolica ware; there is nothing better in the Exhibition. Give the third to Wedgwood for his earthenware *plaques*, or tablets, painted with forms of beauty and grace. In the strictest justice, the most discriminative equity, may such an award be made ; and thus, I hope, everybody will be satisfied. There will be no call for anybody to cut anybody else's throat in the way of trade; and I, who am no shepherd, son of a king, but only a poor scribe, may at least claim the merit of impartiality.

To particularise. Minton and Co., Stoke-on-Trent, standing in Messrs. Johnson's catalogue as No. 11, in the 17th class of the third group, exhibit china, earthenware, majolica, mosaic, inlaid and enamelled tiles. I take this firm first on their admitted " speciality "—majolica. To this, as all art lovers know, the house of Minton principally pin their faith. In " large pieces " coloured, of opaque ware, they make a superb show. Their modellers excel in things *en grand*. They have the Rubens touch, the Luca Giordano power of wrist, the roundness and flowing abundance of form and drapery which we recognize so gladly in the conceptions of Giovanni di Bologna and Donatello. If it be urged against the Minton majolica that it is florid, the triumphant answer is that it is Renaissance. The Cinquecento spreads no Spartan table ; offers you no black broth, with a leek and a pitcher of water by way of dessert. If you sit down with the vigorous, hot-blooded men of the Revival, you must expect to eat your fill and drain your flagon, and leave no heeltaps. " How many days does the Herr Graf expect to be absent ?" Count von Bismarck's valet is said to have asked lately, as he was packing up his master's needments for a trip into the country. " A month," replied Otto of the ilk of Schönhausen. " Then," added the prudent servitor, " we shall require sixty bottles of cognac, *fine champagne*."

Those who do large things are apt to live largely. The Renaissance was a luxurious style. The richest foliage forms the composite column, the juiciest ornaments form the Corinthian frieze. All that the Roman had of racy, all that the Greek had of rare, all that was sumptuous and extravagant in the Gothic, it took and brayed with flowing pigments and plastic wealth in an affluent mortar, adding, however, harmony as a sauce; and from these components it made such dishes as were fit to set before such kings as Francis of France, Henry of England, the Cosmos and Leos of Italy, the Maximilians of Germany, and the Doges of the City in the Sea, who were more and less than Kings. Minton's majolica has the true sparkle and sheen, the veritable gloss and density of 'broidered richness of the age when the wine flowed from the nostrils of Donatello's horse at Padua, and carpets of Persian pile were laid from the Church of San Geminiano to the Molo, when the Doge went to wed the Adriatic, and the two most splendid monarchs of Europe met on the Field of the Cloth of Gold. Minton's models partake of the gorgeousness of the time. His Nereids are bounteous of limb. They disdain to conceal their charms because Mr. Stabb is virtuous, and the " Pure Literature Society," whose stand is close by, ostracise everything printed save the " Bellowsmender's Friend " and the " British Ratcatcher's Journal." The Mintonic nymphs are full of what the Italians term *morbidezza*. They are vascular. Were you to cut them, they would bleed, almost. The Tritons blow so lustily into their shells that you wellnigh seem to hear their conch-music, and the Cupids are as chubby and creasy and dimpled as those colossal babes who brandish the holy-water pots beneath St. Peter's roof of golden mosaic.

I have seen a dolphin caught, and die, in the far-off Antilles; but I prefer Minton's dolphins in majolica. The romance of *my* dolphin was spoilt by the knowledge that the foremast men were waiting round about the moribund with frying-pans to cook and eat him so soon as he had flapped his parti-coloured life out. But the earthenware fish suggest no thoughts so prosaic. You revel, instead, in a world of grace-ful grotesques—of shells and weeds and tridents and branches of coral. Amidst much majolica, you begin at last to be-lieve in mermaids; to think it by no means unnatural that a middle-aged gentleman, of a convivial turn, should have the hind legs of a goat, and ears of the shape of leaves; to esteem it quite an ordinary circumstance for a young lady to let down her hair, and, with that for sole *parure*, disport her-self on the back of a leopard, or tickle a sea-horse till he grins hugely, or embrace the orb of a water-jug, or hold up a dish, or waltz with an inkstand, or take an audacious "header" into a curling green sea—which is, after all, made but of potter's clay. All this is very unreal, very grotesque, no doubt; but it has something human in it, something striving and struggling; and, for my part, I never look at the Renaissance without fancying that I see, endeavouring to emerge from all these mad imaginings, the great, truthful beauty of Reformed Faith freeing itself from the myths of Paganism and the idolatries of Rome.

It must not be thought that the Minton display is entirely confined to the "speciality" of majolica. I marked some stupendous vases of the old Sèvres form, and painted with flowers and landscape, with the old Sèvres skill. Then, there were some notable tea and coffee services in porcelain; some notable statuettes, and some exquisite specimens of white and gilt plates. Let me also mention a pair of vases covered with some of the most charming representations of children in the style of Albano I have ever seen. They are just a trifle too rosy in the shadows; but this may be a fault for which the oven, and not the pencil, is responsible.

Come now to Wedgwood. Nearly a century's history will tell us what the House, whose habitation is at "Etruria," can do. What, indeed, did good old Josiah Wedgwood *not* do? It needs a "Silver Pen" to recount his achievements. He did for pottery that which Hogarth did for painting, Bewick for wood engraving, Flaxman—with whom the name of Wedgwood is indissolubly connected—for sculpture, Soane for architecture, Strange for engraving in line, and Turner and Girtin for water-colour drawing. He proved to envious, sneering, captious foreigners that, if we were indeed a nation of shopkeepers, we could fill our shop windows with things of beauty—the invention of our own quick intelligence, the work of our own strong right hands. While French art was literally rotting and putrefying—while all that Sèvres could do was to cover the mantelpieces of the Parc aux Cerfs with lewd *potiches*—while the masterpieces of the easels of Boucher and Fragonard were sold to make *dessus de portes* for the *petites maisons* of the Farmers-General —while even Greuze was fain to limn for simpering profligacy, and Houdon found his boldest model and his most bounteous patroness in the Dubarry, John Flaxman, "sculptor of eternity," and Josiah Wedgwood, honestest, pluckiest of English potters, struck hands and went to work to bring back the pure and truthful past—the grand antique time before there were hoops and patches and high heels and powdered curls, the days when the youth of Greece, proud of the forms of beauty which the gods had given them, strove to make them comelier and stronger in the arena, in the chase, and in the combat. Some traces of the alliance between Etruria and Staffordshire, between Flaxman and Wedgwood, are still visible in this stall in Paris. The spirits of the two great English worthies still seem to hover over the works of their descendants. There they are: the well-remembered forms, in their modest, graceful livery of blue and white, simple, quiet, unaffected, but unapproachable in excellence of workmanship and purity of design. There are also some noble bas-reliefs in black earthenware, and two or three exquisite services all in opaque ware. There is one in particular, painted with subjects from the fables of La Fontaine by the famous Lessore. This good artist is now an old man, and a generation hence his works on earthenware will be as valuable as a Wright of Derby or a Patrick Nasmyth on canvas. His colour is wonderful, and he has a touch, a quick, incisive, punctuated method of handling, which may well be styled inimitable, for his imitators could scarcely avoid degenerating into carelessness and "spotti-ness."

The modern "speciality" of Wedgwood is, as I have said, *plaques*, or painted earthenware tablets. Some sumptuous specimens of these are exhibited; and all are fully worthy to be put into rich frames and hung up, as real pictures, in the galleries of amateurs. It is only to be regretted that, in the selection of subjects, the artists employed have confined themselves too closely to copying the works of the detestable French school of the eighteenth century. It is Boucher and Fragonard, Fragonard and Boucher, over and over again. *Palsambleu!* have we not had enough of these fat naked

women and sham pastorals? Are we farmers-general or
gentlemen of the chamber privileged to mount *dans les
carrosses du Roi?* Are our wives Pompadours and Dubarrys?
For goodness' sake let us have an end—if it be even for a
time—of Pompadour and Dubarryism. Are there no stately
cavaliers, no "doddy" little infantas in ruffs and farthingales,
by Don Diego Velasquez? Are there no priceless beggar
boys and gitanas and majas by Don Esteban Murillo? Has
Richard Wilson done nothing worthy of being copied on
clay? And the rustic George Morland? I would give
twice as much for a brace of his pigs as for a gilded pigsty
of a boudoir, with Cotillon Premier vagabondising therein.
And the pure and harmonious Stothard? And the graceful
Westall? And Fuseli, with his writhing forms of terror?
And Mortimer, with his monsters and chimeras dire? Let
us have, Messrs. Wedgwood, a revival on earthenware of
these good old British masters; or turn, if you will, to the
courtly Watteau and the sprightly Lancret—at least, they
dressed their nymphs; or abide among the Dutchmen—with
the sweet, patient Gerard Douw, or David Teniers, soft and
silver gray, but a gentleman even among his boors and his
beer jugs; or old Isaac Ostade, subdued, but luminous as a
firefly on the Riviera di Levante on a moonless night. But
spare us any more of those Pompadour *plaques*, which only
seem designed to show the development of the *latissimus
dorsi* and the *glutæi* muscles on the part of nymphs who
ought to know better.

XIV.

GLASS.

Arriving at the consideration of glass in the Exhibition—as applied to the uses of the table and of ornament—it scarcely strikes the observer that any great progress has been made within the last few years in regard to Form. Outline, perhaps, in every department of art (save English oil-paintings) is reaching its acmé. An acquaintance with mathematical canons has been so intimately wedded to proficiency in linear drawing that scarcely a curve remains to be discovered; and on a cunning familiarity with curves, and their multitudinous combinations, rests, I need scarcely say, that invaluable quality in a *gentilhomme verrier*, the art of producing something new in the way of a goblet, a vase, or a tazza. I am constrained to confess that, in outline, I see nothing new, and even nothing striking in the glass ware of 1867. Those versed in the production of ornamental designs must know how many ellipses are to be produced from cunning changes of centres and blendings of circumferences. After all, the most elaborate attempts in vases generally resolve themselves into an endeavour to improve the shape of an egg; and in goblets, expansion and contraction are, as a rule, only involved replicas, the shapes with which we have been familiar since infancy, or which have been transmitted to us by artistic tradition. Coming, however, to this most important branch of manufacture in a candid and willing spirit, I rejoice to register, touching the glass manufacture of England, two capital facts—the wonderful improvement as to colour, the surprising advance as to engraving.

To speak of "colour" in connection with crystal may seem a paradox. The best English glass—and we pride ourselves on *making* the best glass in the world—should, strictly, as I pointed out in my mention of the Copelands, have no colour at all, save that which the laws of refraction give it. Pure crystal is essentially void of tint. The slightest tinge of any hue whatsoever mars its perfection. Its business, as Sir Walter Raleigh would say, is "to warm as snowballs do: not like fire, by burning, too"—*i. e.*, its colours, like the caloric awakened by contact with a sphere of snow, must arise from exterior influences, and must not be contained within itself. How would you like a piece of steel smirched with red? You would say that it was rusty. How would you admire a nugget of gold that had a brown stain in the midst of it? Gold is the only substance whose adventitious presence does not mar beauty : witness the auriferous "splashes" in lapis lazuli. So the highest eulogium which glassmakers can pass upon crystal, when they wish to pronounce it faultless, is this, that it is a "right good piece of metal." To be perfectly metallic it must be wholly colourless; albeit, when cut, its facets may refract a host of rainbows. Looking at our English glass in Paris, it is impossible not to be at once stricken with its surpassing brilliance and purity of "water." The French equal us, and may sometimes beat us, in the elegance of their forms and the dexterous arrangement of their lustres; but their "metal"—their crystal itself—is nearly always dull, pale, and lack-lustrous. This is not the fault of their cutters; it is simply the fault of their "metal." The Austrians carry us away at first with the gay hues, the glowing gilding, the rosettes, the spangles they lavish upon glass; but their ware is but flimsy and brittle, and, without the aids of scenic decoration, would be comparatively ineffective. The North German beer-glasses are very stately, and their dimensions are prodigious; but in artistic productions the Germans have not yet been able to achieve in glass what they have achieved so successfully in iron and steel. Belgium, in respect to the fabrication of glass, is still in a most rudimentary condition; and it would have been, perhaps, an act of wisdom on the part of the Belgium commissioners to have refrained from unpacking the deformed rummers with bloated sides and gouty feet, the meagre, conical wine-glasses, and the ill-blown and worse cut tumblers which are displayed in the Belgian court. From Holland, the Royal Painted Glass Company, under the title of J. Fischer and Co., sent an enamelled glass cupola, gay enough, but anything but tasteful; but Mr. E. Wessel, of Rotterdam, had, on the other hand, some more than tolerable specimens of cutting in fancy crystal. Lest I should be accused of doing injustice to Belgium, I hasten to admit that their window-glass—notably that of the Charleroi factories—seems stout enough, with a good surface and a tolerable purity from colour; and in an entirely different department of the art—that of ecclesiastical glass painting—M. Vanderpoorten, of Molenbeck, exhibits a very splendid "Presentation of the Virgin in the Temple," intended for the church of Notre Dame de la Chapelle, at Brussels. The chemical and glass works of the St. Gobain

Company of Aix-la-Chapelle have deservedly attained considerable celebrity, and are classed, like those of the other Rhenane provinces, with Prussia; but in spite of political accuracy, Aix-la-Chapelle is more a Franco-Belgian than a German town, and the firm of St. Gobain, Chauny, and Ariy, are as French in their manufactures as in their names. The gigantic sheets, or rather walls, of plate-glass, erected by the St. Gobain Company, which flank the grand entrance to the Exhibition building, opposite the Bridge of Jena, are magnificent, These distinguished manufacturers also exhibit some very admirable mirrors, and some remarkably curious glass tiles for flooring. The principal Berlinese exhibitor of glass is Mr. C. F. Heckert. Apart from his lustres, which are pretty, but heavy in design, he shows some exceedingly pretty polished glass mounted in bronze and wood; with a number of thermometers, inkstands, almanacks, door-handles, buttons, and articles in artificial jet. From Morocco, even, there are some quaint looking-glasses of large and small dimensions; but, as is usually the case with Moorish mirrors, their charm is in the design and execution of the frames, and the glasses themselves are unequal in surface and poorly silvered.

The French glass manufacturers—who appear in a bright band no less than seventy-two strong—are most sumptuously installed in a row of lofty, spacious courts, in which their glittering wares are most ingeniously disposed, with a view to the enhancement of their effect. They can hang their chandeliers from great heights, and thus give an idea of the aspect which their enormous lustres would present in palatial saloons. Their candelabra and tripods have ample space and verge enough around them, whereas the English manufacturers of glass are crammed into the narrowest and most inconvenient corners, and have had the greatest difficulty in obtaining the bare hanging and standing room necessary, to say nothing of any margin of circuit whence spectators could admire the objects exhibited. To be sure, the French exhibitors have been made to pay for their space, and that, too, at a most exorbitant tariff per square metre; but so vital is the need for light and space where glass has to be shown off, that I almost wonder that the English glass exhibitors did not protest against being cabined, cribbed, and confined in the interior of the palace, and that they did not run up a shed for themselves in the park.

I have said that the two most shining merits of the English glass are the excellence of its material and the exquisite beauty of its engraving. Engraving as applied to glass is an art which, although exercised to a limited extent from times very remote, has lain until the last ten years in comparative abeyance. Of late years, however, it has received a prodigious impetus; and those who decry trade combinations are apt maliciously to point out that engraving on glass would not have been heard of in modern times but for a fierce strike among the glass-cutters. They remained on strike a very long time, and when they evinced a disposition to return to their work, they found that the masters had called in the aid of engravers from Germany, and that their own services, as cutters, were no longer needed. There may just be a grain of truth in this story as regards drinking glasses and decanters, but there are many more departments in the trade which must always depend on the cutter; nor is it probable that the demand for workmen whose skill can give such matchless and gem-like brilliance to glass will ever cease. It is essential, in the consideration of engraved glass, to remember that there is a true and a spurious method of producing a design by incision upon glass. Precisely as you may *bite into* a copper or steel plate by scratching its coating of varnish with a needle, and pouring aquafortis over the parts left exposed, so may you "bite" into glass by pouring fluoric acid over the parts from which a preparatory coat of some "stopping out" agent has been scratched away. You may "etch" on glass as you etch on steel or copper. To the unpractised eye it is difficult to tell a strong, bold etching from a line engraving, legitimately executed by cutting into the steel or copper with a graver; but the two processes are, as the adept knows, entirely different, and an etching can be produced in one-tenth of the time which would be required for an engraving in line: so is it with glass. Etching on glass is a comparatively cheap and expeditious process, whereas engraving is difficult, laborious, and consequently expensive. It is no exaggeration to state that a glass, very elaborately etched, might be sold for five guineas, whereas the same object, legitimately engraved, might cost fifty. It is error, however, to suppose that glass is engraved by the deliberate incision of the surface with a diamond point. This would only amount, at the utmost, to "scratching," and the effect produced would be very poor and meagre. In glass engraving, as our Dobsons and Pellatts understand it, whole portions of the glass are actually "*tagliati*," or cut away, and a surprising vigour of relief is attained. This can only be done by holding the glass, at an infinity of angles, to a number of copper wheels rapidly revolving in grooves cut in the artist's work-table.

As an engraver on glass, it seems to be the unanimous

opinion of critics, both English and foreign, that the lead is taken by Mr. Dobson, of St. James's Street. Such pre-eminence can be awarded to him without detracting in the slightest degree from the acknowledged merits of Chance, of Pellatt, of Henry Greene, of James Green, of Millar of Edinburgh, of Powell of Whitefriars, or of the Defrieses, at whose stall the Emperor purchased a service of engraved glass. Some of these gentlemen are manufacturers, others factors; some excel in table glass, others in lustres; but Mr. Dobson's speciality is the production of the most beautiful classic and Renaissance designs on glass of exquisite form; and in these I humbly conceive he stands unsurpassed. I have never seen anything more beautiful in elaboration of pattern, in purity of outline, in precision of engraving, and in delicacy of finish, than Mr. Dobson's Renaissance jug, decorated with the composition called "The Chariot of Love." It would be perhaps unjust, in view of the other manufacturers who demand my attention, to dwell in detail on even a tithe of the objects exhibited on Mr. Dobson's stand; else I could say a great deal in favour of another and most wonderful jug, of Rafaellesque design, exhibited by him, and of a gorgeous fifty-four light lustre, with jewel-pattern drops. There are whole services, too, of the most delicious table glass—the slenderest, the most cobweb-looking, and yet of adamantine strength. There are all kinds of claret jugs, water jugs, decanters, flower-stands, champagne cups, tazze, goblets, and vases—some so expensive, from their consummate finish, that only princes or millionaires could purchase them—others obtainable at prices within the reach of persons of very moderate means. One of the most sumptuous of the engraved jugs was purchased by the South Kensington Museum for one hundred and fifty guineas. But, as there were strong men before Agamemnon, so are there doubtless many most skilful and tasteful glass dealers besides Mr. Dobson. I shall, in preference, indeed, dwell more at length on the characteristics of form and cutting displayed elsewhere by his colleagues in trade. I am content to award him the palm as an Engraver —as having attained the highest excellence in a most beautiful but difficult art—as having done on glass that which the incomparable artist employed by Messrs. Elkington has done in *repoussé* work on silver in the " Paradise Lost " shield. Mr. Dobson, I understand, executes himself on the glass the designs which are subsequently to be engraved, and that is the highest praise which can be awarded to an engraver. To their shame, the international jury only awarded a silver medal to Mr. Dobson. If taste and skill in art deserve reward he merited a double gold one.

I mentioned the superb "installation" of the glass in the French department. They have a whole suit of sumptuous saloons to themselves, lofty and spacious, and flooded with light, and, from the largest to the smallest of the productions they exhibit, all can be inspected from every conceivable point of view, and under the most favourable conditions. Withal, as I have already observed, the display lacks that surpassing lucidity and brilliance which are so distinctive of the English glass show. For magnitude and for elegance of design the French deserve the highest praise : but their glass is not crisp, it is not clear, and it is not sharp. For the two last-named deficiencies the cause is obvious. The vast majority of the French works are not cut, but moulded. The primary forms are given over to the cutter to be " touched up " and finished, but the foundation of moulding is always to the experienced eye easy of detection, and the difference is as great as between cast and wrought iron. Many of the French jurors and experts in glass who came round to the English region—say to Henry Greene or Millar of Edinburgh's stand—would hardly believe at first that the objects they saw were really of legitimately hewn crystal. "*Mais ça doit être moulé*," they exclaimed; and it was only after attentive comparison, by applying all the tests of sight and touch to the specimens, that they were brought to recognize our pre-eminence as cutters.

There are, of course, a great many persons, as weak in technics as they are in taste, who are carried away at first sight by the stately proportions and fanciful ornamentations of the French vases and goblets and candelabra, and to whom it matters very little whether the work be moulded or cut. By a parity of reasoning they would esteem a chromolithograph as highly as an original water-colour drawing, a cast cameo as one cut on *pietra dura*, a "machine-embroidered" petticoat as one worked by hand. I do not quarrel with the French for getting through the hard work of glass-making by the moulding process. The genius of their race is essentially plastic, as that of the Anglo-Saxon is essentially incisive. The Frenchman is a modelling, the Englishman a hacking and hewing animal. The latter lays low a whole forest with his broad axe, while the former picks up a twig and fashions it into the sweetest true-lover's knot you ever saw. The only thing I protest against is that inexperienced persons—the Americans, for example—should rush about wildly praising the beauty of the French glass manufactures, and declaring that "John Bull can't come near them." These are the kind of people who would prefer a garish ormolu clock and candelabra from the Passage des Panoramas, the "Wrath of Achilles" or the "Triumph of Galatea" at the top—*toute la garniture cinq cents francs*—to a twenty-guinea hunter by Barwise or Benson. Fortunately there are in France and other continental countries amateurs of glass who can fully appreciate purity of hue, excellence of workmanship, and sharpness of finish. It is probable that the English glass exhibitors will have very few of their wares to take home again. The Princess Mathilde bought a gorgeous service from Mr. Dobson; Prince Napoleon, the Countess de Souza, Madame de Metternich, and Baron Rothschild have made large purchases in the English *verrerie*. Most of Henry Greene and Apsley Pellatt's wares was already the property of English noblemen and gentlemen, and the remainder was eagerly purchased. When Mustapha Pasha arrived; when the Viceroy of Egypt descended on Paris; when Dalaheddin Pasha made his appearance; when the Colossus of the North, the rugged Russian Bear, the Great Duke of Muscovy—when this autocrat and all his boyards stalked through the English courts, nearly a clean sweep was made of all that was unsold in the way of English "crystal fanc glass." The Sultan bought little; he contented himself with giving away vast sums of money. Unsold. It came to this, then; to a mere prosaic affair of buying and selling. Yes; Universal Exhibitions have shrunk to their second cause, and the counter and the till have been set up against the trophy of art and industry. In Hyde Park, in 1851, nobody thought of selling anything. We only wished to interchange ideas: not to truck merchandise against money. We were all for peace and love and fraternity then. But, on the other hand, there were no thoughts in '51 of sitting down in restaurants, and eating and drinking and smoking beneath the very roof of the Palace of Glass. The soul of Superintendent Walker, and of the ubiquitous and sagacious Durkin, would have shrunk with horror from the bare idea of a mild havannah puffed within the Paxton premises. There was no beer to be got in Hyde Park; and poor Alexis Soyer declined to compete for the refreshment contract, and went off to the Symposium because the virtuous minds of the Executive Committee revolted at the notion of allowing him to sell wines and spirits. I am not digressing, I hope. My theme is glass and glasses, drinking as well as looking ones; and it is surely apposite to the subject to mention the fluids which glasses ordinarily contain.

But let me halt now before the grand *étalage* of La Compagnie des Verreries et Cristalleries de Baccarat, in the department of the Meurthe. I thus particularise it in order to remove any impression that this great enterprise has its *locale* at Bacharach on the Rhine, or is in any way connected with the pleasant game of Baccarat as played at the Jockey Club. Table-glass, chandeliers, plain-coloured and mounted glass, engraved and encrusted glass, and fancy articles, globes of enamel, imitations of precious stones, cast, sheet, and other glass, enamelled vases, jars, goblets, and flower-stands—of all these the Baccarat Company make a splendid show. You may buy a pair of candelabra here at the rate of 25,000 francs a piece, and a very pretty vase, to hold your roses and geraniums, for 3f. 50c. The Baccarat will suit all purses and most tastes. Some of their chandeliers are gorgeous; heavy with countless drops; the cluster so thick, so rich, that you almost fancy that you are strolling in some Italian vineyard in the month of September, and the innumerable grapes dangling from the trellises have become magically vitrified.

The St. Louis table glass, particularly the cast specimens mounted in wooden or bronze gilt frames, is likewise very remarkable. The moulded glass of the Cristallerie de Lyon is very elaborate, but somewhat old-fashioned. The mirrors and silvered glass of H. Brossette and Co., of Paris; the enamels and imitations of gems of J. L. B. Soyer; the Venetian mirrors of A. A. Ullman, and in particular the glass frames—although personally I dislike a glass frame as much as I do a gilt painting—of L. V. Gesta, of Toulouse, are all very worthy of notice. Of the ecclesiastical stained glass, both in the French and other departments, I shall speak hereafter. C. Leveque, too, of Beauvais, has a noticeable show of flat and embossed glass frames for mirrors, sufficiently Venetian in fashion and admirable in execution. Glass frames are growing very fashionable in France—what is there that has not its turn of fashion in this country?—but will hardly, I fear, become fashionable in England. We are, after all, a Conservative people; and it is as received a maxim with us that our pier glasses should have gilt frames as that our wives should wear gold wedding rings. The French would change their conjugal fashions as quickly as they change their skirts. You would not be surprised to see on Madame Benoiton's marriage finger a circlet of leather, or of straw, or of peagreen beads, or of peacocks' eyes, if she could get those orbs dried and set.

The Austrian and Bohemian glass demands a somewhat more extended notice than I have yet bestowed on that very prominent manufacture of South Germany. As a traveller who for the last eighteen months has been incessantly wandering up and down Europe, and in whose memory the crystal glories of the Graben and the Kärnthnerstrasse at

Vienna and the Zeil at Frankfort are yet fresh, I must confess that there is nothing in the way of Austrian or Bohemian glass in the Champ de Mars which has surprised me to any extraordinary extent. It is not my fault if, like M. Choufleury above quoted, I have been *chez lui* in every European capital, have had my fill of shopping, and have seen almost every show which the world's showman can beat a gong or cry "walk up" about. I am sure I wish that this were not the case. I should bring then to my task more freshness, more *naïveté* of appreciation; and, although I might occasionally over-estimate a thing, I should not undervalue it because to me it was old and stale. Do you know the Bohemian glass —blazoned, florid, luxurious, iridescent?

Its prime object, as you know, is to look as unlike glass as is possible. It is glass gone to a fancy dress ball, or a masquerade at the Grand Opera. It imitates anything and everything—malachite and cornelian, ruby and emerald, porcelain and Byzantine enamel, gold, silver, and aluminium, mother-of-pearl, Japanese lacquer, Tunbridge ware, Spa wood, and heraldic coach-painting. Mr. Thackeray, talking of Bohemia figuratively, said that Prague was one of the most picturesque cities in the world. Physically, too, the Czech capital is wondrously quaint—full of colours and strange costumes, more than half mediæval, and odd particoloured Gipsy ways. Where in Europe, either, will you find civilization wearing so picturesque a garb as in the Prater at Vienna? Almost every class of society has its characteristic dress, and almost every dress is gay and glowing with many tints. Austrian and Bohemian glass partake of the "fancy" aspect of the realm of Franz Joseph. There is a bit of the mediæval knight and a morsel of the merry-Andrew, and a considerable admixture of Hungarian hussars and Styrian notables, and Slavonic shepherds, with any number of sylphides from the opera and Greeks and Turks from the coffee-houses about Leopoldstadt; and the entire result is Austrian life—and Austrian glass, if you will—not very substantial, but eminently bright and gay and picturesque.

Returning to England, it will be remembered that I accorded to Mr. Dobson the first place as an engraver on glass. Justice compels me to record that in the case of Pellatt and Co.—a very small and unpretending one—there is an assemblage of articles in cut and engraved glass, almost every one of which, both as regards material, design, and execution, is a gem. James Greene, of Upper Thames Street, has a large show of lustres and table glass, excellently worked and finished. To the artistic excellence of the engraved and cut ware of Millar, of Edinburgh, I have already paid some tribute. The show of Henry Greene, of King William Street, in lustres—some of large size and most elaborate in design— in cut-glass services, engraved goblets, &c., is throughout splendid. Some exquisite specimens of porcelain—chiefly from the works of the Royal Worcester Company—may also be seen on his stand; with the delightfully painted service executed for the Countess of Dudley, and lent for the purpose of the Exhibition. Messrs. Defries and Son excel in "large pieces"—pardon me the repetition of a technical term. They show a colossal candelabrum, sparkling like a tower of light, and destined, I suppose, for the divan of some potent Indian Rajah. They have also some large chandeliers glowing with Oriental hues, and obviously intended to suit the somewhat gaudy Hindoo taste, and arranged for either gas or candle; and a variety of table glass, of capital form and finish. Cheapness and durability, as well as splendour, would seem to be within the attributes of the Messrs. Defries, who can give you an elegant three-light lustre for fifty shillings, and go upwards and upwards to three and five hundred pounds.

XV.

JEWELLERY AND GOLDSMITHS' WARE.

THIS world is best seduced by glitter, and always will be
—of that there can be no doubt.   Jewels glitter more brightly
than gold, and are consequently even more powerful agents
in the corruption of mankind than money itself.   There have
been politicians who have refused treasure, rank, and place,
but who have ratted incontinently when a jewelled garter was
dangled before their eyes.   "I never knew but one woman,"
remarked the wily statesman who boasted that "every man
had his price"—"I never knew but one woman," said Sir
Robert Walpole, "whom I could not bribe with money.   It
was Lady S——, *and she took diamonds.*"   A Universal
Exhibition is nothing without a blaze of jewellery.   You cannot
have too much of it.   Its success with the million is certain.
"Oh, if you please," hoarsely whispers a mysteriously-cloaked
person, of unmistakably ticket-of-leave aspect, to an affrighted female in one of Mr. Leech's vignettes, *àpropos* of
the Exhibition of '51, "could you tell a cove the way to the
Queen of Spain's jewels?"   But it was not only burglars *in
posse* who longed to find their way to the *joyeria* of Isabel
Segunda.   The whole world of Hyde Park flocked to those
dazzling caskets; and a squad of policemen was needed to

keep the crowd at a respectful distance from the gilt birdcage which held the Koh-i-noor. So great was the frenzy excited by the last-named gewgaw, that imitations in glass, of the precise form and weight of the priceless " mountain of light,' but which were not intrinsically worth two shillings, were sold for as many guineas. It was the glitter that entranced the public; and the finest statue that Buonarotti ever wrought, the choicest picture that Sanzio ever painted, will never command a tithe of the admiration bestowed on Belinda's diamonds, "which Jews might kiss and infidels adore." Gems will never go out of fashion. They were fashionable in the days when the Hebrew women wore them on 'their " round tires like the moon ;" and a lady with ten thousand pounds' worth of diamonds on her wrists or round her neck may laugh to scorn, now, the milliner who should tell her that her sleeves are obsolete or her skirts *rococo*. Diamonds and cashmere shawls are the only things that are always *à la mode*. Barren, indeed, would be the Exhibition without a "blaze of triumph " in the way of jewels. They are like the stock-pieces of which theatrical managers bethink themselves when the exchequer is running low—old favourites which are sure to "draw," certain to command a "run," which can be warranted to " bring the swells into the stalls." "*Affichez les Mémoires !*" the French manager was accustomed to say, when the *caissier* brought him a beggarly account of empty boxes. He knew that the dramatized version of Frederick Soulié's *Mémoires du Diable* would always secure a tolerable house. A Jacquard loom, a Stephenson's locomotive, a Howe's sewing-machine, a Stanhope press, a Volta's pile, a Galvani's battery, a Daguerre's silvered plate, a Talbot's flask of collodion, have had far more influence on civilization than all the pearls that Cleopatra could have dissolved in vinegar, than all the rubies that Augustus the Strong lavished on his concubines, than all the emeralds with which the Arab soldans encrusted the shrine of the Mosque of Granada, than all the diamonds that ever came from Ind or Brazil—that were ever cut by the Amsterdam lapidaries—that merchants ever chaffered over with kings and emperors; but the world passes by the loom, the locomotive, the sewing machine, the printing press, with a "Dear me!" or a "Very wonderful, I dare say!" and, suppressing a rising yawn, hastens away to fasten down like bees on the glass case which holds the Duchess of Sennacherib's wedding jewels, or goes into ecstasies over the Duke of Pampotter's jewelled hawk; or Mr. Grimgribber's blue brilliant, or Sir Isaac Ingot's sapphire as big as a plover's egg, or the late Prince Evercrazy's diamond breeches. And I do not quarrel with the world for doing so. Give me the Koh-i-noor, and keep it dark, and I will turn Jew to-morrow.

There is a truly magnificent display both of jewellery and goldsmith's ware in the Paris Exhibition. Of what we call "plate" and "precious stones," the French *orfévrerie, joaillerie,* and *bijouterie,* and the Germans *gold-und-silber-geschmieds-waare,* and *edelsteine,* there is a show in which richness of material is only equalled by skill and delicacy in workmanship. Among the French exhibitors are the world-famous firms of Christofle, of Froment-Meurice, of Odiot, of Belleau, of Luquet, of Fontana, and of Beaugrand. Among the English are Phillips, of Cockspur Street, Aubert and Linton, Elkington, Emanuel, Howell and James, Hunt and Roskell, Hancock, Randel, and Watherston, of London. There are Turkish jewellers both from Constantinople, from

Trebizond, and even from the inacessible Mecca. China has sent us some articles in filigree silver. Carlini of Milan, Cortelazzo of Vicenza, Somni of Cremona—whence, by the way, there is not a single fiddle—Pane of Naples, and the well-nigh unapproachable Castellani of Rome—one of the most artistic and the dearest tradesmen in the world—represent Italy. Even non-manufacturing Columbia sends some very sumptuous plate from the Broadway store of the Messrs. Tiffany. The name of the Austrian and Prussian jewellers and goldsmiths is legion. Holland has *affichéd* but one exhibitor, Mr. M. E. Coster, of Amsterdam, who showed the productions of diamond mines, and successive stages of lapidary work, in an *annexe* constructed for the purpose in the park. The Dutch lapidary's workshop was one of the greatest curiosities of the Exhibition. Portugal, Sweden, and Denmark send some beautiful specimens of gold and silver filigree, and plates beaten thin and perforated. Active little Tunis is, as usual, to the fore with Arab goldsmiths' work, rather barbarous, but very pretty; and Russia, whose entire display in every branch is, like herself, grandiose, arrogant, and astounding, has decked herself as richly in gold and gems as Queen Esther before Ahasuerus. Even his Eminence Cardinal Antonelli, Minister Secretary of State for the Holy See, appears as an exhibitor in the department of jewellery; but with commendable modesty and humility—the humility inseparable from Princes of the Church—his Eminence has eschewed the precious metals, and shows only a beautiful cameo cut out of rock crystal.

It will thus be seen that there is enough jewelled and golden and silver sumptuousness in the Champ de Mars to create the anticipated "draw," and to command the indispensable "run." You can hardly get near the jewellery cases. Young ladies clasp their hands and wave their parasols in the agitation of their emotion. A salmon at Grove's, a fine quarter of lamb at Slater's, a haunch of venison at Tucker's, a *botte* of asparagus at the Trois Frères, a *pâté de foie gras* at Chevet's, a *hure de sanglier* at Potel and Chabot's, an Easter egg at Siraudin's—the admiration excited by delicacies such as these is meagre and colourless in comparison with the spasmodic appreciation of the great world for the jewellery and goldsmiths' ware in the Exhibition. But it behoves the critic, I take it, to do something more than clasp his hands, or turn up his eyes, or smack his lips, or murmur "Pretty, pretty, pretty!" like Sir Joshua Reynolds over an amateur drawing. It is his business not only to draw attention—without distinction of country—to the works which he judges to be the best both for conception and for finish, but to endeavour to discern, by reflection and by comparison, what progress, if any, has been made in an art whose professors—albeit they are often ranked with tradesmen—are, in reality, artists of a very high order; and to establish whether the nineteenth century, so far beyond all preceding ages in the crafts which can ennoble, or refine, or usefully serve humanity, has kept pace with its predecessors—has advanced or has retrograded in the pursuit of an industry that may not tend to any distinctly utilitarian purpose, but will nevertheless always extort our admiration, both for its intrinsic beauty and for the extrinsic taste and feeling it fosters.

Universal Exhibitions may be said to have a dual aim. One is sentimental, the other practical. On the sentimental side an immense deal of fine writing has been lavished; but contemporary History—as the Prussian President told the

Polish deputies the other day—has seemed rather disposed to " pass to the order of the day " on the fine sentimentalities uttered. "Congresses of peace," "brotherhood of nations," "friendly emulation, the only honourable rivalry," et cetera, et cetera, et cetera : of the making of essays on this theme there has been no end; and I have made as many as my neighbours. The "order of the day " to which history has passed has amounted to this—that each of the Universal Exhibitions within our own generation has been closely followed by a bloody and destructive war. The funeral baked meats of '51 furnished forth the marriage table of the *coup d'état*. The Exhibition of '55 was held while the three most powerful nations in Europe were engaged in deadly conflict, and four years afterwards came Magenta and Solferino. The Peace Congress of '62 led very gracefully up to Königgratz and Custozza in '66; and in '67, while all nations are supposed by the sentimental to be basking in the sunshine of peace and amity in the Champ de Mars, there is a prevailing smell of saltpetre in the air, and the rumblings of a coming earthquake are distinctly audible. So much for the sentimental aspect of Universal Exhibitions. The practical side is a little more tangible. At each one of these recurring Olympiads, artists, manufacturers, and social economists are enabled to gauge and measure how much has been done towards the development of material and the perfection of execution in most human industries since the last time the nations met. There is not much "fraternity" in the matter; for we are generally anxious to borrow one another's tools, and crib one another's patterns. Very often we forge our brother's trade-mark, and under most circumstances we strive to undersell our brother, and get his trade away from him.

And, indeed, I see no harm in such a system of procedure
for if it be considered quite in accordance with Christianity
and civilisation that we should go to war, and cut our
brother's throat in the tented field, why shouldn't we also cut
his throat in the way of business?   Still, for the purpose of
measurement, a Universal Exhibition is invaluable. Measurement implies inquiry; measurement implies the accumulation
of facts, and the consequent acquisition of knowledge;
measurement implies contrast and comparison; measurement
implies, in the end, Understanding. If you measure a thing
you will afterwards be inclined to weigh it; and in putting a
thing in and out of the scale you will have the priceless
advantage *of seeing both its sides.* Measurement, in fine, is
the irreconcilable foe to dogmatism, which sees but one side
to anything.

To measure accurately, you must have a standard. Am I
wrong in taking for my standard for measuring the advance
made by the moderns in the art of the goldsmith and jeweller
a certain stand, roofed in with glass, and revolving on a pivot
in one of the saloons of the Museo Gregoriano in the Vatican
at Rome? The compartments into which this stand is
divided contain a surprising collection of ornaments, most of
which were found in a single tomb at Cervetri. There are
gold and silver filigrees, chaplets for the priests and magis-
trates, diadems, fillets composed of wreaths of ivy, myrtle,
and olive, necklaces, bracelets, armlets of every variety of
pattern—some elastic, some of the form of a serpent, single
or coiled. There are elaborately-worked "*bullæ*" or amulets.
There are "*fibulæ*" of exquisite workmanship. There are
earrings of every variety of pattern. It has been said, by a
competent critic, "the filigree work of Genoa, the chains of

Venice and Trichinopoly, do not approach these works in minuteness of execution, and rarely approach them in taste ;" that "the models for female ornaments might be worn as novelties in any modern court of Europe ;" that "the brooches for fastening the toga, the chains for the neck, the lace, the embossing, the rings set with precious stones, or jointed, or composed of *scarabæi*, set on swivels, are so beautiful and minute in workmanship, that modern skill can produce few specimens of equal delicacy." This criticism is the unexaggerated truth; but it is also as true that the jewellery so highly praised is—setting dusky old Egypt on one side—the very oldest in the world. The revolving stand in the Gregorian Museum is full of the famous Etruscan jewellery. Do all we can—plaster butter upon bacon, and lard on the top of all—put gold on silver, and gems on both, and we cannot surpass, even if we equal, either in richness or in luxury of execution, the art-workmanship of the mysterious race whom the Romans called Etrusci and the Greeks Tyrrheni, who came from nobody knows where, and overran Italy nobody knows when—if it was not about fifty years before the war of Troy, whenever that may have been; and who, in the time of Tarquinius Priscus—whenever *that* was— had utterly disappeared as one of the leading peoples of Italy. The beauty of their jewellery is fabulous, and the history of the Etruscans themselves is a fable, and antiquaries knock their heads against Etruscan remains in scientific despair; and of their language, chiefly preserved to us through their sepulchral inscriptions, we know absolutely nothing, beyond the theory that "Lar" means king, that "Larne" is the name of Etruria itself, and the oft-repeated "Ril avil" a notification that some Etruscans departed lived a number of years—how many years none can tell. It is one of the most extraordinary phenomena connected with this cloudy people that, although their alphabet has been partially deciphered, their language remains unintelligible. It resembles neither Hebrew, Latin, Sanscrit, nor Celtic. Some of the letters are Greek and others Pelasgic; but the Greek letters have no reference to Greek sounds. So much for the Etruscans, who have bequeathed to us a number of keys without locks, and bridles and stirrups without horses, and the solutions of conundrums without the conundrums themselves, and whose jewellery and goldsmiths' ware, with the aid of a little rubbing up with a tooth-brush and some whiting or vermilion in powder, might be laid out in the morocco and satin-lined cases of our Bond Street and Boulevard jewellers, and command immense prices as the latest novelties from the *ateliers* of London and Paris.

I set Egypt on one side. Albeit her civilisation may be centuries older than that of the Etruscans, the gems and goldsmiths' ware which Egyptian sepulchres have given up have an interest only as rarities and curiosities. Beyond the form of the *scarabæus* ornament—which is not peculiar to Egypt—the designs of Egyptian jewellery are heavy and monotonous, and the workmanship is "clumpy" and uncouth. There is a stolid brutishness, a "chewing-the-cud" kind of immobility, in the decorative art as in the religion of Egypt. They seem to be always worshipping apes, and onions, and cheese. The Chinese, who may be as old as the Egyptians, if not older, marvellous carvers and painters and enamellers as they have always been, have never done anything notable in the way of jewellery properly so called; and even in India, the land of gems and precious ornaments *par excellence*, precious stones have been from time immemorial execrably cut—sometimes worn half cut, or even wholly uncut, and sometimes pierced through the centre and strung in chains like schoolboys' trophies of birds' eggs. Trichinopoly has gained deserved renown for its gold work; but Trichinopoly, like Venice, was indebted for its gold cunning to Arab workmen—the same workmen who, learning the secrets of the goldsmith's art from the Syrians, who learnt them from the Phœnicians, carried proficiency in the making of chains and filigree to Spain, to Malta, to Sicily, and to Genoa. To this day the towns on the Barbary seaboard are inhabited by artisans skilled in the production of precisely the same ware which in commerce goes by the name of " Genoese " and " Maltese."

How, then, do we stand, in regard to any advance in goldsmith's work? I take it that advance on the ancient or Etruscan model is all but impossible; because artistic goldsmithery cannot be done by steam (advertisements of machine-made jewellery notwithstanding); because goldsmithery, pure and simple, cannot be affected by mechanical or chemical discovery; because tiny hammers and chasers and gravers and burnishers have been used ever since the time of Tubal Cain; because, finally, excellence in this art depends al ost entirely on human industry, skill, patience, and taste; and taste, patience, skill, and industry were as much the gifts of God to the peoples who lived five thousand years ago as they are now to us. Yes; you may make a brooch or a bracelet by machinery; of that I have no doubt. I saw some brooches the other day, electro-gilt, and the centres enamelled, on iron, by Baugh's patent, which could be made to the extent of thousands a day at Birmingham, and sold wholesale at twopence-halfpenny a-piece. Earrings may be cast by the ton weight, or watch-chains twisted by steam power, or bracelets cut out with circular saws, of course—just as copies of oil paintings and watercolour drawings may be printed by steam; but the results of all these do not amount to anything artistic, nor would twenty tons weight of them weigh a feather in the scale of taste against a *bulla* or a *fibula* from the Etruscan Museum. I do not see that it is possible to do anything in goldsmith's work superior to what was done in Etruria in the inscrutable past; nor is it possible to give higher eulogy to, perhaps, the five best firms of goldsmiths in the world—Christofle, Froment-Meurice, Castellani, Hunt and Roskell, and Phillips—than to say that they keep the Etruscan models fully in view, and that they have imitated the choicest productions of antiquity with consummate skill and complete success. They have not done better than the ancients, simply because it is not in human nature to do so. It may be admitted, however, that although their work cannot be finer than the Etruscan, it far surpasses in minuteness of finish the Roman jewellery of the Imperial period, samples of which are continually turning up in the ruins of villas or in the bed of the Tiber. These as models are eagerly copied, but modern skill improves on their execution. Modern skill *cannot* improve on the Etruscan; and in the specimens which are extant, it behoves us to remember that they must have once been even more marvellously beautiful than they are now. Gold is imperishable, but it will tarnish; and trinkets, although kept snug in a sepulchre for three or four thousand years, will lose something by the imperceptible but sure attrition of time. You never saw such " old-looking gold " as in the Etruscan ornaments. They are worn thin. They have a weird and shadowy look, like the keys of an old piano, like the colours of old tapestry. They have not been tossed about by time ; they have not been touched ; they have contained in themselves no elements of decay ; but they were antique ornaments perchance, old heirlooms, old and time-worn trinkets when they were first placed in' the tomb beside the warriors and matrons of Etruria.

In the cutting and the setting of gems, the moderns have clearly the advantage of the ancients. By cutting I mean, of course, the mere lapidary's work, and not the engraving of precious stones. Intaglio is an art still pursued in Italy, but poorly patronised and more poorly paid. In France and England, since the introduction of the prosaic "gummed envelopes," seal engraving has gradually declined, and it is to be hoped that we shall not require a new Great Seal for many, many years to come. "Die-sinking" has become a purely mechanical process; and it is to be questioned whether any modern engraver of gems could approach—I will not say the Greek or Roman models, but the famous diamond ring worn by Charles the First, and on whose topmost facet were cut the royal arms of England. We cut jewels better, and set them better, however, every year.

Were I a judge, or a juror, or a connoisseur—and I am not one of the three—I should give my award thus. For monumental goldsmith's work, colossal services of plate, trophies, cups, and so forth, Christofle of Paris, and Hunt and Roskell of London, should have the prize. If I were a king, these gentlemen should make my crown—the mere circlet and bows, and orb and star. Hancock should set the crown with gems ; he has the most splendid stock of jewels in the world. My regalia should be enshrined in a casket made by Froment-Meurice. Elkington should emboss the plateau of silver on which my sword and sceptre were laid. But Phillips of London, and Castellani of Rome, should cover my Queen from head to foot with bracelets and rings, necklaces and tiaras, earrings and brooches, chains, girdles, and stomachers of the real goldsmith-jeweller's work—the exquisite combination of the noble material with the nobler artistic handicraft.

The diamond is the queen of gems, and in diamonds the French exhibitors in the Champ de Mars make a display remarkable at once by its opulence and its exquisite taste. It is hardly to be disputed that, so far as regards the arrangement and setting of gems, and their artful combination so as to derive the greatest advantage from juxtaposition, the French *joailliers* bear away the bell from every other nation in the world. Such enormous gems as Mr. Hancock can produce from his private casket—the casket meant only for the inspection of millionaires and crowned heads—they do not, perhaps, possess; but they make far more of the resources at their command, and the result of their work is a dazzling magnificence far greater than has been attained elsewhere. You may have seen in Turkey a chibouk-stem or a saddle-cloth, or a scimitar-hilt or a pair of holsters, literally encrusted with diamonds; but for the matter of the effect they produced they might as well have been so many glass beads. So is it with the Imperial crown of Russia, which is one mass of diamonds without golden circlet and arches, and yet fails to dazzle; and there is even one of the Czar's state carriages, the very panels of which are adorned with brilliants, of small size certainly, but still brilliants, but which, through their clumsy arrangement, are of no more account than chandelier drops. It is but just to say that both the crown and 'the carriages are nearly a century old, and that the modern Russian jewellers have been very successful in mounting such trifles as rings, pins, and brooches. Some of the presents dispensed from the treasury of the Hermitage to celebrated singers and dancers who have performed before the Imperial Court have been worthy to vie with the best works of the Palais Royal and the Rue de la Paix. The German jewellers, especially those of Hamburg, Frankfort, Vienna, and Augsburg, were pre-eminent in the last century as jewellers; but the tumbling to pieces of the Holy Roman Empire, and the "mediatisation" of the petty princes of the Rhine by Napoleon I., inflicted a sad blow on the High Dutch jewellery trade, which seems destined to receive its *coup de grace* from the hands of the ruthless Bismarck; for how is the *Herr Hof-Juwelier* to live if there is no longer any Landgrave of Hesse-Bootstein to give him an order for so many collars, badges, and crosses of the Pig and Whistle or the Holy Beer Barrel in diamonds? Italy still holds her own in jewellery, not alone in Rome, where she can challenge the whole world to outdo her, but in Milan, in Venice, in Genoa, in Florence, and in Naples.

The standing French reproach against the English style of setting and mounting gems is that of "heaviness;" and it is to be feared that, as a rule, the reproach is not unfounded. But, "heavy" as may be our style, that of the Spaniards and the Portuguese is ten times heavier. The influence of Orientalism is still apparent in the Peninsula; and in decorating a beauty for the market the only thought with an Oriental jeweller is how much beauty can bear. Aurelian was merciful enough to allow the captive Zenobia, a slave, to hold up her golden fetters when she walked behind his triumphal chariot; but no such mercy is shown to the modern eastern belle. Her tyrant continues to load her with bangles, bracelets, necklaces, earrings, and armlets, till, as with the camel and the straw, the last brooch sometimes breaks the odalisque's back. A tribute of admiration, however, is due to the ingenious despot who discovered an additional point of vantage in his odalisques for the display of jewels, and so supplied them with nose-rings.

No, I am afraid that for elegance, lightness, and brilliance, we cannot beat the Parisian *joaillier*. Pray observe that I am not using the French term unadvisedly. We ordinarily translate "jeweller" into "*bijoutier ;*" but gold and silver ornaments may be *bijouterie*, whereas *joaillerie* refers exclusively to precious stones, and the *joaillier*, otherwise *le metteur en œuvre*, is the expert artisan who devotes himself entirely to the mounting of jewels. Of late years the title *metteur en œuvre* has been applied more specially to those who work in jewels of inferior value, or in the daily increasing department of "imitation." It does not appear that "*joaillerie*," properly so called, was much practised among the Romans. Their gems, mainly onyx, sardonyx, and cornelian, were engraved and mounted in rings. Jewellery proper came from the East; but it was not until late in the reign of Louis XIV. that the French became proficient in an art which the Italians had learnt centuries before from the Byzantines and the Asiatics. The first operation in "*joaillerie*" is the sketching in, or tentative arrangement of the stones to be mounted in the form they are subsequently to assume—be it that of a diadem, a *rivière*, a bouquet, or a bracelet. This operation is performed by means of a box or frame, in which is laid a ground of soft wax of a dark colour. The stones are pressed into the wax according to the pattern desired ;

and, from the nature of the ground, this pattern can of course
be varied as the taste of the artist shall direct.   This is called
the *mise en cire ;* and I have mentioned a matter so purely
technical for the reason that on the deliberate settlement of
this tentative sketch depends the ultimate beauty of the ornament.   That wondrous plume of diamonds you see waving
from Beauty's tresses—that superb bouquet of rubies and
brilliants reposing on its satin couch in the Paris shop windows, while poor milliners' girls strain their eyes, and persons
of dishonest mien, " known to the police," lick their lips as
they gaze on the glittering bauble—these are but the perfected reflex of the loose stones picked up by the *metteur en
œuvre,* and pressed, according to his fancy, into the ground of
wax.   The *mise en cire* is to the jeweller what the pencilling
on the block is to the wood engraver or the clay model to
the sculptor.

As for the precious stones themselves, I am absolutely
frightened—through considerations of space—to say anything
about them.   You may know, perhaps, as well as I do, that
the ancients, although they were acquainted with diamonds,
were ignorant of the means of polishing them, and that they
were actually in the habit of throwing away as worthless those
diamonds which were not naturally transparent, or to which
crystallisation had not given regular forms.   The discovery
of the art of diamond-cutting has, like almost every other
discovery or invention, been attributed to a lucky accident.
One Louis de Bergen, of Bruges, amused himself in an idle
moment by rubbing two diamonds together.   He found that
as the friction increased each stone became more brilliant,
and gradually gave signs of alteration of surface.   " Diamond
cut diamond !" cried Louis de Bergen, of Bruges; so he

straightway made him a wheel, and became a lapidary. The first diamonds he cut were for Charles Duke of Burgundy, in 1470. Prior to this period diamonds had been " natural," like the Koh-i-noor before it was given over to the Amsterdam lapidaries. The huge diamond which fastened the coronation robe of Charlemagne was a " natural," and, I dare say, as grubby-looking as a piece of bottle-glass. Nor, perhaps, need I tell you that there are four cardinal points on the diamond-cutter's card. The first is *pierre faible*, or " table," the most ancient of all. The next is *pierre epaisse*, or " Indian cutting." " Table," as its name implies, is flat at the top, with bevelled sides. It is generally a square or an oblong. " Indian cutting " is tabular at the top, but the inferior portion is in the form of an inverted pyramid, slightly truncated. A diamond of this kind is more valuable than a table one; first, because of its greater density, and next because its pyramidal form below increases its reflective power, and consequently its brilliance. The third is the " rose cutting," so called from the resemblance of the section of the diamond so cut to a rosebud *unblown*. This is slightly on the *lucus à non lucendo* principle; but it suffices for jewellers. The entire surface of the rose-diamond is cut into triangular facets, and at the summit it comes to a point formed by six triangles in the shape of a star. A stone approximating to the circular in form is the best one for cutting in rose fashion. " Brilliant cutting " is the fourth and last *taille*, and the brilliant is the most valuable of all diamonds. This method of cutting only dates in France from the time of the Fronde; and Cardinal Mazarin is said to have caused to be cut, brilliantwise, for the crown of young Louis XIV., a dozen of beautiful diamonds, which have ever since gone by the name of the "twelve Mazarins." The entire surface of a brilliant is cut into facets, but it comes to no point at the summit, which is gently convex. It is much more valuable than the rose, because much more of the original stone must be cut away by the lapidary to make a brilliant than to make a rose. There are said to be three hundred and fifty-seven distinct ways of cutting brilliants; which may prove a very sufficient apology for my saying no more on the technicalities of the lapidary's art.

Nor, I fear, would my readers have much more patience with me were I to enter into a detailed criticism, or even a bare enumeration, of the sumptuous specimens of jewellery exhibited in the French courts. There are specimens quite as sumptuous to be seen every day and every night in the shop windows of the fashionable quarters of Paris—things beautiful enough to make poor men envious and rogues desperate, but which are yet so carefully, albeit quietly, guarded by the pursy shopkeeper or the placid lady who sits knitting behind the counter, that they are very seldom stolen. With the supplementary guardianship of a *sergent de ville* outside, and of the criminal code and Cayenne in perspective, diamonds may be said to be much safer in Paris than they are in their native Brazil. There the unhappy slaves who are employed to wash the gravel in which the precious toys are found are forced to work naked, lest they should secrete them about their garments, and to sing lustily while they wash (on the principle of the grocer's apprentice who was bidden to whistle while he filled the jam-pots), to obviate the possibility of their occasionally popping a diamond into their mouths. The slave who finds a stone is bound to clap his hands three times; thereupon comes an inspector, who takes the diamond and weighs it. If it be above a certain weight the burly negro gets a gratification, and in certain cases his freedom. If he endeavours to steal or to hide a diamond, he is mercilessly flogged. With all these precautions it is calculated that one-third of the diamonds found in Brazil are, as a preliminary measure, stolen and "smugged" by their servile finders. After a reasonable time has elapsed the slave-owners are glad to compound the felony, and to buy the jewels from the agents of the thieves; so that in the end, although by a very roundabout and clumsy process, something like a balance of power between capital and labour is obtained.

You will excuse me from cataloguing all the beautiful things in jewellery to be seen in the French Exhibition, although, were I a lady, or were I writing only for ladies, you should have a full, true, and particular account of everything shown by the Froment-Meurices, the Le Blanc-Grangers, the Bocquillions, the Otterbourgs, the Brocards, the Mainpoys, the Boucherons, the Mellerios, *et hoc genus omne*, down to the tiniest diamond butterfly, down to the minutest ear-drop. And I honestly confess that, after a time, after wandering among "girandole" sapphires and "chatoyant" sapphires; among "cymophanous chrysoberyls," and "Lametherian chrysolites;" among "gmelin" rubies, octahedron "spinelle" rubies, and "vinegar" rubies; among "jonquil" topazes and "pale Saxon" topazes; among "smaragdus" emeralds and "honey" emeralds; among amethysts and carbuncles, Cingalese "jargan," pearls, opals, obsidian, jet, and coral; after all this, it is not only that my eyes begin to feel somewhat dazed and blurred, and my mouth uncomfortable from much watering; but I find myself growing melancholy, discontented, and envious. After all, no dog likes being shut up in a cookshop with a muzzle on. In the long run there must come a term to the admiration of things you are never to possess. Have you not experienced a somewhat similar feeling of inward disturbance when paying a visit to a very rich friend in the country? He trots you up and down *his* property, he shows you *his* horses, *his* dogs, *his* pictures, *his* statues, *his* graperies, *his* pineries, *his* laundry, *his* dairy, *his* rabbit warrens, *his* pheasant preserves! "Hang the man!" you cry at last; and you don't want to look at anything else that is his. Thus, also, you may admire other people's jewellery too long for your peace of mind.

But pearls and coral demand a few words, nevertheless. Nor, in mentioning the latter, can I adduce a better exemplar of proficiency in working and taste in mounting this beautiful material than Mr. R. Phillips, in Cockspur Street. Coral is a thing about which a great deal may be said, both for and against. Carelessly selected, clumsily set, and ignorantly arranged, it may become one of the most vulgar and un-sightly of known ornaments. Coral was in fact thus vulgarised a few years since in France and England. People went about bedizened with twisted sticks of seeming red sealing-wax; and coral earrings bore an unpleasant resem-blance to fragments of ginger or orris-root, or even the domestic forked radish, smeared with red ochre. One has seen a coral necklace that looked for all the world like the *débris* of a lobster strung together; and more than once an elaborate attempt to produce something like a pattern in coral has only been productive of the impression that the spectator was looking at a bunch of carrots through the small end of an opera-glass. Sham coral was made in cartloads, mainly of vermilion and resin as a varnish, and the public seemed really indifferent as to whether they wore the genuine or the spurious article. Yet coral has its *fasti*, and should not be spoken of with disrespect. *Corallium officinale*, or *Gorgonia nobilis*—the *Isis nobilis* of Linnæus—"it is a zoophyte strongly characterised by the symmetry of its axis. It is petrous, solid, of a red or rosy colour, striated as to its surface, which has a coating of 'aurora' hue, and full of little cavities, from which proceed polypi with eight serrated tentaculi." This is what M. Fourcroy tells us in his " Système des Connaissances Chimiques;" but I fancy that a fashionable lady would be possibly astonished were she to learn that her coral earrings had formerly given board and lodging to a select party of polypi. Coral has been known from time immemorial. The Greeks call it "lithodendron," the Arabs "morgian." It is fished for on the coast of Africa, in the Straits of Messina, in the Greek archipelago, and in the Indian seas. In the European mind coral is popularly associated with the mermaids' home. Those saline young ladies are accustomed to deck their tresses with coral, and to make the frames of their looking-glasses therefrom ; and if you marry a mermaid at the bottom of the sea, you must be prepared to enjoy the delights of love in a Coral Cottage. As a substance fit for the jeweller's craft, it has long and deservedly enjoyed a very high reputation. The fine and soft polish which it is capable of receiving, the delicacy of its paste, the beautiful carnations which its colours include, the solidity of its tissue, and its unalterability under atmospheric action, all recommend it to the jeweller. In French commerce there are no fewer than fifteen varieties of coral, "blood froth," " blood flower," " aurora "—coral of the first, second, third, fourth rank, and so forth. It must be vividly red or extremely pale to be precious; the medium tints are little regarded. It is cut into facets for bracelets, brooches, combs, and so forth. The Indian faquirs use coral beads for their rosaries; the devout Mussulman places grains of coral on the tomb of the departed to chase away the djinns and ghouls; and an analogous superstition impels the Italian to suspend a tiny branch or tooth of coral to his watchguard in order to ward off the " *gettatura,*" or evil eye. And Pliny, that sage naturalist, gravely assures us that a branch of coral hung round the neck of a child will preserve the infant from all dangers, and that a house which contains coral will never be struck by lightning. Finally, miraculous medical properties have been assigned to this pretty stuff.

I imagine that Mr. Phillips is not very ready to claim for his coral ware that it will cure lumbago or the king's evil; or that, worn as an amulet or talisman, it will prevent middle-aged gentlemen of nervous disposition from being accused of improper assaults on ladies in railway carriages. I am afraid that even pounded mummy has lost its virtues as a specific for ailments, that Miriam no longer cures wounds, and that Pharaoh is no longer sold for balsam; and that a divining rod of coral would not be of much use, without the aid of Mr. Hawkshaw or Mr. Bazalgette, in increasing the London water supply. Mr. Phillips has regarded coral simply as a precious substance, the working of which was by taste and skill to be largely developed and improved, and the result of his enterprise was triumphantly displayed in the English jewellery department of the Champ de Mars. No eulogy can be too warm for these beautiful specimens of art-workmanship. Coral is a section of the jeweller's art which Mr. Phillips has made peculiarly his own; and that his efforts have been unremittingly sustained is apparent in the marked superiority of the work now exhibited in Paris over even the best of the kindred objects shown in our Great Exhibition of 1862. For harmony and delicacy of tint, for richness of texture, for their faculty of forming graceful combinations with the work of the *orfevre*, for the minute sharpness yet tenderness of their carving, Mr. Phillips's productions must be seen to be properly appreciated. They present almost every conceivable variety of ornamental form, but there are also numerous specimens of unwrought coral in its pure and natural state, most delightful to view. Of beads, bouquets, earrings, foliage, and even cameos and bas-reliefs, there is also an abundance in this admirable collection. With regard to the intrinsic value of coral I am not prepared to give any arbitrary opinion. It has been laid down as a general statement that the value of the finest varieties of Neapolitan coral is more than five times that of gold. There may now and then turn up specimens, wellnigh unique for beauty of natural form or for delicacy of hue, which may be worth twenty times their weight in gold. I have heard of a pin, surmounted by a little morsel of coral not much bigger than a shirt button, which was sold for twenty pounds, and the purchaser of which has since refused fifty guineas for it. But all this is an affair of fashion and caprice. Coral can have no determinate value, like the diamond, the ruby, or the emerald. Corals, like pearls, are too abundant for anything but a "fancy" price to be quoted, save for phenomenal specimens. A little pearl may not be worth a penny, and a big one may be worth ten thousand pounds. Coral, as coral, bears out the Hudibrastic axiom, and is worth just as much as it will bring. But coral "worked up" by a Phillips—coral cut as sharply as a diamond, or polished to mirror-like brightness—coral combined with the most cunning goldsmith's work, and grouped in forms of perfect beauty—really possesses intrinsic value, and will command a large price so long as taste and ingenuity are appreciated as human qualities.

It is not alone as a worker in coral that Mr. Phillips claims attention. It may amuse the lovers of sensation to be told that he possesses a necklace of thirty-two coral beads, estimated to be worth two hundred and eight pounds; but higher praise may be awarded to him as an art workman, and next to the celebrity which he has acquired as a worker up of coral must be placed his repute as a goldsmith. In the production of Etruscan jewellery I have already said that he ranks with Castellani; and that should be as laudatory a critique as to say that Edouard Frère ranks as a painter with Mulready, or George Sand as a novelist with George Eliot. Mr. Phillips's specimens of "classic" jewellery might have been newly exhumed from the sepulchral jewel-box of an Etruscan prince; and, in addition to his sumptuous imitations of ancient Italian jewellery, he may be congratulated on the production of some very curious and beautiful examples copied from the goldsmith's work of the ancient Scandinavians. Altogether the objects he exhibits are probably, from an artistic point of view, the most interesting in the English jewellery department. Dazzling masses of gems are to be seen elsewhere—whole rainbows of diamonds and rubies, emeralds and pearls, and mountains of glowing gold and silver plate; but does not one grow rather weary in the long run of all this Belshazzar's Feast redundance of splendour? Have we not been spoiling the Egyptians too often? Take those monstrous race cups and vases—which are often neither cups nor vases at all, but huge, lifeless groups, representing nothing, meaning nothing tangible, menageries of war horses, tigers, and elephants, dead deer, bloodhounds, and falcons, Astley's-looking knights, and Amazons, and troubadours, with palm trees, banyans, and rocks—all very fine in frosted silver, and destined to form very grand ornaments for the sideboard of the sporting nobleman whose trainer has won a race for him, or for the dinner-table of the Anglo-Bengalee Curry and Rice Company, but all wholly dumb and useless as to the marking of any phase in the history of art, or any stage in the record of industrial progress. There is a vast deal said about reform now-a-days. I wish that some æsthetic reformer would set about reforming the style and fashion of our race cups and our "testimonials."

It may be that our English jewellers possess pearls as large, and of a colour as fine, as any the French can exhibit; but they assuredly maintain their claim to supremacy over us in this particular branch, so far as the number and the artful display of their pearls are concerned. They have enough in their cases to furnish forth a thousand *dames aux perles*. I own that I have no very fervent admiration for pearls, save when they are embodied in teeth, in the mouth of a pretty woman, and that the spurious trinkets known as "Roman pearls," or even the imitation beads sold in the Burlington Arcade, or in Bow Street, Covent Garden, to deck the tiaras of tragedy queens, are to me fully as satisfactory as any genuine pearl that amateur ever raved about. I delight in oysters, but anybody may have the shells or the pearls for me. This is, of course, not only ignorance, not only a pravity,

but an absolute lack of taste and feeling for the beautiful.
All I can say is that I do not care about pearls, but that there
are plenty of people ready to go into ecstasies over the
"spherical concretions formed in the interior of certain
shells, which are produced by a mollusc called by Linnæus
the *Mytilus margaritiferus*, and by Lamark *Avicula mar-
garitefera*." This is, I believe, the scientific *signalement* of
the pearl, which is mostly found in the Indian seas, in the
Persian Gulf, and off Cape Comorin, on the coasts of New
Holland and of Mexico.   Pearls occasionally turn up among
the Western Isles of Scotland, and an inimitably droll wood-
cut, in Mr. A'Beckett's "Comic History of England," reminds
us that Julius Cæsar was incited to the conquest of Britain
as much by the repute of its pearl fisheries as by the martial
desire to vanquish the people who painted themselves blue
and burnt their sacrificial victims in market-baskets. "Orient"
pearl—a phrase consecrated by high poetical authority—does
not necessarily imply that the pearl comes from the East.
In the language of jewellers, the "orient" of a pearl is the
beauty and variety of its viridescence. · The "pear-shaped"
pearls are mostly found near Cape Comorin, the flat ones off
the coast of Algiers.   Scotch and Irish pearls are, as a rule,
too milky in hue and too irregular in form. Small or "seed"
pearls are sold by the ounce, and are as plentiful as blackberries, although of a directly opposite hue. The colour of
pearls is not unalterable. They wear thin; and worse than
that, after long contact with the wrists and throat of beauty
they are apt to tarnish and to turn to a muddy yellow. I
dare not inquire whether the chemical productions sometimes applied to the skin of beauty, in the way of cosmetics,
have anything to do with this deterioration of hue. However,

there is a cure for it. I remember reading, in an old number of the *Asiatic Journal*, that, in the island of Ceylon, the native jewellers were accustomed to clean their pearls by mixing them with boiled wheat, and giving them as food to fowls. When the pearls had been about a minute and a half in the fowl's stomach the unhappy rooster was decapitated, and, on a *post mortem* examination, the pearls were brought to light again as fresh and lustrous as when they were first taken from the shell. The Romans and the ancient Persians were as mad about pearls as any "Grande Duchesse de Gerolstein" of our own age might be. Pliny speaks of two "pear-shaped" pearls which served as earrings for Cleopatra. She is said to have inherited them from a long line of Ptolemies, although, according to another account, she purchased them for 60,000 *sesterces*—about as many pounds sterling. One of these earrings was dissolved, as we have all heard, in vinegar, and was drunk at the great banquet given to Mark Antony; the other was taken to Rome, with the rest of her treasures, after her death. Augustus caused it to be sawn in two, to make a pair of earrings for the statue of Venus, by Praxiteles, in the Pantheon. After this all trace of the big pearl was lost. For aught we know, the savage Goths may have dissolved Venus's earrings in Campanian wine, and swallowed the precious potion in unconscious imitation of Cleopatra. There was another big pearl worn by the Emperor Rudolph II. in his crown, which weighed forty-five carats; and Garcilaso de la Vega—a tremendous liar, *du reste*—assures us that in 1579 Don Diego de Temes presented to Phillip II. of Spain a pearl which he had brought from Panamá, "pear-shaped" and as big as a pigeon's egg. It was estimated by the court jeweller, Treco, as being worth fifty thousand ducats. It was called "Perquira," or the incomparable. Philip IV. was likewise accustomed to wear in his hat an Indian pearl presented to him by a missionary, which weighed one hundred and twenty carats. The missionary became not long afterwards a bishop. And with all this I find it very difficult to get up any enthusiasm about pearls. They may be large or small, but they don't look as though they were worth anything; and as for their iris-reflections, I prefer those of the opal. I have a reservation to make, however. Was it not Colonel Esmond who, after paying his addresses in a most violent manner to a very beautiful young lady, discovered that he liked the young lady's mamma much better, and married her? I am in that case. I don't care a fig for Beatrix *la perle fille*. I prefer the matronly Rachel. Give me mother-of-pearl—one of the most exquisitely-beautiful of kind old Mother Nature's products.

Besides, pearl for pearl, do not the sham ones look quite as good? The imitation of pearls in France is as old as the time of Henry IV., who gave a monopoly for forging them to one Jaquin. Italy, and especially Rome, has always been celebrated for imitation pearls. In their fabrication the scales of a little river fish called the *Leuciscus alburnus* are much used. From a precipitate of these scales, passed through several waters, an unctuous paste is formed, called "oriental essence," which, incorporated with gelatine, is then introduced into spheres of very thin glass. The glass, however, is only just coated with the "essence;" the remainder of the cavity is filled up with white wax to give weight and solidity to the whole. Imitations have also been made with pulverised mother-of-pearl. Then there are imitations which are blown from "opaline" crystal, with a basis of minium, soda, borax, nitre, oxide of gold, green antimony, calcined bone, and manganese. Of late years the opal itself, in combination with artificial enamels and varnishes of " oriental essence," has been used to imitate "*perles fines.*" The advance made in these curious deceptions has been most surprising; and the very best judges of jewellery—professional experts even —are sometimes puzzled to tell the difference between genuine and spurious pearls. There is a droll story told in this regard, and *àpropos* of the Exhibition of 1862. A foreign jeweller—I will not say whether he was a Frenchman or an Italian—brought over to London a most choice collection of pearls, some real and some sham. The imitations excited almost as much admiration as did the originals. On his return to his native land the jeweller discovered that, somehow or another, his real pearls had become irremediably mixed up with his sham ones, and, for the life of him, he was unable to distinguish the true from the false. "What did you do?" asked a friend to whom he related this mishap. "*Per Bacco!*" answered the jeweller—or perhaps it was "*ma foi!*"—"I gave myself the benefit of the doubt, and I have been selling them all as real ones ever since."

But enough of pearls. You may see them of all shapes, sizes, and colours in the Exhibition—spherical, hemispherical, flat, button, pear, and egg shaped, white, opalesque, yellow, blue, grey, and even black. I may not dwell upon them; but I have a few words in conclusion to say about jewellery. To the automaton swan, in silver, exhibited by Mr. Harry Emanuel, I have already cursorily alluded more than once. This curious toy is remarkable not only for the ingenuity of its mechanism, but especially as regards the wings and the vertebræ of the neck is a perfect anatomical study. Mr. Emanuel, however, shows other articles, which command attention on more legitimate grounds. There is a beautiful gold cup in *repoussé*, made for Colonel Guthrie, of the Bengal Engineers. This cup was originally intended for the utilisation of a very fine sample of oriental cairngorm, but some difficulties having arisen in cutting this stubborn material, "oriental aventurine" was substituted. As this could not be perfected in time for the Exhibition, a piece of bloodstone has been temporarily substituted, which conveys, however, but a very faint impression of the effect which will be produced when the "aventurine" is introduced. The ornamentation is *repoussé* throughout, and has been raised from the flat gold plates by the hammer of Mr. Thomas Pierpoint. In Mr. Emanuel's cases I also notice the "Dymoke shield," made for the son of the hereditary Champion of England; and four exquisite *tazze* of *repoussé* silver illustrative of scenes from Shakspeare. Then, in Mr. Emanuel's jewel-case there is a large almond-shaped diamond, to which the suggestive title of the "Idol's eye" has been given, and which presumably formed part of a lucky bit of "loot" on the part of her Majesty's forces during the Indian mutiny. The "Idol's eye" is mounted as a "Cellini" jewel, supported between two figures of angels of chased gold and with outspread wings of diamonds. Attention is also drawn to a large diamond coronet with a pearl festoon and two *plumets* of brilliants, which, apart from the gorgeousness of the materials, may be pitted against the best works of the French *joailliers*, as an example of success in diamond-cutting. Altogether, any lady or gentleman of large fortune might have spent two or three years' income in about two minutes and a half at Mr. Harry

Emanuel's stall, and with the highest satisfaction to the
purchaser, as well as to the purchaser's friends and relations.

The Paris Exhibition was yet young, and I was fresh to
my task, and was vain enough to imagine that, in the course
of a couple of months or so, I could furnish the public with
something approaching a comprehensive view of the contents
of this enormous bazaar, when, one morning taking a walk
through that which, to avoid invidious comments, I will call
the Patagonian Department, a distinguished Patagonian
exhibitor, or exhibitor's assistant, advanced hurriedly from
his stand, and thrusting in my face a cut-glass jug, said,
with a strong Scotch accent, "Eh, ye'll just look at this
for yer paper." It was a handsome jug, very well cut;
but I declined to look at it just then: first, because I had
something else to do; next, because I thought the summons
peremptory, not to say rude; and last, because one of the
facets of the jug hit me on the nose, and hurt it, and the
nose is a tender part of the human anatomy. I have visited
Terra del Fuego since, and have looked at the jug, and said
that which I deemed just about it; but I must repeat that it
is not pleasant, when you round Cape Horn, to have a glass
jug heaved, so to speak, at your head. A few days afterwards,
traversing that part of the machinery gallery which is affected
to the display of spinning-jennies, steam-hammers, and
centrifugal pumps, from the Baratarian Islands, I was
accosted by a hairy person in fustian, and whose voice was as
the voice of a compound householder, crying, "Hoy, Mister,
coom ere." I suspect I had been pointed out as a "wroiter"
by one of the compound householder's acquaintances, and
that he thought, in the interest of his employers, that I was
bound to "wroite" a special article about his spinning-jenny.

On another occasion I was seized upon by an individual who was an agent for a new blacking. An industrial who sold biscuits was " down on me " at Bertram and Roberts's lately, demanding peremptorily to know when I was going to say something about his cracknells; and it is with difficulty I have escaped from the importunities of a French inventor of an improved lucifer match. As for patent mustards, my life has become a burden to me through those condiments. I have been waited upon at eight in the morning by patent frilled petticoats, and called up, after I had gone to bed, by elastic spring mattresses and alarum corkscrews. Waterproof garden chairs used to lie heavy on my soul, and I was fearful that if I didn't say something of photography by the new thunder and lightning process, I should have another communication, eight folio pages long, from the photographer, who lives at Tobolsk, and is stereoscopic artist in ordinary to the Aurora Borealis. A gentleman who binds books left an envelope with my *concierge* one day, with this pithy but portentous announcement on the flap, " A pretty kettle of fish—they havn't given me a Medal." What had I to do with the gentleman's medal or his kettle of fish? When to these trifling annoyances I add daily visits and hourly letters from inventive spirits who had devised means for climbing the North Pole and securing the leg of mutton which, as every one knows, caps the summit; from philanthropists who wished me to notice their entirely new process for making brocaded silks out of cobwebs, and copying ink out of black-beetles; and from visionaries anxious to favour me with their views of the intimate connection between the French Exhibition and the Grand Apostasy, the Battle of Armageddon, and the Number of the Beast, you may imagine that my path in

Paris during the hey-day of the Exhibition season was not precisely a highway of roses, and that, on the whole, I consider the lot of a tom-cat on hot coals, and without claws, to have been preferable to mine.

I only.asked one question. How was I to do it all? I forget how many thousand exhibitors there were; but whatever be their exact number, the name of their applications for notice was legion. And they all deserved notice, I have not the slightest doubt; only how was one man to give them what they desired? How was I, if I wished to avoid idiocy or raving madness, to rush from a cotton gin to a packet of darning needles, from a colossal marble statue to an improved mousetrap—from the Swedish dummies to the American pianos—from Australian gold to Chelsea china—from M. Meissonnier's pictures to Brown and Green's kitchen ranges? As it was, I felt sometimes that reason was tottering on her throne, and that a "snake valley" at Spiers and Pond's became imperatively necessary to restore the damaged equilibrium. I was five months in Paris. I was in and out the Exhibition, ever since the 10th of February, day after day, like a dog in a fair, and became at last alive to the unpleasant conviction that unless I was sent elsewhere to do something else, Lord Macaulay's New Zealander, when he visited this continent, on his way to the banks of the Thames, would find, amidst the sands of the Champ de Mars, amidst the ruins of rusty girders and shattered glass cases, and the skeletons of fair-haired barmaids, an old, old man, decrepit and imbecile, sitting on the basis of a decayed refreshment-counter, and, as he pored over his blotted note-book, piteously complaining that he hadn't yet come to Textile Fabrics or Machinery in Motion.

The worst of it was that, even in those sections to which I had been able to give cursory notice, I perforce omitted to mention many exhibitors whom it would be most unjust to pass over in silence. From time to time I strove to rectify these shortcomings; but the arrears were frightful, and I saw no chance of thoroughly clearing them off. For instance, take the highly important department of jewellery and goldsmiths' work, on which I have just been discoursing. At least half-a-dozen times I have mentioned the name of M. Castellani, of Rome, as one of the foremost manufacturers of antique jewellery in Europe, or, perhaps, the world; but I have not yet told you what M. Castellani has to show. May the following brief paragraph make some amends. The Castellani exhibit is of a duplex nature. The first category is formed of that wonderfully beautiful " Etruscan " jewellery, from antique models, in the production of which he has long held the first rank among Continental goldsmiths. The characteristics of this ware I have already described, as accurately as was in my power, in the notice of the goods shown by Mr. Phillips, of Cockspur Street. Among Castellani's special examples of Etruscan art, the most prominent is a sumptuously-worked coronal or diadem of " decussated " and " reticulated " gold—an extraordinary specimen of design and workmanship, which has been purchased by the Earl of Dudley, at the price, I believe, of a thousand guineas. I much doubt whether the intrinsic value of this ornament exceeds a hundred pounds; but there cannot be any cause for complaint in the price asked and paid. The marvellous excellence of the workmanship would warrant the exaction of even a higher price than that quoted. The second moiety of M. Castellani's display is devoted to a very curious and suggestive collection of the gold and silver ornaments worn by the Italian peasantry and lower middle classes—ornaments which are rarely seen in the shops of fashionable Italian jewellers, but which form the principal stock-in-trade of the dealers who keep the poky little shops on the Ponte Vecchio at Florence, and in that sombre colonnade at the southern foot of the Rialto at Venice. Among the queer, coarse trinkets brought together by M. Castellani, are great knobbed silver pins not much smaller than life preservers, and others, in the forms of daggers, arrows, anchors, and javelins, to transfix the "back hair" of the Contadini. There are bracelets as heavy as handcuffs, brooches like fryingpans, and lockets as big as hand mirrors. The earrings are especially exorbitant, and of amazing variety of quaint and uncouth design. For these designs the Italian goldsmiths must be held blameless. These ornaments are heirlooms in Italian families. They are handed down from generation to generation; and if you wish to see the original patterns from which they have been fashioned you must go to the Museo Borbonico at Naples, and inspect sundry gewgaws of gold and silver dug up from the city which was buried in ashes, and sold by the Campanian goldsmiths, in the narrow lane which yet bears the name of their craft when Caius Cuspius Pansa and Cornelius Rufus were Ædiles of Pompeii. M. Castellani is much to be commended for having brought together this interesting collection; but it is to be regretted that he did not add to it a complete series of *"ex votos"*— the rudely-modelled ears, and noses, and legs, and arms, and hands, and feet, which devout Catholics hang over the altars of the saints through whose intercession they believe themselves to have been cured of certain ailments. I have seen some astounding *ex votos*, but none so grotesque as that mentioned by M. Henri Taine, in his " Voyage en Italie."

Rapidly removing from Rome to Bruton Street, Bond Street, or rather to that branch of the parent establishment which occupies a conspicuous situation in the English section of the Paris Exhibition, I find that I have also been treating Messrs. C. F. Hancock, Son, and Co. with very great cruelty. Every one knows that Mr. Hancock is one of the most famous of European jewellers, and on more than one occasion I have alluded to the wealth of goods he exhibits; but, for the same reason that I gave M. Castellani the go-by, I allowed Mr. Hancock to " stand over." I now notice in a more detailed manner his productions. Some of the finest productions of the jeweller's art are exhibited at his stall, and, as regards the size, quality, and water of the precious stones themselves, even the French *bijoutiers*, chary as they are in admitting our superiority in workmanship, confess that no finer gems have been set than those shown by Hancock. One might think that the wondrous diamonds in that necklace which Böhmer and Bossange made for the Dubarry—but the Dubarry died—which they tried to sell to Marie Antoinette, but Marie Antoinette " couldn't afford it," which the Countess de la Motte stole — but she got whipped and branded for stealing it, and part of which the Count de la Motte, her swindler husband, sold to Mr. Gray, jeweller, of London—one might think that half at least, the immortal " *Collier*," had found its way back to Paris: only to the Champ de Mars instead of the " Grand Balcon " in the Rue Vendôme. Messrs. Hancock had other things to show besides diamonds. They had some exquisite suites in opals and diamonds, and of pearls, emeralds, and brilliants. Then there was a string of large-sized pearls of perfect form and the purest "orient," and a sapphire brooch and locket, which for size and colour of stones has rarely been equalled. In this case also was the glorious suite of rubies sold to the Earl of Dudley. Why, we must have been living in the days of Puss in Boots, and *everything* must belong to the Marquis of Carabas! These rubies are worth ten thousand guineas. Messrs. Hancock show likewise the rare assemblage of antique gems belonging to the Duke of Devonshire, and a cameo or intaglio said to be of "fabulous" value. Yes, a good many fables have been told about cameos. Goldsmiths' work on the largest scale is also among the Hancock attributes. There are race cups, groups and vases, goblets and tazze— precious in material, rare as works of art, for they bear the names of such designers as Armistead, Monti, and Owen Jones; but no more: the ten thousand pounds' worth of rubies bring an unpleasant amount of moisture to my lips. I reverence the British peerage; but, oh! if I were a Sallee Rover, wouldn't I lie in wait for the Right Honourable the Earl of Dudley's yacht, and bear his lordship off to my Barbary home, and hold him to ransom!

Here is one other English jeweller whose show is most solid, unpretending, but thoroughly excellent, and who should not be passed over. This is Mr. Watherston, of Pall-mall East. As a jeweller Mr. Watherston makes a good figure. He has a very beautiful coral and diamond necklace and earrings, than which there are few finer things in the Exhibition, with any number of glittering bracelets, lockets, brooches, and rings; but the mere enumeration of articles of jewellery grows at last as wearisome as "*toujours perdrix*" for dinner, and I prefer to consider Mr. Watherston with regard to his more important specialty—that of a first-class English goldsmith. He excels in the manufacture of massive gold chains. Now gold chains, I need hardly observe, are as a rule sadly deceptive things. It is one thing to buy a chain and another to sell it; and, on the whole, I should prefer, were it possible, to sell my chain at the jeweller's price and to buy it at my own. The Watherstonian system, however, as to chains is to charge so much for weight and so much for workmanship or fashion; and this, although extremely praiseworthy, is not precisely an original idea, but the revival of a custom which was prevalent in England in the reign of Queen Elizabeth, and which is still prevalent in the East. For example, I had a large gold signet ring made in Algiers two years ago. I purchased, first, a little lump or slice off an ingot of gold—seventy-five francs' worth. I took the gold to a smith, and he made it into a ring and charged me twenty-five francs. I took the ring to an engraver, and he cut on the plain tablet a certain verse of the Koran, in Arabic, to bear me harmless in all perils by land and sea. He charged ten francs. Total, a hundred and ten francs— say four pounds eight shillings, not much in these Sardanapalian days; but I have still the satisfaction of knowing that the gold of my ring, of eighteen carats Mint-mark, is worth three pounds sterling. Mr. Watherston, I suppose, saves his customers by travelling from the Mint to Goldsmiths' Hall, thence to Clerkenwell, and thence to Pall-mall, to buy their gold and get it marked and hammered into a ring or a chain; but the system is virtually the same. Then an Act of Elizabeth called upon the goldsmith to charge the wearing buyer not more than one shilling per ounce for gold, or one penny per ounce for silver, beyond the price which he could obtain for the same at the Queen's Mint or Exchequer. To this he was of course entitled to add a price to be agreed upon for the "fashion" or workmanship. I wish our fashionable tailors would consent to adopt this simple and comfortable system. A frock coat would then cost four guineas instead of six, and a pair of pantaloons one-twelve in lieu of two-six-six.

It would, of course, be impossible to apply the "weight" and "fashion" test to all the wares sold by a goldsmith. M. Castellani, for instance, might as well shut up shop at once if he were forced to confront every indignant customer who was charged, say fifty pounds, for fashion in a brooch which did not contain, perhaps, more than fifty shillingsworth of gold. But, in articles usually so simple in their workmanship as gold chains, the distinct avowal of how much is their intrinsic value, coupled with a fair charge for the fashion, according as it is more or less intricate, cannot fail to be an intense comfort to the purchaser. Let me put a case. I will suppose that you are abroad—say in a provincial town in France—and that you have been robbed, or that your remittances have not arrived, or that you are, at all events, in that impecunious state which prompted the illustrious W. M. Thackeray to pen the *Carmen Lilliense*. Your watch may happen to be a silver one; but you have a handsome gold chain for which you paid Messrs. Aurum and Boreum, of Cheapside, ten guineas. You have heard of such an institution as the Mont de Piété—the governmental pawnshop, in fact—and thither, with a beating heart, you go. "How much?" asks the governmental expert. "A hundred and twenty-five francs," you modestly make answer. The expert tries your chain with aquafortis and touchstone, and flings it disdainfully on the counter. "*Bas or*—low gold," he replies; "I can lend you forty francs." There are many travellers, now prosperous gentlemen, to whom this little adventure may have occurred; and this is why I have thought Mr. Watherston's "weight and fashion" gold chains worthy of notice.

XVI.

BRONZE.

IN Walker's Dictionary you are pithily informed that "Bronze" is "Brass." Yet a bronze chandelier is certainly not a brass candlestick. Our new pennies and halfpennies are made of bronze; but every true friend of the Protestant succession has prayed, since the days of James the Second, to be delivered from brass money, indissolubly connected as is that debased coinage with Popery and wooden shoes. If you refer again to Walker, and turn up the word "Brass," you will find that it is a "yellow metal made by mixing copper with *lapis calaminaris,*" and that it is synonymous with impudence. The genuine artistic bronzes of which I am about to speak are best made with gun-metal, or with the amalgam used at the Mint for the smaller coinage. Bronze, when it first comes from the foundry, is as bright as a new penny piece. The variety of beautiful tints it subsequently acquires, and of which the most pleasing is a mellow brown, shot in the reflected surfaces with green, and touched with golden yellow in the high lights, are due to the gradual oxidisation which takes place on its exposure to the atmosphere. Among ancient bronzes, you may tell those which have been disinterred from Pompeii by their being covered with verdigris, while those from Herculaneum are quite smooth and polished, and of a lustrous sepia hue. In England bronze, after it has been a year or two in the open air, turns black. The illustrious Charles James Fox has for many years past assumed the likeness of a master chimney-sweep; Mr. Wilberforce, at Hull, may well be called "the friend of the blacks," for he is as dark as old Dan Tucker; and the gaunt grenadiers incessantly on sentry at the Guards' Monument in Waterloo-place are beginning to produce in the mind of the spectator an impression that it was on the Sutlej, and not in the Crimea, that their prowess was displayed. Their rapidly-increasing suit of sables may, perchance, be a reminiscence of Inkermann. But the bronze column in the Place Vendôme is still unsmirched by soot, and the bronze gates before Sansovino's *loggetta*, and the bronze sockets which hold the three staffs for the banners of Venice, Cyprus, and the Morea, in St. Mark's Place at Venice, yet glisten in the Italian sun as brightly as when they were put up, hundreds of years ago.

There is imitation bronze in plenty. Formerly the greater number of imitators used an alloy consisting of tin, regulus of antimony, and lead. This alloy works up very sharply, but it is very expensive, and will not last. At the present day it has been almost entirely abandoned by manufacturers in favour of pure zinc: the kind known as the Vieille Montagne being most extensively used. Zinc, when covered by the electro process with a coating of copper, produces an admirable imitation of bronze. This galvano-plating, however, cannot be executed save at very considerable cost, and in order to produce cheap articles some establishments use a mere varnish of the hue of bronze or gold. Steam power is employed in certain stages of the fabrication of bronze; but bronze-working is essentially an Art, and not a Trade, and manual labour will never be entirely superseded in its production. Machinery is of the greatest use in the turning shop, where it really saves the workman much unnecessary fatigue. The number of workmen employed in the operations illustrated in Class 22, *i.e.*, bronzes and other artistic castings and *repoussée* work, is set down at 11,000. Some are paid by the day, others by the piece. They may earn from four francs fifty centimes to eight and ten francs a day, and even more. Just before the Exhibition, it will be remembered, there was a strike for wages among more than four thousand bronze-workers in Paris alone. The public were amazed to learn that so many skilled hands could be employed in one branch of industry; yet a large number of workmen remained who did *not* strike. The day's work is of ten hours. The annual value of the productions of the bronze trade reaches about seventy millions of francs (nearly three millions sterling). Four years ago the value of the exports of bronzes amounted to forty-four millions of francs; but at the conclusion of 1865 there was a decrease of no less than ten millions. The returns for 1866 have not yet been furnished; but, in the opinion of the best judges, the falling off, when published, will be yet more apparent, owing to the efforts made in Belgium, Germany, and Russia to establish more works for casting in bronze and zinc.

The articles exhibited in the 22nd Class comprise artistic and ornamental bronzes—statues, statuettes, clocks, vases, *tazze*, caskets, inkstands, candelabra, and so forth. There are also a vast number of iron castings of an ornamental character, but upon these I do not intend to touch. The genuine bronze trade is almost exclusively Parisian; and the art, taste, and fancy displayed in the Parisian bronzes have gained for them a special character, which, up to a very recent date, have placed them almost beyond rivalry. Electro-bronzing, or the galvanisation of metals, however, is an art developing as rapidly in England and Germany as in France. The principal metals employed in the manufacture of bronze are, the copper of Chili, Russia, New Zealand, Minnesota, and Lake Superior; but the greater portion comes from Chili. The zinc is either from Silesia or the Vieille Montagne. The tin comes from Sumatra, Banca, and from Cornwall; and, for aught we know, there may be in the antique Roman bronzes Cornish tin procured ages since by the crafty Phœnician merchants who would not divulge where their Tom Tiddler's ground was situated. In the manufacture of bronze the metal represents two-ninths of the value of the production, the rest being divided among the moulder, the founder, the chaser, the mounter, the turner, &c. Thus, if you purchase a little bronze statuette for, say four guineas, you may be certain that the metal alone at the marine storeshop will fetch eighteen shillings, which in these days, when so much is charged for " fashion," and the intrinsic value of your purchase is usually so infinitesimal, is a fact highly satisfactory to dwell upon. To be sure, you must not buy your bronze statuette in the Rue de la Paix, for the reason that, under those circumstances, the retail dealer would pop on another four guineas in consideration of the locality, the rent, the taxes, the gas, and your simplicity.

For most of the foregoing facts—excluding the concluding inference—I am indebted to the lucid official statement of M. F. Barbédienne, member of the committee of admission of the twenty-second class. M. Barbédienne, however, has, with commendable modesty, omitted to inform us that he is—far above all competitors—the first manufacturer of artistic bronzes in France, and, indeed, in Europe and the world. The modern Roman bronzists, skilful as they are, do not pretend to the execution of works on a large scale. It is upon an Antinoüs twenty-four inches high, or a model of the " Biga," which might be put under an ordinary clock case, that you must spend your scudi at Rome. The *ateliers* of Barbédienne, on the contrary, are on a colossal scale, and the resources at his command enable him to produce works of the very largest, as of the tiniest, dimensions. With two Council medals gained at the London Exhibition of 1851; with the grand medal of honour, four silver and four bronze medals—coals to Newcastle, these last—and four honourable mentions, awarded to him at Paris in 1855; and with three medals for excellence in different classes gained in London in 1862, M. Barbédienne may well afford to dispense with any further honorific distinctions. I conceive that, like Gérome and Meissonnier in painting, he is *hors concours,* and can obtain no more prizes; but public opinion—wherever cultivated taste and admiration for the beautiful can govern public opinion—will not desist from conferring on him fresh laurels for the surprising excellence of his work. The man himself is one of the Worthies of France; a hard-headed, large-hearted, indefatigable, self-reliant, busy-brained, honest creature; not to be baffled, not to be discouraged, not to be beaten back from the track he has marked out for himself. He has been the revivalist of bronze working in France. He has added a new glory to the artistic *fasti* of his country. He is a man of whom every Ruler, every Government, and every party might be proud, and yet, I dare say, there are many thousands of persons who will read this paper who have never heard of F. Barbédienne. I do not think I am overstating his merits when I say that he has done, in bronze, in France, precisely that which Wedgwood did in pottery in England.

M. Barbédienne has of course a display, and a very magnificent one, of bronze in the Exhibition. He shows a splendid coffer and goblet of antique form of bronze, encrusted with ornaments in massive gold and silver, chased *sur pièce*. The work lavished on these is amazing. The design—for it is the custom of M. Barbédienne's house to follow the good example of Adrienne de Cardoville in the " Wandering Jew," and affix to a work of art the name of the workman as well as that of the manufacturer—the design is due to M. Constant Sévin, the ornamentist in ordinary to the firm, who was rewarded with a special medal for excellence at our World's Fair in '62. The executant of the cup and coffer is Mr. Désiré Attarge, " artist-chaser." From the same designer and executant come two silver goblets, exquisitely minute in finish, in repoussée and ciseli work. Then there is a magnificent mirror and *cartel* in bronze gilt and silvered, the style Renaissance, and enriched with Limoges enamels by M. Gobert, of the Imperial manufactory at Sèvres. There are two wonderful *cornets* in the luxuriant style, known as *cloisonné*, enamelled and gilt upon the bronze, and with some extraordinary chasings of flowers and fruits. These have been purchased by the King of the Belgians. Take, too, a gorgeous chimney-piece in black marble, composed by M. Sévin, and with enamels by M. Gobert. Take another chimney-piece in the Louis XVI. style, with bas-reliefs of fruits and flowers, with one bas-relief in white Carrara by the sculptor, Carrier-Belleuse, and some beautiful decoration by M. Pernot. Take, again, the " mathematical reductions" of various sizes of the famous bronze statue of the " young Florentine singer " of M. Paul Dubois. Then there are two charming female figures of torch-bearers in gilt bronze, in the Louis XVI. style. There is also a dazzling chandelier in gilt bronze, the drops in rock crystal. As for reproductions of the best antique statues—among which is a noble copy of Michael Angelo's Moses—as for sumptuous clocks and goblets, and pedestals, and caskets in simple bronze, in bronze gilt or silvered, and in bronze enamelled and *cloisonné*, were I to enumerate a tithe of M. Barbédienne's beautiful things, I should be in peril of making this paper read like the catalogue of a sale of articles of *virtù* at Christie and Manson's. It needs not, however, to be a fanatic in admiration for a particular branch of art to appreciate, to their highest extent, the merits of such works as those of Barbédienne. Some people go mad after Chinese and Indian Jade —a species of insanity from which I believe I am secure, for jade, precious as it may be, never puts me in mind of anything more *recherché* than petrified absinthe. Some folks rave about cameos ; I heard the other day of an amateur who gave a thousand guineas for one ; *and there is not a cameo in the world, ancient or modern, except perhaps the one which Pope Pius VI. gave to Napoleon I. at Tolentino, worth so much as four hundred pounds.* Some people go crazy after Palissy ware, which to me is very nasty-looking stuff indeed, a great deal too crustaceous, and fittest to be lectured over by Mr. Frank Buckland ; but what would you have ? Did you ever " take tea in the arbour ?" Did you ever find a cockroach in your cup, a spider among your shrimps, or a snail on your bread and butter? I always think of "taking tea in the arbour," when I contemplate Palissy ware. *De gustibus, et cetera, et cetera.* Mithridates fed on poisons; but I like my tea without arsenic, and if Mr. Palmer, of Rugely, treats me to hot brandy and water, let him put the brandy in one glass and the strychnine in another. *Che n'est pas que c'hest sale,"* as the Auvergnat remarked when he found a blackbeetle in his soup, "*mais cha tient de la plache.*" What is one man's meat may be another man's poison; but there are some things on which we are all agreed as being beautiful and agreeable. I never met anybody yet who wouldn't eat strawberries and cream when he could get them, who, being abroad, did not delight in a number of the *Illustrated News*, and who didn't admire Barbédienne's bronzes.

To judge fully, however, of the merits of these good works, you should go to the bronze factory itself. You should see the many handicrafts—at least a score—which are brought into play ere such a cup and coffer as those of MM. Sévin and Attarge—ere such a statuette as the " Young Florentine Singer" of M. Paul Dubois, are ready for the Exhibition or the shop window. You should see the Machine Collas at work—that extraordinary improvement on the Pentograph which will reduce to any given size and in unfailing mathematical proportion the design to be afterwards worked out in bronze. You would think, to see the needles and gravers of this machine patiently dotting and stippling and shaving the mass of damp plaster, that it was a Machine with a Hand—a hand of flesh and blood and nerve and muscle—that it was a Machine with an Eye—a human eye of taste and justice and exactitude; and when even you have watched all the various processes of the *main d'œuvre*—the moulders bedding Venus in sand, or covering up the Horned Moses in dust and ashes, or forming a " core " for Hercules' torso to swell around—the founders at their furnaces pouring in their scalding metal, the turners at their lathes, the chisellers, and enamellers, and gilders, and polishers, and mounters at their divers tasks; when you have studied all this, you have seen but the body of bronzeworking; the soul, the spirit, are elsewhere. For the spiritual part you must enter the sculptor's studio, and there find the first geniuses of the age busy modelling forms of beauty and grace, to be afterwards copied in plaster, and ultimately cast in bronze. The expenditure on such models, where—as is the case with M. Barbédienne's enterprise—the foremost artists of France are put under requisition to furnish original designs, is necessarily enormous; and this fact alone is sufficient to keep up the high price of artistic bronzes. But the universality of art instruction, and the inculcation in technical training of sound canons of design, in lieu of the present wretched and perfunctory "drawing-master" system, would, in England at least, and in a very few years, give us a class of skilful and accurate modellers ready to work for the foundries; and, looking at what we can do, and have done, in the way of casting metal, I see no reason why we should not make bronzes as big and as beautiful—but not so murderous —as those huge weapons of death and mutilation which are to be seen in our English ordnance shed, the " lovely horrors " of which we are so very proud, and about which we boast so much, but which, to my darkened and prejudiced mind, are a foul blot and disgrace to our character as a Christian and civilised nation. People who make guns think guns; just as those Sheffield wretches who made saws thought saws, and in process of time cut their brothers' throats with them.

It is an old vulgar error to suppose that butchers are not allowed to sit upon juries. For my part, if I started a private Universal Exhibition, I would hang up a placard over the entrance gate, "All bronze Dianas and cast-iron Cupids are welcome here, but no Artillery need apply, and no Bombs will be admitted."

XVII.

ELKINGTON'S WARE.

THE present chapter is intended to be of the " composite " order ; or, to employ a legal term, the paper may be described as one of a series of " remanets," which have been standing over from several sessions. I have found it all but impossible indeed, in taking up some distinctive branch or section of the Exhibition, to make there and then an end of it. Some corollaries of attractiveness are sure to crop up, and divert me from the main line of my narrative. Again, when I have commenced the study of a particular department, it has generally happened that one or more of the countries which should have been comprised in my survey have not been thoroughly " installed ;" and days after I have delivered, as I thought my " last words " on a given subject—say pottery, for instance—I discover, to my dismay, that important nationalities, such as Spain or Italy, have unpacked their cases and displayed their wares since I closed my notes ; and I am thus forced, however unwillingly, to reopen the account. Finally, notwithstanding the painfully elaborate scheme of division adopted at the outset by the Imperial Commission, experience has shown that the objects exhibited do not always correspond with the groups and classes to which they are theoretically supposed to belong. Thus, I have found enamelled iron tablets and mosaics in odd contiguity to Crosse and Blackwell's pickles, Huntley and Palmer's biscuits, and Woolloton's hops. Why stuffed birds and cocoanut matting should be associated with steam-dredgers and centrifugal pumps I have likewise been at a loss to discern; and although a trophy of racoon and opossum skins is a very pleasing and edifying sight, and Stephens's Imperishable Dark-blue Writing Fluid, warranted to withstand tropical climates, is one of the very best inks extant—I have carried a stock of Stephens's about with me, in an inkstand of about the size of a small hat-box, during the last twenty years—I have yet to learn that there is any artistic or industrial connection between the former and Cleaver's Honey Soap, or between the latter and Messrs. Peters's four-in-hand, the very sight of which suggests radiant visions of Wenham Lake ice and Duc de Montebello's champagne; and whose general "down the road" and "Derbyish" aspect is continually prompting me to purchase a betting-book, rush on the turf, and take the odds against everything; thus completing the cycle of human follies, for, betting excepted, I suppose I have done by this time everything foolish that a human being can do.

However, pending my appearance in the "ring," I will do my best to dispose of my "remanets." The name of Elkington and Co. is the first that strikes me as awaiting a long-delayed and well-deserved notice. They should properly have been classed among the gold and silver smiths; but, as you may have perceived, I was forced to diverge into the branch lines of jewellery, and, discoursing on pearls and diamonds, to leave much unsaid that pertained to the nobler craft of the artist in gold. Elkington & Co. have three specialties,

in each of which the firm have gained world-wide renown.
First, they must be taken as the most prominent manufacturers, if not the actual inventors of "electro" plate—a material of which the introduction has conduced in a surprising
degree to increase the comfort and elegance of middle-class
life, and whose history would form a very curious adjunct to
the record of modern civilization. Next, they have achieved
remarkable success as electro-bronzists. I wish with all my
heart that they would "go in" for bronze in the solid, and
thus relieve us from the humiliation of having to purchase
the best of our bronze works of art from the Barbédiennes
and Languerreaus of Paris, and the Cervanis and Marinis of
Florence. It is deplorable to mark, year after year, our continuous neglect of this most beautiful art manufacture.
Berlin, Vienna, Munich are busy as bees in bronze working.
Even Morocco can show a good collection of bronze ewers
and trays, lanterns, incense-burners, and coffee-pots; yet all
that Great Britain can produce in the way of bronze in 1867
is to be found in a pair of doors, intended for the South
Kensington Museum, produced by the electro process by
Franchi and Son, of Clerkenwell—presumably an Italian firm
—and a "hot-water apparatus," also for South Kensington
designed by Mr. A Stevens, and executed by Hoole and Co.,
of Sheffield. We saw the other day that Sir Edwin Landseer
was obliged to go to Baron Marochetti to get his lions cast.
It is a shame—a burning shame. We can cast big guns
enough in all conscience to carry death and mutilation into
the ranks of our enemies. By almost identical processes we
could make the moulds, and form the "cores," and "run"
the metal for Hebes, and Venuses, and Apollos; and the
Birmingham gunsmith, who so daintily finishes a rifle barrel

or a revolver lock, would be precisely the artisan who, with some moderate tuition of a special nature, would chase, and chisel, and polish artistic bronzes. But all this is a parenthesis. I return to Elkington, and mention their third speciality—that of the production of the beautiful and elaborate work known as *repoussé* in gold and silver. They have in their employ the Benvenuto Cellinis and Giovanni Brunelleschis of the nineteenth century. They have one artist, especially, in permanent commission—a Frenchman, too, to our shame and sorrow be it spoken—named Morel-Ladeuil, who, if it be not paradoxical to say so, can paint with his hammer; at least he knows no other pencil. With nothing to guide him but a rough outline sketch, he will take a plate of silver and hammer out a scene of beauty and grace such as the most skilful professor of the palette and maulstick might envy. Take, for example, the Elkington's great *repoussé* shield, in iron and oxidised silver, the compartments of which embody the principal episodes in Milton's "Paradise Lost." Some of the figures, those of Adam and Eve in the centre, for instance, are in such high relief, so "undercut," or rather "underhammered," and in such bold plasticity of *ronde bosse*, that you might fancy a slight touch would detach them from the surface of the shield, or that they have been separately modelled and artfully soldered on. It is no such thing, however; they are a firm and integral part of the original mass. They, and the delicate landscape and foliage, as delicate and highly-finished as M. Leopold Harzé's terracotta leaves and foliage—they, and the angels and demons, the clouds, the gauzy draperies, the intricately foliated ornamentation, have all been steadily and sternly "hammered up" from the back of a hard metal plate. You may look at the back of the shield if you like.   There you see the reverse of the tapestry—the " behind the scenes " of this astonishing art drama.   There you see the traces of the indomitable hammering, punching, pushing, drumming, and dinting, which have produced on the obverse a composition full of harmony and elegance—charming in tone, in feeling, perfect in execution, and replete even through the artfully graduated relief with *chiaroscuro* and atmosphere.   That linear perspective is possible in high relief, some wonderful works in ivory in the Dresden Gallery, and the well-known sarcophagus of the " Battle of the Amazons " in the Museum of the Capitol, have shown ; but in this silver shield M. Morel-Ladeuil has positively contrived to insinuate aërial perspective:—so tender are the *nuances* of distance, so skilfully is foreground insisted upon, middle distance suggested, so imperceptibly does the remotest background melt away into vapour and haze.   All this is hammered out of iron and silver.   Throughout it is what the old armourers used to call " *opus mallei*," a process by which not only *repoussé* armour, but some curious specimens of early attempts in the chalcographic art were produced. The " *opus mallei* " is translated by the modern engraver as- " knocking up."   If you have bitten your plate too deeply, or cut too trenchant a line with your graver, you must " knock up " the plate ; that is, you must steadily hammer away at the back on the part corresponding to the too deeply incised surface, till sufficient metal is forced upwards to obliterate the faulty line, and afford you fresh ground to engrave upon. The worker in *repoussé* is thus, to all intents and purposes, a " knocker up," but he must likewise be an accomplished draughtsman, an adept in composition and perspective, an accurate judge of distances, and, under all circumstances, an artist of consummate taste and feeling. In fact, he should be one of those persons of whom the image-makers of Ephesus were accustomed to be jealous. When those trades unionists of antiquity discovered that any one excelled, they used politely to recommend him to go and excel elsewhere; and I am afraid that M. Morel-Ladeuil would very speedily have been bidden to "clear out" from the city of the many-breasted Diana.

This *repoussé* shield, although the *pièce de résistance* in the Messrs. Elkington's display, is only one among numerous other splendid works in *repoussé* exhibited by them. There is the "Inventors" vase, a charming semi-Renaissance composition, decorated with modelled figures in *ronde bosse*, emblematic of the various inventions of modern times—such as photography, galvanism, the steam-engine, and the electric cable, and surmounted by a wonderfully-executed *figurine* of the "Infant Vulcan." There is the "Princess of Wales's table," a large and sumptuous work in *repoussé*, also by Morel-Ladeuil. There is a tankard, with bas-reliefs of a lion hunt; and this, with its companion plateau and a vase of the same size of the "Inventors," have been purchased by the Emperor Napoleon. Let me also notice a pair of gorgeous electro-gilt vases, on tripod stands, some charming caskets and plateaux in enamelled bronze, quite equal to anything that Barbédienne has done in this pretty branch of the art, and a grand service in electro, of luxuriant Renaissance design, manufactured for Mr. W. Graham, M.P. I have never been accustomed either to qualify censure, or to "damn with faint praise." I cannot find anything to blame in the really splendid artistic works exhibited by the Messrs Elkington; but to my eulogium I add only the reservation of two modest hopes—that, when the next Exhibition takes place—whenever that may be—they will show some genuine English bronzes, not electroed, but cast and finished by hand—statuettes, candelabra, vases, tazze, and so forth ; and, lastly, that they may find time some day to make experiments in *niello* work upon silver—an art which has almost died out in France, is all but ignored in England, languishes in Italy, and though actively pursued to this day in Russia, is associated generally with the stiffest and most mannerised designs.   Let the next table Messrs. Elkington manufacture for a princess—let the next service they make for a Glasgow millionare—be in *niello*.

XVIII.

CARPETS AND TAPESTRY.

THE landlords of the gigantic caravanserai called the Paris Universal Exhibition certainly obeyed the precept inculcated in the old song. They filled the flowing bowl until it did run over. All the world determined to be merry for the nonce, and waited for to-morrow—that to-morrow which is the *grande chose* of Victor Hugo; to-morrow which may be Moscow, which may be Waterloo—to get sober again.

> Ah ! Demain c'est la grande chose,
> De quoi Demain sera-t-il fait ?
> L'homme, aujourd'hui, sème la cause,
> Demain Dieu fait mûrir l'effet.
> Demain c'est l'éclair dans la voile,
> C'est un nuage sur l'étoile,
> C'est un traître qui se dévoile,
> C'est le bélier qui bat les tours :
> C'est l'astre qui change de zône,
> C'est Paris qui suit Babylone ;
> Demain c'est le sapin du trône,
> Aujourd'hui c'en est le velours.

When we grow over-ecstatical about Paris, her exhibitions, her splendours, and her vanities, it is as well perhaps to bear these magnificent lines of Hugo in mind.

For the present it was enough to watch the joyous overflowing of the bowl. Vesuvius never voided such a torrent of lava. The Exhibition " ran over " the confines of its own palace, and overwhelmed the Champ de Mars. It " ran over " into the Seine, and swallowed up the Island of Billancourt. The insatiable flood crossed from the left to the right bank of the river; and the Palais de l'Industrie, in the Champs Elysées, with its monstrous international concerts and *concours* of *fanfares*, was only a succursal to the bigger bazaar that lay over against the Trocadero. Redundance was one of the most marked features of this unparalleled show. There was not only sufficiency but there was superfluity. There was too much of everything. Too much painting and sculpture; too much gold, silver, and jewellery; too many cafés and restaurants; too many puffing advertisements; too much mountebanking and buffoonery; too much griping and grasping after francs and centimes. If that wise and good Prince to whom we owe the Exhibition of the Industry of All Nations held in London in 1851 had survived to see the Universal Exhibition of 1867—could Prince Albert have been permitted to witness the successive development and consummation of his grand idea, it is much to be questioned whether he would have regarded with entire satisfaction the latest and, it is to be hoped, the last of the World's Fairs— the fair which came at last to resemble rather too closely the bygone saturnalia of Bartlemy and Greenwich, and in which, cheek by jowl with the noblest monuments of art, science, and industry, there were to be seen, alive, and for twenty *sous*, a Chinese giant eight feet high, a Japanese dwarf, and a small-footed lady—a Fair, one of whose principal attractions was the stuffed skin of this year's *Bœuf Gras*—a Fair whose alleys were trodden by camels from the Menagerie, ridden by

Bedouins from Franconi's Circus—a Fair in which impudent jades from the Barrier Balls were permitted to dress themselves up in turbans and Turkish trousers and call themselves Tunisians—a Fair in which there were barbers' shops, touters for photographers, wandering minstrels, and boot-blacking establishments, where, at one stand, for twopence you might eat lollipops till you were sick, and to whose attractions was added at last the exhibition for money of an itinerant tooth-drawer called Sallot, nicknamed Casque de Fer, whose claim to celebrity was based on his having been recently tried somewhere down in the south of France for complicity in a most horrible murder, but, luckily for himself, acquitted. The Champ de Mars only wanted gingerbread nuts, catcalls, and " back-scratchers," to be complete ; and in the midst of this *tohu-bohu* of vagabonds, masquerading about in fancy costumes, I have often thought seriously of putting on a false nose, and cramming a dozen of halfpenny dolls into my hatband.

The redundance, the *trop plein* of everything, became very embarrassing and wellnigh afflictive when, in the performance of his duty, the chronicler had to take up some special object of production or manufacture, and endeavour to consider it in its relative and international bearings. I wished on a given day, for instance, to examine carpets and tapestry. I found these manufactures in the eighteenth class; but I was perplexed and confused at the very outset of my inquiries by the multiplicity of things heaped together with carpets and tapestry in this same eighteenth class. I found them associated with silk and satin damasks; with "reps" and table-covers ; with fabrics in goats'-hair, wool, and cotton ; with poplins, Algerian stuffs, and horsehair ; with chintz,

" cretonne," and printed cloth; with embroidered and figured muslins; and with "tick" for furniture, blinds, and bedding. In fact, I found in this class nearly all the textile fabrics used by the upholsterer. My space being exceedingly limited I may be excused for not saying a word either about "reps," " cretonnes," damask or embroidered muslins, and for confining myself strictly to the carpets which we lay on the floors of our rooms, and the tapestry which, occasionally, we still hang upon our walls.

The First Carpet was probably the skin of a wild beast stretched on the clay floor of a hut constructed of mud and wattles or loose stones heaped clumsily together. I am speaking, I need scarcely remark, of the Western World, and, preferably, of Italy, from which nine-tenths of Western civilisation are derived. Those fierce hunters and shepherds who founded Rome, and who, even when the Roman Republic was settled and powerful, used to come down from their mountains and terrify the soft Grecian colonists of Campania out of their wits, were the very men to use the skin of a wolf or a deer for a carpet. Lord Macaulay might have added such an accessory to his brilliant word-picture of an early Roman interior—when the largest lamp was lit, and the chesnuts glowed in the embers, and the kid turned on the spit, and the goodman and his sons, trimming their bows and arrows, or adjusting the plumes of their helmets, listened with weeping and with laughter to the story of how well the bridge was kept by Horatius in the great days of old. Even when Rome was at the height of its grandeur and magnificence that wild-beast carpet kept its place in their interior decoration. What a graphic, *voyant* picture is that! Could all the learning of Bekker—could all the painful archæology in

Gallus and *Charicles*—could all the laborious researches of a Montfaucon, a Gell, a Muratori, give us in so few, broad, sweeping lines, such a satisfying glance at classic life—not the mere scenic, "S. P. Q. R." life of helmets and togas and sandals, but the life of the peasant and the slave?

These primitive carpets were spread in the dainty halls of Pompeian houses for the Domina to rest her pretty feet, or for the naked children to dance upon. But the skin became at last that of a lion or a tiger. It was lined with perfumed leather from Mauritania, and the claws were of gold or silver. It was only in the decadence of Rome, when excess of luxury had brought about effeminacy and corruption, that from the lavish East came bales of glowing carpets, and rich silken stuffs for hangings. The Roman Republican, honest, austere, and simple, wanted neither panelled door nor woven arras to his chamber; but the Roman Emperor, with his infinite dissoluteness, came to need curtains of Tyrian hue and Syrian fabric to veil the portals of his harem. Carpets and eunuchs and perfumes worth their weight in gold, and more, came in together; and then came the Barbarians and swept everything away. The early Christians killed classic art; but the Goths, the Huns, and the Franks killed domestic elegance and comfort in Italy. The Peninsula has never recovered the blow. You may curse Attila now, when you get no soap at Radicofani, and anathematise the memory of Genseric if you find the beds at Perugia filthy; and it is all the fault of Totila if the domestic arrangements of the inns at Ferrara are execrable. Carpets wholly disappeared from the West during the great social earthquake of the Dark Ages, and until the full sunshine of the Renaissance were almost unknown in Europe. The *Rois Fainéants* of France were content with fresh straw in their palaces. Even our Queen Bess's keeping-room was strewn with rushes. Tapestry-weaving had, indeed, become a manufacture of great importance in the Low Countries, but upholsterers never dreamed of laying down tapestries to be walked upon. Floors were made in marble and costly mosaic, and intricate marqueterie; but to this day Italy is the most carpetless country in Europe. It is a country on the second and third floors of whose houses you find hard shining *pavements;* and even in France, within my own recollection, a drawing-room carpeted in its entire length and breadth was a curiosity. There was, perhaps, a small square in the centre, and another by the fireplace; but the rest was prettily arranged oak planking, duly polished every morning with beeswax by the *frotteur,* who for that purpose attached a pair of scrubbing-brushes to his feet, and slid about in a *pas seul des patineurs.* The stairs of French houses, even of the best class, were equally destitute of carpet; and the treacherous slipperiness of both stairs and flooring were provocative of the most involuntary gymnastics on the part of the inexperienced visitor. You "shinned" your way up to the first floor as though you were ascending the Scala Santa, and it was in the position of a Siamese on all fours that you entered the presence of Madame la Comtesse. As for your bedroom, the floor was neither carpeted nor planked; it was simply paved with red tiles—very cool and pleasant in the summer, but far from agreeable to the feet in winter.

Meanwhile the East had, from time immemorial, been luxuriating in carpets. The Orient is, as we all know, the cradle of civilisation, and in that cradle there was probably a carpet for the baby to sprawl upon. But, as there must have been a beginning to everything, I am led to assume, I hope not fantastically, that, as the first carpet of the savage Western hunter was the skin of a beast, so the first carpet of a nomadic Eastern shepherd was the fleece of a sheep, or perhaps a loose heap of wool shorn from his flock. With natural earths he may have ruddled his sheep, or a fragment of a black fleece may have been laid on a white one, and from this may have originated ideas of pattern and colour; and in process of time the sheepskin laid upon the grass beneath the patriarch's tent became the soft and brilliant fabric in which cunning Cleopatra was shrouded when the slave brought that wonderful baggage to Cæsar at Alexandria. The point of contact in phases of civilisation is most curiously marked in the mere fact of the great Western conqueror having a *carpet* brought to him so soon as he had mastered Egypt. It is as suggestive as Clive smoking his first hookah.

While the West was sunk in barbarism, the East was beautifully carpeted; and these delightful adjuncts of comfort and luxury necessarily followed in the train of the Mahometan conquerors, who, during the dark ages, overran a portion of Europe. In the "dark ages" all was light at Constantinople and Damascus and Cordova and Granada. We ordinarily, but, I think, rashly, assume that the renewed use of carpets was brought to the West by the knights and barons returning from the Crusades. I am not of this opinion. The Crusaders brought very little back with them, either of a moral or a physical nature—one or two fresh vices, and one or two fresh diseases excepted. Carpets, with a hundred other luxuries, we owe to the commerce of Venice with India and the Levant. Marco Polo was the prototype of Liéutenant Waghorn. At a time when thousands of Italian princes and nobles were shivering in winter on the icy marble floors of their palaces, the saloons of Venice were thickly and richly carpeted, and the use of these stuffs slowly penetrated through the countries supplied with commodities by the merchants of the Most Serene Republic.

As regards tapestry, properly so called—that is to say, the imitation of paintings in woven or needle-worked stuffs—it has a strong claim to be considered an invention, if not peculiar and original to Europe, at least one which, from the earliest times, has been acclimatised in the West. There is a dim indication of wall-tapestries in the scriptural portrait of the sensuous Aholibah; but it is not defined to satisfaction. Every one knows the history of Rafaelle's cartoons; and it would be superfluous to recount how many illustrious Italian, German, and French artists furnished designs to be translated into silk and wool work by the dexterous handicraftsmen of Arras, and Ghent, and Bruges. Flanders, while it has preserved all its *prestige* in the manufacture of carpets, and still retains a portion of its ancient renown, has all but abandoned the fabrication of tapestry for hangings. The most important establishment in the world for artistic tapestry is at present that of the Gobelins, in Paris, and of the display made by this Imperial manufactory, at the Paris Exhibition, a brief notice may not be out of place.

The Gobelins Tapestry Works can scarcely be mentioned without reference to the cognate Imperial Manufactory of Porcelain at Sèvres. They are almost invariably classed together; and in the Exhibition we find the superb saloon which contains the products of Sèvres most appropriately draped with Gobelins tapestry. The manufactory itself is in the Rue Mouffetard, Paris, and here are made not only the famous "Gobelin," but the less celebrated carpets called "de la Savonnerie." The building was originally the *Garde Meuble* of the crown. In 1662 all the weavers, dyers, embroiderers, and designers who worked in the Louvre, the Savonnerie, and the Tuileries were collected at the Gobelins, and the new organisation was formally installed under the patronage of the Great King. His predecessor, Francis the First, had previously established a manufactory of tapestry at Fontainebleau; Henry the Second's craftsmen worked at the Hospital of the Trinity; and Henry the Fourth established his *tapissiers*, after the expulsion of the Jesuits, at their convent in the Rue St. Antoine. When the R. R. P. P. came back, the *tapissiers* were fain to move to the Palais des Tournelles, near the Place Royale. It is good, however, when we mark the definitive settlement of these artisans by Louis the Fourteenth in the building of the Rue Mouffetard, which had belonged to a wealthy family of dyers called Gobelin, to remember that the *tapissier ordinaire* of the Great King—a *tapissier* who, if he did not weave, saw at least to the arras being hung up in the Royal Rooms—was the father of a certain Jean Baptiste Poquelin, otherwise known as MOLIÈRE.

The first Director of the Gobelins was the notorious painter of ceilings, Charles Le Brun, grandfather of all our Thornhills, Verrios, and Laguerres. Among his assistants were Blin de Fontenay and Baptiste Monnoyer, the flower painters, and that Dutchman, Vandermeulen, *who used to paint battle pictures on the soles of Louis the Fourteenth's shoes.* Most ineffable snob! Do I mean the Dutchman or the Bourbon? Well, perhaps the Hollander couldn't help himself, nor the

King either, for that matter. It must be a dreadful thing to have to paint the soles of shoes for a living: who would not sooner be the little robin redbreast at the street corner blacking "uppers" for pence? To clean boots is a beginning, to paint pictures on them is an ending. It must be a more dreadful thing to have to put on knee-breeches, and walk backwards, with a pair of lighted candles in your hands, up the stairs to a private box at the playhouse, when Royalty comes; yet I dare say, were you or I kings or princes, we should think it a perfectly proper, loyal, and religious thing for people to paint the heels of our highlows, and walk before us as crabs are said to walk, but do not. We are often cruelly hard and unjust to the Royalties. We won't let them know anything, and then we grumble at their ignorance. We endow them while they live with virtues they never possessed, and accuse them after death of vices of which they never were guilty. The little princess who, seeing a funeral procession go by, and asking whose it was, learnt that it was that of a little duchess, her former playmate, expressed her suprise, saying, that she thought it was "only street people who died." This naïve damsel, with her Royal kinswoman, who when told that the people had no bread, asked why they didn't eat cake, *de la brioche*, may point, and have pointed morals and adorned tales five hundred times: but 'tis not altogether their fault. How am I to talk Hindostanee if I have never been taught? How was Mr. Samuel Weller to see through the deal door when he had not a "double million magnifier with him?" We surround our Royalties with an incense-cloud of lies, and fulsome eulogies and fulsome flatteries, and then we wonder at their winking and blinking, and growing purblind. We load the donkey's back with relics, and bow down before them; and then we quarrel with poor Neddy because he thinks we are bowing down to *him*.

The illustrious portrait painter, Mignard, succeeded Le Brun, and among other directors of the Gobelins have been Coypel and Oudry, the animal painter. Boucher, too, of pink nymph and Cupid notoriety, ruled the roast here in Louis the Fifteenth's days, and did his best to ruin the manufactory by insisting that nothing but his own meretricious pictures should be copied. During the Revolution little was done; but the manufactory was not wholly suppressed. Under the Empire the cold hand of sham classicism was laid upon the Gobelins, as upon every other art work which Napoleon I. could touch, and the big-bodied, soulless compositions of David and Vien were copied in the Rue Mouffetard by the acre. The manufacture languished under the Restoration and the Monarchy of July, but new life and spirit have been infused into the Gobelins by Napoleon III.

The history of the Gobelins, apart from mere dates and names, is little but a dismal record of wellnigh incessant squabbles and controversies. Continual quarrels have taken place during two centuries between the directors of the establishment and the artists employed to furnish designs. Rarely have either agreed as to the kind of models to be supplied, or the manner in which they were to be executed in tapestry. Sometimes the director, sometimes the artist gained the upper hand and the countenance of the Government. Frequently the difficulty was complicated by the mutiny of the weavers, who with true Trades-Union doggedness and perversity, insisted that only certain forms of *métiers* or looms should be used, and only certain colours employed.

It has been said of Scotch Sabbatarians that they would stop the "working" of beer, and punish the birds for singing on Sunday, if they could; but I really think that a real wrong-headed unionist, if a certain kind of work could be more profitably done with four digits instead of five, would "agitate" to compel masters to chop off their apprentices' thumbs or their little fingers. To throw some little technical light on these disputes, I may define Gobelins tapestry as "Mosaic in worsted." On a series of parallel threads, which, as in all tissues, form what is called the *chaîne*, the workman traces first the chief outline of the work to be reproduced; then with his *navette* or shuttle he weaves in the elements of colour composing the subject. As, after each operation of "throwing," he must secure, by a hidden knot, the cross thread he has introduced, he is compelled to work on the back or wrong side of his tapestry. In fact, he executes *repoussé* in the "soft." In the velvet-pile carpets of the Savonnerie, on the other hand, the work can be executed on the right side. As regards colours, the old system was to employ only a few primary tints, and to obtain the intermediate gradations, as is done in colour block-printing and chromolithography at the present day, by interweaving of the threads of one colour into another, thus producing the effect of what is called in painting "cross-hatching." The tapestries of the middle ages are, in their high lights, bountifully "cross-hatched" with gold and silver; but the original colours having faded, the precious threads appear only in the guise of splendid but incongruous patches. This system was in vogue until the commencement of the sixteenth century.

It was used more sparingly in the seventeenth, and completely abandoned in the eighteenth, when what may be termed the " Berlin wool " style came in. The colours were now varied, but were placed in juxtaposition without being blended or " hatched." As, however, from imperfect chemical knowledge, the durability of the hues employed was not equal, that which may be called " dislocation " in the harmony of the picture very soon took place. Some colours stood and others fled, and the tapestries of the eighteenth century are cacophonous; their discord in colour reminds you of a puppy dog scrambling over the keys of a piano, and they are now, as art fabrics, comparatively worthless. Some lamentable specimens of the " dislocation " may be seen at the Casino del Principe, at the Escorial, where the walls of one saloon are hung with the curious " Boys and Bullfighting " tapestries designed by Francisco Goya y Lucientes. Many of the figures have assumed hues as incongruous as those you see in porcelain or enamels before they go to the furnace: there are green skies, pink trees, and sky-blue faces; and many more figures have vanished as completely from the tapestry as faces and hands will vanish from a photograph in which bad chemicals have been used.

One cardinal error beset for a very long period this interesting manufacture. The painter executed his model arbitrarily, using whatever combinations of colour his taste or his caprice might direct. The Sultan threw his painted handkerchief, and the odalisque-weaver was expected to pick it up, and be thankful. This model the weaver was bound, slavishly, to copy. We have no means of ascertaining whether Rafaelle condescended to consult the Flemish arras-workers as to the precise gamut of colours they would prefer in the cartoons he drew for them ; but those who have compared the cartoons at Hampton Court with the actual tapestries executed from them, which remain in the Vatican, will hardly fail to discern the difficulties under which the poor Flemings laboured, how sedulously they tried to translate Messer Rafaello Sanzio d'Urbino into a Flemish Mynheer, but how often, and inevitably, they failed ; making coarse and staring in the tapestry that which in the cartoon was subdued and refined.

Rafaelle, it may be assumed, was not highly gratified when he saw what a brilliant hash the weavers had made, say of his wondrous cartoon of the Beautiful Gate. In the present day how often do we find artists grumbling over the manner in which wood-engravers have translated their drawings on the block. That which should be "fac-simile" is emasculated into a "tint ;" and surfaces whose "lineing" should be horizontal are shaded perpendicularly.

And yet the very first tapestry hands in Europe were employed on the Rafaelle hangings. In the Gobelins, at the present day, a more sensible system has been ordained. The artists are required to colour their designs in conformity with the exigencies of tapestry work. The artists complain, and the workmen too, sometimes, but the result is certainly more homogeneous and harmonious. Of course there are critics who contend that this comparatively mechanical mode of operation strikes at the very root of tapestry work as a Fine Art, and that the products of the Gobelins are no longer genuine "tapestry," but so many highly decorative floor carpets hung against walls. The answer to this is that a shuttle is not a paint-brush nor a needle a pencil.

I will not enter into the vexed questions of horizontal as

against vertical looms, of the *haute-* as against the *basse-*lisse, and of both against Vaucanson's rotary looms, which are still in use at Beauvais. I may observe, however, as a curious example of " trades unionism," that to work at a vertical loom was long considered at the Gobelins as a point of honour; and that only the sons of master *tapissiers* were allowed to be apprenticed to vertical loom work. The principal modern reforms in the Gobelins have been the establishment of a school for drawing and painting, attached to the establishment, and the delivery of lectures on chemistry, and a change in the disposition of the models copied by the workmen. Formerly they were rolled on a cylinder, and exposed strip by strip; now they are strained on a frame, working up and down in a "slit" or aperture between the flooring and the wall, precisely as is the case with the "flats" in a theatrical painting room.

The finest specimen of modern Gobelins' work to be seen in England is undeniably the sumptuous piece of tapestry presented by Napoleon III. to the Army and Navy Club, of which that Ruler is, I believe, a life member. It is in every way a favourable sample of the modern manufacture: chaste and correct in composition, grandiose in design, but purposely subdued in colour. *Chi va piano va sano*, says the proverb; and the more recent directors of the Gobelins have arrived at the conviction that a colour not nominally too staring and glowing is apt to keep its hue for a very long time, and that although always sober, it will always remain in harmony with its neighbours. The Sèvrés porcelain saloon contains, among its Gobelins' hangings, numerous pieces as fine, but none finer than that at the head of the club staircase in Pall-Mall. In addition to these, there is in the Exhibition a choice collection of copies in tapestry from the old masters. In particular, I note a superb Titian, and a wonderful boar-hunt after Sneyder.

Sincerely, however, as we may admire Gobelins' tapestry, there can be little doubt that it has had its day, and done its work, and that it is, like lithography, virtually a dead art, galvanised only by imperial subventions. Photography killed lithography, and paperhanging has killed tapestry. The halls of palaces and more palatial clubs may from time to time derive enhanced splendour from a display of these costly fabrics, but for all practical purposes the best use to which we can put a piece of tapestry is to nail it down on the drawing-room floor and stand upon it.

An attempt has been made to revive the use of hangings or panels of stamped and gilt leather ; but the employment of such decorations will never be more than exceptional.

The State establishments of the Gobelins and Beauvais produce all the tapestry used in the Imperial palaces, or pre-sented by the Sovereign to foreign potentates. The tapestry sold in the trade is manufactured at Aubusson. In conclu-sion, it may be noted that tapestry is made of unmixed English wool, which costs, without dyeing, from twelve to fifteen francs the kilogramme. Although the demand for large " arras " is, save among kings and princes, exceedingly limited, the small pieces made by hand constitute a very important branch of manufacture applied to upholstery in France. There are in the Exhibition some very beautiful samples of chairs, sofas, and table-covers in *tapisserie à la main*, among which I notice an exquisite series of illustrations of La Fontaine's fables. These, in design and colour, are simply charming, but somehow I shouldn't like to sit down on the wolf and the lamb, or put my legs up on the fox that had lost his tail. Did you ever know a lady who was addicted to what one may call " pious " Berlin wool? I have seen " Thou shalt not steal " on a hassock, and " Pray without ceasing " on a fire-screen, and I could not help thinking this mode of decorating furniture to be as unseemly as the " moral pocket-handkerchief " patronised by Mr. Whackford Squeers, of Dotheboys' Hall.

The employment, to a greater or lesser extent, of carpets—not as a mere object of decoration, but as a substantial element of comfort—marks, in my opinion, and with sufficient precision, the degree of civilisation attained by any particular country. This postulate is, *primâ facie*, so dogmatical, that it is necessary, in order to avoid the imputation of paradox, to vindicate and explain it. I grant frankly that the use of carpets must generally be affected by the circumstances of climate. In the East, for instance, and in Persia and Syria in particular, it may be assumed that there existed, more than two thousand years ago, a perfection of *material* civilisation which succeeding ages have never been enabled to equal. I emphasise material—meaning thereby that the Persians and Syrians had succeeded in surrounding themselves with almost every adjunct of bodily pleasure and luxury, from paintings to perfumes, from silks to spices, from baths to banquets. But, exquisite as must have been their physical civilisation, these effeminate nations never knew what it was to be morally civilised. Their minds were never opened to the elevating and ennobling influences which, through the channels of the Platonic and Socratic philosophy, fertilised the mind of ancient Greece, and which, through the infinitely grander conduit of Christianity, have permeated, and will continue to permeate, the West.   That the laws of the Medes and Persians should have been unalterable and irrevocable seems eloquent of the morally incurable condition of the Orientals.   They might wrap themselves in silks of Tyrian dye, and bedizen themselves with all the gold of Ophir and all the gems of Iruz; but, morally, their souls remained stagnant and incult.   That which they were morally twenty or thirty centuries ago they are now.   In their higher grades polished and luxurious, but debauched, prejudiced, idle, and depraved; in their lower degrees either nomadic and predatory, or sedentary and servile, but always stationary and hopeless.   In the West, on the other hand, the most pregnant sign of advancing civilisation is the perpetual ambition to advance, to amend, and to reform : not blindly to adhere to old laws, because (as from the Persian point of view) they are old; but, while preserving a due reverence for the wisdom of our ancestors, to revise their enactments, in order that, by bettering our laws, we may make ourselves better, and so strive to approach the Best, which is the beginning and the end of all laws, and was revealed to us, as a reminder, for the second time, in Palestine.

And this has further so much to do with Carpets, weighed against Climate, that a very superficial acquaintance with geography will make it obvious that to carpet a room in Damascus as thoroughly and thickly as we carpet a room in Paris or London would be virtually an impossibility.   Under the sun—in the regions where the real, hot, blazing orb of day rains down his dangerous gifts, it is one of the essentials of existence that we should keep ourselves cool.   Under the sun animal and insect life teems, swarms, pullulates, rots, and is revivified from the midst of its own corruption.   The leaves live, the dust is vital, the air is vascular. Nail down a carpet throughout the length and breadth of an apartment in the East, and millions of tiny creatures would be begotten beneath it. Even a paperhanging is perilous in hot climates. In a week the paste and size will begin to live. Thus, carpets in the East have always been movable. When the Sheik encamps at night, they lay down his carpet for him, and they roll it up again, and sling it over the hump of a sumpter-camel when he sets forth again the next morning. The devout Mahomedan who condescends to patronise the Algerian railway between Moustapha Inferieur and Blidah, carries with him something wrapped up in oilskin, and which resembles Mrs. Gamp's umbrella with the spine drawn out. It is his prayer carpet. At the proper hour, albeit the railway whistle may be screaming in lieu of the Muezzin's voice, your devout Mahomedan unrolls his rug, plumps down on it in the midst of the carriage, turns his face towards Mecca, and murmurs his orisons. All furniture in the domain of Islam is mobile and temporary. In a khan they give you nothing but four bare walls and a clay floor. If you want furniture or cooking utensils for the night you must bring them with you; and I have often thought that one may trace a relic of the oriental origin of the Sclavonic races—I mean the Poles and Russians, who are in reality ethnological brothers, and that is the reason why they quarrel so bitterly —in the custom which prevailed not more than ten years since in one of the principal hotels at Warsaw. You engaged a room, and they charged so much—say two roubles. But if you wanted furniture you paid for it, *pro ratâ*. Thus a wash-hand-stand was fifty copecks, an arm-chair thirty, a towel-horse twenty-five, and a counterpane fifteen, extra. I had to

make a visit once to a lady who kept an industrial school for
Moorish girls in Algiers. I came to order the confection of
some burnouses and *haicks*. I was shown into a room with
an open roof, four bare whitewashed walls, a beautifully-tiled
floor, but containing nothing else. Being set down as a
person of distinction, an ancient female, in baggy white vest
and trousers, but otherwise as black as my hat, brought me a
pipe and some coffee, a strip of carpet, and a couple of sofa
pillows to squat upon. Then one by one a succession of little
brown houris in gay-coloured jackets and knickerbockers
flitted in and *furnished the room*. They brought a sofa, they
brought a chest of drawers, they brought a hanging bookshelf,
they brought a clock, they brought a framed portrait of the
late Mademoiselle Rachel in the character of Roxane. And
then the industrial schoolmistress entered, and I bargained
with her for a couple of goat's-hair opera-cloaks and a dozen
pocket-handkerchiefs embroidered in the corners with the
name of the adored one of my heart, in choice Arabic. She
transacted business in a *fauteuil* of *moquette*, which I could
have sworn came from the Rue St. Denis. She was, from
head to heel, a Frenchwoman of the Frenchiest; and I dare
say she had not the slightest idea that, in the impromptu
furnishing of her reception-room, she was but following a
custom which may have obtained long ere Solomon in all his
glory sat among his nine hundred lady friends, and was weary
of them, and himself, and all else beneath the sun. I have
never been in India, but I can imagine how the prodigious
heat of the climate must render the thorough nailing down of
carpets very rare. That curious event related of the phleg-
matic member of the Civil Service who, sitting after tiffin
with the wife of his bosom, saw her suddenly calcined by a

sunstroke, and coolly summoning a something " badar," said, " Bring clean glasses, and *sweep up your mistress*," could hardly have occurred in a thoroughly carpeted room. The *parquet* must have been smooth and polished for the lady to be neatly swept up. It is sufficiently plain, therefore, on all sides, that in hot climates it is not expedient to indue the flooring of habitations with a compact epidermis of woollen. There must be a cool desert of inlaid wood, or marble, or enamelled tiles, and a mere oasis of carpet.

Understand that in admitting the exigence of climate, I do not budge from the claims I have asserted for the East as regards excellence in carpets. Study every specimen of this beautiful manufacture in the Paris Exhibition, and you must own perforce that the Morning Land still holds its own in softness of pile, in richness of colour, in ingenious intricacy of pattern. In short, the best Persian and Turkish carpets are still as precious to sight and touch as, in their degree, are Cashmere shawls. Lyons and Paisley have done wonders in shawls. All save the most experienced may be perplexed to discover the difference between the intrinsic worth of the Eastern and Western shawls; but to the thoroughly illuminated— and the greatest share of illumination is generally possessed by a pretty woman, who, geographically, can scarcely tell Cashmere from Camberwell—an Indian shawl is " far above rubies," and Cashmere will remain Cashmere, unapproached and unapproachable, to the end of the chapter.

It would be unjust, however, to allow ourselves to be governed in this matter entirely by æsthetic considerations and I am only adhering to my original position, that the quantity of a nation's civilisation may, in one phase, be measured by the degree of excellence it has attained in the

manufacture of carpets, when I draw attention to the sur-
prising development of this industry in France, England,
Belgium, and Germany which the last ten years have wit-
nessed.   The long pile velvet carpets of Arnaud-Gaidan and
Co., of Nismes; the Belleville tapestry of Bercheau and
Geurreau, of Paris; the *moquettes* of Allard and Crombe, of
Roubaix; the short pile *tapis* of Bulot and Lhotellai, of
Amiens; the sumptuous short-cut, velvet piles imitation
Savonnerie, *moquettes*, and furniture-tapestry of Sallandrouze
de Lamornaix, of Aubusson, in the department of the Creuse;
the *chenille* carpets of Moissel-Foye, of Paris and Abbeville;
and the *moquettes* of Liborgne, of Lannoye, all merit a length
of appreciation which the dire necessities of space alone prevent me from extending to them.   For, in this marvellous
collection of the industrial and artistic triumphs of the world,
were I to give every one his deserts few would 'scape—not
whipping, but commendation.

Among British carpet manufacturers the first rank, both
for beauty of design, richness of fabric, and excellence of
workmanship, may, with the strictest justice, be accorded to
Messrs. Brinton and Lewis, of Kidderminster, the largest
manufacturers of " Brussels " carpets in the world.   I need
scarcely premise that I state this only so far as the products
of this eminent firm in the Paris Exhibition are concerned.
British carpet manufacturers as excellent as Messrs. Brinton
and Lewis there might be remaining at home, who had not
thought it worth while to send a sample of their industry to
the Champ de Mars; but, as in a tournament, the awards of
the judges can only be extended to those knights who personally enter the lists and engage in the combat, so in this
great carrousel of arts and crafts, those *preux chevaliers* who

manifest their chief interest in the pageant by staying away from it, put themselves virtually not only *hors concours*, but *hors critique*. He, therefore, to whom the judicial task is assigned, must needs confine his measurement of the standard of goodness to the examples actually before his eyes: and he has nothing to do with the merits or the demerits of those who either neglect or decline to compete.

It is probable that the term "Kidderminster carpet" may convey to a certain number of persons of Conservative, not to say antiquated and prejudiced opinions, the idea of an article not altogether first-rate in quality. Indeed, Kidderminster" carpets have been too frequently—I will not say with how much justice—associated with "Pembroke" tables, with "Dutch" cheeses, with "Irish" butter, with "Brummagem" jewellery, and with "British" wines; as something, in fact, which is cheap and not nice—which may be fit for the servants' hall or the housekeeper's room, but is unworthy of the drawing-room or the boudoir. Your "stuck-up" acquaintance would as soon own that his port was South African, or his sherry potato-spirit from the Elbe; as that the *tapis* of comfortable thickness, but of execrable design, which covers his parlour was from the looms of Kidderminster. He swore stoutly that it was "real Brussels;" and for a very long period, in other than "stuck-up" circles, the deserved fame gained by the Low Countries during the middle ages, in the production of wool-woven fabrics, caused the generic name of "Brussels" to be attached to articles of purely British manufacture. "What's in a name?" has been asked by the greatest of poets. Poetically there may be nothing, but in trade and commerce the Name is Everything. It may take at least a century before British beer-drinkers can be persuaded that any good bitter ale can be made out of the town of Burton-on-Trent; and if our senseless Excise laws were relaxed, if we were allowed, in England and Ireland, to grow, as we once grew, tobacco; if by sedulous and skilful culture we raised a supply—however small in amount—that should equal the famous Vuelta de Abajo of Cuba; and if, with the assistance of the most skilful artisans, we perfected a cigar which in make and flavour should be equal, if not superior, to the finest Regalia which the house of Cabaña y Carbajal ever turned out of its warehouses, there would still be pseudo connoisseurs, who, *if the article were candidly admitted to be of home and not of foreign origin*, would declare that, relatively good as it might be, there was a "something" about it, a *je ne scais quoi*, which must ever render it inferior to the genuine Havana. There is nothing like falling back on the *je ne scais quoi*—on the "you know not what"—when you know nothing. I don't think I have ever seen the influence of name more drolly exemplified than in the section of the Paris Exhibition devoted to Bremen cigars. They are avowedly and unmistakably of North German manufacture, and some of the samples exhibited are really very excellent cigars; but the makers persist in attaching to their boxes Spanish trade-marks which they know to be fraudulent, and Spanish brands which they know to be forged. It may be charitably assumed that they do not mean any harm; that in their wholesale dealings they do not palm off on their customers a spurious for a genuine article; and that they duly invoice their goods as "Bremen," and not as "Havana." But the original bad faith remains, and the final cause of bad faith is that Somebody— preferably a poor man—gets cheated. If I ever travel far afield again on the Continent, and am worried by hotel waiters, as all travellers are worried, to purchase a box of "*ne plus 'ultra*" cigars, warranted genuine and smuggled, I shall esteem it as one of the highest of probabilities that the cedar casket which the *Oberkellner* presses on one with such passionate importunity—swearing by Odin and Thor that he has bribed innumerable officials and run the risk of fifty years' imprisonment and a million florins fine in getting it through the Custom House—I will undertake to wager that the first appearance of this box of cigars on the public stage was in Paris, in the year 1867, and in that part of the Champ de Mars affected to the display of the manufactures of the whilom free city of Bremen.

But we will leave Bremen for Brussels—genuine or simulated—and abandon cigars for carpets. The disparaging manner in which Kidderminster carpets, even within the memory of those still living, were treated, was not wholly undeserved. As fabrics they were undeniably well woven; their pile, if not silky, was comfortable to the tread; they wore well; their colours, such and few as they were, stood tolerably; they were, in fact, as warm and comfortable as Witney blankets; but in design, as in arrangement of hue, they were simply horrible and abominable things. Imagine the stock of a market gardener squashed and trampled down pell-mell into warp and woof, and left there to be "a thing of ugliness, and a disaster for ever." Imagine every law of proportion, every canon of symmetry, every axiom of chromatic harmony systematically and impudently violated, and you may form some notion of the Kidderminster carpet of— well, not so many years ago. The unutterable hideousness of our carpet patterns could only be approached by the staring monstrosities of our paperhangings, and by the dire chimeras with which we daubed our bed-curtains. We disdained to be elegant. We thought it "un-English" to be tasteful. I have read an article in the "Quarterly Review" in which the French are sneered at because they designed such beautiful ribbons. The British lion—noble, purblind old beast—used to account taste in art as something pretty but frivolous, after the manner of fiddling or hairdressing. Dr. Syntax in search of the picturesque was a butt for a wag. Now-a-days Dr. Syntax's name is John Ruskin or Beresford Hope. I know an old gentleman, who declares that the English were fifty years ago a stronger race than they are now. A modern boatswain's mate, he asserts, could not hit half so hard as the terrific *carnifex* with a pigtail who, in the heroic era, scarified the backs of our seamen at the gangway. The very scourged ones were stronger. No modern soldier could endure eight hundred lashes. No modern community could tolerate the spectacle of fifteen human beings strangled in front of the debtors' door on a single Monday morning, for such offences as uttering a forged one-pound note, counterfeiting a hat stamp, returning from transportation, or stealing a silver toast-rack. We were, says my old gentleman, a stronger, braver, more lion-hearted generation. Look at the port we drank at night, and the brandy we swallowed the next morning to "set ourselves right." Look at the beefsteaks we ate; the "rump-and-dozen" wagers we laid; the coaches we drove, the watchmen we beat, the cocks we fought, the bulls we baited, the prizefighters we patronised, the pickpockets whose ears we nailed to the pump! Cigars, seltzer-water, thin claret, and light literature—I still continue to quote my old gentleman—have made us a degenerate and effeminate race. Well, I think we *were* stronger fifty or sixty years ago. We must have had prodigious stomachs and pretty strong nerves to endure the outrages to good taste in our carpets, our paperhangings, and our bed-curtains, without expiring from indigestion or the horrors.

Since the unsealing of the Continent in 1815; since the revival of Gothic, of Renaissance, and of Classic taste; and especially since the greatest of modern revivals, under the auspices of the Prince Consort in 1851, a tremendous revolution has taken place in English art manufacture; and I am not going beyond the mark, I hope, in stating that there is scarcely a plate or a wine-glass, a bread-knife or a salt-spoon, a candlestick or a matchbox, a cardrail or a paperweight—that there is scarcely an object in England, of the simplest and commonest domestic use, in which there cannot directly be traced the influence of the New Birth of 1851. The manufactures of Kidderminster have participated to the full in these beneficial changes. I remember that, about 1852, a special collection was brought together at Marlborough House, Pall-mall, of essentially bad things— things bad in conception, bad in design, bad in colour, bad in execution. There were some specimens, in that House full of Horrors, of villanous carpets, paperhangings, and curtains which I have rarely seen equalled, and which, I am perfectly sure, *could not* be repeated by any English manufacturer in the present day; and the fault at that time was not wholly in the manufacturer. The most crying fault was in Toryism —I don't mean political Toryism (for which I entertain all the respect which the holder of one creed should entertain for him who holds to a contrary confession of faith), but the stupid, blundering, inveterate Toryism of our social polity

—Toryism from which a Cockney is no more exempt than is a country Squire; the Toryism that thought— and in many instances still thinks—it wrong that the great mass of the community should "ape the manners of their betters," and share in recreations and avocations which might give them "ideas beyond their station." The possession of beautiful and tasteful things was obsequiously conceded to the rich and the well-born. Be a duke, or be a dustman with a hundred thousand pounds, and you were allowed to be a Connoisseur. For the patricians or the millionaires was the precious picture; for them the marble statue; for them the porcelain vase; for them the carved work, the enamels, and the "tall copy" of the master-piece of literature. The poor were to have things "according to their degree." Not only their government and discipline, but their knives and forks and spoons, their chairs and tables and beds, their books—have you ever seen the chapbooks and threepenny ghost-stories of fifty years since?—were to be in strict consonance with "the state of life into which it had pleased God to call them." Whom has God "called" into any state, save to one—of being his creatures, coming out of the dust, and returnable thereto? And not among the meanest advocates of this idiotic Toryism was the bitter Radical, William Cobbett—who, I remember, once made a vehement attack on a tradesman who proposed to manufacture cheap and good candles for the poor, on the ground that when he was young his parents, in summer, went to bed at twilight without any candles at all, and in winter, when some artificial light was indispensable, never dreamt of using anything but a few rushes which they had themselves gathered from the brook, dipped in the fat which they had themselves skimmed from their broth. The first blow at this monstrous monopoly of the tasteful and beautiful was struck by Henry Brougham when he declared that "the schoolmaster" was "abroad." Then he, and the wise and good men who established the Society for the Diffusion of Useful Knowledge, started a Magazine, in which you could positively learn who Benvenuto Cellini was, and gaze upon a capital wood engraving after Rafaelle or Titian *for a penny*. Then Charles Knight, and Kitto, and Craik fought their good fight. Then came the *Illustrated London News*, and universal 'Exhibitions, and schools of design, and the cheap press; and I remember, too—although you must be wearying of my reminiscences—that two days before I left England, two years ago, being at Manchester, looking in at the window of Messrs. Agnew's print shop, I overheard a great brawny Lancashire man in corduroy, striking one fist into the palm of his other hand as he spoke, say to a companion in fustian, as he looked at an engraving of the "Horse Fair" of Rosa Bonheur, "*What a dom'd deal o' truth an' vigour there is in that lass, to be sure.*" Lord Brougham yearned for the day when every peasant in England should understand Bacon. I the more earnestly look forward to the day when every working man shall understand and appreciate art as this admirer of the "Horse Fair" at Manchester did. I look forward to another day—not, I pray Heaven, far distant—when it shall be no longer necessary for the workman to emphasise his opinions by an oath, or employ a rude and uncouth dialect for the expression of his thoughts; but when, by means of secular education and Common Schools spread throughout the length and breadth of the land, Cockney and Cornishman, Devonian and Lancastrian, shall alike learn to speak and

T

write the pure and sound and flowing English of Shakspeare
and Swift and Pope, of Macaulay and Dickens and Arnold
and Forster.

But even while I pen these lines, comes to me the remembrance of a recent, "commencement" of a "Working Woman's College," where, for three shillings a quarter, semp-
stresses or servant girls may learn languages and music—
yea, even, and drawing and the mathematics. And it will
not be long, I wager, before the newspapers are deluged
again with letters from "Paterfamilias" and "Materfamilias,"
complaining that their cooks and housemaids are not what they
used to be ; that they have gotten all kinds of "new-fangled
ideas into their heads ;" and that, intent upon superficial
"book learning," they are neglecting their black-lead brushes,
and their pots and pans. Would the evil be abrogated if the
book learning were profound and not superficial? Would
your cook consent to live underground, boiling potatoes and
roasting joints, if she could read Homer in the original?
Would Molly the maid consent to black the stove if she
could play Beethoven's Sonatos on the pianoforte?   Where
are we to set up the hedge? How are we to find the mean?
Must there be ever a Helot cláss ?   No civilised nation in the
world has ever yet got on without one.

> I stout, and thou stout,
> Who's to carry the dirt out?

That is the answer to—

> When Adam delved and Eve span,
> Who was then a gentleman ?

The Americans have abolished slavery, but they have gotten
the Irish, who will do niggers' work, if they are paid for it,

without cowhiding. Gin, ignorance, and parson-conducted schools keep up helotry among us; but should we be able to get waited upon at all if working women's colleges became national institutions?

There could not be a more remarkable contrast between the "horrors" I saw at Marlborough House in 1852 and the existing condition of our carpet manufacture, than the magnificent "Indian Axminster" carpet exhibited in Class XVIII. by Messrs. Brinton and Lewis. As its name implies, this fabric is a close imitation of the textile marvels for which India, from time immemorial, has been famed; but the imitation is confessed and avowed. This is no case of a treacherous simulation designed only to entrap the unwary, or foist upon the market a sham instead of a genuine article. If Mr. Crace gives us a " Pompeian" cabinet, or Jackson and Graham a " Renaissance," or Holland a " Gothic" one; if this potter makes " Majolica," or that " Etruscan ;" if " Limoges " enamels can be made in Paris, and " Roman" pearls in London; the term " Indian," as applied to a carpet manufactured in England, need not be quarrelled with. The principal features of the " Indian Axminster," then, are a remarkable richness and closeness of pile—a velvety crispness, so to speak, combined with exquisite fineness of outline in the design, which, together with the fact that the choice of colours employed is almost unlimited, enables the manufacturer to achieve an effect whose *ensemble* is not in any way inferior to those of India. The finest carpets I ever saw, which were Eastern, but not Indian, were shown me in Algeria, and were stated to have been made at Trebizond, in the days of that short-lived and mysterious empire, of which, perhaps, only Mr. Finlay, of Byzantine history celebrity, knows the secret. These Indian Axminsters of Brinton and Lewis remind me very strongly of the Trebizond carpets. They possess in the same degree that priceless feature in a good carpet, "indistinct distinctness" in pattern and "subdued splendour" in colour. You will pardon the paradoxes; but I can't print a strip of carpet in chromolithography, as a vignette to this chapter, and carpet connoisseurs will understand what I mean. The pattern of a carpet should be "distinct" inwhat are intended by the designer to be the marked and salient points; but it should be indistinct in infinite intertwinements and interlacements of the subordinate parts. There should be, in fact, in a carpet an absolutely aerial perspective—a foreground, a middle and extreme distance; yet the result of the whole should be a perfectly blended and harmonious scheme of design. The "distinct indistinct" can be very aptly remarked in one of the higher class Cashmere shawls, in the last century carpets imported from Constantinople by the Turkey Company— I have not the slightest doubt that the respected papa of Mr. Tristram Shandy possessed such a one—and especially in the wonderful decussations and reticulations of the tracery in the courts and rooms and over the archways in the Alhambra, of which, by the way, there is an astonishing collection of models on a small scale in the Exhibition. As it is with the design in a carpet, so should it be with the colours employed. Have you seen a great bouquet skilfully composed by one of the foremost florists of Covent Garden or the Place de la Madelaine? Well, every colour, every hue under, and it would almost seem over, the sun, are to be found in that nosegay. It is a wilderness of crushed-up rainbows, and yet, beyond the salient points marked by the skilful florist, according to the desire of the customer, who tells her that her colours for that evening are crimson, or white, or violet, not a single tiny flower unduly stands out; every colour gently marries with another, and procreates harmony and perpetuates grace. Or, if I may be excused for adopting so very trivial an illustration, take a thoroughly good, thoroughly studied Parisian bonnet. There is almost everything in it. Gold, silver, red foil, fruit, flowers, seeds, berries, gauze, lace, muslin, tulle, silk, velvet, satin, jet, bronze, straw, corn, wine, and oil, and the whole is not much bigger than a muffin. But nothing unduly predominates; nothing is intrusive, nothing inopportune. The entire affair may be a vanity of vanities, but it is harmonious and beautiful.

In the finest French carpets, majestic as they are in design and splendid in colour, I always seem to hear—for, as blind Professor Sanderson said of scarlet, it is quite possible to *hear* a colour—something like a roll of drums, a flourish of trumpets, or a prodigious clattering of musket-stocks against the ground, swamping and hustling everything else out of their way. Now it is the frame that asserts itself in a series of big bouncing scrolls. Now it is a dolphin, and now a nereid, surging up in a corner, and commanding us, under pain of blindness, to admire them. Now it is a thundering bowpot bursting out in the very middle of the work, like the bouquet in a firework show at Cremorne. Being of a timid and nervous nature, I prefer the indistinctly distinct and soberly splendid carpets of Eastern fashion. Their mellowed richness, their subdued gorgeousness, lead a man, somehow, to calm and contemplation—to the crossing of his legs, and the puffing of his pipe, and the quaffing of his coffee, and the enjoyment of his *kef*—to the stroking of his beard, and the telling of his beads, and the letting of a vain and giddy world go by.

I must not omit to mention that these Indian Axminsters of Brinton and Lewis (to whom a Gold Medal was deservedly awarded) can be manufactured at about one-half the price charged for real Indian carpets, and that the house are engaged in erecting looms to produce this class of goods up to a width of thirty feet without seam, so as to fit an apartment of any given shape, circular or otherwise. Nor must I be guilty of the great injustice of neglecting to state that the designer of these beautiful and luxurious carpets is Dr. Christopher Dresser, a gentleman whose name, it is true, does not appear in any one of the Exhibition catalogues, although it might be fairly affixed to a score of the most remarkable productions in the Champ de Mars. For some years past the taste and skill of Dr. Dresser have been put into requisition by some of the leading art manufacturers both of England and the Continent; and both as a designer of models and patterns, and as a general " art adviser," his talents have been of the very highest service to firms whose principals, as in the case of Messrs. Brinton and Lewis, combining capital with indefatigable enterprise, are laudably determined to bear Art as sedulously in view as they do Industry ; and who scorn, merely because a thing is " sure to sell" and " must find a market," to sow Bad Taste broadcast and perpetuate Ugliness.

XIX.

THE GRAND PRIX.

IT may not be out of place to remark that, in addition to the medals of gold, silver, and bronze, and the certificates of honourable mention, the international jury of the Universal Exhibition had at their disposal a certain number of "*grands prix,*" or exceptional prizes, destined for the recognition of merits which were considered superlative or *hors ligne.* The superior council, acting on the recommendations of the group-juries, arrived, after long and presumably painful deliberations, at the determination as to how these superior prizes were to be adjudged. The following were fortunate recipients-designate. His Majesty the Emperor headed the roll for the workmen's dwelling-houses, which, under his auspices, have been constructed in the Champ de Mars. It is impossible to deny that these dwelling-houses are fabulously cheap, that they are built with as large a view to comfort as is compatible with economy of space, and that the idea which has prompted their erection is thoroughly philanthropic. Architecturally, they are decidedly ugly. We should not, again, as Englishmen, forget that Napoleon III. is not the only sharer of " that fierce light which beats upon a throne" who has bestowed thought and study on the truly imperial question how best to improve the condition of those whose lot it is to labour. It seems but yesterday when, in the stable-yard of Knightsbridge Barracks, there was built a " semi-attached couple " of model cottages for workmen, designed, or at least imagined, by the Consort of the Queen of England. Those cottages were not the most brilliant, but they were among the most practical contributions to the Great Exhibition of 1851. The world is quick enough at remembering names, but it is apt too often to forget the most shining claims to national gratitude of those by whom those names were borne; and even when it bears the deeds of the departed in remembrance it not un-frequently ignores the better to extol the worse part of a man's career. It is to be regretted that the good seed sown by Prince Albert at Knightsbridge in 1851 has not borne better fruit in England. In the rural districts some humane and enlightened landlords have erected or urged their tenants to erect for the agricultural labourer dwellings on the " model " principle—dwellings in which the English peasant, his wife and family, may live a little more like human beings, and a little less like swine. Like swine! In the county of Bucks, for one, I have seen many more commodious pigsties than commodious cottages. A little, however, has been done in the " model " direction ; but every one who is acquainted with the outskirts of Manchester, Liverpool, Old-ham, or indeed any large provincial town in England, must be aware that the " compound householder," or the poor mechanic, or the needy millhand, continues, when he has a house at all, to inhabit a miserable little brick box, stunted, tasteless, and gloomy, with a staircase so narrow and an entry so cramped, that when he dies his coffin has to be lowered from the first-floor window. In the poor suburbs of London.

notably at the East-end, the working man is still worse off. Rows of brick kilns, hastily hollowed out, are run up by "blind" builders, and called households. Some modern Palladios restrict their energies to the erection of "carcases," which they mortgage or sell, to be finished haphazard; and in the interior of the metropolis "vested interests," by which are implied the meanest, the most sordid, the most repulsive forms of human cruelty, selfishness, and rapacity, still conspire to keep, and still succeed in keeping the British workman sweltering in the rotten kennels of Dudley Street, Clare-market, and the Coal-yard, and in the noisome dens of West-minster and Whitechapel. The only real strides in advance —and magnificent strides they are—that have been made are in a diametrically opposite direction to those traced by Prince Albert. The number of "model cottages" erected has been, in proportion to our population, infinitesimal; but the Workmen's Dwelling Association, and the trustees of Mr. Peabody's munificent gifts, and Alderman Waterlow, have already endowed London with numbers of admirable "model" lodging-houses, vast and comfortable structures, which only need a little artistic decoration—and that decoration could be easily applied—to render them palaces.

I have dwelt on these facts because I fear that the scheme of the Emperor Napoleon, admirable as it is in conception, is not likely to find very great favour, at least in Paris. At Mulhouse, and in the suburbs of some other manufacturing centres, workmen's cottages have been erected and are said to be doing well. "*Cités ouvrières*," as congeries of these cottages are called, have also been tried, and many more are planned in the environs of Paris, outside the lines of circum-vallation; but I cannot help thinking that the vast majority of French workmen—eminently social and combinative as they are—will continue to the end of the chapter to prefer to live in " flats."   The *concierge* is a part of French organisation. He need not be a tyrant or an extortioner as he now is, but without some kind of *concierge* or janitor at his door I do not see how any Frenchman, from a senator to a *serrurier*, could get on.   It stands to reason that you cannot have a *concierge* for every hundred pound cottage; and thus, taking likewise into consideration the enormous value of land in Paris, I apprehend that the best workman's colony or *cité ouvrière* would be composed of tall, handsome houses, as many stories high as the building laws will permit, let out in " flats," or portions of " flats."   This is not Baron Haussmann's opinion I know.   He leans to the notion that the bricklayer or the mason should live a good many miles away from the splendid new Boulevard his hands have built; but recognizing the impropriety of too narrowly criticising the domestic policy of a country which is not mine, I may, in parting, take one more glance at London, and express my firm and deliberate belief that if I could only buy up the rotten, filthy, felonious house property that lies between St. Martin's Lane and the Church of St. George's, Bloomsbury—buy it up in a lump— pull down Seven Dials, St. Giles's, and the Broadway, and build up handsome streets of model lodging-houses in their infamous stead, I should in five years' time get a return of five and twenty per cent. on my capital.

The Emperor, however, well deserves his exceptional prize; for, on his side the Channel, Sovereigns who have cared any- thing about the well-being of their humbler subjects have been very exceptional indeed.   Another prize was given to Herr Jacobi, of Prussia, for " Galvano-plastie," or works in electro-bronze. Such a prize might have been gracefully bestowed on our English Elkingtons, but as that firm are doubtless already gold medallists as workers in the precious metals, Herr Jacobi may rejoice in the reversal of the national Prussian legend, "*Ich gab gold fur eisen*," and find that he gets something better than gold for bronze. Mame and Co., booksellers and printers, of Tours, were the next on the list. They are the Cloweses of provincial France, and the Leightons too, if they are their own bookbinders, for their binding is sumptuous. They are the "Bagsters," and the "Society for Diffusing Christian Knowledge," and the "Religious Tract Society" too, of the French Empire, providing any number of Lives of the Saints at surprisingly cheap prices for those who have any taste that way (for hagiology, I mean, not cheapness), and their great Bible, illustrated by Gustave Doré, will long be remembered as an artistic triumph. Then came M. Pellin-Gaudet for "metallurgy;" Mathieu for surgical instruments; the Company of the Isthmus of Suez for—well, what shall I say?—for the Isthmus of Suez, and being well out of the scrape, or well in for it, which ever you please; then came the iron foundries and workshop company of the Mediterranean; M. Fariot for steam-engines; "Algeria," generally, for her cottons; and "Brazil," equally generalised, for her proficiency in the culture of the same product. M. Dufresne was exceptionally rewarded for the discovery of a process by which gilding by mercury can be carried on without injury to the health of the workmen employed; M. Schneider, the director of the enormous foundry of the Crezuot—the glory of mechanical France—earned a well-merited prize; so did Mr. Bessemer, as a worker in steel; and Mr. Hughes, for improvements in electric telegraphy. A prize of honour likewise fell to the share of our admirable Royal National Lifeboat Institution, who had an "exhibit" on the banks of the Seine, close to the Pont de Jena. M. Pasteur gained an exceptional recompense as the inventor of a method of "preserving wines." I conceive this to be the system of subjecting new wine for a few minutes to the action of a very high degree of heat, thus destroying, or ostensibly destroying, the mysterious vegetable or animal fungus which is said to lie latent in wine, and to be productive of after-fermentation. This second fermentation arrested, we are told that it will become possible to ship both port and claret beyond sea without loading the first with brandy or "fortifying" the latter with Heaven knows what—a consummation devoutly to be wished. At present, when we cry for "natural wines" from Spain or Portugal, we are told that unless they are brandied they will not stand the sea voyage; and if we complain that our claret has lost its bouquet and our burgundy its aroma, and that both more intimately resemble an amalgam of red ink and vinegar than anything else, we are assured that "second fermentation" is at the bottom of it, and that we are suffering from fungoid growth in the substance of the wine itself. If M. Pasteur, in addition to preserving wines, could devise some means for improving the morals of wine merchants, he would certainly merit that most splendid reward imagined by "Little Em'ly" in "David Copperfield"—"a cocked hat and a pocket full of money."

M. Maris, for his system of subjecting the vine to the action of sulphur, was among those whom the Imperial Commission delighted exceptionally to honour; and it is in an extreme degree gratifying to learn that the highest reward in the power of the commissioners to bestow was conferred on the Sanitary Commission of the United States of America. Not half enough is known in Europe of the good work of this most excellent organisation, or of the labours of such enlightened philanthropists as Miss Delia Dix, as the Rev. Dr. Bellows, and hundreds of other American ladies and gentlemen, no less humane than patriotic, who, during the four long years of the American civil war, ministered to the wants and comforts of wounded and sick soldiers. The American Sanitary Commission was a corporate Florence Nightingale on a gigantic scale. Many millions of dollars were raised by subscription, or by the characteristic festivals known as "Sanitary Fairs," held all over the Northern and Western States of the Union, and most judiciously laid out in the purchase of food-comforts, even to toffy and " candy," extra bed and body linen, hospital bandages, artificial limbs, &c. The Sanitary Commission supplied the wounded soldier with everything, from a cough mixture to a glass eye, from a buckwheat cake to an order for embalmment. Although always ready with spiritual counsel, it did not ostensibly press religious assistance on the wounded or sick soldier. It took care of his body. A cognate association, called the " Christian Commission," took care of his soul, and fed him with tracts. Together the two Commissions effected a surprising amount of good, and cast at least one ray of blessed light on the darkest page in American history.

When I state, finally, that a " *Grand Prix* " fell to the share of the "International Society for Aiding the Wounded on the Battle-field," I am reminded that early in the summer of the year 1865 I met in the midst of a sandy plain, on the African continent, on a blazing hot day, and sitting on the

stump of a prickly pear tree, under the shade of a white
umbrella, an intelligent Swiss gentleman—I think he was
from Geneva—who informed me that he was the founder of
the aid-giving association in question. You know all about
the society, no doubt. An immensity of the sentimentality
termed " rot " by the inebriated parent who drinks claret by
mistake in Mr. Robertson's play of " Caste " has been talked
about it. That belligerent nations (as in the American case)
should form associations for succouring *their own wounded* is
feasible enough; but to profess to go about pouring oil into
the wounds of those whom you have yourself wounded, and
to leave twopence at the inn for the man whom you have
yourself gone down to Jericho for the purpose of robbing, is
Samaritanism, I take it, of a very questionable nature, and
may fairly be stigmatised as "rot." Yet this "International"
association has received the "adhesion" of most of the
European sovereigns, and its principles have been recognized
by an international convention. The hospital flag is to be
neutral; the ambulance is to be sacred; the hospital attendant is to be non-combatant. I could not help remarking,
however, at the time, to the intelligent Swiss gentleman, that
if nations were to refrain from cleaving each other's heads
and ripping up each other's bowels on slight pretexts, there
would be but little need for his association; and that, so
long as nations indulged in these agreeable pastimes, it
seemed very like the Mockery of Hell to whine internation-
ally over the sufferings of those whom we went out know-
ingly and deliberately to kill and mutilate. The opinion I
ventured to express in Algeria two years since I venture to
repeat now, having read in the papers about a certain battle
at Sadowa—which was " nine times Waterloo "—and having

heard with my own ears the sound of the cannon at the battle of Custozza. There must be something wrong somewhere. If we are to reward the society which prides itself on assuaging the sufferings of wounded soldiers, should we not hang the next gentleman who invents a big gun instead of making him a baronet?

P.S.—At the massacre of Mentana the " Chassepot rifles did wonders." Pity it was that a few priests and members of the Swiss gentleman's association were not present to pour oil into the wounds made in the Garibaldini by the Chassepots. It is not generally known that the butt of a Chassepot rifle is made in the form of a crucifix.

XX.

THE DISTRIBUTION OF PRIZES.

RARELY if ever within the memory of living man has there been witnessed a spectacle more replete with gaiety, with beauty, and with fascination, than that which took place on the 1st of July, in the Palace of Industry, in the Champs Elysées, under the presidency of the Emperor Napoleon III. and of his beautiful consort, in the presence of Abdul Aziz Kahn, Soldan of the Turks; of Albert Edward, heir to the throne of England; of Umberto of Savoy, heir to the throne of Italy; of Ismail Pasha, Vice-King of Egypt; of Frederick William, Crown Prince of Prussia; of Louis Prince of Hesse; of George Duke of Cambridge; of the Nuncio of the Sovereign Pontiff of the Roman Catholic Church; of the son of the Taicoun of Japan; of Napoleon Jerome, foremost among French princes; and of a throng of Dukes and Counts and Senators—of noble men and beautiful women—of personages illustrious in arts and arms, in politics and commerce, so numerous, so brilliant, and so exceptional, that a bookcase full of peerages, of *libri d'oro*, of rolls of honour, of *Almanachs de Gotha*, of *Law Lists* and *Army Lists* and *Court Guides*, would but poorly suffice to enumerate their dignities, and blazon forth the splendour of their renown. The pick and choice of the whole civilized world were gathered in the magnificent area of the Palais de l'Industrie, to do honour to Arts and Industry. No vain gage of chivalry, as in the "Vows of the Heron," was to be asserted. Gorgeous as was the assemblage, this was no Field of the Cloth of Gold, where feudal kings had met to seal feudal compacts, whose end should be to exalt feudality and keep the people down. It was the rather, amid all its glitter and all its glory, a Field of Homespun and of printed calico; for no greater homage could be paid to the real purport of this Congress—no more significant symbols could be presented of its real scope and bearing—than the Ten Trophies which had been erected in the arena of the wonderful amphitheatre in which two-and-twenty thousand persons were massed together this day. These Ten Trophies represented the ten groups or classes into which the products displayed in the Universal Paris Exhibition were divided. The materials of these Trophies varied from the most exquisite art-achievements of the Christofles, the Froment-Meurices, the Barbédiennes, the Elkingtons, the Hancocks, the Castellanis, the Phillipses, the Watherstons, the Hunt and Roskells, the Fourdinois, the Dobsons, and the Roux—from the most stupendous mechanical performance of the Schneiders, the Penns, the Krupps the Armstrongs, and the Whitworths—to the humblest objects of domestic art, to the crudest samples of Nature's bounty. We laughed at the Pickle Trophy in the London Exhibition of 1862; but, symmetrically and artistically arranged in the nave of the Palais de l'Industrie, were things quite as heterogeneous, quite as *bizarre*, quite as humble, yet quite as veritably important, when it was borne in mind that out of the multiplicity of little things, and out of the carefulness of their elaboration, come the development and the infinite enhancement of the grand desideratum we call civilisation. Among these " trophies " were not only bottles of pickles, and sauce, and catsup, and biscuits, and preserved meats, but ears of corn, and cocoons of silk, and lumps of ochre, and nuggets of camphor and nitre, and shavings of wood, and leaves of plants, and the raw fibres of cotton. In strict, ånd perhaps unconscious, attention to the original and astute scheme of the French Imperial Commission, the entire history of modern production and manufacture was traced in these Ten Trophies. He who had tact and intelligence could follow the chronicle of the morsel of ironstone or of silver ore in Group IX. to its apotheosis under the hammer of Morel-Ladeuil in the silver and iron *repoussé* shield exhibited by the Elkingtons in Group II. He would follow the gold, from the quartz in which it was imbedded, to the workshop of a Castellani, and the *atelier* of a Phillips. He could trace the humble potter's clay to the grand painting rooms of Sèvres, to the truthful studios of our Copelands and Mintons. And to me, at least, a writer whose word has been always for the many, but with whom few agree—a writer who for twenty years has blunderingly striven to tell the truth at the risk of being thought coarse and vulgar, there has not been, among the hundred shows that I have witnessed, ONE sight more noble, more comfortable, and more genuine than this: when the judges in Israel and the rulers of the earth met, in their most sumptuous conclave—*not* to pass a Pragmatic Sanction—*not* to chop logic over an *uti possidetis*—*not* to hold an Œcumenical Council, " dealing damnation round the land " on those they judged the foes of Heaven—*not* to accede to a " Holy " Alliance—*not* to devise fresh devices for the enslavement and the obscuration of mankind; but simply to testify that if Jacques Bonhomme had made a good cabinet of walnutwood he deserved to be honoured among men for it; and that if Thomas Smith had fashioned an excellent bracelet, pure in design and solid in execution, the world was the debtor to him for his fine taste and his good handiwork. I should be ashamed to have such coarse and rude things printed, but that the discourse of Napoleon III. bore out in dignified language that which I have endeavoured roughly to inculcate.

The doors of the Palais de l'Industrie were opened to the public at noon. The plan of the arena in which the great solemnity was held is easily given. The Palace is a vast parallelogram, in a line with the Champs Elysées, and standing, with tolerably mathematical exactitude, north, south, east, and west. Within this parallelogram there had been contrived an ellipse, occupying what might be termed the nave of the edifice. Draw out to a considerable degree of tension the area of the Coliseum at Rome, and you may form an idea of the space occupied only by the trophies to which I have already called attention, which intervened between the ranges of seats. There were two concentric ovals—an outer one, carpeted with crimson, which served as a promenade and a procession ground; and an inner expanse, where stood the trophies, and in which were assembled, marshalled under their divers banners, the commissioners, the jurors, and the exhibitors fortunate enough to be the recipients of gold or silver medals. It will thus be seen how a building which, if filled from side to side might have contained 150,000 spectators, was crammed almost to suffocation by an audience which certainly did not contain 22,000. In fact, the auditory only fringed and skirted the *enceinte*, and the general effect of the pageant was thus decidedly heightened. The inner ring had been decorated by perhaps the most luxurious floral display ever seen in Paris since that memorable horticultural festival in 1811, when the Princess Schwartzenberg told Napoleon I. that Austria "designed to crush the French Empire with flowers." The Quai aux Fleurs, the Marché de la Madeleine, the *Serres* of the Ville de Paris, St. Cloud, Bougival, Passy, Vincennes, Fontenay-aux-Roses, must have been rifled to the last petal to furnish forth that wondrous cornucopia of floral gems with which the Palais de l'Industrie was decked. The air was almost sick and heavy with hothouse scents; and Mr. Rimmel's perfumes must have been hard pushed to transcend the natural odours which Flora, at the instigation of discreet market gardeners, had purveyed.

In the centre of the north lateral of this amphitheatre was the throne. Three chairs, of Royal and Imperial estate, oval backed, and of crimson and gold, towered o'er the summit of a high *estrade* and staircases, richly carpeted, reaching to the floor of the arena. The three thrones were flanked by ranges of sumptuous fauteuils. The north-east curve was filled by the orchestra, consisting of three hundred and fifty instrumentalists, and one hundred and fifty male and female choristers from the Grand Opera. The south-west side of the amphitheatre was garnished with a grand *escalier* of egress. Over all this you will be pleased to figure the semicircular roof of glass, with the finials of painted glass, so familiar to us all in 1855, at either end, and, pendent from the girders, the flags of all nations. Your idea will yet be flat and meagre if I omit to tell you that the throne was surmounted by an alcove, a baldaquin, and canopy, topped by the Imperial crown, and backed by the Imperial escocheon, in crimson velvet and gold, forty feet high. These things, I may hint, do not cost our clever, mercurial neighbours a fortune. They have always an adequate supply of crimson velvet and gold, escocheons, Imperial arms, Venetian masts, thrones, carpets, and footstools " in stock." These festive accessories come from " *Le Garde Meuble de la Couronne,*" the great " property room " of French pageantry. The stores of this wonderful magazine are on a par with those of the wholesale funeral-furnishing establishment of the *Pompes Funèbres.* Everything is ready docketed, pigeon-holed, and ticketed, and the consequence is that Paris never requires more than five minutes' notice to be ready either for a *fête* or for a funeral.

On either side the thrones I have just described the rank and file of the Cent Gardes, tremendous, sumptuous, and immobile, kept watch and ward. Have I omitted anything to help the kind subscriber who may read this narrative in a quiet Berkshire village to an understanding of this unequalled sight? Ah, yes; I have left out the very marrow of my matter. It is one o'clock. The amphitheatre, such as I have endeavoured to draw it, is here. Now, in your mind's eye, you must strive to fill it with humanity in its most varied and its most gorgeous aspect. Two-and-twenty thousand ladies and gentlemen, dressed in all the pomp and all the circumstance that the tailor and the milliner's art and the cunning blazonry of the Heralds' College can suggest. Uniforms so multiplied and so magnificent that you grow weary at epaulettes, and are satiate with plumed shakoes and em- broidered dolmans. Senators and members of the Legis-

lative Corps and Councillors of State, whose brocaded cuffs
and collars do not glisten more brightly than the bare necks
and shoulders of the beautiful ladies who have been brought
here by the laudable desire of seeing things as comely as
themselves; members of the Corps Diplomatique ablaze with
orders, radiant in ribbons, staring in stars; Austrian generals,
Prussian generals, Spanish generals, Italian generals, in every
phase of bullion, of lace, and of *passementerie ;* and, relieving
the mass of continental blue, and green, and brown, pray take
into account the bright scarlet of the British army. Our red
tunics were well to the fore—worn by stalwart Britons fully
worthy of their cloth. Add to these the glowing municipal
robes of the Corporation of London, and of a score more
British mayors, and a hundred more British aldermen who
had come expressly to Paris to assist at this grand spectacle.
Do not forget the Turks in their fezzes. Do not omit
numbers of wily and astute Greeks, and especially of noble
and aristocratic Magyars. There was one Hungarian magnate,
in a suit of maroon velvet, trimmed with real sable, which
must have been worth at least three hundred pounds, and
with a collar of enormous turquoises, gracefully meandering
over his breast, who, if he was not the Tavernicus of Hungary,
must at least have been the descendant of one of those enthusiastic Palatines who, when Maria Theresa appeared in the
Diet at Pesth, with her infant son in her arms, clashed their
swords in unison, and cried, " *Moriamur pro rege nostro.*"

This was the scene at half-past one. The orchestra now
gently intoned some music, of which I am not qualified to be
a judge. At two o'clock a general rustle and a universal cry
of " *Assis! assis !*"—sit down, sit down—proclaimed the
arrival of the royal and imperial hosts of this unparalleled

festival. By degrees the great daïs where the thones were became filled with the Salt of the World. Now, up came the brave and handsome son of King William of Prussia and his fair wife, Victoria, the eldest daughter of England. To him quickly succeeded Prince Louis of Hesse. Then came Prince Joachim Murat. Stay a moment. Who is this gallant young gentleman, fair, and franklooking, so sorely tried, so cruelly belied, so unworthily sneered at and libelled, whose chief faults seem to be that he is six-and-twenty, has a good appetite, and is disposed to look upon things from the Tapleian, or "jolly" point of view—but who is still the Hope of England, and the Heir whom we hope some day to hail as Edward VII.? The Prince of Wales goes by, and his stalwart kinsman, the Duke of Cambridge. Now there is a slight pause. *Majora canamus:* here is Cæsar. The Emperor Napoleon looks exceedingly well; calm, quiet, self-contained, but evidently pleased at his reception, for the moment he appears the whole two-and-twenty thousand spectators rise at him and shout "Vive l'Empereur!" By his side is his incomparable empress; and, as usual, the beauty and grace of her form seem but the reflex, patent to all men, of the kindness and tenderness of her good heart. To be beloved by all who have ever beheld her should make a woman vain—for Eve's daughters are much of a muchness; yet I have never heard that the Empress Eugénie was conceited. It was but the other day that the greatest lady in Europe went down among the trulls and queans of the prison of St. Lazare, and insisted that they should have warmer beds and softer benches while they picked their oakum and wove their mats.

The Viceroy of Egypt—he was there, too; but I can spare

no space for a detailed photograph of his Highness. Prince Humbert and his brother the Duke d'Aosta may wait until they have done something worthier ere I care to limn them. Prince Louis of Hesse, *ne m'en parlez pas;* but here is a grand figure who must be finished off in two or three broad lines. On the right hand of the Emperor Napoleon sat the Sultan. He wore his fez and his tunic blazing in gold embroidery. He contemplated the extraordinary scene with concentrated yet calm attention. It is not my province to listen to the conversation or to attempt inferences as to the remarks of sovereigns; but in presence of this scene I cannot help thinking that the Sultan Abdul Aziz will be the last of his race to speak of Christians as "dogs" and "giaours," and to think that nothing good can come out of Frangistan. Let me add that this Oriental potentate, all unused as he was to such company and such environment, comported himself, as every well-trained Turk is sure to do, as a polite and courteous gentleman. We often, when we travel, forget what is due to the prejudices and to the customs of strangers; but, from personal experience, and as a pretty close observer, I can say that not only the Ottoman Sovereign, not only his great generals and pashas, his dragomen and physicians, but his very *vakils,* behaved from first to last as men not of an inferior, but of an equal race with Europeans; not like the soft, sleek Hindoos, all shawled and diamonded as they are, but like Eastern gentlemen, who must not be blamed if they were born Conservatives, in view of the commendable efforts they are making to liberalise their institutions.

Their Majesties being seated, the long-promised inaugural Hymn of Peace—with war accompaniments—the words by

M. Pacini, the music by the illustrious Rossini, was performed. I should prefer to say nothing about the merits of this hymn. I have heard "Semiramide" and the "Nozze di Figaro." Some competent critic may inform you whether the jingling tune and puling accompaniment we heard were worthy of a *maestro* who was brother to Meyerbeer and Bellini.

The hymn being come to an end, and, of course, most vehemently applauded, the general report on the *ensemble* of the Universal Exhibition of 1867 was ostensibly read by M. Rouher, Vice-President of the Imperial Commission. I am wholly incompetent to transcribe it. His Excellency M. Rouher spoke lengthily, and, I have no doubt, to the purpose; but to twenty-one thousand five hundred of the twenty-two thousand persons present his discourse must have been wholly inaudible. He was not exactly coughed down, but there was a universal sigh of gratification when his Excellency concluded.

In remarkable contradistinction to this long-winded and muffled harangue, came, clear as a bell, terse and concise, sonorous and resonant, the speech of Napoleon the Third. You have all read it by this time. The best criticism I can pass on the speech was that we all heard it. Its only fault was that it was too short.

Now followed the distribution of the prizes, a ceremony which, I am constrained to say, was, in comparison to all that had preceded it, remarkably flat and meagre. The prize-holders of the various groups—the gold medallists only—marshalled under their respective banners, and preceded by their commissioners and jurors, passed in turn before the throne, and the great prizes were delivered by the Emperor's own hand. This ceremonial, properly conducted, might have been most imposing. *But a toastmaster was wanted.* There was no Mr. Toole to cry out the names of the fortunate recipients of recompenses. We merely saw lugubrious processions of gentlemen in black defiling in a mournful manner before the Imperial daïs. Their flags might have belonged to Sunday Schools or to the Ancient Order of Foresters. There was no music to enliven the distribution of rewards, and the entire affair hung fire and burnt as though with damp powder. I had been furnished—as indeed had every one else present—with an *authentic* list of the prizeholders. But so far as I am concerned, as a spectator, the gentlemen who passed before his Majesty might, in view of the vastness of the expanse and the difficulty of hearing anything, have been visited with a vote of censure instead of any meed of commendation. The consequence of this oversight in official quarters—by the want of sonorous heraldry proclaiming the merist of the exhibitors, and announcing their title to be recompensed—was that the pageant flagged ere it was three parts completed. An intermediate fillip was given to the proceedings by the tremendous bursts of applause which greeted the concession of "grand prizes," first to his Majesty Napoleon III. as the designer of dwellings for the working classes—a prize which was most gracefully accepted on the part of his papa by the Prince Imperial; and, next, by the thoroughly cordial storm of plaudits on the part of the French which accompanied the bestowal of a "grand prize" on M. de Lesseps, the enterprising "undertaker" of the Suez Canal.

The culmination of this grand scene swiftly followed. The illustrious personages on the daïs, in a slow and stately manner, descended from their high estate, and made the entire circuit of the arena. As this peerless cortége advanced and passed by the sections of benches allotted to the various countries, the band struck up the national air appropriate to the country passed. Now we heard the enlivening strains of the Prussian march; now the sonorous strophes of "*Tsar boge kranze*," the Russian anthem; now the inexpressibly soft and mournful movements of the Sweedish hymn; now the bold and jovial passages of "God Preserve the Emperor Francis." "God Save the Queen" was not played as the Emperor, the Sultan, and their suites passed that part of the English assemblage where the Lord Mayor and Corporation of London, arrayed in their robes of state, were placed; but, as a consolation, the band and chorus struck up an air from an old English oratorio, called "See the Conquering Hero comes.' Take the title who will; but George Frederick Handel belongs to *us;* and "See the Conquering Hero" has played in the entry of a thousand English warriors.

Throughout, the applause which followed the Emperor was prodigious. His popularity was only approached by that of the Empress and of the Prince Imperial, now thoroughly restored to health. The Sultan, also, who looked none the worse for his twenty-four hours' pull from Toulon, was also most cordially greeted. His Imperial Highness Prince Napoleon looked more like the Emperor Napoleon the First than ever, and behaved himself accordingly. With the Prince of Wales came the Duke of Sutherland, looking fresh and handsome as usual; and a round of hearty applause welcomed the honest and good-natured Duke of Cambridge.

And then this scene terminated. I had been down to Toulon to meet the Sultan; had come back (through the kindness of General Fleury) in the Imperial train; had, so soon as I arrived in Paris, hot, dusty, and without taking my boots off, swallowed a fowl and a bottle of champagne, and written four columns for a daily newspaper about the "Sultan in France;" and early next morning I was bound to be in evening costume at the Palais de l'Industrie. I leave it to the *Saturday Review* to sneer at the efforts of the chronicler of a pageant, who, between Wednesday and Sunday, had travelled twelve hundred miles to describe it. *Abi tu, et fac similiter.* I must observe, however, in conclusion, that after the Imperial and Sultanesque processions had been allowed to depart in comparative quietude, a vast multitude of sight-seers fastened upon the equipages of *Le Gran Lor Maire de Londres* and the dignitaries of the Corporation, and accompanied them, with much clamour, to their home.

XXI.

ENGLISH NEWSPAPERS.

IT is stated, I know not with what truth, that some weeks prior to the opening of the Exhibition, the Imperial Commission formally requested the corteous official who was plenipotentiary in all matters concerning great Britain in the Champ de Mars to exhibit "something which might serve as a comparative history of England during the last five-and-twenty years." The request was made in undeniable good faith, and was taken, as it was meant, *au sérieux*. The reading-room attached to the English department was pointed out as the locality most suitable for such a display. But how on earth was Mr. Cole to "exhibit" the History of England ? A complete collection of Acts of Parliament passed since the accession of her Majesty would hardly fulfil the end in view. The Dean of Westminster would scarcely be persuaded to "loan" for exhibition in Paris that very curious collection of waxen effigies of the Kings and Queens of England, in their habits as they lived, which still lies *perdu* in some dusty cases in the old Abbey, and which, if brought to light, might serve as a very suggestive gloss on certain events in English history. The French themselves, I perceive, are exceedingly reluctant to let us have those noseless statues of the Plantagenets from Fontevrault which M. Drouyn de Lhuys rather rashly promised to Lord Stanley; and thus one very remarkable link in our historical annals would be deprived of illustration.   Could the keeper of the jewel-house in the Tower be persuaded to send over the crown and sceptre, the orb and the Koh-i-noor, under a guarantee against all depredations committed by possible successors of Colonel Blood? Could arrangements have been made with Mr. Froude, Mr. Grote, Mr. Carlyle, Mr. Merivale, Mr. Goldwin Smith, and other distinguished historians, to deliver a continuous series of lectures on English history to all whom it might concern* in Paris? There is a mania for oral instruction just now. M. Oscar de Vallée, Avocat-Général, and himself one of the most brilliant talkers of the age, declared, in the course of the late Grammont-Caderousse trial, that " *le triomphe de la parole* " was at hand, and that a time was coming when writers and thinkers would have to bow their heads before speakers. " Conferences " have attained great vogue in Paris.' The Athénée, although its intellectual bill of fare would be considered in England as the heaviest and dreariest imaginable, is nightly thronged with audiences eager to hear sedate lecturers drouthily discourse on Greek plays, Finnish poems, and Egyptian hieroglyphics. A most startling success might be expected, then, for the English historical lecturers in the Champ de Mars, only it is to be feared that Mr. Grote and Mr. Froude and the rest " wouldn't see it." Again, the limitation to a quarter of a century of the historical area to be traversed would sadly cramp us in the exposition of our historical *fasti*. When we talk about our own chronicles we are naturally anxious to say as much as possible about Crecy, Poitiers, and Agincourt—about

Blenheim, Ramilies, and Malplaquet—about La Hogue, the Nile, and Trafalgar—about Salamanca, Vittoria, and Waterloo. We couldn't do this under the five-and-twenty years' limit. And, again, would it not have been the worst of manners to touch, however discreetly, on such invidious topics during a festival which was inaugurated by a Hymn of Peace? Mr. Cole would not have done badly, perhaps, had he endeavoured to satisfy the thirst of the Imperial Commission for historical information by purchasing a double set of the *Illustrated London News* since its commencement, just a quarter of a century since; and, joining the engravings together in due chronological sequence, after the manner adopted by M. Philipon with his *rouleaux* of caricatures from the *Journal pour Rire*, pasted them on screens, and invited all the world to study the abstract and brief chronicle of the world as it has wagged since the year 1842; for therein, indeed, all who run might read the history of England. The annalists of the burin and the wood block, more deft than those who cut the arrow-headed chronicles of Nineveh, or those who limned on cotton bandages the wars and feasts and religious ceremonies of the Aztec Empire, have left us enduring memorials of all that has been done worthy of note in England during a whole generation. On the screens the world might see how we opened a palace of glass in Hyde-park in 1851, and how we took it to pieces and put it in waggons and transported it to Sydenham, and set it up afresh to be a thing of beauty, and—a partial conflagration notwithstanding—a joy for ever. How our great Duke of Wellington died, and how we buried him. How we went to war with Russia in the Crimea, how we suffered in the cruel winter before Sebastopol, and how Inkerman and the Redan made amends for our sufferings. How our Sepoys in India broke out in mutiny; and how, with stern foot, we trampled the rebellion down, and built up an Indian empire grander and stronger than ever. How we held yet another Exhibition of all Nations in 1862; and how, while the enterprise was yet incomplete, the wise and good Prince to whose fostering care our arts and our industry owe so much fell sick and passed away, and left a whole nation weeping. All these things might have been seen, together with portraits of our most famous nobles, statesmen, authors, artists, and divines, and with such extraneous matters as February revolutions and June insurrections, and December *coups d'état*, and August *fêtes*; as discoveries of gold in Australia and California; as wars in China and in the United States; as Royal progresses, volunteer reviews, regattas at Cowes, and races at Epsom. Could not the engravings from the *Illustrated News* have been enlarged by the indiarubber process, like the *Punch* drawings of the late John Leech? Vividly coloured, what an astonishing historical gallery would have been there! Mr. Cole, however, may have quailed before a task so gigantic; but still, in his laudable desire to meet in some measure the wishes of his French friends, he formed and made ready for exhibition a collection which, in one section of English history at least, was unrivalled and unique. With rare industry, patience, and research, he brought together that which may be described as a complete panorama of English literature and journalism. On certain screens in the English department were displayed an almost innumerable series of newspapers, magazines, reviews, and serial publications of every imaginable form, type, character, size, and price. There were seen the daily broadsheet, eight-paged, four-paged, morning and evening, full-priced, half-priced, and low-priced, stamped and unstamped. There the lofty "Edinburgh" and the sublime "Quarterly" filtered down, through imperceptible gradations of monthly, fortnightly, weekly, and bi-weekly publications, to the humble catchpennies of Seven Dials. All the London and all the provincial papers; the most rubbishing farthing ballads, as well as the gorgeously illuminated poetry of Dover and Albemarle streets; all the almanacs, all the cheap books, all the puffing pamphlets of advertising tailors and hatters, found a place in this remarkable collection. It was very much laughed at, but I hold it to have been most interesting and most instructive. The immense mass of printed matter was most ingeniously arranged with a view to the economy of space as well as to that of giving to each publication exhibited its proper prominence. As regards illustrated literature, the panorama was as varied and even more historical, since the gradual progress in wood engraving, which has culminated in such brilliant results, can here be traced step by step. And not only were newspapers and periodicals "historically" exhibited. With a really wonderful assiduity and concentrative patience, the booksellers of Great Britain and Ireland, and of the Channel Islands to boot, had been laid under contribution. From elephant folios to tiny "sixty-four-mos," there was no break in the continuity of the collection, showing what has been published in every department of literature. It was impossible of course to paste the books on screens; and to exhibit only their title-pages, and so mutilate them, would be as tasteless a proceeding as that of the bibliomaniac whose library contained nothing but epigraphs and colophons. He cut off the head and the tail of

x

every book he bought, and burnt the rest. The books, then, were shown in cases, and were accessible to reference. It is no exaggeration to say that this collection—literary as well as journalistic—must, as a whole, be regarded as more complete than that on the shelves of the British Museum. The law gives to our national library a right to the first fruits of all contemporary literature, large and small ; but booksellers are not always very anxious to comply with the provisions of the Act of Parliament, and the officials of the Museum, zealous as they may be, cannot hunt up every remote publisher, say in the West of Scotland, or every obscure newsvendor, say in the depths of Devon, who has published some infinitesimal opuscule and omitted to send a copy of it to Great Russell Street. Mr. Cole, however, as a mere volunteer, seems to have been perfectly lynx-eyed. Nothing printed escaped his survey; and even Holywell Street had a place on his screens. It is very satisfactory to remark that, exhaustive as was the search, Holywell Street and its kindred dens of nastiness occupied a very small place, and made a very contemptible show. The great body of English literature and journalism was as healthy as its best friends could desire.

XXII.

FANCY GOODS.

THE question as to where "fancy" is "bred" was asked a long while since by a lyrical poet; but it has not yet been decided whether the culture concerning which the bard was so anxious takes place in the "heart" or in the "head." It is my more practical business to inquire where the articles usually termed, for trade purposes, "fancy" are made—how they are made—who makes them, and who were the most noteworthy exhibitors of "fancy" wares in the Paris Exhibition of 1867.

Taking as ground-lines for these remarks the official explanations furnished by the Imperial Commission, it may be premised that in France the generic term for "fancy goods" is *articles de Paris*. When the demand for *articles de Paris* is brisk, and their sale correspondingly active—this, by the way, is *not* official—the workmen of Paris are happy and contented, and France, as a necessary consequence, is tranquil. When the demand for the *articles* is dull, and buyers are few and far between in the Rue de Rivoli and the Palais Royal, the Parisian *ouvrier* is given to grumble and to say seditious things about his pastors and masters; and, Paris feeling aggrieved, France is soon in a ferment. The market, indeed, for nicknacks is a kind of politico-social thermometer, which the observant would do well to watch. Several trades, intimately or remotely connected, contribute to the supply of the fancy shops of Paris; leather-workers, wood-workers, and basket-workers, potters and glass-workers, all make *articles de Paris.* The articles themselves comprise pocketbooks, dress-ing and travelling cases, ladies' reticules and châtelaines, handkerchief boxes, cigar boxes, cases, and holders, pipes, tobacco jars, purses, &c., &c. They are principally made in the Third Arrondissement of Paris. In their production an immense variety of materials is used. For example, sheep, goat, kid, boar, and other skins, specially prepared; paper, silk, rosewood, mahogany, oak, ebony, and maple; bone, horn, ivory, tortoiseshell, gold, silver, iron, steel, platina, bronze, aluminium, copper, and the "white metal" of China. A vast number of machines and tools are employed to work the different materials, such as turning lathes, presses, stamping and drawing machines, dies to cut out and pierce, paring, polishing, and hinge-making machines. Some of these engines are moved by hand, others by steam. One-third of the artisans employed are women, earning from fifty sous to three francs a day. The wages of the male artisans vary between five and six francs per diem. Two-thirds of the articles made find a market in France; the remainder is dispersed over the European continent, the United States, and England. Germany, I should say, takes the smallest proportion of *articles de Paris,* for Germany has her own *articles d'Alle-magne,* and makes them excellently too. America, her im-moderate tariff notwithstanding, must buy large quantities of nicknacks; for, albeit New England manufactures a variety of small things called "Yankee notions," and New York has a home fabric of "dollar jewellery," the manufacture of fancy goods—even in toys—is still in its infancy on the American continent. The reason for this I could never well understand; for it is certain that the most skilful artisans from every part of the world emigrate to America in order to be free. Yet America will not condescend to make her own gloves, her own portemonnaies, or her own portable inkstands; and even if you walk into a store and buy a toy model of an American fire-engine or a papier-mâché statuette of Abraham Lincoln, the candid dealer will inform you that these essentially American "notions" have been imported from France or Germany—preferably the last-named country—where they are manufactured specially for the American market. That I am not overstating the case will be plain, I think, from the fact that only six exhibitors from the United States appear in the fancy ware class in Paris. Two firms from Massachusetts send samples of "wax flowers and fruit;" one house from New Jersey exhibits "ornaments of skeleton leaves," which must be considered rather as "curios" than as fancy goods; a German house in New York sends meerschaum pipes; and two more New Yorkers exhibit wax flowers and rustic basket-work. There must be some cause for this dependence on foreigners—certainly not more ingenious and industrious than Americans—for articles which, albeit not strictly useful, are indispensable adjuncts to the luxury and elegance of life. The cause may be a duplex reason: first, that Americans find it more profitable to sell these articles than to make them; and next, that the skilled artisans, when they arrive in the promised land, are filled, by the very vastness of the scene around them, with a contempt for the merely small and pretty. Their soul begins to thirst for "big things," and they plunge into the most colossal enterprises. He who has been vegetating for years as a lucifer match-box maker turns gunpowder manufacturer or patents monster guns; and he who was glad to engrave cockrobins on beer-jugs for twenty groschen a day starts a lager-beer brewery, makes a gigantic fortune, or "busts up" for a million of dollars.

France still considers herself to be at the head of the fancy goods trade of the world; but other nations have made within the last few years surprising advances, and ere long may approach and even distance her. Berlin and Vienna are making a varied assortment of articles in which the highest qualities of art workmanship are combined; and the rest of Germany, even to the very smallest states, absolutely flood the Continent with tiny articles of a "fancy" kind, whose principal merit is their amazing cheapness. There was a time, unhappily a far distant one, when the Italian fancy goods, known under the name of *galanterie*, were eagerly sought for in every market in Europe; but at present the traveller in Italy, when he has laid in a stock of the "fancy" staples of each city—mosaics at Florence, alabaster vases at Brescia and Bergamo, fans at Milan, filigree and shell work at Venice, mosaic and bronze at Rome, coral at Naples, and inlaid cabinet ware at Sorrento—will find nine-tenths of the fancy ware shops full of nicknacks from the "third arron-dissement" of Paris. From Spain nothing fanciful comes save statuettes from Malaga, embroidered garters from Leon, and "ribbon" sword-blades from Toledo; and even the two last are said to be mostly manufactured in Paris and smuggled over the frontier. Russia, however, especially since the Crimean war, has been doing a most gratifying trade in fancy ware, home-made. I will not dwell now in detail on the pretty things she makes, and which the Russian peasant —willing, good-natured, intelligent, crassly ignorant fellow as he is—seems to have a special aptitude for making, as I have noticed Russia separately elsewhere, in the hope of doing justice to a country whose industrial and artistic display must be held as one of the most brilliant successes in the Exhibition of 1867.

A very few more items of mere statistics are necessary ere we can take a comprehensive view of this highly curious branch of commerce. The articles in fancy wood and basket-work fill, of course, a large space in the catalogue. They include small articles in mother-of-pearl, cocoa-nut, and hard veneers, in addition to the materials I have already named. Ivory statuettes, small bronze figures of animals, billiard balls, combs, snuff-boxes, brushes, fans, screens, chessmen, dominoes, draughts, parasol, umbrella, and "fancy" whip-handles, all come within the same category. They are made not only in Paris, but at Dieppe, St. Cloud, Beauvais, and in the cantons of Méru and Noailles, in the department of the Oise, and in those of the Aisne, Maine-et-Loire, Moselle, and Vosges. The principal artisans of the male sex employed are sculptors, engravers, painters, modellers, lacquerers, horn-flatteners, bronzists, pasteboard cutters, decorators, filers, inlayers, polishers, turners, gold and silver smiths; and, among females, pasteboard cutters, polishers and piercers, colourers, gilders, and mounters. It is computed that Paris alone makes eleven millions' worth of *articles* every year.

When we take into consideration the immensity of things produced, the vast number of factories, firms, and agencies connected with the fabrication, the wholesale and retail sale

of these small wares, and the universality of the trade itself
in a metropolis which otherwise cannot be considered, like
London, a manufacturing centre, it would be something like
a work of supererogation to enumerate even the principal
makers and sellers of *articles de Paris*. Nor even when I
cull at random from the list of exhibitors such names as Marx,
Gerson and Weber, Chatelain, Fournier, Filmont, Cassella,
Chouquet, Manin, or Pinson—all eminent firms in their several
departments of fancy production—shall I be serving, I am
afraid, any very definite purpose. I shall only be conveying
so many series of sounds to my reader's ear, without adding,
in an appreciable degree, to his stock of information or his
resources of comparison. This, indeed, is a case of the
"strong Gyas" and the "strong Cloanthus," if we mention
only two, three, or five hundred manufacturers equally strong
and equally deserving of notice, but who obviously must be
left unmentioned. In fine, if a Parisian manufactures anything, he is pretty sure to manufacture *articles de Paris*.
There are exceptions, of course, to the rule, and among them
I hasten to note pianofortes, porcelain, bronzes on a large
scale, such as those of Barbédienne, furniture, and some little
paper and *carton pierre*. But beyond these the Parisian throws
his energies exclusively into *articles de Paris*. He is not a
founder, an engineer, a soapboiler, a candlemaker, a silk-
weaver, an indiarubber and gutta percha manufacturer, a
crucible maker, a "chemical works" proprietor, a tanner, a
sugarbaker, or a sizemaker, as are our great manufacturers
at Bow or Vauxhall, at Whitechapel or at Bermondsey. At
least he is not so in Paris. Industries of the nature just
mentioned he may carry on at Lyons or at Marseilles, at
Mulhouse or at Roubaix, at Lille or at Rouen ; but at Paris

he is a Parisian, and makes *articles de Paris*. Monotony of excellence need not be mediocrity; but this monotonous excellence is really a characteristic of the Parisian fancy goods trade. Cæsar at Montmatre is as skilful as Pompey in the Faubourg St. Denis; and the nicknacks of the Rue du Temple run a dead heat with those of the Rue Turenne.

Their final Parisian home, however, is not there. From the *usines* and wholesale houses in the low, cheap, and dingy quarters which M. Haussman has left standing, but which he continues to regard with ominous eyes, as a cruel school-master might eye the little boy whom he has not yet thrashed, but surely will when he has made his mind up " where to have him," these bright trifles come down to the boulevards, the Rues de la Paix and de Rivoli, and the Palais Royal. Without the slightest wish to disparage the transcendent attractions of the Exhibition in the Champ de Mars, I may say that nothing in the shape of *articles de Paris* exhibited there can surpass the display of similar wares made every day in the shops of the leading thoroughfares of the capital of France. Nay, in the last-named localities the fancy goods have their attractions enhanced to a degree impossible of attainment in the galleries of the Exhibition, which can only be visited by daylight; whereas on the boulevards and their tributaries the shops remain open until the hour of eleven o'clock at night; and all that can be done with a blaze of gas, heightened by artfully disposed reflectors, is done to increase the charms of the show, and to fascinate the spectators. It will sufficiently complete the purpose I have in view if I observe that, among the ninety-three exhibitors of *articles de Paris* in the French department, stands conspicuously as an exhibitor of " small furniture in wood, workboxes, caskets,

and fancy articles decorated with gilt bronze," the name of
A. Tahan, 34, Rue de la Paix. Tahan may be taken as the
very incarnation of an *article de Paris*. What proportion of
the astonishing collection of tiny and beautiful articles he
exhibits are made by M. Tahan himself—I mean in his own
workshops, for he can scarcely be, like Henri Fourdinois, his
own designer—it is no business of mine to inquire; but
whether he makes some things, or has others made for him,
it is not the less certain that his house has acquired a celebrity
which is European, and that his "exhibit" in the World's
Fair shows no derogation from the fame he has legitimately
acquired.

Comparisons are proverbially odious; but to compare, or
at least to establish a parallel, may be often useful and sometimes unavoidable. So, turning towards England, and
endeavouring to ascertain how we stand with regard to *articles
de Londres*, the proverbial inhibition may be left to take care
of itself for a moment while I state that as the house of Tahan
is to Paris so is the house of Howell and James to London.
Both enjoy a world-wide celebrity. Both are essentially
"West-end" houses, intended for the supply of articles of
virtù and luxury to persons whose taste is on a par with their
resources. You would not, for instance, think of walking
into Tahan's to ask for a couple of cribbage pegs; and I dare
say Messrs. Howell and James would not care much about
you if you sent them an order for one box of wax matches
and an electro-plated toothpick. For my part, I acknowledge
that in the days of my youth I never passed that serene
mansion, up the steps, in Waterloo Place, and saw the great
golden clocks, looming, dimly gorgeous, through the plate-
glass windows, without fear and trembling. Surely the

treasures of Golconda, supplemented by those of Potosi and the Washoe diggings, were collected behind those walls. Who dealt at Howell and James's? The cream of the cream. The Emperor of Samarcand always went to Waterloo Place when he wanted a diamond bootjack. The Cacique of Cathay always bought his emerald nose-rings and his under-waist-coats of cloth of gold there; and the officers of the Life Guards pink never thought of going anywhere else for their gold latchkeys and their dressing-cases with jade and malachite mountings. I looked on Howell and James's as a kind of ante-chamber to St. George's, Hanover Square. The elect of Hymen passed through the Waterloo Place rooms before they entered that vestry in Maddox Street to affix their names to the *libro d'oro*, equally insisted upon by the Established Church and the Registrar-General; and there hung about Howell and James's a vague yet unmistakable aroma of orange flowers and bride cake, white satin favours, and lemon kid gloves. The place might have been lit with the smiles of bridegrooms and the tears of mothers-in-law. I fancied that the post-boys from Newman's always lifted their whips respectfully when they passed the great emporium for wedding presents, and that the young man from Gunter's always sighed sentimentally when he passed with that green box on his shoulder.

This is an age in which we must all strive to " popularise our institutions," and Howell and James, so far as their display in the French Exhibition is concerned, seem to have made up their minds to be as popular as the strongest ad-vocate of " popularity " could desire. They have kept nothing back, and not only the " cream of the cream," but all the world and his wife, or the young lady on whom he intends shortly to confer the enviable distinction of wifehood, are privileged to gaze upon all the treasure collectors of Waterloo Place possess in the way of nicknacks and fancy ware generally, and especially of jewellery. Their show was a very brilliant and tasteful one indeed, and it is only to be regretted that, through some mismanagement, oversight, or under-blundering on the part of the officials to whom had been intrusted the bestowal of space on the exhibitors, the area marked out for Messrs. Howell and James's case was precisely in that part of the English section where it can be viewed with the least possible advantage. One of the most meritorious " exhibits," indeed, we possess is stowed away in a dark corner, almost necessitating a compass, a chart, and a dark lantern to discover it. However, it is there, and when found, as Captain Cuttle would say, should at once be made a note of. The beautiful Italian façade of Goldsmiths' Hall is not one whit the worse, intrinsically, for being hidden by George IV.'s heavy and ugly Post Office, which may serve to console Messrs. Howell and James, if they need consolation.

The variety of fancy goods for the boudoir, the toilet, the drawing-room, and the library, exhibited by this eminent firm, is most remarkable. All these tiny, tasteful things, toys if you will, but in the highest degree conducive to the cultivation of good taste, are, it should be remembered, of English manufacture. We can purchase as many French clocks and bronzes in Waterloo Place as we choose ; but the articles of which I speak—mainly in morocco, raw woods, oxydised silver, and gilt metal—are of a nature in the production of which English fancy manufacturers are daily making wider strides. There are now on the boulevards of Paris actually a number of genuine English shops for the sale of English-made

fancy wares; and this, in the very heart and home of the
articles de Paris, is, at least, a most significant fact. I
notice among Howell and James's more important articles a
sumptuous dressing-case of ormolu, ornamented with onyx,
and the fittings of silver-gilt, coral, and turquoise, which is
doubtless dirt cheap at three hundred and seventy-five guineas.
Were I a duke, or a Boyard, or a railway contractor, I might
order, too, that exquisite writing set of ormolu and malachite
to be sent home to my hotel; but, not having been yet called
into that state of life, I experience more gratification in
expatiating over the more moderately-priced nicknacks, *bric-
à-brac*, and toilet ornaments.

This house made likewise a very superb show of jewellery,
mention of which it would be unjust to omit, although it
would with greater propriety have come into my special papers on jewellery and goldsmith's ware. Take, for instance,
the "butterfly brooch"—the butterfly whose head is a black
pearl, and whose body is made of rubies and diamonds. Take
the fourteen hundred pound *rivière* and cross in diamonds.
Take also two big emeralds and the two bigger sapphires.
Take the "peacock locket," whose tail is all diamond eyes
and emerald eyebrows. Take the locket with the Imperial
Crown of France and the intertwined initials N.E. on the
exterior, and inside the portraits of the Emperor and Empress
of the French, most cunningly limned. Take the suite of
bracelet, earrings, and necklaces in turquoise, pearls, and
brilliants. 'Tis only five hundred pounds—a mere bagatelle
—the price of the first volume of your next novel, Mr. Trol-
lope. Half-a-dozen pages about a Cornish fisherman or a
Zummersetzheer varmer. Anything for a change, Mr. Tennyson. But I will say no more, out of consideration for the

ladies. I don't want to make any one die of envy. I will only discreetly hint at another "specialty" of Howell and James—that they deal in textile fabrics, that they sell the most gorgeous silk dresses imaginable. In what, to conclude, do they not deal? I am reminded, on this head, of having travelled once in a railway carriage with two gentlemen, presumably in the army, whose conversation I could not choose but overhear. Captain A. was going to Norway, intent on the sports of the field and the fjord, and he was telling his friend how he had ordered guns galore, and fishing rods, and wire cartridges, and mercurial unguent to anoint his gunlocks in case they froze. To him said Captain B., " Got a thermometer ?"—" No," replied the candid A. ; " confounded West End tailors don't sell thermometers." They seemed, in this case at least, to have sold everything else. I wonder whether I could get a thermometer at Howell and. James's. It would be of malachite, of course, with a tube and bulb of pure topaz.

XXIII.

FURNITURE.

The readers of novels and the students of poetry will open their eyes very widely when a grave and deliberate assertion is made that the two greatest master upholsterers of this age have been Walter Scott and Victor Hugo. I am not speaking in any way figuratively. I mean that the writings of the two illustrious authors I have named—that their genius and their example—have brought about a radical change and revolution in the chairs on which we sit, the tables at which we eat, and the beds on which we sleep. Their inexhaustible invention and glowing language inspired the reading world with admiration and appreciation of the beautiful and the picturesque in domestic decoration. Painters and modellers waited on their text, and in time illustrated it with graphic and plastic skill. A new taste was formed, a new demand created. The practical upholsterer, the decorator, the cabinet-maker, the worker in marqueterie and buhl, in carving and gilding, had then nothing to do but to step in and supply, by the *main d'œuvre*, the new æsthetic want which had arisen. David painted sham-classic pictures, because the taste of the Directory and the Empire tended, in all things, towards the sham-classic. Benjamin West produced conventionally Scriptural paintings, because the Church of England was, in his day, conventionally pious. The decoration of an epoch naturally and inevitably partakes of the character of its men and women. The debased designs and clumsy execution of the early Christian sculpture and painting are eloquent of the iconoclastic intolerance of a people who hated idol worship, and who, on throwing down the gods of Greece and Rome, had destroyed the most exquisite exemplars of beauty and symmetry, and who, in abolishing the bloody contests of the amphitheatre, had abolished, albeit unconsciously, a never-failing "life academy," in which the anatomy of the human figure, both as to its bone and its muscle, might be studied in the very highest perfection. It is a canon in the whimsical philosophy of Mr. Carlyle that the individualities of mankind may be best studied through their clothes; but the works of the tailor cannot teach us more significant lessons in the history of our species than can those of the maker of chairs and tables. The furniture, the tapestry, the mirrors and dressing-glasses, the carved chests and jewelled caskets of an epoch are a sure guide to its wants and pastimes, its passions and its feelings; nor will the exceedingly composite nature of the upholstery of our own age be without meaning to the generations which are to come. When our "drift" shall be turned over by posterity, and our relics collected in museums, when from the astonishing *pêle-mêle* of Greek and Roman, of Gothic and Byzantine, of Saxon and Arabesque, of Italian and Scandinavian imitations and reproductions, antiquaries yet unborn shall strive to arrive at something like a conclusive opinion as to the civilization of the nineteenth century, the verdict will, perhaps, amount to this: that we were not quite certain as to what was best, or what we really required, but that we experimented in all things, and could be, from the very structure of our society, consistently constant to none; that our civilization was of no particular or prevalent hue, but was multicoloured, like a harlequin's jacket; that we professed to believe in a great many things, but in reality were in scarcely anything *certain* in our creed, that is to say, immovably persuaded and convinced; that we were, in fine, not a settled generation, not an original generation, not a generation given to doctrines of finality, but that we tried and tried, and gave everything a chance, and copied most things of antiquity that were good, and many that were bad, and continually expected something to "turn up;" but that, on the whole, although almost entirely destitute of definite ideas or thorough convictions, we endeavoured to do the best we could, in the hope of better times and a New Revelation.

But how, and to what extent, it may be asked, is upholstery indebted to the authors of "Kenilworth" and "Nôtre Dame de Paris?" For an answer let the questioner look back upon the "furniture" of English literature for a century prior to the appearance of the Waverley Novels. The gorgeous picturesqueness of the Shaksperian, the Spenserian, and the Jonsonian poetry had disappeared. There is but a passing glow of the superbly decorative in "Comus" and the "Allegro." There is but a transient, meteor-like flash of picturesqueness in a few of Dryden's dramas. What is the *mise en scène* of Wycherly, and Congreve, and Farquhar? The Temple Gardens, rakes' dressing-rooms, gambling-houses, usurers' counting-rooms, demireps' parlours, and roystering taverns, where Brandy-faced Nan is serving out strong waters to the gentlemen, and swords are crossed in tipsy quarrels.

The " Spectator," charmingly, tenderly as the papers of Steele and Addison are written, is coarsely and meanly "furnished." Sir Andrew Freeport spends his nights at a mug-house with a sanded floor, and Sir Roger de Coverley regales on hung beef and takes a pipe of tobacco with a hackney coachman. Johnson's "furniture" is gloomy and not grand. The Orientalism of Rasselas is impossible. Goldsmith did not attempt handsome "furniture;" and when his Duke called out three times to Mr. Jerningham to bring him his garters, we gained a pretty close insight into the commonplace character of the age. Horace Walpole thought he had some taste, and was gifted, perhaps, with an infinitesimal grain of that rare quality. But Strawberry Hill was as falsely Gothic as Rasselas was falsely Oriental; and the Castle of Otranto was a very small oasis indeed in the midst of a Sahara of powder and pigtailism. Chatterton seemed, for a moment, to have had a genuine glimpse of the glorious mediæval and the more glorious Renaissance past. Some things he has attempted might be illustrated by Gustave Doré; but Chatterton was a cheat, and, being convicted, also, of poverty, poisoned himself. As for Fielding, Smollett, and Richardson, the heroes and heroines of the two former sat on inn-parlour settles, drank brown October out of Staffordshire jugs, beat the watch till they were lodged in the round-house, or slept off the effects of debauchery in night-cellars or in market-baskets; while the only "furniture" in "Pamela" and "Clarissa Harlowe" belongs to the servants' hall, the housekeeper's stillroom, Squire B——'s dining-room, and a milliner's shop. And even if we take the most brilliant and accomplished writer of the eighteenth century, how do we find that he has "furnished" his poems? Pope's "Iliad" is as polished and crisp as a crystal chandelier, and as colourless. It needed Flaxman, full fifty years afterwards, to show us the warriors who sate down before Troy in their habits as they lived. There is just a touch of the picturesque in "Windsor Forest;" and the machinery of the gnomes and sylphs in the "Rape of the Lock" is real "furniture"—real *bric-à-brac*, real *mise en scène* which William Beverley might paint, or John Gilbert draw on wood. But does any interest attach to the chairs on which Pope and Arbuthnot or Bolingbroke sat, or could there have been anything more tasteless than Lady Mary Pierrepoint's screen or old Sarah of Marlborough's mob-cap? If you doubt my right to draw inferences as to the "furniture" of an age from its literature, go and look at Hogarth's pictures. There you will find the clumsiest, unshapeliest chairs and tables and beds, the coarse homeliness of which is common to the dwellings of the poor and the rich, but which in the houses of the latter is glorified by coverings of gorgeous stuffs, while fundamental nakedness is concealed by a crowd of bizarre and ill-chosen pictures and chimney-ornaments brought from Italy, and belonging to Italy's most corrupt and degraded period of art. "Burlington Gate" and the second scene of the "Marriage à la Mode" are unerring indices to the taste in "furniture" of the eighteenth century.

Sir Walter Scott came upon an age which, lately upheaved by two tremendous democratic revolutions — in America, and in France—had abandoned powder, and patches and hoops, cocked hats, high-heeled shoes and silver-hilted rapiers, to become, in France, ultra-Græco-Roman in its dress and furniture, and ultra-extravagant in everything; and, in England, through the mere sulkiness of Tory hatred to freedom, had lapsed into a more than Quaker-like simplicity.

Nothing could possibly be uglier than the dresses our fathers wore, the houses they built, and the furniture with which they garnished their dwellings. From the death of Louis XVI. until the downfall of Napoleon, taste and style lay dormant, and even all but dead in England. Some weakly attempts to revive the pastoral were made in literature; but the picturesque was almost untouched. Scott came to his work to find such "furniture" as may be seen in Dr. Moore's "Zeluco," or in Mackenzie's "Man of Feeling," or Hayley's "Triumphs of Temper," or in the "Spiritual Quixote," or the "Fool of Quality." Miss Edgeworth had a right insight, but her *mobilier* was mainly confined to the description of Irish shebeens and rack-rent castles. Coleridge had an inkling of the artistic future—witness his "Christabel" and "Genevieve" —but he resided, mostly, in cloud-land. Wordsworth gave the world little beyond the interior of a cowhouse, or the configuration of a market-cart. Now came the Great Wizard of the North, and turned upholsterer. He took up a crowd of moss-grown towers, of ruined abbeys, of crumbling castles, of haunted mansion-houses, of cottages, and desolate manses, and he furnished them—furnished them with an affluence and copiousness of grandeur and comeliness and glowing colour such as the world had never seen since the days of Jean Goujon and Andrea Sansovino, of Pierino del Vaga and Maître Roux. From the enchanting romances of Walter Scott came forth a bright band of knights and men-at-arms, of noble damsels and comely bower-maidens, of seneschals, pursuivants, halberdiers, and dwarfs and jesters in spangled gear. Out they came to the waving of pennons and the brandishing of Andrea Ferraras and the sound of the sackbut and the dulcimer. Pigtail, powder, and patches fled, their wearers howling in affright; and the grand men and women of Shakspeare's time,—of Tasso's, of Brantôme's, of Florio's, of Chaucer's, of Froissart's time, trod the stage once more. Whose blood has not leaped up in his veins when in "Ivanhoe" disguises after disguises are thrown off, and the Black Knight bursts upon us as Richard of England, and the fat hermit as Friar Tuck, and Locksley the yeoman, as Robin Hood? "I am Robin Hood of Sherwood Forest," he says, simply. There is an epic in the words. These people brought their "furniture" with them. They brought the glowing tapestry from the looms of Arras and Louvain. They brought the jewelled casket, the hauberk, and corslet of Milan steel, so curiously damascened; the ebony cabinet, with its infinite inlaying of ivory; the great silver-chased tankard, the tall Venice goblet, the high-railed chair, with its carving and velvet; the oriel window, with its stained glass; the great missal, glowing like a lamp before a shrine with illuminated pictures; the trophy of bright weapons and stags' antlers, the shining keys at the châtelaine's girdle, the jingling bauble of the fool, the hood and jess of the falconer, and the great dungeon-door of the castle, studded with rose-headed nails. This was the kind of "furniture" Sir Walter Scott, in a score of books, brought back to us. He struck a chord, and the whole heart of a people, sick of paint, powder, pigtails, and patches, answered him joyously and gratefully. I have heard ere now the revival of taste in the mediæval and Renaissance art ascribed to the late Mr. Pugin, to the "Tracts for the Times," and to Mr. Ruskin; but, to my mind, this revivalism must be traced much further back. Its real source is in the novels of Sir Walter Scott. The library at Abbotsford was the precursor of innumerable picturesquely-furnished English houses. The influence of Sir Walter in this direction has been durable. Although his novels are not half so eagerly read now as they should be, the love for the good old times and the good old furniture which he awakened has not declined, and carved oak and stained glass have held, and will hold, their own through the fiercest mutations of fashion. He did more than the author of the "Corsair," more than the author of "Lallah Rookh." They tried, and succeeded for a while, in making the East fashionable; but it was not long ere the public discovered that the Veiled Prophet of Khorassan was a humbug, and that out of Paradise there was no such being as a Peri. The impress of Mr. Thomas Moore's genius did not extend beyond the landscape annuals and the walls of the Water Colour Society. The belles of fashion declined to array themselves in snowy turbans and spangled gauze trousers, and sit, cross-legged, on divans, playing on the mandolin. The light of Mr. Moore's harem was very soon put out, and his bulbul whispered to the rose in vain. The influence of Lord Byron was, for a season, more powerful, as his genius was immeasurably greater. But the "furniture" he bestowed on his dramas was false, and in the end the public rejects that which is not true. "Lying is not permitted by the Eternals," writes Mr. Carlyle. Byron's stay in the East had been brief; his acquaintance with Eastern languages was almost nil; his knowledge of Oriental manners and customs superficial. Compare his written "furniture" in "Lara," or the "Giaour," with a picture, say, by Lewis or Holman Hunt—compare his Gulnares, Medoras, Gulbeyaz, and Haidees, with the real Oriental women—the dusky, flabby, lazy, stupid creatures who make themselves sick with sugarplums and tobacco-

smoke in real Oriental harems—and the failure in durability
of the Byronic furniture may be at once accounted for. It
was very pretty when it was new, but it would not last. A
number of silly young ladies believed the scoundrel Conrad
and the egotistical Childe to be heroes, for a time, and a
number of sillier young gentlemen turned up their eyes and
turned down their shirt-collars in a vain attempt to look like
the noble bard; but it would not do. It very soon became
apparent that Conrad and the Childe, Lara and Manfred,
Werner and Marino Faliero, Don Juan and Jacopo Foscari
were all one and the same person, and that person was the
Right Honourable George Gordon Noel Byron. The intrinsic
selfishness of the Byronic philosophy accounts for the very
slight hold which Byronism obtained on the customs, the
costume, or the furniture of his age; but Sir Walter Scott
was a true man from head to heel, and the mediævalism he
inculcated, traced back to the original models, and found to be
as true, has become an integral part of domestic decoration.

The revolution in the adornment of our habitations commenced in Britain by Sir Walter Scott was continued in
France by Victor Hugo. I shall be accused, I hope, of no
overdue tension of chronology, in order to suit my text, if I
name as a contemporary of him who wrote "Waverley" the
illustrious author of "Les Misérables." Byron might have
been contemporary with Tennyson, and yet Byron seems to
have been dead a hundred years; and, without any violation
of the laws of time, Napoleon the Great might have lived to
witness the funeral of Wellington. Although much the
younger man, Victor Hugo had yet obtained European
celebrity ere the fame of Scott had begun to pale. The
"Odes et Ballades," the "Orientales," and the "Chants du

Crépuscule," were published before the " Fair Maid of Perth " or " Count Robert of Paris " had made their appearance ; and the gorgeous series of Waverley Novels had scarcely been brought to a close—their author, I believe, still lived— when from the lurid smoke of the Revolution of July arose the superb Renaissance romance of " Nôtre Dame de Paris." That romance, as all the world knows, is as full of old-new furniture as the Hôtel de Cluny. It was gorged with sumptuous appointments—with carved fald-stools, and cunningly-woven arras. It resounded with the clanking of men in armour and the clattering of halberts and partisans. It brought back the Moyen Age to France as completely as " Ivanhoe" and " Kenilworth" had brought back the days of the Plantagenets and the Tudors to England; and the gauntlet thus thrown down in literature was continued, in successive defiances on the stage. In " Lucrezia Borgia," in " Ruy Blas," and in " Le Roi s'amuse;" all Renaissance dramas, all abounding in oratories, and torture-chambers, donjon-keeps, and Venetian palace-gardens tenanted by mysterious personages in ruffs, and *sottanelli,* and long rapiers, by gallants with guitars, and ladies in black velvet masks. What had the French stage seen before for upwards of a hundred years ?—the sham shepherdesses and sham marquises of Marivaux and Crébillon, the sham Greeks and Romans of Voltaire and Delille, the sham Shaksperians of Ducis. As for " Nôtre Dame de Paris," it is not unadvisedly that I style it a gage of defiance. It was flung deliberately in the teeth of the classical romancists, of the Vicomte d'Arlincourt, with his " Solitary," of the sublime but stilted Chateaubriand, with his impossible Indian chieftains and maidens, and his ideal American lovers, who, in their exile in Florida, are able to hear the roar of the Falls of Niagara.· As is usual, when a revolution in "furniture" takes place, the painter and the musician hastened eagerly to wait on the poet and romancer. M. Victor Hugo found, first designers to illustrate, and ultimately upholsterers to put his glowing tableaux into solid and practical shape. Delacroix, Delaroche, and, to a certain extent, Ary Scheffer, boldly ranged themselves under the "Romantic" standard. "The Murder of the Duke of Guise," "Mignon Regretting her Country," would have been impossible pictures under the Empire. Even the art anchorite Ingres—the disciple of David, the devotee of Raffaelle, lifted his cap, as it were, in passing, to the "Romantic" School in his picture of the "Odalisque"*—an undraped young woman whose orientalism is problematical, but who is still infinitely preferable to the Medeas and Atlantas, the daughters of Danaüs, and the Mothers of the Gracchi, who poured from the school of David while Cæsar reigned. The struggle, however, of Victor Hugo and his followers was a bitter one, and the battle was with no mean or feeble opponents. The Bourbons, " sleeping in the sheets of Napoleon," had condescended to patronise that " classic" style which he so passionately admired. Napoleon hated the Renaissance. He thought that he loved the Romantic, but he fell in love with a lay figure, in Ossian ; and it is worthy of remark that the hero, whose life was one long-continued romance, and replete with adventures of almost incredible picturesqueness, should have tolerated, in literature and art, only the coldest, most colourless, most unreal reproductions of remote antiquity. The straight, formal, lavishly gilt yet poorly enriched, and thoroughly

* See chapter on the Fine Arts.

uncomfortable drawing-room furniture belonging to the "*Style Empire*," is as characteristic of Napoleon's reign as the spurious Greek dresses of the ladies of his Court—as the interminable laurel and olive-leaf embroideries on the coats of his senators and prefects, his chamberlains and his academicians—as the bas-reliefs, monstrous in their ugliness, of coats without wearers, helmets without heads, boots without legs, and gloves without hands, which sprawl over the pedestal of the column in the Place Vendôme. The chairs and tables, the sofas and *guéridons*, the very clocks and candelabra of the Napoleonic epoch, are of a piece with these bas-reliefs, with the laurelled and olive-leaved coats of the courtiers, with the short-waisted and shorter-sleeved ball-dresses of the Grand Era. There was no reasoning with Napoleon on the subject. He believed only in Plutarch as an historian, in Virgil and Ossian as poets, and in David as a painter; and he thought the pedantic mandarin of the Academy, Baour-Lormian, to be the legitimate successor of Voltaire as a dramatist. As I have said, the Government of the Restoration were content to adopt the spurious classical bantling which had been reared by Bonaparte. The Hebes of antiquity were less displeasing to M. Sosthène de la Rochefoucauld, who strove so hard to lengthen the skirts of ballet-dancers, than the curt and diaphonous garments of an Esmeralda. To the Classicists the Renaissance meant licence, effrontery, free speech, free living, free thinking—in fine, horrible thought, it meant Liberty. When the Bourbons fell, and the cause of Legitimacy was lost for ever, some legitimists of course remained. Not all the Carlists followed Charles X. to Holyrood, or the Duchess of Berry to Venice. Carlism, pigtailism, classicism, call it what you will, still.

held its own, in the Faubourg St. Germain, in the columns of the great newspapers, in the jury of the exhibitions of paintings at the Louvre, in the best-known saloons, and among the arm-chairs of the Academy. It was this classicism which M. Victor Hugo—himself deeply imbued with classic lore—himself in the outset a legitimist, prior to his becoming a Bonapartist, and previous to his subsequent phases as an Orleanist and a democratic and social republican—undertook to vanquish. The fight, as I have said, was fierce; but the rout of the classicists was complete.

The actual aspect of French decorated furniture is one of repose. It is all but universally either Renaissance, or a combination of the styles which flourished at the end of the sixteenth and the beginning of the seventeenth century, and of which the magnificent travelling *bureau*, made for the Maréchal de Créquy, now in the Hôtel de Cluny, the *portières* and *lucarnes* of Pierre Collot, the chimney-pieces of Jean Berain—to say nothing of that which Jean Goujon has left in the Louvre, and Maître Roux and his disciples at Fontainebleau—are, perhaps, the best examples which have come down to us. An analogous and kindred order, but one more quaint and less lavish in decoration, more sober and less elaborate, is to be found in what we term the "Elizabethan"—a style in which the heavy but noble characteristics of the furniture which was fitted for the sleeping rooms of Tudor houses, and the guest-halls of "courts" and "granges," were blended with those more graceful lines of Italian-Renaissance architecture which Inigo Jones had learnt from Palladio and Sebastian Serlio, and with the bounteous but always dignified enrichments of the frames, and cabinets, and cornices of Venetian manufacture—a manufacture most attentively and beneficially studied by Englishmen of taste during the Elizabethan period, when the intercourse between England and the Great Republic of the Adriatic was much greater than it is now, or ever can be again. [This is not the place in which to show, from internal evidence, that William Shakspeare must have made a voyage to Venice, probably as the supercargo of a vessel— which would account for the sea scene in the "Tempest"— else he never would have placed the villa of Portia, a Venetian lady, at Belmont, *on the main land.* To this day the Venetian nobility have their villas, not in Venice, but on the banks of the Brenta, on the *terra firma ;* but it is well to bear in mind our close and friendly relations with Venice between 1580 and 1620, when we examine our Elizabethan frames and bedsteads, cabinets and bookcases. Compare their bosses, cartouches, and cornices with the ornamental borders to the "costumes of Cesare Vecellio," so recently and so admirably reproduced by the house of Firmin Didot, and it will be found that there is a most remarkable similarity between them and the Elizabethan carvings and decorations with which Mr. Nash's great work has made us so familiar in England.]

The Renaissance in furniture, as in architecture, would seem to be best suitable to the genius and character of the French people. They never favoured the strictly classical, save during the short frenzy of the Directory, when, as Madame Tallien and other daughters of Eve chose to dress or rather undress, *à la Grecque,* obsequious upholsterers took to the study of Montfaucon's Antiquities, and provided them with the *cathedra,* the *triclinium,* and other articles of furniture designed after classical models, and executed in bran-new

Paris satin damask and ormolu. They never endured the classical, save under the coercion of Napoleon, who, strong-minded as he was, was crazy after pseudo-classics. He had the Arch of Septimius Severus on the brain, and babbled of the Forum Boarium. There is nothing more tasteless, perhaps, nothing at once so cumbrous and so meagre, so redundant in ornament, yet so poor in real elegance, as that "Empire" style to which I have more than once made allusion. Ostensibly classical as it was, it had about it a *je ne sais quoi* of the cavalry parade and the barrack-room; and only the other day, on the forty-sixth anniversary of his death, when I saw the veterans of the Grand Army feebly trotting towards the Place Vendôme to hang their garlands of immortelles on the Great Man's column—when I looked upon those valiant ghosts, with their huge helmets, their busbies with shaving brushes at the top, and ladies' work-bags hanging on one side, their embroidered pantaloons, their dolmans heavy with tarnished lace and sugar-loaf buttons, their sabertaches for ever getting between their legs, their pigtails, their sabres, their spurs, their white locks and withered pippin-faces, their shrunken limbs and quivering hands, all apparently belonging to the Year One—or rather to that more definite year when Austerlitz was fought—when I beheld that half-solemn, half-grotesque procession—*le sublime du ridicule*, as the French have dubbed it—I would have given much to dismantle, there and then, the old furniture shops of the Rue Louis le Grand and the Rue Basse du Rempart, and to have seated those old warriors down on the chairs, sofas, and footstools of the Napoleonic period. Indeed, the charm of association is the only one which can make the furniture of the First Bonaparte tolerable. The upholsterers had, it is true, studied Montfaucon, but they had understood him badly. Their minds were in a state of artistic confusion as to whether Lucius Junius Brutus or Mutius Scævola were really antique Romans, or whether they were *forts de la halle* who had turned *sans culottes* and Jacobins, and danced the Carmagnole. The classic gold was in the quartz, and of the quartz was made the furniture. Mr. Hope had not yet written, Canina's book was in embryo, the Elgin marbles were yet the target for the soldiers of a Turkish pasha to shoot at, and the treasures of Etruria were not yet disentombed. The classicism that reigned was that of the "Young Anacharsis" and Fénélon's "Telemachus." To complete the debasement of the classic model set up for artists, the great authority in all matters of taste during Napoleon's reign was Dénon. The Emperor and King who knew no human will but his own until the day when he found that he must defer to that of an English sergeant of the guard—the Imperial organiser and dogmatist who, at one blow, by one passage in one decree, "enregimented" the theocracy and made the Gallican Church a church militant indeed, by declaring that a bishop should have the pay of a general of division, had made up his mind that as Dénon knew a great deal about the Pyramids, he must know quite as much about the Parthenon or Adrian's villa. Napoleon virtually gazetted Dénon as Field Marshal commanding the Army of Connoisseurs. Now, if Napoleon had Septimius Severus on the brain, Dénon had Egypt. The consequence was that the Pyramids got mixed up with the Parthenon in the furniture of the *Style Empire* as inextricably as King Charles I.'s head in Mr. Dick's memorial; and thus, while you are scrutinising Imperial clocks, and sofas, and consoles, you are often astounded to find the sphinx sitting on the top of a Corinthian column, Isis piping to the Hours while they dance, and Pharaoh's daughter weeping because Adonaïs is dead. We all know that when Greek art was in its infancy Egypt was a nursing-mother to her; but that when Greek art was old, and effete, as in the time of Cleopatra, Egypt came in as a step-mother, and strangled her. This is plain enough in the " classical " furniture of the Emperor, as " improved " by the influence of Dénon. An unnatural alliance has been essayed between Cleopatra and Pallas Athené, and the result is confusion. Judged by any strict canon, tried by any pure standard, the furniture of the Empire is as " unclassical " as the stucco abominations committed by Nash—not the " old-mansion " Nash, but the George the Fourth one—in Regent Street. But the " charm of association " I have mentioned adheres to those uncouth and over-ornamented pieces of furniture, and it is a charm that will not easily or soon be unwoven. The tawdry, tasteless gear belongs to a heroic age —to the age when there were giants in the land—the age when *cocottes* were not the leaders of patronage and *boursiers* the doubles of statesmen, and when diplomacy was used to serve other ends than to procure a " concession " for the pulling down of a back street or the keeping of a cookshop. Wander into one of those old furniture shops in the Rue Louis le Grand. Make the *brocanteur* drag from the labyrinth of darkness and cobwebs the old squabby sofas, gouty arm-chairs, and rickety tables of the Empire, plethoric in body yet with spindle-shanks like tavern " rummers." Look on their faded satin and their tarnished gilding; admire those griffins and chimeras, those sphinxes and dragons, those endless scrolls, those Gordian knots of carving and gilding.

They are old, they are æsthetically ugly, they are hopelessly *rococo*; yet gaze upon them attentively, and association will give a fresh glow to their pallid draperies, and make their shabby gilding shine again. They are tenanted once more by the brave men and the beautiful women of the Grand Epoch. Over that dingy sofa leans a cavalier handsomer than D'Orsay, more splendid than Esterhazy, braver than the Cid. He is all gold and diamonds and white plumes. He is the *beau sabreur*, the innkeeper's son, Joachim Murat, Grand Duke of Berg and King of Naples. Then, do you see the graceful gracious woman who is talking to him, flirting her fan meanwhile. That is Madame Récamier, the banker's wife. Do you see those two wicked old men at the green-covered table, chattering over their *bouillotte*, and sneering at the world as they cut for deal. They are old Cambacérès, arch-chancellor, and old Talleyrand, arch-rogue. Yonder slender dame, with the long, long satin train winding behind her, who rises with infinite dignity and grace of mien from her *fauteuil*, and walks towards her aviary to " put her birds to bed "—do you know who that lady is to whom belong that sweetest of smiles, those tenderest of eyes? That is the incomparable Joséphine Beauharnais. And here is a stern, massive, austerely gilded arm-chair, a heavy *bureau*, an *escritoire* at the side, where a secretary is writing busily. They are all *Style Empire:* arm-chair, *bureau, escritoire,* secretary and all, down to the very inkstand, belong to the Empire—to the Empire who is There, too, incarnate, with the beautiful Græco-Roman face—the face of the young Augustus in the Vatican, and with the lock of dark, silky hair careleslsy sloping over his white forehead. He is in the uniform of the Chasseurs of the Guard, with kerseymeres and silk stockings;

but he is the same Empire whose incarnation you have seen limned a hundred times, clad in the grey great-coat and the little cocked hat. This is the *Lui* of Béranger and Victor Hugo—the Emperor and King who grasped the world, and died upon a rock.

But I leave the First Empire for the Second and existing one.

The productions of Henri Fourdinois of Paris exhibit, in the highest degree, the qualities of which I spoke as characteristic of the most modern phase of French cabinetmaking. The force of imitation of Renaissance and sixteenth-century models in French "fancy furniture" can perhaps no further go. Perfection in the reproduction of the masterpieces of the past has been attained; and it may be said even "plus-quam-perfection" has been reached—since French grammarians acknowledge such a tense as the *plusque parfait*—in delicacy of fitting, in evenness of workmanship, and in luxuriance of enrichment. It would seem as though the French *ébénistes*, having succeeded in all that art-workmen could achieve in the way of noble modelling and glowing harmony of line, had found a new impetus to excellence in the study of those marvellously intricate and elaborate performances in carving and inlaying which increased acquaintance with China, with India, and with Japan has brought within our reach. Beautiful and astonishing as are those works, they seldom fail to bear internal evidence of a state of civilisation which is imperfect, or which, at least, is diametrically opposed to our own. They bear some mysterious Paynim stamp. They have vaguely but unmistakably the impress of belonging to a country whose conditions of existence can ever be ours—of having been fabricated by workmen who will never be brought to wear the coats and trousers and chimney-pot hats of the western world, and who, while their manipulative dexterity confounds and abashes the European artisan, always show, in their works, the faultiness inseparable from the absence of that mathematical neatness and regularity which the use of machinery and machine-made tools alone can give. A very striking example of this was brought to my mind recently when visiting the bronze works of M. Barbédienne, in the Rue de Lancry. I was shown a goblet in the enamel known as *cloisonné*, most rarely and beautifully chiselled—by hand, it is true, but by a workman provided with the very best tools, and with every kind of machinery at command for squaring and proving the accuracy of his work. And then, when I had sufficiently admired this goblet, the gentleman who showed me through the works produced a Chinese or Japanese goblet of a pattern very similar to the French-made one, but in which the effect of chiselling was given by means of thin wire carefully soldered on to the surface in infinite intricacy of pattern. It must have been the work of months, if not of years. Such a piece produced by a French artisan would have been worth, from the mere cost of the *main d'œuvre* bestowed upon it, much more than its weight in gold; and yet, turning from this ineffably curious trifle you saw, in your mind's eye, the native workman with his shaven crown and long pigtail, and his jerkin and breeks of blue cotton, squatting in a dark, evil-smelling little hovel no bigger than a cobbler's stall, and lavishing all the cunning of his eye and hand on this toy, day after day and week after week, for a meagre bowl of rice and a few "cash" a day. This wonderful thing may be said, emphatically, to be finished the Lord knows how; and equally does the Lord know why these strange nations should have attained proficiency in these arts centuries and centuries ago, and yet have never grown to be anything better than dirty, bloodthirsty, dishonest, sly, silken barbarians. Is it not the same with Eastern carpets? You know what kind of work are those of Aubusson. You know all about M. Sallandrouze de Lamornaix, and Sir Francis Crossley, and Bright Brothers. I shall have something to say, by-and-by, of Brinton and Lewis of Kidderminster. You have been told of the immensity of the capital invested in their enterprises, of the various and splendid machinery they use, of their gigantic profits, of the magnificent social position the *Princes de la Tapisserie* assume, of their munificent gifts in parks, schools, and libraries; and yet have we not seen in the East, in some dirty bye-lane, the swarthy carpet-weaver, a ragged turban on his head, and a raggeder cloth round his loins for all gear, crouching on his hams before his loom, in a dark hole with a clay floor, chickens feeding about him, and a stolid camel looking through the unglazed hutch of his workshop? There he squats, seemingly indolent and half asleep. We know what a paltry wage of piastres is his. We know that he has no certificated student of the Government School of Art to design patterns for him, no skilful chemists to dye new yarns for him, no accomplished Dr. Dresser to teach him the canons of polychromatic harmony; yet, day after day and year after year, working only from some dim traditions of colour and design, handed down, perhaps, from the days of Father Abraham, he will toil on, turning out carpets as beautiful and as gorgeous as any that our tapestry princes can produce. *And he is none the better for it.* The sheik will not abate him a penny of his poll-tax for his cleverness' sake; the cadi will bastinado the nails off his toes if he be too poor to bribe him; the pasha will spoil him of his goods if in an odd year he has contrived to lay by the price of a few yards of carpet. He has never been the better for anything. The Curse of the East is upon him—the curse that blights all and everything in those delicious regions. He who makes attar of roses lives like a pig, and never knew what it was to use a pocket-handkerchief. He who so exquisitely damascenes sword-blades and pistol-rods has never a knife and fork, and he who covers the caftan with that sumptuous gold embroidery, has not a shirt to his back, and his breeches are like unto those of the Needy Knife-grinder. More than that, he does not care about mending the holes. Father Abraham, perhaps, wore no trousers at all, and the Koran says nothing about the franchise or compound householders, or Mechanics' Institutions, or Industrial Exhibitions. If the Imperial Commissioners could have shown a few real Eastern workmen in the Champ de Mars, and provided for the delivery of a few lectures on the real condition of the Oriental "proletarian," more practical service would have been done to the great cause of social economics than by dressing up a score of Orientalised Frenchmen and rapscallions of the towns on the Levantine seaboard in fezzes and caftans, and passing them off as Turks and Egyptians, or by allowing the French manager of the Hippodrome to palm off jugglers from Franconi's circus, and acrobats from the Foire, as genuine "Celestials" in the "Chinese" theatre of the Champ de Mars, which was about as Chinese as the Bains Chinois.

To return to M. Fourdinois. His masterpiece is a carved cabinet of light woods—in which I at first suspected some of the more delicate *nuances* had been tinted by hand—in the late sixteenth-century style. The columns and pilasters are so architecturally true to the laws of Vitruvius, that the work might be called a combination of sixteenth and seventeenth centuries. A little more, and the richness of the decoration would become redundant, and fall into that class denounced by some, admired by others, of which the Jesuits have left us such dazzling examples in Rome, and Venice, and Seville. The Jesuit draughtsmen excluded, however, the female figure undraped, or semi-draped, from their designs. Their Virgins and angels had, like the Queen of Spain, no legs; it was only in their little naked children—theological Cupids, so to speak —that they ventured to portray the human form in all its majesty of " nothingondom." The Renaissance, on the contrary, from its birth, under the joyous influence of Francis I., to its death, under the intolerable incubus of the crowned pedagogue Louis XIV., scorned not to admit the nymph and the satyr, the dryad and the faun, into its upholstery, and the cabinet-work of this long and glorious epoch of French art abounds with statuettes, and masks and medallions in *rondo bosso*—in carved *alti-rilievi* with mythological subjects, and with those figures supporting cornices which, if females, are called "Caryatides," and if males, " Persians." In classic decoration these figures are usually of severe aspect and flowingly draped; but there was a dash of the Bohemian, a spice of the grotesque, and a kindly remembrance of the Gothic in all the Renaissance did; and so we find the Caryatides of this era frequently half human or half vegetable, or half monstrous. The Renaissance artists were not at all inclined to agree with Horace as to the absurdity of representing a beautiful woman with the tail of a fish. M. Fourdinois' cabinet resumes and sums up all the conclusions I have hazarded here. This work, taken in its chronological aspect, is the *dernier mot* of decoration prior to the ponderous scroll-work of Jussieu, and the sprawling allegories of Lebrun. In this work we see that the Medici, from Catherine to Mary, are going out, and that La Vallière and Montespan are coming in. The ruff, the 'broidered doublet, the plumed cap disappear; and, under the Grand Monarque, we must look only for carved and gilt periwigs and high-heeled shoes in polished ebony.

I hold M. Fourdinois' cabinet to be the masterpiece, not only of his own stock, but of the entire French furniture department. A very accomplished connoisseur who was with me when I studied this piece took exception to its decoration as excessive in finish, and to the delicate gradation of the tones in its substance as "finicking" and pallid. "It is not like wood," he objected; "it is like wax." I have heard objections precisely similar urged against M. Leopold Harzé's terra cottas. They do not resemble clay, it is said; they resemble wax. So also may you tell me that Elkington's repoussé shield does not bear the appearance of having been beaten up with a hammer. It looks as though it had been carved out of the solid. Giving due value to all these reservations, I think that praise, and praise of an unqualified nature, should be awarded, in a manufacture of which the mainstay is *workmanship*, to him who shows the strongest, brightest proof of hard, patient, skilful, conscientious work and labour done. And this praise belongs, I opine, to Henri Fourdinois. He received a gold medal, and he is a Knight of the Legion of Honour; but had I to distribute rewards, the names of every one of his carvers should be published, that all art-Europe might honour them.

Work of another kind—work in perfection as great, yet as

different in degree from Fourdinois' as light from darkness, as summer from winter—is shown in Jackson and Graham's great ebony cabinet inlaid with ivory. It was found impossible to complete inlaying the last of the three panels into which the substructure is divided in time for the Exhibition; but the hiatus was most skilfully filled up by a photographic reproduction of the corresponding panel, which, tastefully tinted and covered with glass, so admirably compensated for the yet unfinished portion that, but for a notification of the means resorted to affixed to the panel, few but professional critics would have discovered that aught was wanting to the perfection of this noble work. The missing panel was, later in the season, adjusted in its place. The engraving of the inlaid ivory is as fine as anything that Cellini or Maso Finiguerra ever conceived, or that the Florentine or Milanese niello-workers, or the *grabadores* of Toledo or Damascus, ever executed. The inlaying of the ivory itself into the ebony is astounding. The white lines, for example, bordering the flutings of the pilasters are as geometrically true as though they had been dropped by a plummet into their place. There must be many joinings, there must be much "mitreing" of the joints, yet so artful has been the fitting of the pieces that not a hair's breadth of fissure is visible. It appears as one pure and perfect piece of cutting through ivory—like a screen or a shawl of lace, taken up bodily and laid, in one mass, into wood made soft to receive it. Yet we know that such has not been the case; we know that the workman, with an almost *religious* persistence in his work—and Carlylians will not quarrel with the term—has laid in the ivory morsel by morsel, strip by strip, curve by curve. The result is most perfect unity, solidity, and natural grace. You might pass your finger—as connoisseurs try fine porcelain—over·the whole of these surfaces without finding a prominence or an inequality. In fine, in this cabinet of Jackson and Graham's I recognise a superlative degree of excellence in the "flat," as Henri Fourdinois has reached superlative excellence in the "round." No reproach, however, can be levelled against Messrs. Jackson and Graham on the score of their work's resembling some material of which it is not really composed. It is not like wax, or like marble, or like bronze, or like *carton-pierre*. It is simply like what it is : ebony inlaid with ivory, sober, simple, well nigh severe in the purity of its lines, yet a triumphant and amazing example of what sedulous *work*, aided by chastened taste, can achieve. I do not like the lapis lazuli and porphyry *plaques* on this cabinet. They disfigure its wonderful unison of tone. They blend with nothing and jar with everything in the work, and the best thing Messrs. Jackson and Graham could have done would have been to take them off again.

The employment, however, of *plaques*, either smooth or in low relief *à la* Wedgwood, in porcelain, imitation jasper, and especially in the glorious blue and white Limoges enamels, is gaining ground every day in the accessory decoration of furniture, and is, to my mind, infinitely preferable to the high reliefs in red terra cotta with which some cabinet-makers have taken to filling their panels. In the first place, terra cotta—unless its design be in the highest sense artistic—looks too cheap for employment in the rich and rare woods of which cabinets are usually composed. Ivory, or gilt, or silvered bronze, or Parian, or porcelain, serve fitly and grace-fully for this purpose ; but a staring mass of red terra cotta— as in Mr. Gillow's "trophy" sideboard, otherwise a noble piece of work—reminds one of the vulgar saying about "putting a beggar on a gentleman." Who would fill up a Florentine picture-frame with a hodful of bricks? Yet this is precisely the effect produced by the importation of a ponderous mass of baked earth into the midst of most delicate and graceful carved work. The Limoges enamels, on the contrary, with their gem-like surface and their glowing backgrounds of richest ultramarine harmonise admirably with an environment of dark wood, say of stained oak, but especially of ebony. M. Roux, in the French department, has an exceedingly beautiful specimen of what can be done with enamelled *plaques* as panels to an ebony cabinet. There are numerous other examples of furniture in the French department in this funereal material; but in the majority of cases, although their design is admirable and their carving elaborate, they are intolerably lugubrious in appearance, and were it not that the "performer" of funerals, when away from his trestles and his trays of feathers, is usually as merry a man as the deceased husband of the nurse in "Romeo and Juliet," I should recommend these sable articles of furniture as chiefly suitable for the drawing-room of an enriched undertaker. One needs only to look at a pianoforte to become aware of the value of ebony when placed in juxtaposition with some other hue; but alone, without a line or a " beading " of white or of metal to relieve its monotony, it gives one the horrors. Oak is the only wood that can stand alone. It is the gold of the forest, and to gild it is as idle a work of supererogation as to gild a guinea.

I may be excused for a few " more last words " on the question of the employment of earthenware or porcelain in the decoration of furniture, for I hold it to be a most vital one. The use of such a material, incontestably beautiful as it is, and even more durable than the wood on which it is encrusted, bids fair to supply one pressing want felt by the purchasers of decorated furniture; to wit, moderation in price. Such a wondrous cabinet as the ebony and ivory work of Jackson and Graham may be cheap at fifteen hundred guineas—indeed, the firm declare that they would not care about making another for less than two thousand; but it is obvious that such masterpieces are within the reach of millionaires only. A room filled with similar furniture *en suite*, combined with an unlucky Derby, and a little dabbling in the Portland, Dartmoor, Spike Island, Botany Bay, and Norfolk Island Junction Railway would suffice to ruin a Crœsus. Moreover, such works must be, virtually, unique. Messrs. Jackson and Graham could find an adequate number of art-workmen skilled in inlaying; but they experienced the very greatest difficulty in lighting on artists who could execute the rare and delicate engraving work with which the whole surface of the inlaid ivory is covered. Even then, the experts who could engrave the scrolls and cartouches could not touch figures, of which the original design comprised a considerable number. In fact, the manufacturers awakened to the conviction that a Maso Finiguerra or a Marc Antonio is not born every day; and when he is born, and the art-upholsterer is so fortunate as to catch him, the rare Marc or Max expects a sumptuous retaining-fee. So it is with the carvers. Surprising developments in this difficult art have been made within the last ten years, and carving, to some extent, can be executed by machinery; but the Grinling Gibbonses or the Alvilas are still few and far between, and, when found, must be remunerated in accordance with their merits. For such a work, for example, as M. Fourdinois' cabinet, not alone the skill of the artisan, but the genius of an accomplished artist was required; and genius now-a-days has taken to be very businesslike, and demands a very high price for its inspirations. In any case, be the wood carved or inlaid, its decoration is apt to become monotonous without the introduction of panels or medallions appropriately decorated. On the principle of *pâte sur pâte*, these panels are frequently bas-reliefs, carved, like the surroundings, in wood. The only objection against their use is the enormous expense. That which can be urged—and validly urged—against the employment of ponderous terra cottas, I have recently pointed out. Such enamels as those of Limoges, or such mosaics as those of Rome and Venice, are in every way suitable to the purpose of adornment; but still the middle-class purchaser is warned off the premises by the exorbitancy of the price. Paintings in oil or in distemper by distinguished artists might fill the vacuum, but modern painters are still too haughty to do on cabinets and sideboards that which Giulio Romano and Paolo Veronese were not too proud to do on ceilings. Porcelain and earthenware remain; and these, although in the highest degree artistic, can by the amount of skill, capital, and enterprise brought to bear on their production be produced at a comparatively cheap rate. The gradual progression in the use of ceramic art in decoration has been very curious. In the last century painted tiles— and the earthenware *plaque* is but a painted tile—were only to be found lining the sides of fire-places. Then a few dairies were tiled in white. Then we began to adopt the practice in our halls and conservatories. I have recently seen tiles adopted—after the fashion followed from time

immemorial in those Moorish and Turkish interiors, which
Mr. John Lewis so exquisitely reproduces on canvas—as
panelling for walls.   For a smoking-room there could not be
a more charming decoration than slabs of painted pottery.
Of late, as we have seen, ceramics have been promoted from
stationary to movable articles, and the gaily dight *plaque*
relieves the sombre hue of ebony, and heightens the mellow-
ness of oak and the sheen of rose and satin wood.   This
universal pottery has risen even higher—even to the ceiling.
There is in Paris, just now, an "Exhibit," albeit it is not
displayed in the Champ de Mars, than which there is nothing
more curious or more beautiful among the myriads of marvels
collected in the World's Fair, and which shows in an eminent
degree to what truly practical uses the potter's art may be
turned.   I allude to the ceiling of the vast saloon now in
course of construction for the accommodation of readers
at the Imperial Library in the Rue Vivienne.   The architecture of this new reading room in no way recalls the
inimitable rotunda which we owe to Mr. Panizzi and
Mr. Smirke, and which is among the chief glories of our
British Museum.   The French architect, however, has worked
out his idea—a very peculiar and original one—with much
grace, and with infinite good taste.   The style of the saloon
may be qualified as quasi-Alhambresque, dimly reminiscent
of the Hall of the Ambassadors at Granada, and consisting of
a number of cupolas supported on slender iron columns.
There might be some reason to fear a multiplicity of echoes,
were not silence an observance rigidly insisted on in the
reading-rooms of public libraries.   That the ceilings of these
domes should be composed of earthenware slabs was, I
believe, part of the primary design, and continental Europe

was explored, and explored in vain, for potters willing to undertake a task so colossal. But Dresden hung back; the Dutchmen confessed that such tiles were beyond their ken; the Chinamen who covered the Porcelain Tower of Nankin were not forthcoming; and even Sèvres shrank from what the Americans would term such an "almighty big thing." At length the Messrs. Copeland expressed their willingness to grapple with the difficulty. The firm of which Mr. Alderman Copeland is the head went to work, brought all their resources into play, and the result of their labours is a veritable triumph of ceramic art, unequalled save in the monuments of Arab antiquity which continue to excite the wonder and delight of the wanderer in Andalusia and Granada. As for the famous "Camera di porcellana," in the Palace of Capo di Monte at Naples, it is a mere toyshop compared with this vast hall. There are nine cupolas lined with painted slabs, *all on the curve*, and each cupola contains four thousand slabs. These thirty-six thousand tiles have been fitted with a dexterity and faultless neatness of finish which is only to be attained in English workmanship. The artistic decoration of the slabs is on a par with the excellence of the pottery, and the effect of the whole is wonderfully light, graceful, and airy. The great defect in modern ceilings is that they are so overloaded with stucco ornaments, or with carving and gilding, that they always seem to be threatening to come down on our heads; but the Messrs. Copeland's *plafond* at the Bibliothèque Impériale conduces to an impression radically different, and far more encourages the idea of additional space and altitude.

Ere I dismiss the names of Jackson and Graham, let me mention their magnificent oval marqueterie table with a centre-piece in amboyne wood, manufactured for Mr. Alfred Morrison, of Fonthill, and the beautiful articles of library furniture in ebony and ivory designed by Owen Jones, and described as *cinque cento*, but which are surely more akin, by the mother's side, to the Gothic, and, by the father's, to the Mauresque. These also are commissioned by Mr. Morrison. I do not quarrel with Mr. Owen Jones for blending the Alhambresque, however vaguely, with all he does. It is all very well for this accomplished gentleman to say that he wears a round hat, but everybody knows that "all round his hat" he wears an embroidered turban, and persons of good repute have alleged that Mr. Owen Jones has been heard ere now to murmur "La Allah, il Allah!" and to spread his prayer-carpet on the roof of his house whenever the Muezzin's doleful summons was heard from an adjacent chimney-cowl. It is the same with Mr. John Lewis, who, all member of the Athenæum Club and rector's church-warden as he may be, notoriously entertains a party of dancing dervishes, fallen upon evil days, in his back drawing-room, and, under the plea of rusticating at Walton-on-the-Naze, makes every autumn a pilgrimage to the Kaaba of Mecca.

Throughout the English court I continue to mark solid, noble, conscientiously worked-out furniture ; not garish, not redundant in embellishment, but decorated with grave splendour, the decorator never losing sight of the fact that in modern furniture comfort as well as grandeur should be considered. The leather-backed dining-room and library chairs of the Messrs. Gillow are admirable in construction and design. They are chairs meant and fit to be sate upon, which is unhappily not always the case with the articles fabricated by upholsterers, who look more towards fantastic elegance than to the real uses of their wares. The remaining articles shown by this firm are of equal excellence. I may observe, in passing, close to their section of the English furniture court are a pair of white lace curtains, thirteen yards long and seven and a half wide, stated to be made on "the widest lace machine in the world." These are exhibited by Messrs. Copestake, Moore, and Crampton, of Bow Churchyard; and it is a pity that a house so celebrated, with the Leafs and Morrisons, the Cooks and Pawsons, *et hoc genus omne*, cannot give our neighbours in Paris some adequate notion of the resources and organisation of their gigantic establishments. How a quiet draper of the Rue St. Denis would open his eyes at the sight of a Manchester warehouse! But we cannot show these our most monumental examples of wealth, industry, and perseverance. The Americans, too, have reason to complain—not that they cannot bring over Niagara, on which Great Britain has a territorial lien to the extent of fifty per cent. of the entire property, but because they cannot astound the Parisians with the view of a mammoth "up-town dry goods store," such as A. T. Stewart's, in New York. The Magasins du Louvre and the Compagnie Lyonnaise would sing very small, it may be guessed, after *that* show.

Messrs. Wright and Mansfield have a very sumptuous *armoire* cabinet in the English Louis Seize style, of satin-wood, elaborately inlaid with coloured woods, and panelled with delicious little slabs of Wedgwood ware in pale blue and white. The cabinet is the sunniest and gracefullest thing imaginable; but it is just the shadow of a shade too light and jocund. It looks as though it had been made to be eaten; and although it may contain some day "sugar and spice, and all that's nice," you don't want to eat your cupboard. Messrs. Holland have a large *dressoir*, or sideboard, in wainscot oak, magnificent in carving, in brass work, in picked-out bits of colour, and draped, even in front, with some most mediævally-figured hangings. It is Gothic—domestic Gothic—to the backbone; Gothic in every quoin, crocket, and rib. The late Mr. Pugin would have clapped his hands over it. Mr. Ruskin might weep over it, M. Viollet-le-Duc go into ecstacies over it. I am ignorant and tasteless enough to think it exceedingly ugly. It is pure Gothic, no doubt; but its beauties must be appreciated by the Goths. It is glaring and inharmonious in colour—a very "warden-pie" of dissonant tints; the composition is singularly undignified and the ornamentation confused and *criarde*. Of course, there are hundreds of judges more competent who will declare this work a masterpiece. I daresay it is; but I don't see it. It is to me devoid of meaning and purpose, and, with its crowd of ledges, shelves, and pigeon-holes, looks as though it had not made up its mind whether to be a sideboard or a bureau. The green mediæval hangings are especially unsightly.

Messrs. Heal and Son show a very sumptuous semi-canopied bedstead of satin-wood, so beautifully polished and finished that the wood might really be mistaken for Algerian onyx. A wardrobe, as elaborately finished, is in admirable keeping with the bedstead. Let me also mention a superb carved ebony cabinet, with enamels in its upper portion, by Messrs. Gillow; and a really marvellous cabinet in the Pompeian style, by Mr. Crace.

The all but complete absence from the French department of the exhibition of furniture in the cumbrous, gaudy, and tasteless styles prevalent during the latter part of the reign of Louis XIV. and the whole of that of Louis XV. is assuredly matter for congratulation. Although affection for Renaissance models may have been carried in certain cases a little too far, and the school of Fontainebleau accepted as the only true academy for design and ornamentation in France, the worst productions of the sixteenth and early seventeenth century are certainly preferable to the most sumptuous examples of Louis Quatorze and Louis Quinze, with their monstrous chimeras of carving, their griffins and human-breasted lions, their cornucopiæ, like overgrown strawberry-pottles in convulsions, their heavy mouldings and never-ending scrolls. This furniture is all ablaze with gilding; yet so ponderous is the general effect produced, that it is difficult to avoid the impression that some baser metal lies beneath the gold, and that the head which conceived and the hand which executed these tawdry things were alike of lead. However, the upholsterers of the Louis were, perhaps, not altogether to blame. They only obeyed the watchword of their epoch. False grandeur, external . magnificence, serving only to veil internal poverty and. misery, were the *mot d'ordre* of that long reign, which from its birth, amidst the convulsions of the Fronde, to its death, amidst the collapse of Blenheim and Malplaquet, served but to illustrate the pride, egotism, and ambition of one man, the dissipation and idleness of a corrupt nobility, and the inconceivable apathy and stupidity of a great European people, who could permit themselves, for more than fifty years, to be tyrannised over, trampled upon, cheated and despoiled by the most arrogant, the most unscrupulous, and the most worthless of mankind. Place but a full-bottomed periwig on the head of that colossal Sphinx whom the Hebrew bond-servants in the Royal Academy picture are dragging, beneath the taskmaster's lash, over the burning sands of Egypt, and a closely typical picture may be obtained of the Most Christian King who, at the bidding of a shaveling, revoked the Edict of Nantes, and drove a million of the most upright and most skilful of his subjects into exile, and who, after a long life of the most shameful and selfish profligacy, married a worn-out demirep turned devotee, who bullied and browbeat him, but his marriage with whom· the vain old man had never, to the end, the courage to avow. The descendant of St. Louis, pottering over the details of discipline of the widow Scarron's girl-school at St. Cyr, was a fit consummation to a drama which had been throughout false, hollow, and pretentious. And he had his Pyramid, too, this Sphinx-Scapin. By the plain of Satory his bondmen reared a monument grander than was ever dreamed of by a Cheops or a Rameses. Its vast slabs were cemented with the blood and sweat of France. The gold which should have rested in the pockets of his people, or fructified in banks and markets, was spread over the gewgaws of the Galerie des Glaces and the Œil de Bœuf. The furniture of Versailles was the most gorgeous the world had ever seen, and its fate was to be knocked to pieces or kicked downstairs by the *poissardes* and *sans-culottes* of the Revolution.

When we come to consider the furniture of the Fifteenth Louis, we find only as much tawdry and tasteless splendour, to which is superadded a great deal of meanness. Versailles was too big for the great-grandson of the Grand Monarque, and he took refuge in the snugger alcoves of the Trianon and the Parc-aux-Cerfs. The difference between his reign aud that of his predecessor might be as that between a debauched giant and a debauched dwarf. The wickedness of Louis Quatorze was on a grand scale. His many mistresses were, at least, of noble blood. Even the widow Scarron was of gentle birth. But Louis Quinze was throughout one of the *infiniment petits*. Cotillon Premier was but the wife of a farmer of the revenue; Cotillon Deux could trace her ancestry to the fish-market. Louis XIV. revelled in acres of painted ceilings, and his sideboards were as big as sarcophagi. The mirrors were on a scale of grandeur sufficient to reflect the image of him who thought himself so great a man. But nothing was too small for Louis Quinze. Beneath his auspices flourished the *petites maisons*. His suppers were as little as his soul. As his vices grew more heinous they grew punier, and his harem at last was recruited from boarding-schools and nurseries.

It is good that the French should have made an end at last of the big abominations of Louis Quatorze and the little abominations of Louis Quinze. A fantastic kind of Nemesis would seem to have fixed on the locality where the odds and ends of the *bric-à-brac* of this lying, impudent, worthless age has found refuge. If you want Louis Quatorze or Louis Quinze furniture you must go to the Quai Voltaire for it; and those ruins are indeed appropriately housed in the quarter once inhabited by the man who, above all others in his time, contributed to shatter the French monarchy to pieces. If I peopled the old furniture of the empire with ghostly occupants, with the Murats and Talleyrands and Récamiers of the Napoleonic era, might one not fancy the spectre of Claude Marie-Arouet wandering about the old furniture shops of the Quai Voltaire, and with that sardonic leer for ever on his lips, pointing with mocking finger to the vanities once prized so highly by the Chateauroux and Montespans, the Pompadours and Dubarrys, which are now of no more account than an old madrigal by Rameau, or an old scandalous historiette by Bachaumont and Tallemant des Riaux, the Hervey and the Horace Walpole of the French monarchy. Their point is gone, their savour has departed, and, for all a few vestiges of gilding, a few scraps of brocaded damask that remain, they are but dust and ashes.

It is only to be regretted that in the Champ de Mars in 1867 very few examples are to be seen of a species of decorated furniture belonging to the Louis Quinze period, which alone, among the trumpery elaborations of that century of decadence, seems really worthy of preservation and of adaptation to the needs of the present generation. I allude to the beautiful work called Buhl or Boule; the incrustation of thin *laminæ* of brass into ebony, rosewood, and especially tortoiseshell. There is scarcely any Buhl to be seen in the French court; and were it not for Germany, which continues to make a fair show in the art so highly appreciated by Grimm's correspondents at the Northern courts, one might be entitled to believe that Buhl was a mode of decoration the use of which had entirely died out in Europe. The only answer I could obtain to numerous inquiries on this head among French manufacturers was that Buhl had ceased to be "fashionable;" nor does the chance of its ever coming into fashion again appear aught but the remotest. This is to be regretted. The art was graceful, conscientious, and durable, and brought into play the highest qualities in taste, skilfulness in design and execution, industry, and patience.

Has tortoiseshell become rare, or is there—as is more probable—a growing dislike among artisans to work in brass —a material of which the manipulation has always been held to be extremely unhealthy?

In the Louis Seize style—which may be defined as a semi-reaction towards the Renaissance, and a semi-intuition of advance towards the Empire, a transition style indeed, and, like all transition styles, weak, undecided, but comparatively innocuous—there is a very splendid specimen in a cabinet by M. Grohe. The price demanded, thirty-eight thousand francs, seems audacious; but audacity in price is one of the most prominent characteristics in the modern revival of French fancy furniture. I hear of larger sums being asked year after year for completed examples of art-workmanship; but I have *not* learnt that the art-workman is in the habit of earning a napoleon a day, or anything like it. From five to six francs would seem to be the mean retribution of an ordinary *ébeniste,* while if a skilled carver or inlayer can earn eight or ten francs he may esteem himself lucky. These observations, however, imply no disparagement to M. Grohe's Louis Seize cabinet, which is, in all respects, a most remarkable and meritorious performance. It is elaborately carved and gilt, but it is *not* meretricious.

The specimens of beds and bed-furniture in the Exhibition are very numerous; and, as a rule, these couches are so gorgeous that it is difficult to imagine any personage under an Emperor, or a Grand Duchess of Gerolstein at the very least, reposing under their carved testers and canopies rich with satin, velvet, and bullion. The satin-wood bedstead and appurtenances of Messrs. Heal and Son I have already mentioned; but while halting at the court of Henri Fourdinois, I omitted to notice a bedstead he exhibits—a very marvel of grace and elegance, but so sumptuous that one might imagine it designed for the *lit de justice* of the next Most Christian King who, thanks to the whirligig of Time and the caprices of Fortune, may be permitted to afflict France with his wantonness and his extravagance. May the time be far distant and the fortune long removed! For the nonce, unless M. Fourdinois' bed find a purchaser in Governor Brigham Young as a *cadeau de noces* for his eighty-first wife, or unless some Gramont-Caderousse yet in his minority put it into an *œuf de Paques* as an Easter gift for some Hortense Schneider of the next age of *ceintures dorées*, I do not clearly see where M. Fourdinois had best look for a market for this very grandest of bedsteads. Ere I dismiss M. Henri Fourdinois from my chronicle, I may be permitted to rectify one or two errors of detail into which I unavoidably fell while criticising his cabinet. The gradations of tone among the light woods of which the cabinet are composed—mainly box, pear-tree, maple, walnut, and oak—are not in any way helped out by artificial tinting. Every wood employed stands on its own merits, and is the unsophisticated representative of its own peculiar hue. Again, it is worthy of remark that the enrichments of the panels are not carvings *laid on* the surface, but are inlaid right through the wood : they are carved marqueterie in fact. Finally, when I expressed my opinion that the designer of this cabinet deserved the cross of the Legion of Honour, I was ignorant of the fact that Henri Fourdinois— who has been designated for one of the exceptional grand prizes—was himself, from beginning to end, the designer of the work. His first professional training was that of an architect, and he is an admirable draughtsman. He first made a rough sketch of his cabinet on paper in charcoal, and, effacing this first sketch, followed it with a carefully pencilled outline, from which a model was made to scale in common deal. The enrichments and carvings were modelled upon this in wax, and successive photographs were taken, in order that ideas, both general and detailed, of the ultimate effect of the work might be gained. Then, but not till then, the sectional workmen—the carvers and inlayers and cabinet-makers—were called in, and the real cabinet was produced.

Summing up the results of that which I have studied in the French furniture department, I cannot refrain from expressing my sorrow that so little really cheap furniture is exhibited. That the articles exhibited are, almost beyond compare, splendid, graceful, and tasteful, I frankly admit; and that the present condition of French upholstery shows a surprising advance, development, and improvement, from an æsthetic point of view, is undeniable. I very readily endorse the introductory remarks prefacing the "Furniture" section of the new edition of the Messrs. Johnson's excellent catalogue: "A few years ago the manufacturers of elegant furniture in France were almost exclusively confined to Paris; but of late some important firms have arisen at Bordeaux, Lyons, Nantes, and in many other towns, such as Troyes and St. Quentin. . . . The reports on the International Exhibition of 1862 showed, in relation to all the trades connected with furniture and decoration, the valuable assistance obtained by great establishments from artists of approved merit, and the great improvement thus produced both as regards taste and practical fitness. The manufacturers have understood the advantage to be derived from art, together with that technical ability that French industry possesses in so high a degree, and have boldly entered into the new path which has already, in some cases, led to the most brilliant successes. The most important improvements to be noticed during the last twelve years are these: Considerable increase of production; the introduction, in the case of ordinary articles, of the use of cutting machines and mechanical processes, *often producing the cheapest possible results*, and the employment in all the trades connected with furniture and decoration of distinguished artists, whose co-operation has introduced good taste into the manufacture." With all this, with one exception, the critic may cordially agree; but I seek in vain for the " cheapest possible results." Now and then you light on an arm-chair covered with " American leather-cloth," ostentatiously labelled " fifty-five francs," or a *meuble* " contrived a double debt to pay," and which is a bed by night, a chest of drawers by day, and is considered astonishingly cheap at four pounds sterling: but as a rule the gorgeous avenues in the *Mobilier* part of the Exhibition display only the appurtenances of the palaces of kings and the garniture of the mansions of millionaires. There must be a section of the people, and a very vast section, too, whose requirements are not comprised in carved bedsteads, inlaid cabinets, damascened bookcases, and lacquer-worked billiard tables—in furniture glowing with precious marbles and Limoges enamels—in mosaics and silvered bronze, in imitation Venice looking-glasses and consoles in *carton pierre*. Surely the sole aim and end of Universal Exhibitions cannot be to show how much luxury can be applied to the use of mankind, or how much material wealth and invaluable time can be squandered on the production of toys which can never be brought within the reach of the lower or even of the middle classes of society. I cannot, however, shut my eyes to the probability that, were the simply cheap and useful made—as they should be—the most prominent articles of display in a Universal Exhibition, that Exhibition would be anything but an attractive gathering. Crowds gather round the cabinet-work of a Fourdinois, a Roux, or a Grohe, a Jackson and Graham, a Crace, or a Wright and Mansfield. The Russian bronzes at a thousand roubles apiece, the Leopold Harzé terra-cottas at a hundred and twenty pounds each, the glistening gems of Hancock, Howell, James, and Watherston, attract swarms of sight-seers; a Phillips finds out that he has "sold out" all his coral, and Dobson or Copeland cannot take orders fast enough for engraved glass or painted porcelain; but if you wish to know that ordinary breeches for the working classes can be supplied at seven francs fifty a pair; that waterproof coats can be made as low as ten francs apiece; and that double-soled boots need not cost more than half a dozen francs, you must seek out some obscure annexe in the Park, where such miracles of cheapness have but few visitors to inspect them, and where the inspection, when it does take place, is of a yawning and listless character. Cheapness and ugliness are, in the opinion of the unthinking portion of the public, indissolubly connected, and people will not give a franc to see that which they hold to be ugly. I am afraid that if we want to examine really cheap furniture we must wander into the workshops of exhibitors who would never dream of sending their "exhibits" to the Champ de Mars, and to whom "small profits and quick returns" are of infinitely more consequence than grand prizes and gold medals. For, in France at least, the art manufacturer frequently finds his prize cabinet remain unsold on his hands; while, without even an honourable mention from an Exhibition jury, a working upholsterer of the Faubourg St. Antoine or the Rue Mouffetard can contrive to sell a good many deal chairs and tables.

XXIV.

ENGLISH WORKMEN IN THE EXHIBITION.

THE wind set so strongly in the quarter of pomps and vanities, during the Exhibition season, and the wicked world of Paris was in such a whirl of excitement with receptions of crowned heads, Imperial balls, civic fêtes, and diplomatic banquets, that I am almost ashamed to chronicle a solemnity —if that be not too big a word for an affair so very unpretending—which took place one Monday, in June, very early in the morning. Humble, however, as was the event and tiny the gathering, a brief account may be neither uninteresting nor devoid of significance to those who are accustomed to look beneath the surface, and are of the opinion of the illustrious historian of the Consulate and the Empire—that gild, and sweep, and polish the crust of sulphur as you will, *le cratère bout toujours*—Vesuvian humanity beneath boils eternally Pardon the magniloquence of this exordium to the narrative of the modest Whitsuntide outing of one hundred and seventy British working men. An association, of which Mr. Layard, M.P., was president, and Mr. Hodgson Pratt secretary, was formed in London, to bring over to Paris, at divers times during the Exhibition, as many working men as might choose to avail themselves of unusual facilities and capital accommodation at a really cheap rate. As we are a practical pounds shillings and pence people, the onus lies upon me, I know, when I mention "cheapness," to prove my words. Here was the tariff of the association. You, John Bradawl or Timothy Teesquare, were very anxious for a trip to Paris, not only to see the World's Fair in the Champ de Mars, but to take a peep into a few French workshops, and shake hands, for the first time, with a few shopmates who, dullards and rascals used to tell you, were your "natural enemies," but who only need the brushing away of a few international cobwebs of prejudice and ignorance to become your fast friends. Now, John or Timothy, you had only to pay the sum of thirty shillings, and the association passed you by rail and boat to Paris and back again, *and gave you comfortable house room close to the Exhibition building for one week.* There were plenty of cheap restaurants, notably the "Omnibus" one, in a line with the Ecole Militaire, where you could get wholesome victuals. In eating and drinking —I bar guttling and guzzling—you need not spend more than five francs a day—say thirty-five francs, a very good imitation of thirty shillings, for the entire week. Thus, for *three pounds sterling* you might consider your hat as on, and your house as covered. If you had an extra pound in your pocket, the sensible interpreter attached to the association— he was Richard Cobden's dragoman, and that is saying quite enough—would put you in the way of buying something cheap and pretty for Betsey and the children. I wish Betsey and the children had come, too, with all my heart, but that could not be managed. Paying the minimum of thirty shillings, you slept in a four-bedded room. Paying the maximum of thirty-three shillings, you were entitled to quarters in a room with only two beds. I went to see the artisans' lodgings close to the Porte Rapp. They consisted of rows of comfortable, clean, airy huts, with every needful fitting and good beds, where one might sleep as snug as an insect, unmentionable to ears polite, is said to sleep in a rug, but without any fear of having that insect for a bedfellow. The association agreed with the person who farmed these lodgings from the French Government to provide a certain number of beds every week during the whole of the time the Exhibition remained open. The interpreter showed the travellers about, and prevented them falling into the hands of the Philistines. If they were thirsty they could obtain wholesome and cheap Bordeaux wine, and there was not the slightest necessity for getting tipsy for the "good" of anybody's "house." If the tourists wanted a pipe, tobacco was plentiful, and not dear. The French Government distinctly made known their readiness and their anxiety to open to foreign workmen all the museums, galleries, and factories supported by the State, and private manufactories were equally liberal. If sickness overtook any of the visitors, medical attendance was at once forthcoming; and there was a porter up all night. And, mind, while I should have liked to see the Bradawls, the Teesquares, and the Painters, Glaziers, and Blacksmiths coming over in force, I knew no reason at all why their number should not be supplemented by as many clerks, assistants, or "odd men," as chose to come. Among the many humbugs of this age is the one which conduces to petting and patronising our brother as a "working man," merely because he wears a fustian jacket with a footrule peeping out of his pocket, and which refuses to see that the bearer of those insignia may be *less* than a mechanic, and that if he have skill, industry, and integrity, he may become something immeasurably *more* than a mechanic, some day. To my mind, the real working man is he who toils hard for his livelihood and earns but very little money. The potboy, who means, with God's help, to be some day a Member of Parliament; or the barber's clerk, who reads " Tidd's Practice " in his intervals of lathering, with a view to being admitted a solicitor; or the boot-black, who buys a sixpenny Euclid, and sits up at night fagging over it—that is my real working man: that is the working man as he is understood in the United States of America: that is the working man who becomes Senator, Statesman, Ambassador, and President. I can't see the drift of the gentleman who having once assumed a fustian jacket sticks to it, half as a robe of triumph, half as a badge of servitude, and is always calling on you to observe how very horny his hands are. Let him save up his money and buy some Cleaver's Honey Soap, and soften them. Thus, I was very glad to see that the association of which Mr. Layard is President—a working man himself if ever there was one—took the term " workman " in its true acceptation —viz., a person who works, and hasn't more money than he knows what to do with; and if among the hundred and seventy there were, in addition to the " horny-handed sons of toil," a considerable admixture of lawyers' clerks, shopmen, cellarmen, omnibus cads or cab drivers—and *they* all work hard enough, Goodness knows !—I can only say that I wish there had been more of them.

The first band of " working" tourists who arrived in Paris one Saturday and Sunday were received at nine o'clock on the Monday morning at the Artisans' Lodgings by Mr. Layard, who, in a most business-like manner, took his seat at the receipt of custom, and delivered the tickets of admission for the Exhibition.   It was a very edifying sight to behold the ex-Under Secretary of State and explorer of Nineveh, the scholar, artist, legislator, and diplomatist, booking Mr. Bradawl's name and ticking off Mr. Teesquare as "paid." These trifling formalities accomplished, a procession was formed, and the party marched over to the Porte Rapp, and so into the Palace.   In the English section of the exterior zone, close to the English Money-Order Office, of which excellent institution good use was made, there had been provided by Mr. Cole, C.B., a spacious and commodious reading, writing, and reposing hall for the "working" visitors. There they might write their letters.   There they might sit and rest.   There they found Mr. Layard or Mr. Hodgson Pratt, if they needed any advice or information.   In fact, the hall was their club room, in everything save in the way of refreshments, which could be obtained close by, at Spiers and Pond's, at Bertram and Roberts's, or Trotman's.   As many of the party as could be kept from straggling by the fascination of the first view of the Exhibition were assembled in this hall, and addressed in a few plain and practical sentences by Mr. Layard, who, at the conclusion of his remarks, was greeted with three hearty British cheers.   And then the workmen dispersed into the mazes of that wonderful labyrinth in which all the treasures of the world seemed collected, but in which, thanks to the zeal and sagacity of the French police, admirably aided by Mr. Superintendent Howie and his merry men from Scotland Yard, very, very few robberies were committed, or even attempted.   A *badaud* among the French *feuilletonistes* has stated that eighty pickpockets, *all of them English*, were captured in one afternoon; but what will not a French *feuilletoniste* state when under the exciting influence of syrup of gum arabic and halfpenny cigars? I read the other day that her Majesty the Queen had presented a million of money to *l'Hôpital de Bedlams, asile pour les pauvres sans logement*. If the *feuilletoniste* took the name of the hospital in St. George's-fields literally, he might at least have written *Bed*slam, for a good many beds could be provided for a million of money.

No better day than the 10th of June could have been chosen for inducting the English visitors to the glories of the Paris Exhibition, for it was Whit Monday, and the French keep Pentecost in even more joyous observance than we do. It is said that ninety-eight thousand persons paid for admission at the turnstiles on this particular Monday; and if to these be added the season-ticket holders, the bearers of *billets de faveur*, and the multitudinous *gens de service*, to assume that there were altogether a hundred and fifty thousand persons within the ring fence of the Champ de Mars would be no exaggeration. The King of Prussia and the Crown Prince were among the visitors. They came soon after ten o'clock, and were, of course, mobbed. It is all very well to speak of the indelicacy and discourtesy of such a proceeding; but, if you are a crowned head, you must expect to be treated as such, and to be mobbed. "The pit rose at me," wrote Edmund Kean to his wife, describing some exceptional outburst of public enthusiasm in his favour. The Athenians used to cast their garments at the actor or the statesman they admired. Voltaire, the last time he went to the opera, complained of being "smothered in roses." Garibaldi was all but kissed to death at Covent Garden; and the American citizen who emerged, his coat split and his hat crushed from a blow, at the White House in Washington, and was asked if he had seen Mr. Lincoln, replied, "Seen him! Lawful Saker! Why, I've trod all his toes into sass, and all but shook his hand off." This is the fate of those who wear the crown. To be shot at if people don't like you, and to be "smothered in roses" if they do. Some sovereigns are nervous, and hide themselves away, and then the obvious cry is, "Why any kings at all?" They must go through with it, even if they die at the stake. The King of Prussia took his mobbing very cheerfully. He was a jolly old gentleman, and when the hustling grew rather too violent he used to take refuge in a café and light up a cigar.

XXV.

THE "EMPEROR OF THE BLACKINGS."

Is it unfair to laugh at the blunders committed by foreigners when they attempt to write in English? Well, perhaps it is; but one can't help laughing sometimes at their droll handling of our difficult tongue. Besides, they may laugh at us—and they *do* laugh—when we try our hands at writing French, or German, or—no, not Italian; for the considerate Italians never do laugh at the bungling foreigner. There fell beneath my notice, in the Exhibition, perhaps the funniest prospectus of a Sevillano gentleman, who makes blacking, that it was ever my lot to read. Here you have it *verbatim et literatim* :—

The First of Andalucia.—Grand Manufactory of Blacking, ocly, and resinous, titled the Emperor of the Blackings, Black Ink and of all colours to write with of D. Joseph Grau, Member of the National Academy of Great Britain, revvarded in the Sevillan Exhibition of 1858, and that of London in 1862. Spain: Andalucia: Seville: O'donnell street, N. 34. This blackings is knoconed to be the most useful for the conservation of the shes, for its brilliancy, solidity, permanency, flexibility, and complete discomposition of the black animal. Mr. Joseph Grau dus a present of 20*l*. sterling to the person that.will present hum a blacking in paste, that will reunite the same conditions as the Emperor of the Blackings.

Now who can the "Emperor of the Blackings" be? Theodorus of Abyssinia, or the President of the Ragged

School Shoeblack Society? I shall certainly patronise the "Emperor" if he can bring about the "conservation of the shes." I have always found the "shes" most difficult to "conserve," and as I have been all my life endeavouring to "discompose the black animal," and get him off my shoulder, if Don Joseph Grau can accomplish that result, the Don is the man for me. The Spanish version of this amazing document is eloquent of the superiority of the pure Castilian over our rough and rude tongue. How nobly sounds, " *El Emperador de los Betunes!*" How grandly do twenty pounds sterling swell into " *dos mil reales!*" And how courteous and delicate is the intimation that Don Joseph Grau will "regale" (*regalará*) with the two thousand reals in question any one who will produce a superior blacking !

XXVI.

AMERICAN RESTAURANT.

THE Exhibition was very grand, very wonderful, very amusing, very instructive, very windy, very hot and very cold, very damp and very dusty, according to the variations of the barometer and thermometer. It was not a very agreeable place, but it comprised within its concentric ellipses a whole curriculum of education. So Humboldt's "Cosmos" is said to do, and Humboldt's "Cosmos" is certainly not an agreeable book. For myself, I can candidly say that since the 1st of April I never passed through the Porte Rapp without reluctance, or emerged from it without exultation. There was a malady called the "Exhibition headache;" there was a tendency to expansion of the facial muscles termed the "Exhibition yawn;" and once I met a gentleman who was suffering from the "Exhibition toothache," and a lady who declared that she had caught the "Exhibition sore eye." Whether the Imperial Commissioners, with a kindly regard to the interests of the restaurant concessionaires, were in the habit of causing the asphalte of the Palace to be sprinkled with salt and cayenne pepper, I don't know; but I can vouch for the prevalence of a serious malady, to which, not being a scientific authority, I will give the name of the " Exhibition thirst." It was endemic, epidemic, chronic, and catching. Its morbid symptoms were a continual clutching at the throat, and a "palpation" of the waistcoat and pantaloon pockets, with a view to ascertain the amount of coin of the realm which might be lingering there. The "Exhibition thirst" led to wandering, both in spirits and mind. You asked a friend what o'clock it was, and he replied huskily, "Spiers and Pond." You asked him how long he had been in Paris, and he replied, "Bertram and Roberts." You inquired about machinery, and he told you about Dunville's V.R. Whisky and Clossman's clarets. You talked high art, and he murmured "Allsopp." On being pressed for an explanation, he pressed his hand to his fevered head and mentioned Duff Gordon's sherries. In fact, the "Exhibition thirst"—super-induced, I suppose, by the heat, the noise, the dust, the long distances to be traversed, and the deficiency of cabs—caused the majority of mankind in the Champ de Mars to look at life after the manner of the General in the "Orpheus C. Kerr Papers;" that is to say, through the bottom of a tumbler. The "oath" was taken incessantly, with sugar, lemon, and ice; and the dexterity with which the French ladies con-trived to suck up sherry-cobblers and gin-slings through straws only added to the admiration and amazement with which I regard the people who do so well that which they have never done before. Haven't you known people who, after going afoot during half their lives, have suddenly come into money? How wonderfully well they drive their mail phaetons! How admirably they ride their park hacks! The young Irish gentleman opined that he dared say he could play the fiddle if he tried. I wonder, if anybody made me a present of an Erard's Grand, or an Alexandre Harmonium, whether I could play a sonata in X minor after a fortnight's possession of the instrument.

While thirst is my theme, let me mention, with gratification, a great establishment for the slaking of human lime which was in the exterior zone. Messrs. Dows and Guild, and another and kindred firm, who added to their *raison commerciale* the familiar name of " Van Winkel," started a grand American bar, and a grander American restaurant. At the bar, and from syphon tubes decorated with silvery figures of the American eagle, were dispensed the delicious "cream soda" so highly recommended by the faculty. "Cobblers," "noggs," "smashes," "cocktails," "eye openers," "moustache twisters," and "corpse revivers" were also on hand; and I dare say you might have obtained the mystic "tip and tie," the exhilarating "morning glory," the mild but health-giving sarsaparilla punch, to say nothing of " one of them things," which is a recondite and almost inscrutable drink. I remember being treated to " one of them things " at Boston, by a young gentleman who was a "Sophomore" of Harvard College; indeed, I think we took two of "them things." The effect produced on me was an impression that I had set fire to the Temple of Diana at Ephesus, combined with an ardent desire to slay Professor Agassiz, and take refuge from justice at the top of the Bunker-hill monument. In fact, " I felt bad." The kindly Sophomore at once suggested a curative whose action was instantaneous and efficacious. I may not mention its components; but it is called "one of them *other* things." Upstairs the American *intrepreneurs* opened a capital restaurant, which could be patronised in all safety and comfort by English and American ladies; and the bill of fare contained such American delicacies as " tenderloin" and "porter-house" steak, "green corn," "stewed oysters," "succotash," "terrapin," "soft-shell crabs," "canvas-back ducks," and "prairie hens." Quite an elegant drawing-room, with a pianoforte, harmonium, and *cabinet de toilette* for ladies, and a reading-room, well furnished with newspapers, for gentlemen, completed the arrangements of the Dows, Guild, and Van Winkel establishment, which was certainly as remarkable an "exhibit" as any that could be found in the section of the U. S. A.

XXVII.

BURGLAR-PROOF SAFES.

THERE is a song, or there was one some years since, very popular at evening parties, entitled " The Wolf." The ditty may have faded by this time from the post-prandial anthology; but in my day " The Wolf" was a very favourite *lied* indeed. It is usually associated in my mind with the vision of a broad-shouldered gentleman, with a big beard, an expansive shirt front, plaited, very small jean boots, with varnished tips, and a tremendously gruff voice. The lower notes of " The Wolf" were absolutely appalling. The song was a decidedly striking one; but, for my life, I never could make out the connection between the predatory animal, whose reputed affinity to the canine species is a reproach so bitter to all respectable dogs, and the commission of burglary, accompanied by violence, in a gentleman's dwelling-house. What had the wolf, whose " midnight howl" disturbed the peaceful snorers of the rural districts, to do with the startling announcement of the flying asunder of " locks, bolts, and bars," and the stern summons of " your jewels, cash, and plate," thrice repeated, if I remember aright, in the song— fortified by a pistol presented at the right ear of the trembling householder ? Perhaps the poet intended to insinuate that Bill Sikes is only a wolf in human shape; but then a housebreaker doesn't "howl" when he goes about his naughty business. He shuts his mouth as tightly as the slide of his dark lantern, puts on list slippers, and walks as stealthily as a cat in a pantry. In a word, I hold "The Wolf" to be, poetically, the most inconsequent song ever written. ·

Walking up and down the machinery gallery of the Exhibition, and picking out for examination and comment the various fireproof, waterproof, and burglarproof safes exhibited, I could only arrive at the conclusion, if the appearance of the articles themselves and the assertions of their manufacturers were to be accepted as conclusive evidence, that it was high time for "The Wolf" to become an obsolete and purposeless ballad; and for country householders, to say nothing of merchants, bankers, and shopkeepers, to hold in scorn, not only the inroads of that "devouring element" of which the Duke of Sutherland and Captain Shaw are such distinguished extinguishers, but also the efforts of the depraved persons who go about with masks, "jemmies," "aldermen," and skeleton keys, and whose business it is to make "locks, bolts, and bars" fly asunder. "Love laughs at locksmiths," they say; but a "Chatwood's septible patent intersected steel invincible bank safe" is warranted to laugh at the cunningest cracksman, even to the famous Casey and the renowned "Scotty" and the illustrious "Velvet Lad." Indeed, Mr. Samuel Chatwood, who hails from the highly-appropriate locality of Bolton, in Lancashire, offered long since, as the managers of the "limited" company into which he has formed himself, to pay a reward of six hundred pounds to any person who, with burglar's appliances, should succeed in opening his septible patent bank safe. Messrs. Casey, Scotty, Sykes, and Co. being themselves temporarily residing in another kind of "safe," of which only the governors of her Majesty's convict prisons have the key, the "burglar's appliances" must be intrusted to mechanical engineers. But no sooner did Mr. Chatwood hang out his defiance, than Hobbs, Hart, and Co., of Cheapside, London, were to the fore with invincible locks, and impregnable safes, and inexpugnable doors for bullion vaults. Not to be affrighted, the illustrious Chubb, of St. Paul's Churchyard, came up smiling in Paris with a whole arsenal of shining steel locks, and bolts, and bars, and safes. Robbins and Son, of Wolverhampton, made a most formidable display of locks; so did John Harper and Co., of the Albion Works, Lillenhall; while little could enhance the modest confidence with which John Tann, of Walbrook, London, informed the world that he had been making iron doors and "reliance" locks and latches ever since the year 1795. Not to be worsted in the honourable race of emulation with their English brethren, the French made a considerable show of locks and safes. Arnauld, of Bonnet-le-Château, Delcloy, of Boulogne-sur-Mer, and Rebour, were the principal exhibitors of locks and keys. Coutant Hantemont and Co., of Paris, showed some very ingenious safety locks with alarm bells; Grandhomme, of the Faubourg du Temple, exhibited padlocks and "combination-figure and letter-locks without keys" —very amusing to study as examples of ingenuity, but which in this age have come rather to be considered in the light of mechanical toys. The principal exhibitors of safes, bullion vaults, and iron doors, were L'Hermitte, of the Boulevard Beaumarchais; Raoult, of the Boulevard Bonne

Nouvelle; Fayet-Baron, of Fismes, Marne; Kaffner, Yoernel, Haffner, all of Paris; Delarue, Petitjean, and the well-known house of Fichet. Holland exhibited no safes. That tough little country probably considered her guilders to be quite safe enough under the guardianship of her dykes and dams. Out of Belgium there came a fair show of locks, and one or two safes. Prussia exhibited some remarkable specimens of the latter, very solid and neatly finished. In Austria the only noticeable safe exhibitor was Wenduth, of Marburg, in Styria. Switzerland contributed, from Geneva and from Salenstein, a few iron cash-boxes, not of much account. No safes had been sent from Spain; but Señor Juderias, of Saragossa, had an assortment of "secret locks," and Hermosel Duvan, of Madrid, sent some locks with "protective firearms," pretty in design, but, practically, quite useless. "Secret padlocks" were also numerous enough in the Russian, Danish, and Swedish departments, and in the Italian section there was a very commendable fireproof safe, with combination lock, by Vago, of Milan. Turin has been ·from time immemorial celebrated for the manufacture of stoves; but in that of safes she did not excel in 1867. From Turkey and Tunis and Morocco we had an array of picturesque-looking locks, and keys, and iron caskets for the holding of sequins and piastres; but it would be, I opine, within the resources of science and the attributes of the youngest locksmith's apprentice at Bolton or Wolverhampton to "double up" the most intricate of the "safety" apparatus from Oriental climes. I have purposely left to the last the United States of America. In a land where the "dollar" is "almighty," it is a natural sequence that human ingenuity should be taxed to the utmost to keep the dollar, or its representative in greenbacks, safe from the persons who unlawfully thirst for its possession.   The Americans are the best bank-note engravers in the world, and they are also the best bank-note forgers.   As locksmiths, and as manufacturers of safes and bullion vaults, they equal us in activity and in subtlety of combinative chests and contrivances; but I do not think they approach us in power of resistance or in excellence of workmanship.   Baffled by the marvellous ingenuity of American locks, Transatlantic burglars have of late years taken to blowing up the locks themselves with gunpowder; but among the inventions of Mr. Chatwood is a lock into which no gunpowder can, efficiently, be introduced. I say this without the slightest wish to disparage the well-deserved fame of such a practitioner as Mr. Asa Hobbs, who in '51, about the time that Commodore Vanderbilt was beating all our yachts at Cowes, came over to England and picked all, or nearly all, our locks.   Our cousins may beat us once more at a regatta, but I do not think they will ever vanquish us again in locks and safes.   Sixteen years are a very long period; and neither London nor Lancashire have failed to profit by the lesson taught us by Hobbs, the new "Leviathan" of locks in '51.   I looked for a very large show of "anti-burglarious" appliances from America in the present Exhibition; but the exhibits tended more towards the display of locks than of safes.   Thus, Hyatt, of Greencastle, Indiana; Bawn, of Boston, Massachusetts; the Talc and Winn Manufacturing Company, of Shelburne Falls; the United States Combination Lock Company, of Providence, Rhode Island; Johnson's Rotary Lock Company, of John Street, New York; and Dodds, Macneale, and Urban, of Cincinnati, Ohio, shewed very remarkable specimens of bank and door locks and fastenings; but the only "safes" properly so called were those of Mr. Silas C. Herring, of New York.

It is to be regretted that a complete exhibition of international locks, keys, and safes was not made in a special annexe in the park, instead of being scattered about the machinery gallery. Safes might with perfect propriety have formed a class by themselves; but it is as difficult to track them out among the machinery as to discover the traditional needle in the bottle of hay; and even in the catalogue we find them huddled into "Group six, class fifty-five," under the vaguely generalistic head of "Civil Engineering, Public Works, and Architecture," and in the eminently dissonant companionship of woodwork and parquetry, specimens of precious stones from Mont Blanc, "Greek capitals in plaster," brick machines and "pug mills," baptismal fonts, leather pumps, "a model of a Gothic church in cork and cardboard," photographs of the monuments of Perugia, and the Right Honourable Lord Willoughby d'Eresby's adamantine bricks. When it is remembered that property to the value of seventy-five millions of francs was stored in the Champ de Mars, a compact arrangement of burglar and fire-defying safes, in some central and isolated building, might have been most interesting and instructive, if only to show what a tremendous "haul" might have been made of the treasures collected in the palace, but for the combined efforts of the Sapeurs Pompiers and the French and English police.

I have been through the bullion vaults of the Bank of England. I have explored those deep solitudes and awful cells, where Plutus may be supposed to dwell in perpetually placid contemplation of the "Rest" belonging to the old

Lady of Threadneedle Street. I have been through the catacombs of Rome,—a gaunt friar stalking before with a taper, and flaming it about to show us the empty graves in the *arcosolia* and the niches in the *loculi* which once contained phials full of martyrs' blood. I have been favoured with a tasting order for the London Docks, and have watched the thoughtful cooper spiling casks with insinuating gimlet, and shedding the golden vintages of Xeres on the impregnated sawdust. I have studied those wondrous festoons of cobwebs in the Dock cellars, and subsequently, coming out into the open air, have discovered that some malignant spirit had popped twenty hundred-weight of rapidly revolving wheels, red hot, inside my hat. About the same time I have become aware that the bow of my cravat had changed its locale from Adam's apple to the nape of my neck, where it hung like a bag wig. And I have walked about the English Cloaca Maxima at Crossness ere Thwaites, the magician, turned on the tap, and allowed impurity to roll its disemboguing streams to Thames. But of all subterraneans I prefer the Bank Bullion Vaults. They are so clean, so quiet, so refreshing; and the fittest genius of the place is that plump Bank Porter, in his handsome livery, wheeling leisurely along that truck piled high with shining ingots. Dear me! you can buy anything with those ingots! Horses, parks, grounds, and all Mr. Hancock's diamonds. Rank, place, respect, beauty, and sleeping draughts, even, for conscience. The "still, small voice" may be temporarily hushed with Godfrey's Cordial, mixed with *aqua d'oro*. Everything in the world is to be bought with these golden bricks—except, perhaps, relief from the tortures of indigestion and the gout.

An article upon iron safes would be incomplete without a

passing allusion to those vast receptacles of wealth whose propinquity must ever shed an odour of financial sanctity over Lothbury, and invite respectable men to haunt Bartholomew-lane. There are plenty of bolts and bars, and iron doors, and granite arches, and concrete walls in the Bank vaults, and the skill of the Hobbses, the Bramahs, the Chubbs, and their compeers, has often, I doubt it not, been put into requisition to devise fresh means for rendering the Old Lady's cupboard thief-tight. Yet I cannot help thinking there is a kind of divinity which doth hedge about the Bank; and that were the " Rest " merely stowed away in hampers under the counters of the Drawing Office, Bill Sikes and Company would somehow be afraid of breaking into the sacred place. The Bank of England is not a place to be spoken of with levity. I never heard of an omnibus conductor who was rude to a Bank clerk. Who would not sooner accept a bidding to lunch in the Bank Parlour than an invite for Lady Methusaleh's Thursdays, or Mrs. Canton's " kettledrums ?" In most of our minds stand ineffaceable a triad of great men. My three are—my first schoolmaster, the Beadle of the Burlington Arcade, and the Governor of the Bank of England.

"Safe as the Bank," is a true British motto, and, all " antiburglarious " contrivances included, the Bank itself is one vast " safe " designed by the late Sir John Soane. And should cracksmen dare to approach the shrine of Mammon, is there not posted every night the Bank Guard? There were legends current in my youth, that every one of the bold Grenadiers who marched from the Tower to take care of the Old Lady's money, received from the Directors eighteenpence in new sixpences, and as much bread and cheese and beer as he could carry; while for the officer of the guard there was laid every evening a sumptuous dinner from Birch's, with a crisp £5 note under the first plate of clear turtle. Break into the Bank, indeed! Bold indeed would be the burglar who should attempt such a feat, under the noses of the Grenadier Guards.

I happened, while travelling in the United States, to be permitted to inspect another treasure-chamber, quite as remarkable in its construction, and even more fertile in food for reflection. It was at Washington, and in the Treasury Department. The chamber, big enough to serve as a dark cell for fifty "roughs," was of iron, embedded in concrete, with another layer of brick round it, and an outer wall of massive granite slabs. The ponderous door was huge and fearsome to look at, as the portal of some Egyptian temple. Inside there were bolts as big as bowsprits and locks as large as tombstones; but the gate of the treasure-chamber could be opened only with one small key about the size of a toothpick. Millions and millions of dollars were stored there; but the drollest thing about the chamber was that, with the exception of a silver teapot and some spoons belonging to a senator's wife, who had sent them to the Treasury for safe custody, as our dowagers send their plate to Coutts's when they go abroad, there was not a cent's worth of bullion in the entire vault. The hard cash was elsewhere. This was the home of greenbacks; and the *genius loci* was no plump porter with his barrowful of ingots, but the sculptured effigy of Salmon P. Chase, smiling from the midst of a "spondoolick."

Bullion-vaults and treasure-chambers, with envelopes of concrete and granite, may very well suit the purpose of

Governments, and National Banks, and Crédits Mobiliers ; but the ordinary banker, merchant, manufacturer, or goldsmith, requires a comparatively portable receptacle for his cash and valuables. I do not mean that it should be portable in the sense of being carried away—the very last thing the proprietor desires—but it should be portable enough to admit of its being brought to an office and deposited in its place by means not quite so expensive and elaborate as those used, say for raising the obelisk of Luxor, or lifting the engines out of an ironclad ram. You don't want your stationary cash-box to weigh ten tons. Thus, what I may term the " model " safe, should not be of greater dimensions than Jackson and Graham's cabinet, and should be quite as devoid of extraneous and excrescent ornaments as that celebrated work of art. You may have observed that a barman in a Whitechapel gin-palace, whose calling frequently brings him in unpleasant collision with " roughs " of a felonious nature, rarely wears a coat or a neckcloth. His throat is bare ; he dons, instead of a coat, a light, knitted, sleeved vest—a " polka jacket " I believe it is called—so that when Mr. Sykes jumps over the counter, intent on robbing the till or strangling the barman, he is unable to tear his garment to tatters or to twist his fingers in the cravat of his foe and strangle him. So, too, do the gentlemen who dispense juleps and cocktails in the underground bars "down town " in New York City, usually wear their hair cropped close to their heads. By these means they baffle the designs of the rowdies with whom they have occasional " difficulties," and who, did the bar-tender wear lovelocks, would infallibly use those ringlets as a kind of twisted fulcrum, giving due leverage to the thumb with which they gouged his eyes out.

Now, the constructor of a safe should, in the outward bearings of his design, always bear that Whitechapel barman and him of New York in mind. The outside of a safe should be quite bald and smooth. It should as much as possible represent a cannon ball squeezed square. There should be no unnecessary protuberances or projections, no convexities or concavities, designed merely for ornament. There should be "nothing to lay hold of." A safe, even, is the better for having no knob or handle to its door. There should be nothing to give "purchase" to the burglar's implements. It should be a compact, homogeneous, continuous body—an iron nut, not to be cracked—a thing which the thief should walk round, vainly looking for an interstice into which to introduce a tool, or a projection to serve him for leverage, until at last, foiled and despairing, he knocks his head against the Gibraltar Rock of Safety, and beats his wicked brains out.

One glance at the French safes in the Exhibition will convince the observer that, ingenious and tasteful as they may be, they totally lack one great desideratum in safes— they are full of "purchase" and "leverage." The ineffaceable Gallic penchant for luxuriant design has encumbered them outwardly with cornices and consoles, with pilastres and pediments, with panels and beadings, all absolutely tempting to the burglar's tool. I am satisfied that Caseley would be able to open the best of the French safes in half an hour. Take a magnifying glass with you and peer into the work, *as* work, and you will find it full of inequalities, full of fissures and interstices, mainly due to this pernicious taste for decoration. The French may make very admirable wrought steel cabinets; but for commercial purposes they are scarcely entitled to the name of "safes." One of them has a beautiful looking glass in the centre panel, and the cornice of another is upheld by two caryatides!

Mr. Samuel Chatwood, it may be remembered, is the enterprising Bolton engineer who, after the Cornhill jewel robbery, when a " Milner's safe " was opened, to the detriment of Mr. Walker, by the Caseley gang, requested permission from Sir George Grey to send one of his own safes to Millbank Prison, there to be " operated " on by Caseley, who at his trial had boasted that he could open any safe in England. The Secretary of State for the Home Department did not think fit to accede to a request so very unusual; but in 1867 Mr. Chatwood brought his safes to Paris—double, treble, quadruple, quintuple, sextiple, and septible—and pitted them against the whole world for impregnability. So far as I can discern, the claims asserted by the Chatwood Company are these : That they are fire proof, on the principle of steam generation and non-conduction ; that they are " drill proof," even against the terrible " Ratchett lever," on the principle that their walls are of " intersected " metal, alternately hard and soft, so that neither can be acted on separately. As a necessary consequence, they must be screw proof; for if you can't drill a hole how are you to insert your screw? Then it is claimed that they are wedge proof, the edges of the door being curvilinear, and a wedge being incapable of following a curve. Being wedge proof, they become, *ipso facto*, crowbar proof. To render them gunpowder proof the lock is furnished with a safety valve, which, instead of resisting the explosive force of gunpowder, allows it to escape harmless. They are also stated to be acid proof and picklock proof. The inside of the chamber is preserved from oxydation by being coated with a composition which successfully resists the chemical action of the water of crystallisation; the centres on which the doors hang are all hardened, and fitted into hardened sockets; duplicates of the keys cannot be taken in wax; and, finally, the small key. cannot be taken out of the lock without locking the bolts of the large lock. The safe can never thus be left inadvertently open. The greatest stress, however, is laid by the Chatwood Company on the fact that theirs is the only safe yet patented in which any provision is made for the escape of the explosive force of gunpowder. These are "brave 'orts," and Mr. Chatwood was prepared to prove them. His treasure chamber stood in the Machine Court, side by side with the safes of Chubb and Hobbs. Both these last-named eminent manufacturers have been granted silver medals, while to the Chatwood safe only a bronze one has been adjudged. This, however, proves absolutely nothing; and, for all the prize medals in this section are worth as real evidences of merit, they might just as well be made of leather or prunella. The proof of a pudding is in the eating thereof; and what should we say of a jury of cooks who awarded a prize to one pudding, simply because it was the biggest and the brownest? What should we say of a jury of musicians who passed judgment on an array of grand pianofortes, every one of which was locked? We should say that the verdicts of such jurors were profanatory and untrustworthy; and I am afraid that such will be the ultimate decision of the supreme jury, the public, on many of the awards made at Paris in 1867. With respect to safes, it is manifestly absurd to pronounce an opinion on their nice gradations of merit unless they be put to absolute and bodily proof. I ventured to doubt the goodness of the French safes because they failed, *ab initio*, to comply with certain conditions indispensable to a "practical" safe. They were, on the other hand, obviously "practicable"—that is to say, their ridiculous external ornamentation gave them, from burglars' point of view, a sheer "come eat me" aspect. In the English and American safes, however, the primary conditions are observed; and there thus remain three points of controversy which it is impossible to decide without actual physical tests. First, excellence of quality in the material; secondly, ingenuity of contrivance; and, thirdly, which is but the corollary of the first and second, "unopenability."

A great testing tournament took place during the month of August between the Herring and Chatwood interests. Silas C. Herring's safe, it is said, arrived too late at Havre for the jurors to report upon it. Mr. Herring, however, hung out, or rather wafered on his safe, a cartel offering a reward of fifteen thousand francs to any one who should open his impregnable coffer. Chatwood took up this wager of battle, and preliminary articles of agreement were drawn, providing that Herring and Chatwood were both to deposit fifteen thousand francs in "safe hands." A committee of five engineers—two Americans, two English, and one French —were then appointed, and proper operators were set to work upon the two safes, to test their relative superiority. The winner of the fifteen thousand francs agreed, after all expenses had been paid, to divide the balance among the charities of London, Paris, and Washington. M. Le Play, ot the Imperial Commission, acted as stakeholder.

The safe-breaking conflict assumed all the proportions of an international struggle, and absorbed the attention not only of scientific men, but of the general public in Paris during many days. I now proceed to describe the transaction in the successive phases into which it entered, even "unto this last," which is not by any means a satisfactory phase, and tends to show that, difficult as it is to decide when doctors disagree, it is still more difficult to arrive at a conclusive decision when practical engineers fall out.

Properly to understand this vexed question, it will be necessary briefly to recapitulate. Mr. Silas Herring, a very eminent manufacturer of *fire-proof* safes in the City of New York—and whose pamphlet, "Fighting with Fire," I have recently read with great interest—arrived in the Paris Exhibition with a certain safe, the which he pitted for heavy stakes against the productions of any other safe manufacturer in the world. The glove thus thrown down was taken up by Mr. Samuel Chatwood, the patentee of a renowned *burglar-proof* safe. It will be as well to keep in mind the difference between these two orders of safes, " fire-proof " and " burglar-proof," as they have much to do with the existing controversy. It may also be noted that Mr. Walker, the watchmaker of Cornhill, whose premises were so recently ransacked by the Caseley gang, has, ever since the discovery of the pregnability of the Milner safe, used a Chatwood one; and, by a curious coincidence, at the very moment the safe question was agitating the Paris mind, Mr. Walker, a prominent exhibitor of watches and jewellery, received a letter from the convict Caseley, dated from his *locus penitentiæ* in Fremantle, Western Australia, in which that worthy announced that he had completed the draught for a model of a safe which he considered to be thoroughly thief-proof, and which, with touching candour, he begged to place at the disposal of Mr. Walker, as some compensation for the injury he had formerly suffered at his, Caseley's, hands. The challenge between Herring and Chatwood ultimately assumed this form: A sum of 15,000 francs was to be deposited on either side in the hands of M. Le Play, of the Imperial Commission. The prize was to be awarded to the safe which best resisted the action of the common implements used by burglars, and which, in the opinion of a committee specially appointed, should be shown to combine the greater number of qualities requisite in a good safe. M. Le Play accepted the custody of the money, or, the rather, caused the 30,000 francs to be deposited in the Imperial Treasury of France. The committee were named, and consisted on the American side of Mr. Holmes and Mr. Pickering, American engineers; on the English side of Mr. Mallet and Mr. Fairlie, both C.E.'s; and of one French member, acting as chairman with a casting vote, M. Douliot. To these gentlemen were adjoined a Mr. Hoyle, as secretary. The actual trial took place on Tuesday, the 13th of August, in the English Testing House. It is very sure that after some hours' desperately hard work the operatives employed by Mr. Herring succeeded in breaching Chatwood's safe, laterally, and getting out a block of wood, deposited in the cavity, and which quite erroneously was supposed to be the test of the safe's pregnability or impregnability. But it is likewise true that the workmen employed by Chatwood to break into Herring, although foiled on the point of time, and unable to continue their work through twilight closing in, succeeded the next morning, *in less than five minutes*, in breaking open Herring's burglar-proof coffer, not at the side, but in front. It must likewise be borne in mind that Herring's men, whose tools were much heavier than Chatwood's, utterly failed in making the slightest impression on the English safe with common burglar's appliances. They tried to drill it for fifty-seven minutes, and failed. They tried to pick the lock; they tried to drift the handle hole; they essayed to wedge the door; and in all these attempts they were miserably worsted; and the claims put forth by Mr. Chatwood thus fully justified. Baffled and perplexed, they were forced to abandon the *modus operandi* of burglars, and proceeded to break or smash the safe up bodily. It became a question of boiler-making, or rather of unmaking a boiler; for it is obvious that great machines must be taken to pieces as well as put together; and it is equally obvious that, given a sufficient amount of force and time, the resistance of any organic body must be overcome. It happened that an Austrian workman employed by Mr. Herring had formerly possessed peculiar opportunities for examining the construction of the Chatwood safe. Mr. Chatwood, indeed, had himself explained the chief peculiarities of the safe to him. This crafty man, aware that the edges of the English safe were dovetailed, and not welded, awoke to the feasibility of skinning the walls of the safe laterally, and thus effecting an entrance. It is needless to point out that no burglar could have done this, as the safe would, in a counting-house or vault, have been imbedded in brickwork or masonry, and its only accessible point would have been the front or door. However, by the introduction of massive wedges, and repeated blows from a monstrous sledgehammer, the three outer plates of one wall of Chatwood's safe were forced away, a hole was battered in the last sheet of iron, and the block of wood was obtained; but the front, the door, the hinges, the lock, were still, and are still, entirely intact, and the safe had not been opened as burglars would or could attempt to open it. So manifestly was this a case of smashing to pieces a machine which could not be opened by legitimate means, that an English captain of Engineers present sarcastically asked why an Armstrong gun or a Nasmyth's steam hammer had not been sent for.

In the meantime we must recollect what Chatwood's men were doing to Herring's safe—or rather safes, for there were two of them, one inside the other. Mr. Chatwood had originally taken the safe exhibited by Mr. Herring to be the one on which the challenge rested; and, indeed, with my own eyes I saw Silas Herring's challenge posted on this same outer safe. But when the terms of the contest were settled, the American stated that the outer safe was only a fire-proof" one, and that to open his "burglar-proof" safe, a heavy steel coffer, which he called a "banker's chest," imbedded in the base of his safe, must be entered. Mr. Chatwood agreed to assail two safes, while his adversaries had only to contend with one; and Mr. Herring, on his side, agreed to furnish accurate working drawings of his "banker's chest." But these working drawings were *not* furnished. An equal weight of tools was likewise to be accorded to each party; but whereas Chatwood's men came into the Testing House with their implements slung round them, as house-breakers would do, Herring's men brought their infinitely heavier appliances on a truck. The Chatwood men worked for a very long period without a sledge-hammer—which is no more a burglar's tool than a hydraulic press would be; but when the tremendous play the Herring side were making with their sledge-hammer became manifest, the committee were in common justice fain to allow the Chatwood party to send for a sledge-hammer; but it was then too late to make up for lost time and insufficient force. The Herring party, also, had wedges of enormous size, whereas the English only brought a modest supply of those used by burglars. The result you know. After opening the outer safe in twenty-nine minutes, the English workmen had not broken open, in front, the banker's chest by the time the Americans had—certainly not broken open—but smashed a hole in the side of Chatwood's safe, which they had "skinned" by their manual strength, and with an amount of noise which no burglar in his senses would dare to risk.

Of course, the Americans claimed the victory: had they not produced Chatwood's block, while Herring's yet lay *perdu* in his "banker's" chest? The impartial award of the committee had yet to be given, and the real question at issue remained yet to be decided—which was the machine combining the greater number of qualities to be expected from a good safe? In the opinion of most impartial persons the Chatwood safe, in principle and in construction, was undeniably the best one. Although a hole had been dug in its side, it remained, as a safe, intact—not thrown a hair's-breadth out of its perpendicular, after hours of battering by professed boiler-makers, and with its door as sound as a rock, and scarcely scratched by the repeated attempts at drifting and drilling which had been made upon it. On the other hand, the Herring safe was torn literally to ribbons, and scarcely a feature of its original construction could be recognized. However, there was the fact of the block having been got out by the Americans. That the bet would be declared a drawn one was expected, and might have satisfied a very large section of those interested. But up to the time of the

consignment of these sheets to the press, no definitive settlement had been come to. The committee had been dissolved,
an attempt to reconstruct it had failed, and the members
were "left squabbling." As I am neither a burglar nor a
civil engineer, my verdict in the matter is of no consequence ;
but as one of the public who witnessed the "Battle of the
Safes" from its commencement to its close, I humbly record
my opinion that the Chatwood safe was by far the superior
one.

As regards time, the actual periods in the contest, as
registered by Mr. Walker's chronometer, were as follows :
The experts on both sides began work at 2·45 p.m., and
allowing forty-five minutes for rest to both parties, the wood
block was out of Chatwood's safe at 7·25 p.m. The net time,
therefore, was three hours and fifty-five minutes. Messrs.
Mallett and Fairlie were of opinion that the material of Chatwood's safe was much superior to that of Herring's and that
the strongest point in Herring's safe, his "banker's chest " or
coffer, was highly objectionable, on the score of the possibility
it offers of being wedged open from the front. Indeed, it
was from the front that this coffer was wedged open by
Chatwood's men. It is allowed that, in the first instance, Mr.
Herring consented to throw open the doors of his outer safe,
allowing the assult to be made only on his banker's chest ;
but he afterwards withdrew this consent, and the consequence
was that the Chatwood party lost a good half-hour in opening
the first safe, and that, had the doors been left open, Chatwood's men would have penetrated into Herring's front
before Herring had breached Chatwood's side. For these
reasons, and for others which I have already gone over—the
absence of correct working drawings of the American safe,

the disparity in the weight of tools, the larger wedges used by Herring's men, the deprivation of sledge-hammers suffered ⟶for a long period by Chatwood's party, and the incontrovertible fact that Chatwood's safe, although pierced at the side, where under normal circumstances it could never have been vulnerable, was never opened, whereas, in Herring's safe, his outer and inner doors were fully and fairly entered from the front—the English section of the committee gave their verdict in favour of Chatwood. The Americans, on their side, and very naturally, swore by Herring, and, indeed, there was as much hard swearing as hard hammering heard throughout the business.

THE END.

LONDON: PRINTED BY WILLIAM CLOWES AND SONS, STAMFORD STREET
AND CHARING CROSS.